Mother and Child

ANNIE MURRAY
Mother and Child

MACMILLAN

First published 2019 by Macmillan
an imprint of Pan Macmillan
20 New Wharf Road, London N1 9RR
Associated companies throughout the world
www.panmacmillan.com

ISBN 978-1-5098-9538-0

1 3 5 7 9 8 6 4 2

A CIP catalogue record for this book is available from the British Library.

Typeset in Stempel Garamond by Jouve (UK), Milton Keynes
Printed and bound by CPI Group (UK) Ltd, Croydon, CR0 4YY

Visit **www.panmacmillan.com** to read more about all our books
and to buy them. You will also find features, author interviews and
news of any author events, and you can sign up for e-newsletters
so that you're always first to hear about our new releases.

For Martin, with love

FOREWORD

First of all, if you have bought a copy of this book, let me say a very big thank you. While this is a story mainly set in Birmingham, it has also been written, unapologetically, with the aim of raising money for the Bhopal Medical Appeal. So, in buying it, you have already helped to make a difference to someone.

It has been written out of love and anger. The anger will be self-explanatory. The love is something I feel for two places. One is the city of Birmingham, our old industrial heartland, which I have been writing about for many years and where people, in the not-so-distant past, were no strangers to industrial accidents. The other is Bhopal, a city also located at the heart of its mother country, India. Bhopal was one of the princely cities; it is sited on two lakes and it is old, beautiful and fascinating.

In Britain, most people who remember Bhopal at all think of it as a place in which a catastrophe happened a long time ago. In December 1984, its name became associated with what is still considered the world's worst industrial accident. The poison gas leak over the northern area of Bhopal tends to be remembered as an event involving thousands of deaths, horrific physical suffering and shameful corporate callousness.

However, the contamination of Bhopal by the American-owned Union Carbide pesticide plant did not begin with, nor was it confined to, the events of December 1984. Less well known than the gas leak, but still wreaking terrible effects in this part of the city, is the ongoing poisoning of its water through chemical contamination from the plant, which has never been cleared.

There are of course still many survivors of the gas leak, living with pain, disability and a bitter sense of injustice. An estimated 150,000 still require health care as a result of 'that night'. Their agony went untreated, or was inadequately treated, for many years. It was to help alleviate this suffering that a charity, the Bhopal Medical Appeal, was set up in 1994. Now, however, the toxic legacy of Bhopal continues into the second and third generation. Children of gas- and water-affected parents are being born with extreme deformities, suffering a variety of agonizing, debilitating conditions.

Nor, of course, is Bhopal the world's only toxic hot spot. There is an urgent and ongoing question of how we enforce the idea that 'the polluter pays'.

There is more information and more stories at the end of this book and on my website at www.anniemurray.co.uk, especially about some of the women and children of Bhopal.

However, this is, in the end, a story and I hope you will enjoy it. I have written it as a gift for Bhopal – and for you.

With warm wishes,
Annie

An Ugly Pair of Shoes

I am wearing a pair of shoes.
They are ugly shoes.
Uncomfortable shoes.
I hate my shoes.
Each day I wear them, and each day I wish I
    had another pair.

Some days my shoes hurt so bad that I do not
    think I can take another step.
Yet, I continue to wear them.
I get funny looks wearing these shoes.
They are looks of sympathy.
I can tell in others' eyes that they are glad they
    are my shoes and not theirs.
They never talk about my shoes.

To learn how awful my shoes are might make
    them uncomfortable.
To truly understand these shoes you must walk
    in them.
But, once you put them on, you can never take
    them off.

I now realize that I am not the only one who
    wears these shoes.
There are many pairs in the world.

Some women are like me and ache daily as
    they try and walk in them.
Some have learned how to walk in them so
    they don't hurt quite as much.
Some have worn the shoes so long that days
    will go by,
Before they think of how much they hurt.

No woman deserves to wear these shoes.
Yet, because of the shoes I am a stronger
    woman.
These shoes have given me the strength to face
    anything.
They have made me who I am.
I will forever walk in the shoes of a woman
    who has lost a child.

Author unknown

CONTENTS

One

NEW ROOMS

25 November 2014

Two years, one month, three days and roughly five hours ago, our son went out to work and never came home. It was the last time we saw him alive. Six hours. Seven. This is how I count my life out now. He was twenty-three years old.

Today, we moved into this house. Tonight, I am lying in a new bed, a new room. If I get up to go into the bathroom, I'll have to think carefully about where to step – the cupboard to the left now, not the right, that chair close to the door. Beside me, my husband Ian is lying with his back turned to me, which is how it is now, or how it feels, anyway. I suppose he is asleep though I can't be sure.

Before, we lived nearer the middle of town, in Moseley. Now we have come to the southern rim of the city. Our old house was an Edwardian terrace; this one is in a row of houses built in the seventies. It used to belong to an elderly lady and is decorated in her style: neat and clean, beige carpet in the hall and living room, wallpaper with big bronze-petalled flowers above a dado rail, pale coffee colour below; a kitchen with white cupboards and black-and-white chequerboard floor; all double glazing and thick white door frames with security locks. And I am glad. One day in some distant future I will feel like redecorating, but for now I want it to be new and quite different from before, the paint colours not chosen by a past version of me; not haunted. Somehow, differently, I have to learn to want to go on.

Eyes open in the dark, I'm listening for his feet on the stairs, the way I used to hear them in the other house, long after he was gone. There would be the tiny noise of the front door latch turning very quietly, Paul trying not to wake us after a shift, that pause as he pushed each of his trainers off with the toe of the other foot. The still-laced shoes would be there in the morning. He might go into the kitchen for a drink before creeping up the stairs, his bedroom door closing almost silently. He was good like that, always sweet, considerate, even at his worst.

I feel bad if I don't listen for him, guilty if I forget, even for a second, guilty if I smile – even the briefest of social smiles – which up until now I have not felt like doing, hardly for a second.

'Jo?' Ian's voice comes to me up the stairs the next morning as I'm cleaning my teeth. 'I'm off now.'

I look down at the basin so as not to see myself in the mirror in this bright white bathroom, this woman hearing a man calling to her from downstairs who is my husband of almost thirty years. *Answer him,* I command myself. It seems to take an ocean of energy to force words past my lips.

''K,' I spit out. 'Bye. Hope it goes well.'

'You going over to Mom's?' he calls.

'Yeah – course.'

He's taking the car. He doesn't ask if I'm going to the cemetery. I went every day in the beginning. It's two buses from here to Selly Oak, just as far as it was from Moseley.

'Great, thanks.' A few seconds of quiet. 'OK, bye.' He pauses again. 'See you later.'

The front door closes. The latch sounds different from the old house with its dark-blue door and ancient Yale. Here we have one of those clicky white jobs, the sort where you have to jam the handle up to lock it. The unfamiliar sound tilts me back into anguish. I'll never hear that old lock turning again, the door opening, the creak of the stairs, each tread familiar. Everything has gone, been taken away . . .

Losing caution I raise my head and the woman in front of me stares back, frozen and at a loss. God, who's that? I try to reckon with her. Skinny. I wasn't always skinny. Haggard? Yes. The best thing you can say about my face is that it's 'heart-shaped', and I used to have good skin as well. The woman I see in front of me has a complexion about as grey and saggy as her old T-shirt. Then there's the mousey hair in an overgrown bob, dull blue eyes looking out from under a too-long fringe, toothpaste round her lips. God, she's a state . . . It's too much for me and I quickly look away again.

It's very quiet. Outside somewhere a car door slams. I'm dazed by all the newness. The old bathroom had pale blue tiles. The walls were lumpy, decades-old dirt creeping out from behind skirting boards. This house came on to the market after Mrs Parsons went into care. Everything is so square and clean. The downstairs walls are smooth, Anaglypta in the bedrooms, everything spotless.

We even have three bedrooms, one small as a monk's cell looking out at the back.

'We don't need three,' I said to Ian when we were looking round. I could hear the savage tone of my voice. 'We don't even need two.'

'But that one's hardly more than a boxroom,' he said, peering into the tiny one. 'Look – it's fine.' He turned, wary with me, the way he is now. 'It's perfect for what we need, isn't it?'

It's just along the road from his mom's and of course he was right, but I was scratching my nails against everything because I didn't know what else to do with all that was inside me.

For a moment now I glance back at the mirror. I must get a haircut, buy some new jeans. Pull myself together. I'm the only person allowed to suggest that to me. If anyone else says it – my mother, for example – they'll get their head chewed off. I can't remember when I last went to the dentist. I need to start something – yoga or Pilates – something healthy, no more sleeping pills and all that. Get some sort of life, now we're in this new place. And this is the most difficult thing of all – to accept having a life, when my boy, my dear, lovely boy, is lying in Lodge Hill Cemetery. How can I have a life, be allowed to go on? But I can't escape the fact – the cruel, unjust fact – that I am one of those still alive.

'Breakfast,' I murmur to myself. 'Eat.' I am trying to think of my body as someone else's, an objective thing that I have to look after, like a pet tortoise.

My phone goes off as the smell of toast is drifting through the kitchen. *Ange,* the screen says. God, when did I last speak to Ange?

'Jo? How's it going?' She sounds really, really nervous.

Dear old Ange, so perky and kind, so distant now, someone from a completely different life – my different life. I suppose it's my fault, but that's how it feels.

'Oh, fine.' I wander into the living room. It's all one room knocked through, light streaming in at each end. Feeling the pile of the carpet under my toes, I realize I haven't put any shoes on or even socks. 'Did you know we've moved?'

Of course she doesn't know.

'Oh?' Startled. 'Have you? Where to?'

'Hollywood.'

'*Hollywood?* What – you mean, *America*? Film stars?'

'You know, near Wythall, down near Ian's mom. Seemed a good idea. We only got here yesterday.' Does my voice sound normal? I can't tell any more. I'm trying to sound light and cheerful – heaven knows what I actually sound like. Probably shrill and a bit crazy. 'Just getting settled in. I'm going to see Dorrie in a bit.'

'Good for you.' Ange sounds awkward and not really like herself either. I've become one of those people who others are not sure how to talk to or what they can say.

Say the right thing.

'You'll have to come over.' It would be great to see Ange, wouldn't it? To have a friend, a life. I can't remember when I last saw her – has she deserted me or was it me who did the damage?

'Yeah,' she says. I hear a small sound, her dragging on a cigarette. 'Yeah – hey, I'll be over to see you soon, chicky.'

I leave it a beat. 'Who says chicky?'

Ange lets out a relieved snort of laughter. 'Soon, yeah?' Nothing definite then. She's cautious, hurt, I think. A

5

tiny window must be opening in me if I even realize now, how I've shut everyone out.

'All right – yeah. That'd be great. Thanks, Ange.'

'TTFN then. Glad you're OK, Jo.'

Afterwards, I sink down on our navy sofa which is pushed against the wall, bare as yet because I haven't found the cushions.

One day, a few months after Paul died, before I finally broke down at school and had to leave work, Ange and I were in the staffroom at breaktime. She was in the corner, making us both a cuppa amid all the chat and stressed outbursts around us and the photocopier churning away in the corner. And suddenly, quite softly, Ange called across to me.

'Hey – how're you doing, chicky?'

I was just sitting there, at least my body was, but I was not there in my head at all. I looked across at her, managing, God knows how, some sort of grin and I saw this great glow of relief in Ange's face, as if she'd caught a little glimpse of me, her mate, the old Jo, the joking, messing-about Jo.

'*Chicky?*' I said. 'Who says chicky?'

Ange shrugged, mocking herself because when she'd said it, the *way* she'd said it, was really tender. She grinned back, bringing me a mug of coffee, a pack of Jammy Dodgers under her arm. 'I do, apparently! Must be getting old.'

'We're growing old together,' I said.

We met when we were doing teacher training. The first day in class, I spotted this flame-haired girl with interesting cheekbones. And there was something she did with those pouty lips and her bright eyes which made it look as if she was trying not to laugh quite a lot of the time. She looks good fun, I thought. We quickly became friends and through the years we had jobs in separate schools and, now and then, in the same one. But never, in all that time which was the best part of thirty years, had Ange ever, *ever* before said 'chicky'.

Thinking about it now, in the drifting scent of toast, my eyes fill with tears. At last – *please*. I ache for tears, a proper flow of them to release me. But I can't cry – hardly ever have since Paul died. I'm ashamed of it – of not being able to do it. So why this, now?

Covering my face with my hands, I breathe right down into myself, into the blockage, like a stone, lodged in my chest. But I'm dry – the tears do not flow. So many things were destroyed with Paul's young life. I shut Ange out – shut everyone out because the pain locks you in with it by yourself, won't let you escape. And it never ends. You can never wake up one day and say ah, it's over now. It goes on and on until I bore even myself and still can't get out of it . . . I rejected Ange, wouldn't answer the phone, wouldn't see her after I left work . . . Because even people who are sympathetic want you to talk about other things sooner or later – day-to-day things, their kids, their lives. And how can you, when you feel eaten up with rage at them for having kids who are still alive and getting on with it and with guilt for still having a life yourself? And when every moment, of every day, all you can think about is him, and getting to the cemetery because if you don't you'll have let him down . . .

And now, Ange, bless her, doesn't say all those crass things, *Are you getting over it? Have you moved on . . . ?*

All her helplessness and feeling of being shut out pops up in that one word, chicky.

I drag myself up to sort out the toast. I want Ange to come round – but then again I don't. Her two kids are going along fine, her life is as it was. She's part of the old days, which for me are closed behind a door of steel. Many things die with a death.

And, I realize, as I stoop to get the marge out of the fridge, she didn't actually ask for my address.

Two

'Dorrie? It's Jo.'

Ian's mom's house is only a few doors along the street. I'm about to knock, but I try the door, right in my guess that she's left it unlocked.

'Come in, bab – I thought you'd be along any minute.'

Dorrie makes her usual attempt to sound cheerful, but there is a quaver, a new thinning of her voice. We thought the stroke had not affected her at first. TIA did not sound as bad as 'stroke'. But we're beginning to realize that it's done more damage than we thought. Nothing you can exactly put your finger on. It's more as if it's knocked the stuffing out of her.

I step in and close the door. Dorrie's house is similar to ours – bare paving stones at the front, white plastic-framed double-glazing and high-security locks. Even though we had the new front door put in for her a while back, she often, out of old habit, just leaves it unlocked, even swinging open sometimes. *What've I got to steal?* she says. *No one round here's like that anyway.*

A plastic runner covers the swirling black-and-mustard pattern of the carpet all along the hall. Another strip of plastic branches off at right angles into the living room, across the cocoa-brown carpet, as if the paving-slab

9

geometry outside has continued into the house in transparent form. There's a faint smell of the cat's tray from the back kitchen, the gas fire, a hint of Vanilla Blossom air freshener.

'Hello, Dorrie.' She's the one person for whom I can push my face into a smile. And she's my saving grace – having her to look after.

The room feels changed somehow, but Dorrie is seated as usual in her chair by the fire, a shrunken Dorrie now, thin and gristly, but she still has her head of soft white curls. Someone comes in to do it for her every week. Sweep, the black-and-white cat, is curled up in the warmest spot close to her feet.

'You can just lock the door, you know,' I say. 'I've got the spare key, remember? Best to be on the safe side.' I don't want to alarm her but you never know . . .

'Oh, I don't like to shut you out, bab, when I know you're coming. Fancy a cuppa tea?'

'Don't you move, I'll make it.'

'No need to go in there,' Dorrie says as I am turning to go to the kitchen. 'It's all here – look.'

Of course, that's what is different about the room. There's a table now by the window, arranged with all the things she might need: tins and packets, a tray with the kettle on it, the flex connecting to a gang plug on the floor, a jug of water, cups, teaspoons, a container of powdered milk.

'Oh!' I say. 'That's a good idea.' But it feels sad. Dorrie – springy, invincible Dorrie – no longer feeling up to a walk to her own kitchen. 'Who did that for you?'

'Wayne next door. I had him pop in and move every-

10

thing for me, bless him. He's a good lad when he wants
to be, whatever they say about him.'

I manage another smile, emptying the carrier I've
brought with me. 'Here – brought you some milk. And
more teabags.'

Dorrie gives me a vague nod and I realize she's actually
just as happy with powdered milk.

I boil the kettle, locate the tin with Tetley teabags
pressed inside and pop them into Dorrie's thin china
mugs, decorated with trailing honeysuckle. I add two
spoons of sugar to hers. *Keeps me sweet . . .*

She sits quiet, watching me. One of the great things
about Dorrie is that you can talk or not talk and it's comfortable either way.

She's wearing a pair of silver-grey slacks, the fabric old
and bobbly, and they look too big on her now, her thighs
like sticks. And she's cuddled up in a big purple jumper
and has comfy slippers on with a rim of fake sheepskin.
Somehow, even in winter, she still looks tanned. Her col-
ouring is brown-eyed and sallow-skinned with dark rings
under her eyes. I never met Ian's dad because he died
when Ian was small. His name was Tom Stefani, from an
Italian family, which is where Ian gets his dark looks, but
even though Dorrie Stefani had not a drop of Italian
blood, she evidently looked every bit as Italian as her in-
laws.

'Here you go.' Passing Dorrie her mug of tea, I can't
miss seeing the tremor in the old lady's hands. It's definitely getting worse. Her fingers are curled, the blue veins
twisty as worms. 'I'll pop it on the table – it's too hot.'

'Thanks, bab.'

I sit opposite her in the wooden-armed chair, and

reach down to stroke Sweep, who stretches out under my hand, fur luxuriously warm. I start to feel the heat, with the gas fire blasting out next to me, and shift my chair away a bit.

The wooden mantel above it is crowded with knick-knacks and pictures. At the far end, the old framed photograph of Dorrie, dark-haired with shapely eyebrows and wearing a glamorous frock, black or maybe navy, with white spots, collar-length hair styled in tight waves, on the arm of her fiancé, Tom Stefani. Tom, in a natty suit with wide lapels, grins at the camera. It's a lovely, classic fifties look and both of them are handsome and radiant. Beside it, there's another black-and-white picture of Dorrie standing in the street in a winter coat and hat with Ian as a little boy in short trousers and hair slicked across from a parting. She's still beautiful but her expression is tense and she can barely manage a smile. It must have been taken after Tom died.

The photos go into colour then: the picture of Ian's sister Cynthia, who lives down south with her twin boys, taken a few years back. Cynth has gone up in the world a bit – husband does something financial though I've never been interested enough to ask in detail. She doesn't come back here much. Ian's and my wedding photo, Ian looking strange in a suit instead of his oily work clothes, me in a short white dress, plain as I could find. And there are three little pictures which tug at my eyes, but which also make me quickly look away: Paul – as a toddler; as a cheeky, gap-toothed seven-year-old; and as the introverted, troubled teenager, but still raising a smile from under that thick fringe for his nana, who loved him to bits. My chest tightens and I have to reach for a breath.

'You all settled in, love?' Dorrie says, clasping her hands in her lap as if to still them.

I swallow, looking back at this dear, loving old woman. She is the one person who I have been able to be with, have not wanted to shut out because she is steady and kind and knows how to just sit, waiting quietly like a bird on its eggs.

'Getting there. You'll have to come and see.'

'Oh, when you're all straight. I don't want to get in the way.'

'You wouldn't do that, Dorrie. Never.' Our eyes meet and she smiles faintly. 'Shall I pass you your tea?'

Dorrie nods. 'There's some biscuits in the tin.'

'I'm all right, I've not long had toast. D'you want one?'

'Oh, *no*,' she says, as if biscuits are an entirely foreign concept that she would never think of indulging in.

After a moment she says, 'Ian at work?'

'Yes, he's busy. The new place is getting going all right, though. He's turning into a tycoon – two premises now!'

'And that lad – Gideon, is it?'

'Yeah.'

'Like the bibles.'

'Yes, very religious family, I think. He's getting on fine – eager to learn, Ian says. But he's more of an apprentice – they'll need someone else as well.'

Dorrie nods, holding the mug with both hands. Carefully, she lifts it to take a sip. I try to look as if I'm not really watching, waiting to leap across and help. It's costing Dorrie effort to keep her hands steady enough. The mouthful, a pause, a swallow. All slow, deliberate. My mind flashes up the memory of a day when Dorrie came with us to the seaside in Wales. It was one of those bright, gleaming afternoons, sunlight dancing silver on the waves, the wind scouring our faces. Paul was about four then and Dorrie had run up the beach to the ice-cream van, legs stringy-strong and tanned in her shorts, hurrying back beaming, hands full of Mivvis and ninety-nines.

'Cold out, in't it?' She interrupts my thoughts.

'Yes. Windy as well.'

'Well – only four weeks 'til Christmas.' She says it with a roll of her eyes that seems to ridicule all commercial folly.

'Don't.' I really don't want to think about it. 'Can I do anything for you, Dorrie, while I'm here?'

'No, bab – just sit with me. It's nice to see you.'

That's Dorrie. *Sit with me.* Paul once said, 'Nana's like an old tree, isn't she? She's just always there.'

Dorrie sips her cooling tea, staring ahead of her. I wonder if she is going to fall asleep.

'Funny how things change, isn't it?' she says suddenly, her voice dreamy and slow.

'They've certainly changed fast in your lifetime, Dorrie,' I say. 'What made you think of that?'

But she shrugs.

'I dunno. Places had more character somehow, in the past. Neighbourhoods, proper ones. People used to know each other's names. D'you know . . .' She sits forward, seeming to come to life. 'I can remember when they used to bring all the pigs and sheep in along the Stratford Road on the way to the slaughterhouse. You'd see them of a morning, a man and his dogs, driving them along – on cold mornings you could see all their breath. You can imagine the state of the road after they'd been by . . . But

14

then we was used to that with the horses. The lads used to pick up the muck and sell it, a penny or two a bucket for anyone with a garden.'

'Nice memories.'

'Oh –' Dorrie straightens her spine and gives me a look. 'Oh, no. Not all nice at all. There was more character to the place but they were hard times – cruel. You don't want to go always thinking the past was better.' She sinks back as if suddenly running out of energy. 'It were different, that's all. I just can't get over it sometimes.'

She sits silent for a long time, reclining in her chair, still holding the mug, half-full in her lap.

'People take more notice of things now ... All that health-and-safety sort of thing.' She sounds drifty and I feel a moment of unease. Is something happening? Is she having another turn?

But she looks up at me suddenly and says, as she has said several times before, 'It'll get better you know, bab.' And then something else happens which has never happened over these two terrible years: her own eyes fill and she starts fishing for a tissue in her sleeve as the mug tilts dangerously. 'I know it don't feel like it, but it will. You learn to live with it.'

I reach across to take the mug from her, then kneel down at her side, my throat so hard and swollen up I can't speak. I have never once seen Dorrie cry, not over anything.

'I know I dain't say much –' Dorrie dabs her eyes. 'What's there to say?' She shrugs. 'No use going on – it don't change anything. But I think of you – you and my Ian and young Paulie. It goes round and round in my mind, why it all had to happen again like that. You've had it hard, the pair of you.'

The dammed-up tears inside me feel as if they're straining at the walls, waiting to burst, but I still can't seem to let go, even here, with Dorrie.

'You don't give in to it much, do you, bab?' Dorrie says. 'You're not one for blarting. I was like that.' She thinks for a few seconds. 'More a case of can't than won't, I think.'

'Yes,' I say, my voice husky. If I could just manage it – to weep and weep a flood up to my waist, if I could break through, allow the river of emotion to flow, then maybe something would change. But it won't come. A few tears at the funeral, welling up now and then as weeks then months have passed – but the straining bulk of my tears feels trapped inside me. And I can see that Dorrie understands. I also realize that Dorrie was not just talking about Paul, but about when her husband died. A heart attack, Ian said, though he was barely old enough to remember.

Handing Dorrie back her tea, I return to my chair. 'Thanks,' I say, because I can't think of anything else and we give each other a *What can you do?* sort of look.

'Will you get summat for me?' She seems to rouse suddenly, sits up straighter. 'In the other room. In the drawer of the sideboard. You'll find an envelope.'

The back room, almost never used, is her dining room – a modern mahogany-veneered table, six chairs and a sideboard, the carpet so immaculate it looks as if no one has ever walked on it before. I find myself tiptoeing.

'The right-hand one!' Dorrie calls.

Best cutlery lies neatly in a velvet-lined holder, the

spoons nuzzled sideways against each other. Beside them, a brown envelope. Inside I can feel a wodge of folded paper. I wonder for a second if it's her will. But no, surely it's too thick for that? What does she have to leave, after all, apart from her house?

Dorrie takes the envelope from me, looking so serious that for a moment I go back to my guess that it contains her will. She has put her mug on the table and sits with the envelope on her lap, resting her hands on it. Once I've sat down again, she says, suddenly formal:

'You've been a daughter to me, Jo, as much as my Cynth has, you being around the place always . . .'

'Oh, Dorrie – don't.' I'm not feeling strong enough for this, for what I guess might be coming: talk of after she's gone, who must have what.

'It's all right, bab. I just . . .' To my surprise Dorrie blushes, looking bashful. 'Well – a while ago I started doing a bit of writing, here and there. Odd memories and such. That's how it started. And then . . . Well, I never finished it. I thought Ian and Cynth should know a bit more about their family. I've not always . . . Anyway.' She rallies, handing me the envelope. 'It's not finished, as I say, and I can't write now, not with these hands.'

'You want me to give it to Ian?' I ask carefully.

Dorrie hesitates. 'You have a read first, bab. And then . . .' She looks down into her lap. There's a solemnity to her face and I can't tell what it means. 'After that, we'll see.'

Back in the house I am tempted to sit down straight away and read what Dorrie has given me, but I really need to get on with some more unpacking and sorting. Towels

17

into the chest of drawers in the bathroom, the kitchen cupboards to be rearranged. As I work, forgetting – no music, I don't do music – I click the radio on in the living room, turned up so I'll hear it in the kitchen. For a few minutes, adverts chatter out of it.

On my knees on the chequerboard floor, head half in the cupboard under the sink arranging bottles of cleaning stuff, the tune coming from the radio clutches its jigging melody like a strangling hand about my heart.

I struggle to my feet, bashing the back of my head on the cupboard.

'*The tide is high . . .*' Blondie.

Paul, aged about eight, would dance to almost anything we put on the hi-fi but this was his favourite . . . I click the radio off and stand with my hand pressed to my chest, caught in the vision of his skinny little body swaying, his face given over to a daft, dreamy expression: *Am I a good dancer, Mom?*

How did I manage to pack away his bedroom, over two slow-moving afternoons? Just me, not Ian. Ian said he couldn't. Bagging up clothes was bad enough and his heavy metal CDs, magazines. But shoes . . . The sight of his shoes, shaped by him, his trainers, his black-and-white flip-flops, worn wafer thin, that he wore that last summer and almost nothing else, that blue football shirt he kept on even in bed which I practically had to wrestle off him to wash. On his chest of drawers, with a photo cube showing faded pictures of us on holiday and his old *Toy Story* figurines, sat the chocolate-brown bear, Lucy, we had given him when he first came home with us. Lucy, with her love-worn fur and missing eye, went into my tissue-lined box, with dinosaur Rex, his favourite *Toy Story* character, his first pair of shoes, the football shirt, his pyjamas and favourite *Tintin* books, that painting he did, painstakingly one summer, of the little lake he used to run around. From his desk I took the few biros still lying there, seeing his long, strong fingers holding them. They went in the box as well.

One box, stacked amid the others, to contain all that remains of my boy. How did I survive it? And now this . . . I sink to my knees on the navy-and-cream striped living-room rug, curling into a ball the way you do to nurse your heart, my eyes squeezed shut.

Three

'Hiya!'

I force myself to call out when I hear Ian come in, soon after six. It feels like jumping over a wall, the energy needed to get my voice out of my mouth, to sound like a person whose man has just come home, a person with energy to welcome and care. It's only lately I've begun to manage this at all.

'Hi.' Ian drops his bag in the hall. As I make myself go to greet him, he straightens up from taking off his work boots. Every day, for years and years, he has done the same thing. All through the years of working his way up. The stint at Kwik Fit, starting his own business in Moseley – four lads there, one promoted to manager now, pick-up service, the lot. And now he's set up the second workshop here, only a mile away.

Every day, door, bag, boots. I used to be so happy to see him. Now, always, there is pain, swirled like mould through each of us. Our faces have forgotten how to smile. In the old days our arms would be round each other, we'd be laughing: these days he stands back, forbidding, not looking into my eyes. Our greetings are like waves that never break but just move on past.

'All right?' I fold my arms, leaning against the side of

the staircase. The house is warm and I have cooked sausage and onions, jacket spuds, comforting smells to greet him. But I surfaced from my trance on the floor full of wanting. I want *something* – even just one small thing – to be how it was, to be alive between us. The jokes, the affection. My eyes are begging, *Look at me!*

'Yeah.' Ian pats his pockets. His overalls make him look even stockier. He is taller than me by two or three inches and strong, like his father, according to Dorrie. 'Yeah – it's going OK. I'll just go and change.'

He leaps up the first few steps, then slows, as if realizing how tired he is. I follow him to the foot of the stairs and watch him from behind. His brown hair, cut neatly at the back, is still surprisingly dark, though there is a slight thinning at the top. When he reaches the landing and turns to go to the bedroom, I almost can't bear him disappearing. For a moment I wonder about going after him up to the bedroom, holding out my arms to him. But I can't do it. Which of us has shut the other out, decreeing that their way to grieve was the only way?

He'll be down soon. Perhaps then.

I wander into the kitchen to check on the spuds, then forget to do it and stand leaning against the counter.

For a moment I've managed to spark enough in myself to reach out to him, but it was as if he was here, yet not here. We are like bodies going through the motions with nothing left to radiate to another person.

I put my hands over my face and draw in a long breath. It's as if he did not even see me and I know I have done the same to him, over and over again. Two lost people who cannot meet each other's gaze. Absent, missing in action, since the night of 22 October 2012.

'I found the cushions,' I say.

We sit opposite each other at the white table in the kitchen, which is pushed against the wall to make sure that there is only enough room for two people. White plates, sausages in gravy with a dab of mustard, potatoes, frozen peas. Ian knifes butter on to his potato. I have already asked about his day, which apparently was, 'Fine. Good, yeah.'

'And the DVD player turned up as well.'

'Great,' he says, mouth full. 'You got on all right then?'

'Yeah.' I won't tell him about the two hours spent crouched on the floor. 'I'll finish off tomorrow. Mom and Dad said they were coming over this afternoon but Mom phoned to say they had to look after Amy today, all of a sudden.'

Ian looks up and for a second there's a connection, a glimmer of sympathy between us. My mom and dad live in Redditch. Their life revolves round my brother Mark and his wife Lisa and their girls, Emma and Clare. Emma, the eldest, is thirty and is off being a busy career-girl dentist. Clare, the younger, stayed close, married Matt her school boyfriend and had Amy a year ago. What with the caravan and a great-grandchild, Mom and Dad are run off their feet. They like things to be local, to look after their own; relations mean blood relations, not incomers like Paul. Once again, thank heaven for Dorrie.

'Mom all right?' Ian's thoughts seem to have travelled in the same direction.

'Yeah. She is . . .'

His eyebrows lift at the reservation in my voice. At last our eyes meet for a second. 'I mean, she *is*. But she's frailer, isn't she? Shaky. It was a job for her just holding her mug today. It's a good thing we're nearer – specially as I'm not at work at the moment.'

'Yeah.' Ian puts down his knife and fork, the plate cleared, picks up his can of lager. 'It's a godsend, that is. You do a lot for her.'

'She's more than worth it,' I say.

He gives me a quick, nervous smile, then looks away.

Now we are in the new house, things are supposed to ease, to click into something different.

Our old pine bed came with us but I bought a new duvet cover, patterned with spring meadow flowers in green and yellow. I felt guilty going shopping, as if I was being trivial and letting Paul down – again. The top of the chest of drawers in the corner looks unnaturally tidy without the normal piles of bits and pieces that never quite get cleared away.

When I come out of the ensuite bathroom, already in my nightshirt, Ian's sitting on the side of the bed, bare to the waist, staring ahead of him as if he's forgotten what he was supposed to be doing. I stop in the doorway and he doesn't seem to hear me. The sight of him catches my breath. Ian. My husband. He doesn't usually just sit like this and it's as if I haven't seen him, not looked at him, for years and years.

We're middle-aged, I realize suddenly. We know in theory, of course. Both of us are on the wrong side of fifty-five – though me only by a few months. Ian's fifty-eight now. During these two hellish years, we have noticed nothing, forgotten ourselves, each other.

Now in front of me I see a fleshy man, sallow-skinned, with good muscle tone. Yet in both his face and body I can see a look of such extreme weariness, a sort of inner exhaustion, that I start to panic. Is he ill?

He senses me looking and turns his head. So many times when we were young, those eyes used to fix on me full of Ian's mischief, his desire. 'A pair of brown eyes,' I used to sing to him, tumbling into his arms. Now he doesn't seem to see me, as if he's staring straight through me. Just for a second he focuses, then, as if looking into a light that's too bright, he closes down again, warily. I feel so alone, more alone than if he wasn't here.

'Ian?' My voice comes out high, begging almost.

Our eyes meet for several seconds before he looks down. It feels as though we have both been pushed right out to the edges of ourselves, away from each other, as if we are moving round a vortex that has opened in the ground between us. We exist day to day, apart. But now he seems so afraid of me and I feel terribly guilty, until I realize how frightened I feel as well.

I force myself forward, barefoot, towards this stranger. It seems to take great effort, like pushing through some opposing force. I stop in front of him, just beyond the V of his legs. He looks up at me and I try to fix him, to keep him with me.

'I'm sorry.'

Pain fills his face. For a moment I think he is going to cry, but instead he just wipes his hand across his forehead. 'Yeah. Me too.'

Even now, his voice is flat. I feel flat as well. Neither

25

of us can reach our feelings. What I want, I realize, desperately want, is for us to make love. It's hardly happened, since Paul. I can barely remember when we last did anything physical – so few times in the past two years. Isn't this somewhere where we can find each other again, be close, lose the terrible barriers between us?

I step closer, between his thighs. Putting my hands on his shoulders, I start to stroke him, his neck, his strong, straight hair, clean after his shower earlier. I can see his scalp showing through where the hair has thinned on top. There are only a few white hairs among the dark brown even now. Ian closes his eyes. All at once his arms are round me, pulling me to him so he can rest his cheek against my belly. My hands move down his back, stroking, soothing, myself as much as him. Gradually I slide down until I'm kneeling in his embrace, adjusting my arms under his so I can hold him and his arms tighten round my shoulders.

'D'you mean it?' he whispers. He's frightened to give in to it. We've both switched off the physical part of ourselves for so long and now it's hard to trust it.

'Yes,' I say, trying to, wanting comfort and closeness and release.

'It's just . . . It's been so long. I hope I can . . .'

We start to tip back on the bed, trying to find echoes of our old rhythms, awkward. I push up on one arm, looking down at him, bend to kiss his cheek, then his lips, deeply, as if breathing life into him. But he is passive, not like my old Ian, as if something in him is frozen and he can't allow himself to trust or let go.

Tears sting my eyes. I have to break through this somehow, have to save us. Reaching out my hand I start to caress his thigh, very slowly, circling my hand, keeping my eyes fixed on his.

We make love, but I do not cry and do not come. Ian, at first seeming to hold back, suddenly lets go in a frantic way, moving almost roughly in me as if he has to prove something. Afterwards we lie silently in each other's arms for a while. It's sad and I still feel alone – none of the talking or laughter of closeness that we used to have. But it is warm and I have to seize my mind and stop it going down that frozen track where everything is about loss.

We are both still here, we have each other's warmth – it's something.

Four

Waking in a new room again there is the feeling of strangeness. But the next morning, I have energy and a thread of hope. Ian kisses me goodbye, stiffly, but at least he kisses me. And standing in the kitchen, absent-mindedly eating toast after he has gone, I remind myself that this is how the days go. On one I'll be jumpy with an almost crazed energy, as if a crack into the future has opened, filled with light and possibility. The next, every-thing slams shut and I'm cast back into darkness – like yesterday afternoon – and can't do a thing.

Today is a good day. Best make the most of it.

There are several boxes of things left to unpack, but I know that there is one that I am not going to touch. Paul's things. A life in a box. I drag it along the hall, turn-ing my mind away from the objects inside – our young man's few possessions. Today I want to keep my energy. I will find a time for this, but today I push it into the cupboard under the stairs.

I spend the morning sitting on the carpet in the living room with Radio 2 on for company – some of the time. I keep the radio close to me and click it off if music comes on that's too much for me. It's progress being able to stand hearing anything. I pull things out of the other two big boxes. Books go on the waist-high shelves – cook-books and a few favourite novels, Ian's manuals on photography and DIY. A couple more cushions come to light, a small lamp with a shade to go in the hall, the book with phone numbers written in it.

At the bottom of the second box I find the photo albums: one brown, the other navy blue. I kneel with them resting on my legs, hands hesitating on the covers, thinking maybe I'll put them under the stairs as well. How eager I was to fill these albums. I used to spend evenings arranging and rearranging the photos. Shared memories, the adoption people told us. It's one of the most vital things in making a family. Build up lots of shared experiences you can all look back on. It's how you bond as a family. And it was true.

If I open the first page of the blue one I know I'll see the picture of Ian and me on the day we were finally allowed to bring Paul home. One of the advisors, a nice woman called Karen, offered to take it. Ian and I squatted down, Ian holding Paul sitting on his knees, his little legs dangling in his snowsuit. You can see Ian's hands, which look huge holding Paul's body, padded out by the little blue suit. Paul's treacle-brown hair was all curls then. He was fourteen months old, barely even standing, and he sat perched there solemnly, not hostile, just unsure, too young to understand. But we were both beaming, hardly able to believe it after all this time, both full of ecstatic, terrified joy.

And then on the next page and the next and all the others, that growing, smiling little boy . . . And in the brown album, more of the same. I can't open them, but I don't want to hide them under the stairs either, as if burying our whole life. I lay them sideways along the bottom of the bookshelf.

A papery clatter comes from the hall and I get up, stiff-legged, to look. A sheaf of garish leaflets on the door mat in a slanting patch of light. Ads for pizza delivery. Someone calls a greeting to the postman outside.

'More flaming junk.' I pick it up to go into the recycling box at the back and head off to put the kettle on.

'Hello, Dorrie!'

Once again the door is unlocked.

'Hello, love. Come in.'

'Brought you a bit more fresh milk – it's nicer than the powder, eh?' In a rush of fondness, I go to kiss Dorrie's cheek, soft as a rose petal. She seems a bit bemused by this as we're not all over each other usually. The cat looks lazily up at me.

'Nice of you to pop in.'

'*Course* I'll pop in. I can come every day for now – whenever you need anything. You can phone as well.' It's not as if I know anyone else in the area. It's a relief to have someone to visit. 'You all right?' I keep my tone light.

'Oh, I'm all right. As I'll ever be, anyhow.' She grins gamely. 'I'll be even more all right if you get that kettle on, bab. I'm not so quick off the mark these days.'

I fill the kettle, wash mugs and busy myself with tea-making. Despite the gas fire pumping out, Dorrie has a blanket over her knees, a fuzzy mohair thing in dusty blue. Sweep is curled on the mat in front of the fire as usual, nose tucked in.

Again, we sit each side of the fire. Dorrie's armchairs

are rather austere things, brown fabric and wooden arms, a bit like something out of a hospital. The faces gaze down at us from the photographs – my younger self, Ian, Paul . . .

'Heard from Cynthia?' I ask, for something to say.

Dorrie nods, cradling her mug. 'She phoned as usual. They're all right.' Her hands look steadier today but she seems withdrawn, despite the warm welcome. Is she tired, I wonder, or is it something more?

'Would you like me to get you any bits of shopping? I'm going up Sainsbury's later.'

'Oh, yes, please, bab. I've done a little list. Look – there. A couple of tins of food for His Majesty here –' she nods at the basking cat – 'and . . . well, you'll see.'

A sheet of lined paper is on the table by the kettle.

We sit quiet for a moment, then Dorrie says, a little stiffly, 'I don't s'pose you've had time for any reading?'

'Your memoir?' I say, regretting that I haven't got round to it.

Dorrie chuckles. 'Oh, is that what it is?'

'I'm sorry, Dorrie, I haven't, I must confess. It's been a bit busy.'

'Don't you worry – just a few of my meanderings,' Dorrie says. 'I just thought . . . Well, anyway, they're not finished.'

There's something in the way she says it.

'How d'you mean?'

Dorrie strains to lean down and stroke Sweep, who rolls luxuriously on to his back. ''Ello, boy – ooh, you're a lazy old thing, aren't you? I just mean, I haven't written all of it,' she says, still looking down. 'I only got so far, like.'

32

'Oh,' I say. 'All right. Well, I'll have a read. I'm looking forward to it.'

Dorrie straightens up and changing tack abruptly, says, 'And what are you going to do with yourself, now you've got the house unpacked? You can't spend your time sitting about with an old broiler hen like me.'

'Oh, Dorrie!' I manage a little laugh. 'You're so rude about yourself – I like your company! But yes – I'm going to go out and have a look around. Join something. Get my hair cut.'

'Umm,' Dorrie says, eyeing me. 'Well, that's a good idea.'

A quick online session turns up three hair salons within walking distance, the Maypole Dental Clinic and a promise of various classes in one of the church halls.

What I am trying to do is to see my guilt at having a life, at still being here, as a black cloud following me around. Several times a day now I find it hovering over me and I catch it in a big fisherman's net and force it down into a box which I close and padlock shut. *Life has to go on.* Clichés have an annoying way of being true, whatever you might feel about it.

So in the afternoon I go out, squinting in the bright sunlight, nose cuddled into a scarf in the wind. The immediate neighbourhood is residential; road upon road of houses shoulder to shoulder, all built in the past forty years, many with their frontages completely covered in tarmac or paving slabs, mostly very neat and well kept up. But we are the last fringe at the south edge of Birmingham and once I'm on the main road, there's a wooden fence on the other side and beyond it, farmland stretching into the distance. Narrow, rural roads leading off it have interesting names, like Dumblepit and Baccabox Lanes.

We've been here often enough to visit Dorrie, but we mainly went to her house, or occasionally to the park with Paul when he was small: even that feels a lifetime ago. I catch myself in the thought. A lifetime – Paul's lifetime. But the unfamiliarity of much of the area is a relief.

I book an appointment in the first hairdresser's I come to. They treat me kindly and manage not to look too disapprovingly at my straggly locks as if to say, *Yes, well, it really is about time, isn't it?*

The church, a few streets away, is a modern brick building with a wooden-walled hall built on the side. I hesitate outside. I've never been a churchgoer and I'm not really sure what to do or how to behave with religion. But I've got to do it. What's the worst that can happen? I haven't come about religion – and they're supposed to be Christians these people, aren't they?

Something seems to be going on in the hall – some kind of sing-song. There are outer doors at the end which are standing open, and glass inner doors the other side of a little lobby, noticeboards on the walls and signs pointing to toilets.

As I go to look at the posters on the noticeboard, the piano starts up in the hall and the singing begins again. I vaguely recognize the song: something from the 1940s.

'Yoga with Lauren,' one poster says, showing an ink outline of a woman sitting in an improbable position. The class is at seven-thirty on a Tuesday evening. I can't see myself turning out of an evening at the moment. It's the days I need to fill. And the poster is intimidating.

I am just heading for a scruffier sheet of paper held on by rusting drawing pins, when someone comes out of the ladies' toilet, an energetic-looking lady, probably in her late sixties with short, styled grey hair and a tomato-red jumper hanging long over dark blue, straight-legged jeans. She tugs the back edge of the jumper down in a business-like fashion.

'Hello, love – can I help you with anything?'

'I'm just having a look . . .' My voice seems faint and weak, which is suddenly how I feel. 'I'm new to the area and I wondered about joining a yoga class.'

'Ah – well, we can help you there. Day or evening?' The woman has a vaguely bossy manner but is friendly and seems eager to help.

'Day, I think.'

'That,' the woman says confidentially, 'is a very good choice. So you see, here –' she points at the first poster – 'we have Lauren's group. The Lycra Lot, we call them. All very accomplished.' This is said drily, with a roll of the eyes. 'And then, here, on a Tuesday morning, we have the other mortals – the Creak and Groaners.'

I can't help laughing. 'That sounds more like me.'

'Yes – me too.' She smiles. She's not pushy about it, but kind. 'I'm Sheila – I go to that class. It's a very nice group, small, but perfectly formed. Kim who runs it is a lovely girl – used to be a midwife. Very caring. We meet most of the time except the school holidays. And it's not expensive – five pounds a session. We'll be here this week, if you fancy it.'

'Thanks – I might do that. I suppose I need a mat?'

'Yes – I don't think there are any spares although someone might be able to help you the first time. The

35

supermarkets sometimes have them but buying one online's the easiest, really.'

'Oh. Right. OK.' Sheila is evidently one of those silver-surfer types.

'Best get back in.' She nods towards the hall. 'Singing for the brain. You know – dementia. Marvellous. They'll want their tea soon.' She makes another comical face as if to say, *Woe betide me if we're late with tea,* and backs into the door to push it open. 'Hope to see you on Tuesday.'

Five

It's a strange feeling, getting back to the house, to those new rooms. Home is where you come back to over and over again. A place where you have to sleep and wake night after day after night until it is your known habitat. It all takes time, like building a nest, twig by twig. And home is somewhere visited by the people you know. As yet, not one familiar person has stepped inside except Ian and me – not even Dorrie. In the old days she would have been straight round. She was like that with our first house, having a good look and poke around, making suggestions.

I push the key into this strange lock, pressing on the white handle. Everything feels alien and that swelling feeling comes back. I breathe, trying to force it away. *It's going to take time.* That's what everyone says. Don't I know it. It is two years and almost two weeks since I last saw my son. The past must recede further and further away – what choice is there?

And yet, since that one night, there come rip-tides of pain which can almost knock me down. Something, a tune, the thought of a key turning in a lock, a head of hair that looks like his from the back, can make me want to run screaming along the street. *Look, look, I beg you – see all this that's inside me! Take it away, help me!* How could anyone tell, otherwise, just by looking at me, that I have a cauldron of agony in me, seething, threatening to boil up over the sides?

Exhausted, I sink on to the sofa, unlace my trainers and tuck my feet under me. The house is nice and warm at least. God, I'm like an old lady myself, needing naps in the daytime. How does Ian manage to keep going, working so many hours? But work, it seems, is all he wants to do.

Just as my eyes are closing, my mobile starts throbbing on the arm of the chair, jerking me awake. Mom and Dad's landline number shows on the screen. I drag a deep breath in and brace myself.

'Jo?' Mom starts talking in a rush. 'Are you all right, love? We were so sorry not to get over to see the new place yesterday, only Amy has been ever so poorly and of course poor Clare was expected at work even though it was the last thing she needed. She's looking a bit better today – Amy, I mean. We were afraid it might be something like measles, or – you know, well, she didn't have that injection and I remember when you had it – anyway, it isn't as it turns out. But then you'll never guess what happened! Mark went out to fix something outside and has somehow sprained his wrist – badly. They spent three hours in casualty last night and he's all strapped up, so we've had a bit of a time of it . . .'

'It's OK,' I say, trying not to think, But she's your *great*-granddaughter – isn't there anyone else who could have looked after her? What about Lisa? But of course, Lisa, my sister-in-law and Amy's grandmother, was out, busy as ever. Lisa is not really into being a grandmother at the age of forty-eight.

'We thought we'd come over tomorrow, if that's all right. It'll have to be the afternoon – we've got things on in the morning . . .'

'That's fine.' Saturday's as good a day as any other in my hectic social calendar, I think, but don't say. And at least Ian might be there as well.

'Oh, *good*.' Mom suddenly sounds enthusiastic. 'It'll be lovely to see it. Now, is there anything I can bring? A cake – rubber gloves?'

'Not that I can think of,' I say, in the face of this random selection of offers. My mother and father do brisk at all times.

'Well, all right, we'll see you tomorrow, love – about three, I expect.'

I click the phone off and stare out of the front window. I've taken the nets down – I don't like them. The houses facing ours are almost its mirror image, except that the one opposite has two little bay trees in pots each side of the front door, cut into leafy globes like lollipops, the one green thing permitted amid a sea of paving slabs. Big, sharp-edged clouds move across the blue sky.

Mom and Dad never quite coped with Paul, no matter how hard they tried. They weren't unkind, nothing like that. But something in them, some primitive reflex, meant they couldn't quite bend to an outsider, someone not of their blood. I remember once, we were all down at the caravan. They keep it on a site outside Redditch, where they live. Paul was about six and Dad was trying to teach him to play cricket. I was standing in the doorway of the caravan watching. It was late in the afternoon and they were in a patch of sunlight, between the shadows from the trees. Paul's hair was dark, curly – that made him stand out as a stranger to begin with. Of course, Ian's family, the Stefanis, all have dark hair and Paul blended right in, but no one else in our family has hair as dark as that. And he kept dropping the ball, seemed bewildered by the whole concept of the game.

'Come on now, lad!' Dad kept saying, impatience veiled by a forced jollity. He's a dapper man, my dad, always very tidy, in his white summer shoes, short-sleeved shirt tucked tightly into grey trousers, belted high on the waist. He's a clever man, but it's the cleverness of calculations, categories, things fitting into place. 'That's it – pick it up and throw it back to me. That's it, lad – no, over here! Oh, dear, oh, dear!' He chuckled in a despairing way as the ball veered off in the wrong direction.

Watching them, my heart clenched. Paul never quite did what boys were automatically supposed to do, not in Mom and Dad's eyes, not the way my sporty brother Mark did – has always done. And Dad made him nervous.

'We had a nice game, didn't we?' Dad said afterwards, too jolly, a hand rumpling Paul's foreign hair as he stared unhappily at the ground. 'But I think stamp collecting might be more his line.'

Paul raised his head and looked at me, frowning. He had no idea what stamp collecting was.

Six
CHILD'S POSE

The yoga class is at ten-thirty on Tuesday mornings.

A long roll of a parcel arrived for me on Saturday. Ian, who had agreed not to work that day as my parents were coming, brought it through from the hall and looked questioningly at me as I sat eating toast.

'Yoga mat. I've found a class in the church hall.' I had told him this before.

'Oh, yeah.' He forced a joke. 'I thought it might be something to keep your dad busy. A club for attacking weeds?'

I stared back at him, not in the mood for jokes. Having to cope with Mom and Dad's arrival later was bad enough. Dad's one of those people who are lost without a little practical task, however futile, to keep him busy. Come to think of it, Mom is much the same.

Ian seemed to realize he'd said the wrong thing – or at least maybe the right thing but at the wrong moment.

'I can get him sorting out these window security keys,' he said. 'I haven't had time to try them.' So far, we've not been able to open any of the windows.

I relented. 'Yeah. Good idea.'

As I walk along the road to the yoga class, I can't stop thinking about Mom and Dad's visit last Saturday. The thought of it is lodged in me heavily, like an undigested meal. It always takes me time to recover from seeing them. Always? Maybe not. I suppose it really started to get to me as Paul was growing up, his not fitting into their prearranged ideas.

Within moments of arriving, my mom, in a workman-like yet pink tracksuit, with packs of J-cloths and bright yellow microfibre cloths, was buzzing about squirting Cif and wiping down already clean surfaces, saying how a new start always made all the difference.

'You can move on properly now, can't you, love?' she said, conscientiously scrubbing at something.

I stared at the back of Mom's head. Her not-to-be-allowed-to-go-grey hair was dyed a glossy chestnut with blonde highlights, cut in a neat bob, the ends blowdried under. It looked so immaculate that I realized this was what she had been busy with this morning – the hair-dresser's and a long session of trimming and dying. She must have felt my murderous eyes boring into the back of her head because she turned, hands encased in her yellow Marigolds, and looked seriously at me. I was so close to boiling that I said nothing.

'There's got to come a time,' she said. Then she looked down at herself for a second and added cautiously, 'Would you be able to find me an apron, love?'

Still saying nothing, I found her a blue-and-white striped apron and took myself into the front room where I sat on the edge of the sofa for ten minutes until I could breathe properly again.

We spent an uneasy couple of hours. Ian kept Dad busy with a drip feed of Allen keys, WD40 and spanners (which brought me closer to him with gratitude than anything else had for a long time). Of course, Dad had his own tool kit in the boot of the car. After all, hardware and tools used to be his business. My grandfather started Gilby's, the family's big, successful store, in the 1930s and Dad inherited it. It's still one of the few non-chain survivors. Mom used to work in the office and they had a lot of loyal customers, *So much better than B&Q.*

We drank tea. Mom had brought an M&S lemon cake. *I knew you wouldn't have had time to bake.* We chatted about the caravan, about the neighbours' doings and Amy's. For all of her eleven months, Amy has been an endless source of anecdotes. They kept looking at each other, egging each other on to tell another story and laugh. And I sat, full of rage and hurt and yet telling myself, This is what people do – you have to talk, to go on with life. This is normal. But I wanted to get up and scream – *Talk about my boy! I want to talk about him, not about Amy!* But we never did talk much about Paul – even when he was alive. And their relief as they got up to go was unmistakeable.

'Take care of yourself, love,' Mom said, giving me one of her hugs which somehow involved minimal bodily contact. 'Mark and Lisa said they'll be over to see you soon, once you're settled in.' Her well made-up face, the grey eyes, lids tinted with something shimmery, looked pityingly into mine, that look which said, *If only your life had turned out like Mark's, with his nice wife and girls and grandchild . . .* She fumbled in her bag and pulled out a twenty-pound note which she pushed into my hand.

'There – put that towards a nice haircut, eh? It'll cheer you up.'

I stood out on the pavement as they got into the car. I

felt as if I had been scraped all over with something, my skin all sore and sensitive. I stood next to Ian, waving, with my other hand closed round the money.

It's always taken time to get over seeing my parents and this felt worst of all.

Three days later I'm not feeling much better.

Reaching the church hall, I hesitate out in the little lobby. I can see there are a couple of people inside. I don't even know why I'm here now. I didn't feel like coming, but the thought of staying home was worse.

To buy time I go into the ladies. Five minutes later there are half a dozen people in the hall. My heart is hammering and I want to turn and run. New people. I never used to be like this, but now thought of even saying hello feels like a mountainous obstacle. But then someone else comes up behind me and I can't just block the way, so I push the door open.

There is a handful of women, a couple over to one side, chatting, one unrolling a mat, another standing by the windowsill writing in a notebook. Mats of various colours are laid like petals round a fat candle in the middle. Two women are sitting quietly, one cross-legged, the other with plump little legs stretched out, clad in grey tracksuit trousers. But I can't see Sheila, the woman I met the other day.

The notebook woman looks up and smiles and comes over to me. She must be in her mid-forties, a nice curvy shape in navy leggings and grey vest, long brown hair caught up in a trendily messy sort of topknot. I like her face immediately, her wide smiling mouth and kind eyes, and something inside me relaxes a tiny fraction.

'Hi, I'm Kim and I run the class – have you come to

join us?' She speaks gently, cautiously, as if not wanting to seem pushy.

I nod. 'If that's OK.'

'Of course it's OK – you're very welcome.' Her voice is deep and silky, but it has in it an appealing hint of laughter. 'Let me just get my little book.' She retrieves it from the windowsill. 'Have you done yoga before?'

'A bit – not much.' I find myself feeling timid and tongue-tied. I never used to be like this. I tell Kim my name and hand over the five pounds.

'Lovely –' Kim writes her in the register – 'Jo Stefani ... Great, Jo.' She puts the book down and touches my shoulder to guide me across the room and it makes me feel cared for. She is that kind of person. Nurturing, as they say. 'You can come on a drop-in basis – that's fine. No need to book ahead or anything. Now, if you just find a space ...'

I unroll my mat in an unoccupied segment of the circle.

'That's it – you come here next to me', says the lady who is still sitting with her legs stretched out. 'I'm Sunita.' She's a middle-aged Asian lady, plump, with shoulder-length, rather chaotic-looking hair, round, dimply cheeks and a motherly manner.

The woman on the other side of me also says hello, in a reserved sort of way. As an afterthought she says her name is Pat. She is probably in her late fifties, slender in black leggings and a white striped T-shirt, and with a round, blue-eyed, fresh-faced look. She has greying brown hair which has a natural curl, a few tendrils falling over her forehead; her smile, showing big, square teeth, makes her look cheerful and suddenly youthful, like a girl. Once I have laid out my bright blue mat, which smells new and rubbery, I see Sheila come in, wearing a black tracksuit, a mat under her arm – 'Sorry I'm late' – and followed by another neat-looking, short-haired woman.

'No Fred today, Pat?' Sheila asks the woman next to me.

'No – he's had to take the car in,' she says, rolling her eyes. I'm not sure why she's rolling her eyes but it makes everyone laugh.

'Right –' Kim comes over, squats down to light the candle, then settles into a limber, cross-legged position. She smiles round at us all. Somehow, she is a person who makes things seem fresh and possible, as if she has eternal energy. This makes me feel rather tired but sort of hopeful at the same time. The room quietens. 'Welcome, everyone. As you can see we have someone new today –' she smiles at me – 'so shall we do quick introductions?' Everyone nods.

'Well, I'm Kim, as you know. I've been teaching here for – goodness, three years now. I used to be a midwife but I started to find it . . . Well, let's just say I needed a change. So –' she shrugs humorously – 'here I am.'

Sheila and Sunita introduce themselves, just giving their names, and suddenly it's my turn.

'I'm Jo. I'm new to the area. And I feel – well, I think I need to do yoga.'

The others laugh. Again, I'm not sure why but it feels sympathetic, as if to say, *Don't we all?*

'I'm Pat. I usually come with my husband, Fred.'

'I'm Liz,' the short-haired woman the other side of her says. She seems quiet, rather shut in on herself.

'I'm Hayley,' says the girl who slipped in even later than the others. She's beautiful: startlingly young amid

46

such a middle-aged group, with thick blonde hair in a high ponytail and a pretty face, even more striking for the wide, dark brown eyes. Her voice is soft and lispy. 'Sorry I was late, Kim. Bit of a hold-up this morning.'

'No worries, Hayley,' Kim says. 'Right – well, we'll get started. Let's all begin by sitting in a comfortable position, legs crossed if you can and eyes half-closed. Take a deep breath, breathing right down into your abdomen.'

I let my spine straighten. I rest my hands on my knees and began to think about breathing. Air courses down my windpipe and I feel myself expand, as if the breath is plumbing down into forgotten folds of me. The air is lightly scented by the candle, something sweet and musky. It feels amazing, as if it's the deepest breath I've taken for months and months. As if I am just discovering breathing for the first time.

We exercise our necks and shoulders. I keep my eyes half-closed through a lot of it, enjoying the feeling of doing something physical, of noticing that I have a body. For all these months, all I have known has been the pain inside me, my body a shell for that pain, otherwise disregarded and untended. Now, in noticing, the old guilt surges up – You're alive, how can you be alive? I try to breathe it away, to alter my mind's direction of travel.

With each position I try deliberately to think of the part I am moving: arms – I have arms! – legs, belly, neck, spine. And muscles. We stand up and begin on the Salute to the Sun. I used to be quite fit. Now with each move, my stretching muscles prod me with reminders of neglect; reminders that I have a body, that I am a living, physical being.

Legs stretched wide for Warrior pose, thigh muscles

shaking from the effort, I find myself thinking of a tiny, bedraggled bird emerging new-born from an egg. After about half an hour, listening to Kim's soothing voice, following the movements of stretching and extending myself, something frightening starts to happen. At first, I start to feel a bit sick and wonder if I am overdoing it for a first time. I gulp in air, trying to overcome the feeling.

'Right,' Kim says. 'Now – we'll go back on to all fours, knees under hips – yes, legs back a bit further, Sunita, that's it. Cat-Cow – take a nice deep breath, flexing your spine . . .'

As instructed, I stare at the blue mat between my hands, beginning to wonder if I should escape to the bathroom. The weird pressure is notching up inside me. Blood pumps in my ears. I'm not exactly sure that sick is what I feel. I can't work it out. It's more the feeling that something is coming at me from a distance, like knowing somehow that a huge lorry is hurtling towards you along a street but not yet being able to see or hear it.

I breathe in deeply, then let the breath out, back arching, head between my shoulders: I breathe in again, belly down, back flexing, head up. We repeat the movement several times and the feeling swells into raw panic. My arms start to tremble, as if something is pressing down on me.

Don't give in to it, I tell myself, frightened now. But I start to wonder if I'm in fact having a heart attack or something. What are the symptoms for women – aren't they different from men's symptoms somehow? I can't remember. All of me is starting to shake and I keep my head down, hoping everyone else is doing the same so they don't notice the state I'm in.

'Right,' Kim says. 'Now we'll go into Child's Pose. That's it – knees together, lay your arms back alongside your legs, head down – just let everything relax.'

As I sink down on to my knees, it sweeps through me like a massive surfers' wave, turning me over and over, helpless. The sound that started to press out of me feels far in the distance at first, high, tiny, like a kitten mewling somewhere until I just can't stop even though I know it's me and it grows into a howl that just keeps coming, on and on, seemingly all on one breath.

'Jo?' A hand touches my back with soft caution. I am locked down, my forehead on the floor, in a darkness that has taken me right over and the hand is the only other thing I know. It begins to stroke, slowly back and forth along my back, just managing to connect me. 'Jo – it's OK. It's OK ... Don't worry, it's all right. You're safe, everything's all right – it's going to be all right.'

She keeps saying those words over and over and I can just about hear them and hold on to them from in the depth of swirling water and the churning and the sick press of the sobs that begin to choke up from inside me.

Once the weeping stops, after who knows how long, I push myself up on to my knees, my hands over my face. I can feel someone's warmth right next to me and I know it's Kim.

'You're OK.' She's kneeling, right there so I can feel her thigh against mine, her hand still on my back. The hand that has pulled me through, a wire-tap back into the rest of the world. 'It's all right, love. Don't worry. Everything's fine. Whatever it is, we're all here for you.' Her arms reach round my shoulders, holding me close, and I cry a little more, but the pressure has gone, has been blasted away. Gradually I take in her closeness, smell her perfume, something spicy, sweet and lovely.

Eventually, as Kim releases me, I dare to take my hands away from my face. Stunned, I realize I am in a circle of women, all watching me, the candle still flickering in the middle. I am beyond embarrassment. I feel exhausted, wrung out. And their eyes are full of kindness and concern and seeing this brings on more tears.

'I'm so sorry,' I say, dragging my hands down my cheeks. 'I've spoilt your class.'

'Don't be silly,' everyone chimes in and they make sympathetic noises. 'We're just worried about you . . .'

'Here you are, love . . .' Sheila reaches across with a packet of tissues.

'Thank you.' I try to smile but more tears course down my face. It feels as if, over the course of a few moments, I have been befriended and it wrings my heart. 'Oh, God – I'm so sorry.'

'No – don't be.' Kim keeps stroking my back again, tender, motherly. 'It does happen like that sometimes. Something physical like yoga can set things off. We don't always understand it or have any idea it's going to happen.'

I shake my head. I feel so bewildered, and yet so safe in this room, among these strangers. It's as if it has shifted a huge block in me, the stone jammed in at the door of a tomb.

'We don't even always know what it's about,' Kim says softly. 'We don't always have to know.'

'Oh, I know.' I look down. I can't look into their eyes at this minute, but I want the door to stay open, for this flow to continue – I *have* to let it. I can't look up, but I want to speak, *have* to. Looking at the edge of my blue mat, where it reaches the wood of the floor, blue on brown, I say, 'My son, Paul – he was our only child – was taken from us ... Killed, just over two years ago. Just after his twenty-third birthday. I just ...'

I hear their gasps of shock and sorrow.

'I haven't ...' Again the emotion hits me, another wave, though nothing like as overwhelming as the first. 'Haven't been able to cry ... Not really properly cry. All this time. And then suddenly, I come here and ...' I shrug. More tears run down my cheeks.

'Oh, you poor, poor girl,' Sheila says.

'It's a long time since anyone's called me a girl.' Wiping my cheeks, I manage a brief smile at them all, then look down again.

Kim puts her arm round me again and squeezes my shoulders. 'It's OK, love. It's what you need – it's fine.'

I look at her. 'You must have been a really good midwife.'

'Oh –' Kim gives a quick smile, but I can sense her flinch somehow – 'thanks.' And I see her brown eyes fill with tears.

Seven

The first thing I noticed about Ian was his eyes.

It was the summer of 1982. Ange and I had just finished our teaching degree and we were out celebrating. We'd never done much clubbing, partly because we were short of money and by the end of the week we often didn't have the energy. We'd go and sit in the pub instead. But now we decided to take ourselves into town with a couple of the other girls and dance the night away. We started off at Kaleidoscope and moved on to Sam Wellers.

Ange was always the dressy one. She had glammed up in a silver sequinned skirt, all layers of ruffles, and a sparkly bronze top. Her eyelids were coated in spaceman silver and thick black eyeliner. With her copper hair she didn't half stand out, glowing and metallic, unmissable. Some bloke was forever coming up to her, show-off dancing, giving it a try.

I felt like the quiet, mousey one next to Ange. After all, my hair *is* mousey, although then I'd just had it cut, short and neat – *gamine*, Ange said when she first saw it. I didn't – and still don't – like feeling overdressed so I'd usually go for a simple look. That night I had on a straight, short, strappy black dress and I was glad of it as I danced myself into a lather on the floor of Sam Wellers, my head all swimmy with the Malibu Ange had insisted we drink and the hot air thick with sweat and smoke.

Everything felt great. We'd finished training, that long slog was over and we'd soon get a job! But first Ange and I were going Interrailing round Europe. I always loved travelling then, saved up, did pub jobs, anything to earn myself that free feeling of taking off, the adventure, exploring new places. (Mom and Dad thought I was mad of course. Why go to all those foreign places when you could be saving for a nice little flat?) The first summer it had been India and Nepal – on my own – the next doing Camp America, teaching kids in Pennsylvania, then two weeks of freedom, heading south on the Greyhound bus.

'Come on ...' We'd sat out for a rest, but Ange stubbed out her fag and pulled me back on to the dance floor. 'We've got to do this one!'

Alison Moyet's voice belted out, 'Don't Go!' and a rhythm you couldn't help falling into. I was spacey, half drunk, mouth oversweet with the pineapple mixer. I closed my eyes but it made me feel as if I was going to fall over, so I quickly opened them and the room was a kaleidoscope of broken shapes and colours all swimming about. When I blinked, whole people came into focus. 'Don't Go!' And I found my rhythm again.

Eyes, just opposite me. Brown eyes. A nice face, good hair, nothing too fancy, just dark and wavy and sitting right with the shape of him. Medium-sized, not overly tall, jeans, shirt. That was what I took in under the flashing lights. I looked away, looked back. Our gaze danced back and forth. The third time, we both smiled, at the same time. For the next couple of dances, it was just eyes, glancing away, drawn back, his smile – a nice smile.

'I'm just a grease-monkey,' he said, once we'd sat down to talk – shout almost – over a drink. He'd bought me a Coke, a lager for himself. We were at the side of the dance floor but I suddenly wanted to be somewhere else, in a quiet place, talking. I couldn't just go off and leave Ange, though.

'I want to set up my own place one day,' he said. 'I'm working my way round – getting as much experience as I can.'

He was impressed by me being a teacher. 'You must be brainy.'

'No, not really,' I laughed. 'I just need to be one step ahead of them. That's my mate, Ange –' I nodded towards the dance floor where she was with yet another bloke. 'We trained together.'

He glanced at Ange, then back at me. 'Whoa,' he said, laughing.

'She's all right,' I said. 'We're going off travelling together next week – round Europe.'

Ian looked at me in amazement. When I told him where else I'd been, he seemed almost bewildered, as if travelling anywhere was another life that he could not be part of.

'I couldn't go away for that long anyway,' he said. 'I want to keep this job.'

We had to lean close to talk. I liked his face, liked the attentive way he tilted his head to hear everything I said. And I liked the way he sat, the shape of his forearms close to mine, the curved muscle under the skin, his fingers round the glass, strong, with wide nails he must have scrubbed clean before coming out. There was something right about him from the start.

He said his name was Ian Stefani. He was twenty-six: I was twenty-three.

'Isn't that an Eytie name?' Dad said, when I told them about Ian, weeks later. His face wore a little frown. Even the war had not managed to widen Dad's horizons. He was in RAF ground crew and never left British soil.

'He's born and bred here.' I laughed to cover my annoyance. 'His mom's name was Doreen Parsons before she was married. He's not foreign or anything.'

'Oh,' Dad said, nodding. 'I see.' He didn't quite add, *Well, that's all right then.*

And of course they always liked Ian, from when they met him; he was polite and, like them, practical and a hard worker, so they approved of him.

Ange and I went on our travels and after that, Ian and I started seeing each other seriously. After my first year, teaching in a school in Lozells, I moved across the city to Greet, to be closer to where Ian was working in Balsall Heath. We moved in together, to Mom's disgust. I knew Dorrie was none too impressed either, though of course, she wasn't one for making harsh judgements. With her it was just a bit of a 'Huh,' and, 'In my day you got married first,' half-joking, even if she was actually quite shocked.

She was always good to me. I was nervous meeting her. Ian is her only son and I thought she might be over-protective and determined to criticize me whoever I was. Ian had never made out that she was like that, but I was still a bit scared. But I remember us going round to her neat little house when she still lived in town. When she opened the front door, she looked at me – really looked – and there was something lovely in her eyes, as if she liked me on sight and didn't mind showing it. She'd laid out a nice tea for us – a tablecloth with proper cups and Mr Kipling's slices and Bakewells and would I like some toast as well? And she was warm and kindly and interested. I think I actually loved her from the first day and not just because I loved Ian. There was something all-embracing about Dorrie. In her simple, straightforward way she gathered you in and you knew she was on your side.

By the Easter of 1985, we gave in to the pressure and got married in the registry office in town, Ian in that grey suit, me trying to look just enough like a bride to keep Mom happy. Then we spent a week away in Wales and it rained almost all the time. There were long mornings in bed; afternoons being almost blown off the coast path, laughing our heads off. We were very, very happy and we laughed at most things then.

The first time it happened, I was terrified for days afterwards. It was soon after we'd got married, as if the very fact of this legal contract made some sort of difference to being careful. We were in our little rented terrace in Balsall Heath and had had a Friday night pizza and a few beers.

Tumbling muzzy and tired into bed, we made love – matter-of-fact, end-of-the-week love, but love all the same. We lay cooling afterwards, side by side, the curtains still open to the marbled grey of a summer night sky. Ian turned sleepily to give my bare shoulder a goodnight kiss. And it hit me.

'Oh, my God!' I jerked up, horrified.

'What?' Ian sounded jarred and indignant.

'My pill – I haven't taken it! Not for two days!' My

heart was pounding, stress beating through me. What the hell was I thinking? We had no plans to have kids – not yet at least. We needed to work for a few years, try and get a place of our own, get Ian into his own business – and have some fun and freedom.

Ian stroked my back. 'It'll be all right. Two days won't matter, surely?'

'*One* day can matter.' Furious with myself, panicking, I scrambled out of bed. 'I'll take one now. Maybe that'll do the trick.'

The next morning, Ian seemed to have forgotten all about it. He got up early for work, brought me a coffee in bed, pulled his overalls on and kissed me goodbye.

I'll never forget that day because in the end, it was so bittersweet, so ironic. There I was, crouched with my mug under the striped duvet, staring at the weird coffee colour of the wood-chip wallpaper, my mind revolving. I told myself I was overreacting. Most women took ages to get pregnant, didn't they? One time of being careless wasn't going to matter. But I just couldn't stop obsessing about it. I felt as if all my future was changing shape. My mind kept whirling round the same track: what if I *am* pregnant? No, I can't be – but I might be ... Calculations. When would it be due if I had conceived last night? It was 21 May, so roughly ... next February. Maternity leave would take me up to the summer holidays and how were we going to manage everything? Everything I had thought and planned up until last night felt suddenly fragile, subject to being punctured open by the disruption of another life.

Finishing the coffee, I lay back down and rested my

hands on my belly, wonder and dread mingled so closely I could hardly tell one from another.

The moment I got my period – in the middle of the day, at school – I sat on the staff toilet, hands over my face, and sobbed. Whether it was relief or grief I was not sure. I hadn't said anything much to Ian because while it was so uncertain I felt silly. He didn't really get it anyway – he had not spent almost every waking moment of those weeks wondering and worrying, that was for sure.

I sat up and stared at the dark red lino of the toilet floor. However relieved I was, I also felt bereft, as if a new little presence who had been standing just in the corner of my eye, waiting to move into my life, had crept away. Everything felt suddenly dulled. I pulled off a strip of tissue, wiped my face, blew my nose.

'Still,' I whispered to myself. 'Just as well really.'

It happened again, once, about eighteen months later, and again it was a false alarm. Looking back, I took the pill unnecessarily for the best part of five years. I might just as well not have bothered because when we did at last decide to go for it and try to conceive, months passed and it made no difference whatsoever. My body remained like an unlit candle.

Eight

I feel shy going back to the yoga class the next week, but drawn to it all the same, to the feeling I had from them of acceptance and friendship.

As I push open the door to the hall, the few people in there – Sheila, Pat and Sunita – all turn and call out hello. With Pat is a man who I take to be her husband, a lean, bald, suntanned bloke not much taller than she is. They are both laughing at something with Sunita.

'You all right?' Kim asks as I go over to hand her the money. She ticks me off on the list. I feel ridiculously happy to be on any sort of list – to belong somewhere again, even just a little.

'Yeah. Not too bad, thanks.' I manage a smile. In fact, the week hasn't been too bad. Up and down, of course, but I've kept busy, popping in to see Dorrie and gradually getting the house straight.

I'm just laying out my mat in the circle when Hayley comes in and takes the spot next to me.

'Hello.' She gives her rather dreamy smile as she settles cross-legged on her mat and I'm struck afresh by just how pretty she is, and how lovely her thick, honey-coloured hair. Hayley also has a sweet, friendly manner, hesitant, as if she has no real idea how beautiful she is.

'How are you?' she says as we sit side by side and I feel touched. Hayley can only be in her mid-twenties, but she has a calm, self-possessed manner that makes her seem older.

'Not too bad, thanks,' I say again. Not wanting to go into anything about me, I say, 'You're not exactly what I'd think of as a "Creak and Groan" sort of person.'

Hayley laughs. 'Well – I love doing a yoga class and I can't come to the one in the evening 'cause I'm at work. This one suits me, and it's a lovely group.'

'We're all a bit old for you, though,' I say. Being beside Hayley suddenly makes me feel old. I certainly could be her mother.

'I don't mind.' She rummages in her bag and brings out a bottle of water. 'To be honest, I live with my nan and help to look after her – I quite like being with older people.'

'Oh. Right.' I nod, wondering about this.

'I don't really get on with my mom – she and my dad split up when I was quite young – and I'm close to Nan. She sort of brought me up, you see.'

I say, 'That's nice,' as I'm not sure what else to say and then Kim comes over to sit on her mat. 'Right – everyone ready? Let's make a start.'

We begin, as before. The group is much the same as last week – Hayley and Sunita, Kim and Sheila, and Pat and me; there's also Liz, the quiet lady, and Pat's husband Fred. He's wearing sporty grey tracksuit trousers and a white T-shirt and cracks little jokes all the way through the class. I find myself wishing he'd shut up.

I'm quite scared to start with that something might happen, the way it did last week. I went home afterwards and managed another cry that afternoon. I felt quite a bit better – lighter, as if each tear had literally carried a heavy weight. But today I want to enjoy the feeling of stretching my body, of breathing deeply, just a quiet time to move in and out of the postures.

And I do. And I feel a bit calmer.

The next week, Kim says, is the last one before Christmas – I'm trying to ignore Christmas but of course every single tinselly, jingling place you go forces it to your attention. Afterwards Sheila comes up to me.

'By the way, Jo, every Thursday afternoon, three-thirty, some of us meet up from this group for a cup of tea and a chat – at my house. You're very welcome to come.'

The others make encouraging noises about it being a great chance to talk without Kim putting them through various tortures etc.

I hesitate, almost automatically. Since we've been here I've hardly been anywhere except Dorrie's, yoga and Sainsbury's. And, of course, the cemetery when I can get there – when Ian leaves me the car, or on the buses, which takes up a good portion of the day. It's so much easier to be alone in some ways, but I tell myself not to be stupid.

'That's nice. Thanks. Yes – I'd like that.'

'We're a friendly lot, you know, out here in the sticks,' Sheila says. 'Here, I'll write down my address for you.' During these last two classes we haven't chatted much – we've all just got on with it and as my mind adjusts to it I realize the tea idea is a really nice one.

'You're not working then?' Hayley says as we pack up our things.

'Not at the moment,' I say, rolling my mat. 'We've just moved in and I'm getting sorted out. I suppose I'll have to look for a job round here soon.'

'That must be nice.' Hayley looks wistful. 'Just not having to work for a bit.'

'Why – where do you work?'

'Oh, I've got a bar job in the evening at the moment. It suits me – I can help Nan out in the day, and do things like this class.'

As I walk home in the freezing wind, promising to go to Sheila's on Thursday, I find myself thinking about work. I feel bad that Ian is having to carry all the burden of our income even though he says he doesn't mind.

'I'm not ready to go back into the classroom,' I said to him, just before we moved here. We were lying in bed together, a Sunday morning and the one day Ian doesn't rush out to work. He's devoted to his business but he doesn't hold with opening seven days a week.

'One day maybe, but not yet.'

The very thought of work fills me with panic, as if all my inner resources have drained away. 'Maybe I should just get a little job in a shop or something.'

'We'll be all right,' he said. He had his hands behind his head. I missed us snuggling up, putting our arms round each other like we always would have done before, just lying there nattering for ages. But Ian stayed where he was, distant again. 'We'll have enough money coming in. And to be honest at the moment I'd rather you were around for Mom –'specially after what's happened. She doesn't want to go into a home – it'll make all the difference you popping in.'

I really can't face work yet and I'm grateful to him.

For Ian, the opposite seems to be true. Work has been his way of coping. Since Paul, and that night, he seems to have done almost nothing but work. There always seems to be a rush job, someone off sick, setting up the new business, needing to take on more staff . . . But what it feels like is him avoiding me, avoiding feeling anything about Paul, and avoiding what I'm feeling and *my* way of grieving. He doesn't want to know. He won't even look me in the eye, as if he's afraid of what he'll see there.

Sheila's house is about a mile from ours. As I turn into the street, a cul-de-sac, I see a dumpy little figure trundling along ahead of me in crimson trousers, a brown coat and a pale blue woolly hat, topped with a jaunty pompom. When we both arrive, almost the same time, at the door of Sheila's neat, modern semi I realize it's Sunita.

'Oh, hello!' She smiles at me, dragging her hat off so that some of her shoulder-length hair lifts with it, drawn by static. She rubs vaguely at her hair to settle it. 'How are you?' she asks, so cheerfully that it does not feel like a loaded question.

'I'm fine,' I say.

Sunita presses the doorbell. 'Fine is all very well.' She turns and looks very directly at me. Her face is round, dimply, good-natured. 'Not easy for you, though. You poor girl, terrible – terrible.'

My throat aches, but I like her matter-of-fact way of speaking. I swallow and try to smile. 'Thanks.'

Sheila opens the door, dressed once again in jeans and her big red sweater.

'Hello. Come in.' She does have a bossy manner and it makes me wonder if she has been a teacher. (I can be bossy too – it becomes a habit.) 'There – hang up your coats.' She points at a row of hooks along the hall. 'Pat's here already. I've got the kettle on.'

The living room, like ours, runs from front to back of the house. On each side of the front section, there is a chocolate-brown sofa along the wall opposite the fire-place, a gas fire encased in a stone surround. At the back end, under the window, is a round table on which there are already cups and saucers.

I say hello to Pat, who gives her big-toothed, friendly smile. Sunita pulls the table out further and squeezes her-self round and on to a chair. Passing through the room to join them, I catch a glimpse of photographs on the mantel: one or two portraits and groups of young people in some sort of uniform – Guides, I think. And on the rug in front of it, head raised to look blearily up at me, is an old, white-muzzled black Labrador.

'Oh!' Warmed by the sight I squat down to give him a stroke. He settles his head again, making appreciative little noises. 'It's nice to see you. You like a bit of fuss, don't you? What's your name then?'

'I think he's called Herbert,' Pat says. 'But she calls him Herbie.'

Pat and Sunita chat a bit though I sense they are shy of each other. After a minute I get up to join them at the table.

'No husband?' I ask Pat, though I'm quite glad that endlessly chirpy Fred is not here.

'Oh, no,' Sheila says, before Pat can reply, as she car-ries a large teapot to the table, swaddled in a padded cosy with country cottages on it. 'We're golf widows on a Thursday – Roy and Fred play together.'

Hayley arrives then and everyone makes a fuss of her, the baby of the group. I can see why. She's so gorgeous-looking of course, but as well as that there's something about her that makes you want to protect her. She looks very tired, with dark circles under eyes, despite her loveliness.

'Oh, dear – look at that,' Sunita says, as Sheila brings in a big sponge cake, oozing jam. She runs her hands up and down over her hips. 'Looks lovely – but I'm getting fat, isn't it?'

'You're all right,' Sheila says, pouring tea. 'Anyway, you get enough exercise running around after those grandchildren.'

We sit round the table, the five of us, and it's nice – more than nice. I feel so grateful to be invited because I realize how much I have isolated myself. We stay mostly on the surface of things, but it's cosy, with the flames of Sheila's gas fire flickering away when the day outside is so cold and raw.

'This is really our core yoga group,' Sheila says, as we all start on the cake. 'With Kim, obviously. There are a few others who come and go but they don't often come round on a Thursday. Kim makes it sometimes, but she has kids to pick up from school. We've become quite a little huddle, haven't we?'

'A coven,' Hayley says, and we laugh.

'You don't look much like a witch to me,' Pat says.

'As for the rest of us . . .' Sheila adds, in her wry way. She stands again to top up everyone's cup.

We drink several cups of tea and eat Sheila's cake – Sunita accepting a slice with a shrug and a chuckle, despite her protests, and then another one. They ask me harmless questions and I say we have come to live near my mother-in-law, who is not well. They do not ask about Paul and I know they will one day and that they care but that this is not the time.

And they tell me things about the neighbourhood, the best doctor, a reliable plumber, the good shops, that it's a lovely neighbourhood, very caring. That I should come to them if I need to know anything.

I learn a sprinkling of other things that afternoon: that Sunita's husband is a solicitor and they have two daughters, each with a daughter of her own, and that one of the families is living in Canada. That Pat works as a receptionist in a busy medical practice. She and Fred married as teenagers and seem to have been joined like Siamese twins ever since. They have two sons. Pat's conversation is sprinkled with the words 'Fred says . . .' at which I occasionally see Sheila roll her eyes. Sheila makes us laugh with stories about 'my Roy', who seems to be a bit accident prone – even getting a lawnmower out of the garage is an activity fraught with danger and don't get her started on his DIY . . . Hayley giggles and everyone talks about day-to-day things – plans for Christmas, a broken-down washing machine, the disappearing window-cleaner. And I am warmed and grateful that they do not starting interrogating me. I am glad just to be included.

The person who surprises me is Pat. I had pigeonholed her, I suppose, as someone a bit dull, a housewife who always has her husband's tea on the table at six. But whenever she says anything, although she is quiet, she has a gentle sort of authority. And there's that lovely fresh-faced smile. I realize I am starting to warm to her.

Hayley is the first to look at her watch and get to her feet.

'That was lovely, Sheila – thank you. I'd better go. Got to get to work.'

We all start to make a move.

'Where do you live, Jo?' Pat asks me. 'Do you need a lift?'

'It's OK,' I say. 'Thanks – but it's not far. And I need to go and see my mother-in-law on the way.'

There is nothing dramatic about the afternoon, nothing much happens, but afterwards I walk home in the dying light, the red tail-lights of the crawling rush-hour cars glowing in the winter gloom. The wind is icy against my cheeks, but inside I feel just a little defrosted. I feel included, and I have received kindness. It makes all the difference.

Nine

Is this what normal parents feel?

I used to wonder that, all the time. 'Normal' parents by blood, not adoptive parents. How does that bond feel? Does it give you an absolute, instinctive insight into this child who you have carried for nine months, have felt moving inside you, have spoken to, sung to and dreamed of? I suppose I thought it did and I struggled with the difference, the mystery that was Paul.

All we knew about Paul's birth mother was that she was young – sixteen – and had not been able to cope. Had she felt that bond, though? How had she managed to sever it and let herself part with him? Had she not known him through and through?

When I asked Rachel, one of the other moms I knew when Paul was small, she said, 'Oh, no. I don't think it's quite like that.' She was watching her four-year-old, Emily, clambering over a frame in the playground as she said it and her eyes never left the child. 'I mean, I may be her mother, but I've no idea what's going on in her head – she's a funny little thing.'

But she said it in that confident, casual tone which belongs only to the very secure. She had the bond, it seemed to me – she knew it without question. The bond of a positive pregnancy test, of vomiting for weeks, of back-ache and indigestion, of feeling the little one stirring inside like a simmering pot, of their first acquaintance face to face in the delivery room. She didn't know what it was to question it, the way I did constantly.

I never was sure of anything – all the way through, never felt quite good enough. But it was not as if I had no bond with Paul. When I first saw him, there was a right-ness. I liked the look of him, quite literally. I liked his dark, bouncy curls and solemn brown eyes; liked him all over, even though his second foster mother Elaine (the first had fallen sick), who had had him for about nine months, had held him back. She had been keeping him in his cot a bit too much and not encouraging him to stand, so that whoever adopted him might feel they were getting a baby. He was moon-faced and still only just getting to his feet at fourteen months. And (though it was men-tioned that he found transitions difficult) we were not there to see his heartbroken wails when he had to be parted from Elaine. But both of us – Ian just as much, I think – liked Paul from the start and very quickly grew to love him.

There was the amazing feeling of taking him home for good, just before Christmas, the tree already up to wel-come him to a pretty, magical home. When we stepped, that day, into our little terrace in Moseley and shut the door behind us, parents for the first time, we were like children ourselves with a new gift, a gift so long waited for that we were fizzy with excitement. All we could think of was him. I didn't want to dwell on Paul's birth mother. I just wanted to pretend she never existed, that we were all there was.

We wheeled his buggy into the front room and saw his eyes widen at the sight of the tree. He made a sound and reached out his hand towards it and we both laughed, enchanted.

And then we looked at each other almost in horror.

'Oh, my God,' I said. 'What have we done?'

Ian pulled me into his arms and we stood for a few moments, awed and close, so close.

'Come on,' Ian said, as Paul started squeaking. 'We've got a family to look after.' I'll never forget his voice as he said that, how proud he was, how right and happy. We were both ready to bathe Paul in love and attention. 'Let's let the little guy out.'

On Paul's first day at school, he clung to me so persistently – first my cardigan, then my leg – that it took both the teacher and the teaching assistant to separate us. His screams filled the room so that the other children quietened and watched with sober expressions.

'Maybe I should take him home again?' I said, utterly chewed up by the sound of my little boy's desolate grief. Ian and I had agreed that I would not go back to work full-time before Paul was doing a full day at school himself. I had been doing bits of supply teaching, leaving him at home with Dorrie for a few hours here and there and taking him to playgroup myself. He and Dorrie hit it off from the start. She was wonderful with him. But I had never been apart from him for long.

'No,' Miss Akhtar, the class teacher, said. She was young, gentle but firm, though she was having to raise her voice over Paul's howls, his hurling himself about trying to get away from her. 'That wouldn't be a good idea. I know it's hard, but the best thing is for you to say good-bye and leave. You'll come back – and he'll see that you come back. I promise, if there's any real problem, we'll give you a call.'

Miss Tennant, the young, plump assistant, was nodding away as well. They looked pretty desperate for me to leave, so I did as requested, feeling like the most terrible traitor. I never did receive a call, even though I spent the morning hovering near the phone, not daring to go out. What I didn't realize then was that this was how it was going to be for weeks and weeks.

Paul was content enough with us at home. In fact, he would have been happiest if he had never had to leave the house at all.

He grew, slimmed down, and his curls relaxed to waves of dark chestnut. Later, his moods darkened, became mysterious, but as a young child he was a cheerful, funny little lad when he felt secure and we had so many lovely times. We took him on as many trips and holidays as we could manage. There were winter afternoons after school, snuggled by the telly with tea, friends round. Paul was not terribly sociable but there were a couple of kids he hit it off with all right. And he was a bright little boy, quietly did well at school. At weekends, Ian sometimes took him out, lads together, or the two of them sat side by side doing Lego or watching TV.

We were always honest with him about his having been adopted. Every year, on 18 December, we had a celebration day, as well as his birthday in October. 'The best day of our lives', I always told him. 'The day you came to us. It's a bit like your royal birthday!'

He asked questions. It was only as he grew older that the questions became more painful to answer. *But why did she have to give me away?* Questions I could never give answers to that would repair that rupture in him. What turned out to be worse was when he stopped asking.

Ten

2005

'Paul, love? Dinner's ready.'

As I said it I tapped on the door and walked in. For a frozen second I stared at the figure stretched out, prone on the bed. Afterwards, I asked myself why I had been so frightened. Paul was lying there, dressed, still wearing his trainers. His hair was all scruffy, head tilted to one side. His face was pale and he was lying so still . . .

'Paul?' I could hear how shrill I sounded.

'Uh?' His eyes opened, registered me standing there. He sat up, the bed, its dark blue sheets and duvet cover, wrinkled about him. The room, painted steel grey, was a messy cavern of books, graphic-art comics and CDs which had long ago left Blondie behind. Bands with names like Aborted, Meshuggah, Apocalyptica. There was a stale, shut-in smell, tinged with sweat.

He put his hands over his face and rubbed them up and down, yawning.

'I thought you were doing your homework?' I didn't mean this as a reproach but it sounded like one. GCSEs in a few weeks. He'd be lucky to scrape through any of them, the way things were.

'I must've fallen asleep.' He shook his head. 'Sorry.'

He was never rude, not to us. He was still my boy. But

he had retreated somewhere even harder to reach. Rudeness and stroppiness might have been easier. All the things I worried about – dope-smoking, drug-taking, bunking off school, trouble and crime – none of these were in evidence. But trouble – sadness, self-loathing, disappointment? – hung about him like a kind of body odour. And I did not know what to do.

'Coming down for dinner?' I was turning into one of those mothers who resorts to being all bright and breezy. 'It's sausage casserole.' His favourite, as if sausages could heal the primal wound of having been given away, which, whatever I said in the way of love and acceptance, of having chosen and wanted him, was deep and unhealed, perhaps unhealable. I felt ridiculous.

'Yeah. Coming.' He got slowly to his feet, rubbing at the chaos of his hair, which I did not dare suggest he go and get cut.

His grades slipped year on year in secondary school. I tried to get to the bottom of it. I knew he was bright. Was he being bullied? No, it seemed not. Classmates liked him, or at least left him alone. He was not completely friendless, because he was nice-looking and amiable, could be funny at times. He did not bunk off school, set cars on fire, burgle houses. Nothing like that.

But it was as if he was being eaten away from the inside.

I read all the books about adopted kids, and their feelings of not being the child that was really wanted, being second best; even being chosen by us was second best because it implied being rejected before that by *the one who mattered most*. The anger and sadness, and the feeling that you never belonged anywhere, not really. The rupture of separation from the woman who had birthed you, however unprepared or unable she was to mother you, the sound of her voice, her smell, the rhythms of her body. This woman about whom I knew next to nothing.

It was heartbreaking, helpless-making to read. I loved Paul as my own – or as close to that as I ever could, because I could never be sure exactly how loving 'your own' would be. Would I have given my own life to save him? Yes, without a doubt. He was my boy. But I had not been able to give him the launch-pad of my own body, the safety of a continuous thread within and without a mother's physical being.

It was not even that we had never talked about it. Paul would sometimes say, hesitantly, sweetly, that he loved me but was not sure where he belonged. It was hard for him to explain. Sometimes we took walks together in the little park, in Moseley, a circle around a small lake, big, ornate Edwardian houses on the skyline above.

'It's not like I want to go and find her or anything – you're my mom and dad. I don't mean I don't belong with you and Dad. I just mean . . . in myself. I think.'

'I think all teenagers feel that to some extent,' I said, guessing, trying to remember. It was not as if I had ever really felt compatible with my parents – even my brother Mark and I were never close. And I told him so.

'Oh, right, yeah,' Paul said, watching his feet on the path. But even then, I could tell from the way he said it that this was no help. Is it ever, knowing how other people feel? I said it to make him feel less alone, but I could see that alone was exactly how he felt.

'Would you like to talk to somebody?' I asked, that day.

His brow crinkled. 'Who?'

'Someone . . . professional. About how you feel.'

He shrugged. 'Maybe.' But he did not seem to welcome it.

'Let's wait and see,' I said to Ian afterwards. He left me to handle all the emotional side. He said he had no idea what to do – as if I did. But I knew he was worried as well. 'He might feel better after the exams.'

He scraped through his GCSEs. The only fail was in science, which he hated anyway. The rest were Cs and Ds. Without any enthusiasm he chose to do A levels in English, philosophy and geography.

'Well, where's that going to get him?' Dad asked, in his usual *I never had any education and look where I ended up* sort of way.

'You can hardly get any work these days without A levels,' Ian said quickly, glancing at me. He didn't have any either.

Dad tutted. 'They'd all be better off with a stint in the army, teach 'em some discipline. None of this lying in bed 'til midday. No wonder we've got hardly any industries left in this city.'

Before I could open my mouth to start on Margaret Thatcher's legacy, Ian said quickly, 'D'you need some help with those paving stones out there, Ron? Looks as if you've got a job on.'

Paul never sat his A levels. Year by year, the bright little boy who had been, if not at the top of the class in his primary school, at least near the middle, sank lower. Teachers spoke to me, concerned. It wasn't that he was unpleasant, they said. He was a nice boy. But he seemed distracted, sunken into himself. There was talk of tests, of ADD, but no one seemed sure about anything. Paul managed to do most of the first year of A levels, going through the motions, making out that it was all right.

In the summer of 2006 he broke down. Being Paul, even this was a quiet event, no histrionics, no outward anger or blame. It was as if he disappeared, slowly, then suddenly. One minute he was revising for his AS exams, the next it was as if he had disappeared, like someone crawling into a large concrete pipe by the roadside for shelter.

He slept, hours at a time even in the day. He had hardly any appetite. When I asked him questions about how he felt he could not seem to answer, as if there was nothing to grasp hold of and an emptiness had taken over. That was how he seemed: empty.

From the outside he appeared like someone who had been unplugged. Watching him try to get up and do anything, I could see it required an enormous amount of effort and he was often defeated. On one of the mornings of the summer half-term, I went up, mid-morning, thinking I really must try and help him get going. The room smelt. He was not washing, or not enough, and he had a sweaty, unaired smell about him, like an old man.

When he swung his long, pale legs over the side of the bed, I sat beside him, full of frustration, of sorrow and tenderness, because I knew he never meant any harm, my boy, not to us. It was only himself he was harming and he could not seem to help it.

'Come on, lovey.' I put my arm round him and squeezed him gently.

Paul sat, impassive.

'I'll wash your sheets today. Let's take them off together, shall we? You can go and sit out in the sun – it's a lovely day.'

He did not react. He sat sunken into himself.

'Paul?'

No answer.

'Love?' I leaned down, trying to see into his face. 'I'm worried about you. I think we need to ask someone for help. The doctor for a start, maybe?'

He moved his head fractionally, almost a nod, but not quite.

'I think we need to, don't we?' I put both arms round him then, hugging him close, kissing his oily hair, babying him as tears stung in my eyes. I didn't want to do anything against his will, this gentle boy, who was frightening me now with his inner sickness. 'Someone who can help you feel better? We all want you to feel better – I hate seeing you like this, my love.'

There was a faint, defeated nod. 'Yeah. OK,' he said.

Eleven

18 December 2014

Dorrie complained that her sight was cloudy and I made the optician's appointment on that particular date for both our sakes. Keep busy, something else to think about – Paul's 'royal' birthday. And in the afternoon, tea at Sheila's with the Creak and Groaners. I'll barely have time to stop all day.

Dorrie is waiting for me in her chair. When I arrive, she makes moves to get up, struggling, pushing down on the arms.

'Can you manage?' I hurry over to help, seeing how much she is shaking with the effort. Looping an arm under hers to pull her up, I can feel her bones actually creaking and how thin and insubstantial she is, the frame of something which has lost its substance.

'We ought to get you one of those chairs,' I say. 'The ones that help you get up. You press a button and—'

Dorrie gives a dismissive flick of her spare wrist. 'I don't want one of them things. Throw me half-way across the room one of them would.'

'I think you can adjust them,' I'm saying, but she's shaking her head, the stubborn old girl.

But it really hit me this morning. Since I have been coming to see Dorrie regularly, we've just sat and talked.

Have I seen her get up and move about, even once? How could I have been so stupid, so wrapped up in myself that I have not tried to find out how things really are for her? She, dignified and stubborn to the last, has probably not wanted us to know what a struggle her life is. And there is part of me that does not want to know. I want to think that this loving old lady will just go on and on . . . I can't bear the thought of her not being there any more . . . I am awash with guilt. I haven't even read the stuff in that envelope she gave me because, to my shame, I have hidden it away and forgotten all about it.

'Ah – that's it,' Dorrie says valiantly, once upright, though she doesn't seem steady on her feet.

Questions nag at my mind. How is Dorrie getting up and down the stairs? Is she struggling to get dressed? Has no one from the hospital asked or offered help? But Ian and I are her closest family and even we have not thought to ask.

'D'you think you're going to be able to manage?' I ask gently.

'I'll be all right, bab.' Dorrie looks down, bracing herself. She holds out a clawed hand. 'Pass me my stick.'

As I help Dorrie into her old mac, looping a scarf round her neck, my mind speeds over needs and possibilities: a Zimmer frame, a wheelchair, one of those stair lifts. The bathroom has already got some handles and she has a shower. But there's a step up into it . . . I don't say any more to her then though, not wanting to chivvy Dorrie with all of it at once.

We inch down the front path to the car, Dorrie a sharp-boned weight on my arm. Ian got a lift to work today so that I could have the car. I help Dorrie fold herself slowly into the seat, lean down and strap her in, pull her coat straight over her knees.

'Thanks, Jo.' She sits upright, steeling herself, then looks up at me. 'Never get old.'

'Dorrie,' I say brightly as we head out to the main road. 'How about we get one of those stairlifts put in for you?'

Dorrie's head shoots round. 'A Stannah?' I'm surprised she is so clued up. 'Oh, I don't need one of them things. I can get up and down the stairs. I'm slow, but I can do it.'

There are times when it's better not to argue. I'll talk to Ian about it all later.

We get through the whole business of parking and getting her into the optician's, an epic journey across a small patch of tarmac which suddenly seems ocean wide, Dorrie pressing down on my arm. Seeing Dorrie in her own house is one thing. Outside she seems shrunken and terribly frail.

It takes her a while to get her breath back in the waiting room. Sitting in the bright, white space, she seems somehow exotic, like a little old owl brought indoors.

'Nice and clean in here.'

'When did you last have an eye test, Dorrie?' I enjoy the feeling of sitting beside her. It's a time for a little chat, mother and daughter. Almost.

'Oh,' she says vaguely. 'I don't know. Years back.'

After a comfortable silence, she says, 'Ian all right?'

'He came in to see you on Sunday, didn't he?'

She nods. 'But is he?'

'I think so.' I hesitated. 'As much as he ever is. It's not always easy to tell.'

'That's what I meant, bab. He bottles things up.'

I know we are both thinking about the same thing.

'It's twenty-five years today since you took him home, in't it?' Dorrie says very softly, with a sideways tilt to her head.

'Twenty-four,' I whisper.

'Oh. Oh, yes. Twenty-four.' She nods slowly.

'Mrs Stefani – are you ready to come through?' A young woman in dark-framed glasses has emerged through the door facing us.

Back at the house, I make tea and a sandwich for each of us, slices of gleaming ham, wafers of tomato, no skins, the way Dorrie likes it.

'Cataract operations are very straightforward – she said, didn't she?'

We are each side of the fire, Sweep sprawled out between us. I can see now what I have not chosen to see before – the milkiness of Dorrie's right eye.

'Ar – I s'pect so.' She takes a sip of tea, hands shaking.

'You don't need to worry, Dorrie – really. It's all done in five minutes. They do loads every day.'

'I'm not worried.'

I follow her every move – just in case – as she painstakingly returns the mug to the table and stares down at the brown, saggy hearthrug. Her fire is an old-fashioned electric thing, hot coils of orange with thin silver bars in front.

She seems preoccupied and I assume it's because she is fretting over her eyes. In fact, I start to wonder again if something else is going on, something physical. I quickly finish my last mouthful of sandwich, lay the plate on the floor. I wonder whether to ask my mother-in-law if she's feeling all right. She doesn't much like questions of that sort. I must go home and read her thing, whatever it is – her collection of papers. She wants me to read it, to know something, and I haven't even bothered to get it out yet. I'm fretting, guilty and worried, when Dorrie looks across at me suddenly, apparently lively as a cricket.

'Put the telly on for me before you go, will you, bab? There's one of them old films on. Pass us the remote control and I'll settle in for the afternoon.'

Twelve

ROSES WITH THORNS

Our house seems terribly quiet when I get home. I don't want to start thinking, to sink into myself, so I hurry to fetch Dorrie's envelope from upstairs and settle down on the sofa with it. I find myself feeling nervous. I would never have put Dorrie down as someone who would find the time to write. It's like discovering a hidden side of her.

I had pushed the papers she gave me into my chest of drawers upstairs, under some T-shirts. The Manila envelope, with Dorrie's typed address crossed out, is old and soft with wear. I draw out the sheaf of cheap bits of paper folded inside and flick through them. The sheets are all lined, of varying sizes, and one side of each is covered in Dorrie's childlike copperplate, in blue ink.

ROSES WITH THORNS *by Doreen Mary Stefani,* I read on the front page. The words are underlined, rather like a school writing exercise.

> *I've decided to write down some memories from my life which most of my family don't know.*

I frown. 'My family don't know.' What does Dorrie mean – that she has never taken the time to tell her children about her own childhood? That wouldn't be so surprising. She was left a widow with two small children so there could not have been much time for leisure or for looking back. Judging by the steadiness of the writing and the yellow tinge to the paper, she must have started on it some time ago and written bit by bit, when the mood took her.

I ease off my ankle boots and tuck myself up on the sofa, pulling my jumper down over my jeans to keep my legs warm.

> It's my own walk down Memory Lane and I suppose they might find something in it interesting one day. I've called it <u>Roses with Thorns</u> because my life has had some very happy times so often cut short and there were always thorns along the way, however much the flowers smelt sweet.
>
> I've come to realize the only way through is to try and snip off the thorns and smell the blooms and be kind where you can, don't get too caught up in yourself. I don't have any great philosophy of life apart from that, even after all these years.

Already, reading the words of this younger Dorrie, tears start to blur my vision. It's as if what happened in the yoga class two weeks ago has taken the stopper off my feelings. Since then I feel in danger of crying at any time – in the supermarket, at odd moments walking down the street, late at night . . . I draw the heels of my hands across my eyes to clear my sight.

> I was born in 1929 near the middle of Birmingham, city of a thousand trades as they called it and

certainly it was humming with industry. It was a big, hard-working, mucky old place, but we had our grand parts and some are still standing, for all the bombs and bulldozers have done their best to flatten it – the Council House and Art Gallery with its tea rooms. The old library is long gone though. It was all musty and dark in there then and you had to whisper, not like today.

There's not many left now remember our old city as it used to be when it wasn't smothered in concrete and neighbourhoods where we all knew everyone's names 'up our end' even if we didn't see eye to eye. The streets were lit by gas lamps and a man came round every night to light them. There was yards of little houses – slums they seem to have decided to call them now – almost up to the Council House itself, before Joseph Chamberlain came along and redesigned it all. That was even before my time. Course Hitler did his bit to destroy us, but we stood proud even with bricks and bombs falling all about us. He failed in the end being a bully, they always do. It was bulldozers did the rest in the name of progress though some would say it had to come.

Our house would seem a very poor thing now, on a cobbled street, another house behind it facing on to the yard at the back. 2/18 we were, two back of eighteen. Truth to tell, they were half houses, built back to back, a bug-ridden row of damp, cramped hovels all holding each other up. There was one room downstairs with a scullery at the back and we all lived and died in that room. There was two bedrooms upstairs, a brass bedstead in each – Mom and Dad in one and us kids all together in the other. Our door opened direct on to Fazeley Street from the front room, no inside toilet or hot water or all the comforts taken for granted in this modern world. There were some roses – like my Aunt Beattie, our mother's sister, who was the saviour of all of us – but there were plenty of thorns from the start, cold and hunger being just two of them.

I'm wandering. The floor of the front room was of brick and we bodged rugs to cover it – old strips of material, the best colours we could find, threaded through a bit of sacking. There were a few sticks of furniture and the iron range where our mother did all the cooking and kept her pots and pans. It was the only thing kept us warm. The hearth was always the heart of a house in those days as we all had to huddle up together. I wonder if it's not central heating that's broken up families.

There was no water in the house – we went out with a pail along the entry to the pump in the yard. That was always a job for us kids. Many's the time I've staggered along between the houses with a full bucket banging my legs and my shoes filling with water. My legs would be all bruises from the metal pail, not to mention my brothers kicking me in bed. The yard was where the lavatories were as well, shared with the neighbours. No running water or that sort of fine living – they were dry-pan lavs and not nice in the summer. And if you took too long in there someone'd come banging on the door. Nothing was clean and safe like now. If the water was dirty *for some reason, whole yards and streets would go down with diarrhoea.*

Our mom didn't have much of a start. Ethel Parsons was her married name, but she was born Ethel Timmins, in a house off a yard in Milk Street, Deritend, Birmingham in 1913. In all her life she only moved a stone's throw away.

At seventeen she walked up the road to Fazeley Street to get married, a decision that, she did not trouble to hide from anyone, she regretted for the rest of her life. She was the middle child of seven, Beattie the eldest. Our grandfather worked in a factory somewhere nearby but he didn't go away to fight in the Great War because of his health, which must have been bad because by the end they were after anything that could move on two legs to send to the front.

They hadn't been too bad off to begin with but Grandpa's health went downhill and soon our Grandmother Alice was left a widow, sometime during the Great War. Our mom used to say she could remember spending hours on the floor as a small child, with just a bit of sacking between her and the bricks, helping her mother, Alice, glue matchboxes together. Mom used to say she'd never forget the foul stink of the glue they used, made of boiled old bones.

I see them in my mind's eye, in one of those cramped, cold rooms with the bugs and silverfish and the damp seeping in, our grandmother at the table with a candle or perhaps an oil lamp once the darkness drew in, the kids round her. Sometimes it

*was sewing buttons or hooks and eyes on cards to
go to the shops, or any other outwork she could get
from the factories around, though the matchboxes
was the thing our mother seemed to remember.
Maybe they were easier for small children's fingers.
They'd be there 'til late at night to notch up enough
of them to earn a few coppers. That was how the
poor made shift in those days.*

*But then at the end of the war Alice passed away
as well, in 1918, when the scourge of Spanish
influenza stalked our neighbourhoods. Our aunt
Beattie was left as head of the family, at seventeen,
with six others in her charge. The youngest, Lizzie,
was three when Grandma Alice died. Poor Auntie
Lizzie was to have a tragic life but I must stick to
the main story, there are so many byways leading off
from it.*

I look up from the page for a moment, surfacing. What is
it that Dorrie wants me to know? So far it's just a rather
rambling account of her childhood.

*So many years have passed since those days in our
Old Brum, so many of the family drifted off and
never came back – especially the four boys, my
mom's brothers. Uncle Charlie was the only one I
knew and he suffered badly with his chest which
seemed to run in the family somewhere, or was it just
the filth of our beloved city that we had to breathe
in day after day? They're all long gone now, those
uncles and aunties, on to another and I hope better
place now, shadows of the past.*

Aunt Beattie used to say that Ethel, her sister and our mother, was born angry, even before she married my father and her own marriage troubles started. Beatt said even as a child Mom was always discontented and mardy. You'd have thought Beattie would have been the one to have more reason to be angry with life, left like that, a mother to six others. But I remember her as always kindly and of good cheer and she outlived the lot of them. She was the one who helped me later on through all the worst times with Mom, bless her heart.

One day Beattie took it into her head to have her portrait taken and I've still got it somewhere. It's like a postcard. Her hair was long and thick and she wore it swept back but softly, in a bun. She wasn't a beauty but she had a round, smiling face and to me it was always one of the loveliest I ever saw. I'll never forget Beatt. She never married, you might say a shame, but I suppose she had had had her fill of children at a young age and she was an angel to me, always. I wish I'd asked her more about how she managed. I can hardly imagine now in that cramped little hovel with no money coming in. She always said she had good neighbours and she went out and collared hard for all her brothers and sisters. There were plenty of factory jobs if you were prepared to knuckle down. And she did outwork as well – buttons and boxes for a jeweller's and the others helped as they could.

Our mom got married to get away from home. Or maybe she thought she'd escape her own unhappy nature, but of course she took that with her in her little bundle of clothes and brewed up an even worse one once she got there.

Never were two people more mismatched than our parents, Alf and Ethel Parsons. Pa slunk away to the usual hideouts of an unhappy husband – the pub and the bottle. He was never even blessed with a drunkard's luck. Mom played the role of the miserable nagging wife, turning to the bottle and screaming at her husband. They had us four, me first, closely followed by Eric, then Irene who had terrible asthma, bless her and passed away when she was barely six, then Bert. Apart from that Mom and the Old Man just about managed to 'cohabit' as they say these days. That was the best you could say. I wonder now, if our mother and father had met by chance in the street, whether they would have given each other the time of day. All I can say is, easier divorce is one of the best things ever to happen in this country.

Thank heaven for Aunt Beatt, the one source of real love and light in our lives. I bless her for ever.

What are my memories of my mother, in our little house in Deritend?

This sentence ends at the bottom of the page but when I turn to the next it does not seem to continue. I find myself surfacing from the world to which Dorrie has taken me, this old city of cobbled streets and back-to-back houses on yards and factories and workshops at every turn.

'Oh, God,' I remind myself. 'I really must go and get the shopping.' I'm intent on getting to Sheila's later.

I have already got through quite a number of the pages. It's obviously important to Dorrie that I read it. I felt that coming off her, a kind of urgency. And for some reason she wants me to read it, not Ian. Is that just a woman-to-woman thing? It's hard to tell.

But we are almost out of milk and I really must get something for Ian even if I don't care all that much about eating – it's the least I can do, with me not working.

Reluctantly I slide the papers back into the envelope and take it upstairs. Hardly knowing why I am still being secretive, I lift some of the shirts in my drawer and lay it underneath again.

Thirteen
FLAGS

'Hello, love.' Sheila welcomes me with a kiss, which makes me extraordinarily happy. 'Come on in, make yourself comfortable – we might have a few extra today as it's Christmas.'

Christmas. Something Ian and I have been determinedly trying not to think about. But the shops are jangling and bulging with it and it hits me with a tinsel shock when I walk into Sheila's house. The tree, with coloured lights, is already visible through the window and there are coloured bulbs taped all round the mantelpiece, candles burning in little holders between the photographs, reflecting in the mirror behind, and a candle centrepiece on the table in a nest of holly and mistletoe. The dog is basking, the cat is on the sofa smirking and all is cosy and lovely.

So far at home we have managed to deny it is happening and not do anything about it. Ian hasn't said anything. So, as usual, we are not saying anything about . . . anything.

Sunita is here already and Liz, who I've met once at the first class. I join them at the table, feeling vaguely embarrassed that Liz's one impression of me will be as a sobbing wreck. As well as the candle decoration there is a pile of white side plates on a red crêpe paper cloth, cups and saucers and red paper napkins.

'Who else is coming? Sunita asks.

'Mary said she might,' Sheila says, passing through towards the kitchen. 'Oh – and Kim, of course.'

'Mary?' Sunita's brow crinkles. She's looking especially cuddly today, in a red mohair jumper with a woolly brown reindeer's head on the front. 'Oh, yes, Mary,' she says vaguely. 'The old lady?'

Sheila, at the kitchen door, looks at her with some asperity. 'Not that much older than me, if you don't mind.'

'Oh –' Sunita rolls her eyes at Liz and me – 'I suppose not. Sorry.'

The bell rings and I'm nearest to the door, so I turn myself into door monitor.

The first time, I find Kim outside.

'Oh, hello, Jo!' She gives me a big hug, which immediately starts up tears in my eyes. She releases me but keeps her hands on my shoulders and her brown eyes look into mine. 'How lovely to see you. Great that you can come to Sheila's – I wish I could get here more often.'

As Kim goes inside and I hear sounds of greeting, I see Pat hurrying along the road, so I wait, half closing the door.

'Hello,' Pat says as I open again, hearing her on the path. She gives her reserved smile, but there is warmth in it.

'I seem to be the door person,' I say, glad to have something to do. 'You go on in.'

Hayley arrives a bit late, looking cute as usual in a fuzzy pink hat and gloves, and gives her gorgeous smile.

'Come on in, Jo,' Sheila calls, in her semi-commanding way. 'If Mary was coming she'd be here by now.'

I'm touched to see they have kept my seat, which is now between Liz and Kim. Everyone looks round and smiles as I come in. Sunita's hair looks ruffled as usual and Hayley has hers up in an immaculate French pleat.

'Now,' Sheila says, standing over us all. She has lit the candle in the middle of the table and is holding a sheaf of paper under her arm. 'Before we start filling our faces, I thought we'd do a little icebreaker – just for fun. It's a way of us all getting to know each other better. So – here, each take a sheet or two of paper . . .'

'Ooh . . .' Sunita says, pulling her mouth down as if to say, *We'd better do as we're told.*

Oh, no – really? I think, feeling dismayed and trapped. Why can't we just talk and have tea without all this? We're not children! I like Sheila, but I find her head-teacher-ish ways a bit difficult. I've had enough of this sort of thing at work. Two packets of coloured felt pens appear on the table. We all look at each other, apparently caught between amusement and a reluctance to be bossed about. But we are in Sheila's house, accepting her hospitality, so we play along.

'Now – what you need to do,' Sheila instructs us, still standing, 'is to draw a flag. In fact, the paper *is* a flag.' She pauses as we all look up at her, baffled. 'Not just any flag, but the flag of *you*. So . . . you draw about four things, more if you want. Three things which say something about you and who you are and one which says something about a dream for the future – you know, if you've always wanted to go sky-diving or to – I don't know – write poetry . . .'

101

We all laugh politely.

'OK.' Kim seems hesitant but willing and reaches for a sheet of paper. 'Come on then, ladies – let's give it a go.'

After some muttering and sharing out of pens and paper and Sheila sitting down, we all go quiet. I still feel resentful about being forced into this. For a moment I sit feeling really annoyed and trapped and wonder whether to just get up and leave. For some reason being obliged to share anything in this artificial way feels really threatening. But I don't want to offend Sheila, or lose the beginnings of the friendships I might make here. Sunita gives a little sigh and sets to work. Hayley is drawing away and Kim, to my right, also sets to and begins to sketch something with a lime-green pen.

What the hell? I think and pull the lid off the orange one nearest me. It smells pungent – of childhood. I sit thinking for a moment, then start to draw.

'Right . . .' Sheila, who has been drawing herself, breaks into the unusual quiet. I don't know how much time has passed, maybe as much as ten minutes. 'Everyone finished? I'm going to fill the teapot and then we can tell each other about them.'

Kim gets up to help her and soon we're scooping the pens out of the way and holding our 'flags' on our laps to make room for the tea and milk jug, the plates of stollen and hot mince pies.

'That was fun!' Hayley says. She seems enlivened by the exercise.

'Are you missing school?' I tease her.

Hayley puts her head on one side. 'D'you know what, in a way, yes. I'm saving up to go to college. One day I just thought, I'm twenty-five, all this time I've been doing dead-end jobs, retail and all that sort of thing. And I thought, what was it I wanted to do with my life again?'

'Do you want to go first and tell us about your flag, Hayley?' Sheila asks. She's pouring tea and we all offer the plates of cakes round.

'All right!' She giggles, sitting up straight. She has on a cream polo-neck jumper, fluffy, like most things she wears. Hayley draws the paper from her lap and holds it up.

'Ok –' she points – 'so that's me when I was little, doing ballet.'

Everyone laughs with recognition. 'Hey, that's lovely,' Pat says. 'You're really good at drawing, Hayley!'

I'm impressed – the little ballerina cartoon with a swinging ponytail is really good.

'Oh, well . . .' Hayley blushes. 'I used to do a bit. Anyway –' she points at a cartoon face with glasses and curly hair – 'that's my nan. She's a star, Nan is, and I've always spent a lot of time with her. And this is our cat, Piggles.'

'*Piggles*?' Sunita chuckles, bemused. 'I like Piggles.'

'He's gorgeous – all big and fluffy, he's a tabby,' Hayley says. 'Anyway, this last one is my dream.' It just shows a young smiling face, again with the swinging ponytail, and big cartoon glasses. 'That's me going to college . . .'

'To do what?' Sheila asks.

'Oh – I haven't quite decided. A beauty therapist, maybe? I just want to do something better with my life,' she finishes earnestly.

Sheila looks as if she might have things to say on this subject but she seems to decide not to.

Liz, next to me, goes next. She's a shy woman, not much of a talker. She has drawn a rough Union Jack – 'Well, I'm English, so I thought . . .' A band of dark blue and white stripes – 'We're big Birmingham City fans –' and some flowers because she loves doing her garden. 'My dream at the moment,' she concludes, 'is to get the extension on the house finished.'

Everyone smiles politely.

'Why don't you go next, Sheila?' Kim says.

'Oh, mine won't take long.' Sheila seems quite bashful and I realize that though she's orchestrating this game it's not because she's dying to talk about herself. And I'm beginning to see that this is a good idea after all. Already we're loosening up, learning things about each other. And it dawns on me, with shame after my annoyance at the whole thing, that she might even have thought of doing this to help me.

'So,' she begins. 'I was a teacher, middle years and assistant head. That's a blackboard, by the way, and chalk, in case any of you young things have never seen one! That's a mushroom and a cross. I've been Brown Owl with the Brownies for years and years, then a Guide Leader – now I volunteer with the Red Cross. That odd-looking thing is a mortar board – I did a degree with the Open University eventually, after I retired.'

'Wow – good for you!' several voices say, including mine.

'And that, believe it or not, is me sitting cross-legged. So, my dream is to carry on doing yoga and to be able to tie my shoelaces and put my own knickers on for the rest of my life.'

Amid the laughter, Kim reaches out and puts a hand on her shoulder. 'We'll see what we can do, Sheila!'

Sheila gives her a wry smile and touches Kim's hand in return. 'Go on – you go next. After a top-up, maybe? Let me go and make another pot.'

There's an intermission of chat and people popping to the loo and I eat a piece of stollen, sweet and delicious.

'OK,' Kim says, once everyone is back. 'Well – this is the OM symbol in the Devanagari script. As you know, yoga has been – is – very important to me. It's helped me through a lot.' She looks down for a moment, seemingly emotional. 'Anyway, these are my kids, my lovely Laura and Joe – don't know what I'd do without them either. Laura's fourteen and Joe's twelve.' She glances at me for a second, as if having a horrible feeling that she's said the wrong thing, but I smile at her. What is she supposed to say except what is true? I like Kim a lot and I don't want her to feel bad about the fact that she has two living, healthy children. And I feel surprised and pleased at being able to feel this. 'Oh, and this is Eddie, of course – he's my partner!

'These hopeless little wavy bits are supposed to be the sea in Devon – my happy place. We've been there lots, with the kids. And this – this is me trying to draw hands reaching out. So this is my dream. I've just decided . . .' She puts the paper down and looks round. 'The thing is . . .' And suddenly she's talking directly to me, as the newest person in the room. 'I was a midwife until quite recently. Various things happened – mainly because of the pressure of the job. I mean, sad things do happen sometimes, of course, but one of our patients died and it should never have happened and I . . .' She looks down for a moment. 'Well, I had a bit of a breakdown, wasn't coping, so I stopped. I really miss it. I miss helping and I miss the women . . .'

'You help us,' Pat says in her quiet way.

Kim smiles. 'That's sweet, thanks, Pat. And I'm going to carry on with yoga – I love it. But I've just decided, I can't face going back into midwifery, not the way the Health Service is at the moment. I've just booked to go on a course to train as a doula.'

Everyone looks blank except Pat, who says, 'Oh – fantastic idea!'

'It's a growing thing,' Kim says. 'I mean, it's a very old thing, actually, but it's coming back – a doula accompanies a woman through her pregnancy and the birth. As well as the midwife, I mean. You get to know them beforehand and support them, especially emotionally. You sort of go through the journey with them. It'll be such a privilege – if they'll have me.'

'Of *course* they'll have you!' Sunita and Hayley both say.

'Will you get paid?' Sheila asks.

'Yes – a bit, I think.' Kim beams at us, her lovely dark-eyed face all lit up. 'I'm really excited about it.'

'You'll be really good,' I say, before thinking, How would I know? But she will, I can just tell. Kim is exactly the sort of person you'd want alongside you when you were giving birth.

'Thanks, Jo, that means a lot.' She puts her hand on my back for a moment. 'Would you like to go next?'

My heart starts to thud really fast and my breathing goes shallow. Why is this so hard?

'OK.' Get it over. Feeling shy I hold up my paper. 'I'm not much of a drawer either. So this is me in my old job.' I have done a little cartoon of myself from the back, looking into a small group of faces. 'I'm – or I was – a teacher too. Primary. This is –' I seem to be gabbling – 'me and Ian, my husband, and our son Paul.' Between Ian and myself and Paul, I have drawn a jagged line. But I know I have to talk about it. They know already that something happened, this new group of people, in this new life I'm trying to make. I must, must . . . 'That's how it feels – like a broken window.'

Everyone listens and I can feel I have all their attention on me.

'I suppose one day it might ease off.' My chest is tightening now. 'I might not think about him, almost every minute of every hour . . .'

I look up and meet Kim's eyes which are already prepared with sympathy. I can feel them all listening, quiet and attentive.

'OK,' I say quickly, 'so this is the past. This is a little aeroplane and this is a railway track – it *almost* looks like one!' They all laugh. 'I used to do a lot of travelling before I settled down. I loved it; saw a lot of interesting places. In fact, we'd been saving, Ian and I – we were going to take Paul on a big trip, before . . . Well, anyway . . . And this – the smiley face. That's my dream, really. I hope one day I can get to that. Learn to live with it. Feel brighter, life more worth living and all that. That's it, really.'

They all smile and thank me and Kim squeezes me round the shoulders for a moment.

'Come on – Sunita and Pat. Who's going first?' Sheila says, offering round the mince pies again.

'Go on, you go.' Sunita nods at Pat.

'All right.' She looks reluctant. 'Mine's very boring.'

'No, it's not,' Sheila says, looking at the neat little pictures on Pat's flag. 'Those are good drawings for a start.'

'So – that's me and Fred and the boys.' Pat laughs with an air of apology. 'I loved being a mum. Loved it when they were little. I've never quite known what to do with myself since. I've never had a career, as such. Worked in the Post Office a while before we were married. Then I've got my bit of childminding – it's taking and collecting from school some days now. Not Thursdays, luckily! This here is supposed to be a drawing,' she says. 'Well, a painting. I've always liked art . . . And that's me running. Not that I do that much any more but I used to like it. And that aeroplane . . .' She sighs and looked comically at us. 'I've never been anywhere very much, but I'd like to travel and see a bit of the world. Fred won't go anywhere – says nowhere's better than England for a holiday so we always go to Tenby. Not that Tenby's not nice . . .'

'And it is in Wales,' Sheila points out. 'Not England.'

'Well – yes.' Pat laughs and I see again what a nice smile she has. 'That's about it for me.'

We all look at Sunita.

'Oh, I didn't know what to put,' Sunita says dismissively, dragging her piece of paper from her lap. 'It's all very silly.'

'Go on – tell us,' Kim says, then bursts out laughing. 'Oh, Sunita – what's that?'

An impenetrable cluster of lines and dots and squiggles adorns Sunita's page. Hayley holds one side of it for her.

'Well, I can't draw!' she protests, wide-eyed so that we laugh all the more. 'These dots ... this is my family – husband, daughters and their husbands, granddaughters ... I got married when I was seventeen, my husband is ten years older. That's what I have spent my life doing. Cooking, looking after my husband, children ... No time for any more things, more education ...' Sunita talks with her free hand, making sweeping motions.

'So – these are my knitting needles. I like knitting – knitted this jumper ...' She looks down, puffing her chest out like a pigeon, and we all make admiring noises. 'I am always knitting – for children, grandchildren. Just now I am knitting a Postman Pat jumper. But this here, this is a book – because I would like to do something else. Reading and study are important ... And my future dream, that is these curves here – this is me. This is when I am going to have a perfect body like a film star, sometime in the future.'

The drawing looks something vaguely like a Barbie and we all laugh again. But Sunita's face sobers as she lays the paper back down and says, 'Sometimes I get fed up with being fat and old. It feels as if my life has hardly begun and I am an old woman already.'

There is a silence as her honesty reaches into all of us.

'Sunita – you're not even sixty yet!' Sheila says, but Sunita waves this away.

'Yesterday,' she goes on, her voice becoming indignant, 'I was looking after my granddaughter – I do every

109

Wednesday. And she said to me, ' "Nanimma, come and sit down here" – because my daughter has bought her a little table and chairs, small size, for playing at making dinner and so on ... And I sat on the chair – it was plastic – and I said, "No, I won't fit," but she said, "Go on, go on" ...' Sunita tuts. 'And then when I wanted to get up I couldn't get my bottom out of the chair ...'

She seems to swell at the neck and her face presents such a picture of flustered indignation that we just can't help laughing. Her face is so funny that I find bubbles of mirth rising in me and popping out, like something long forgotten in a wine cellar.

'I even stood up and the chair was stuck on my bum – and Leela said, "You kneel and I'll pull it off" – she's only five years old!'

'And did she?' Kim says, her shoulders shaking.

'I am pushing and she is pulling the other side ...' Sunita gestures, eyes popping. 'And I wiggle a bit ... And yes, finally we got the damn thing off. And my granddaughter says to me, very serious, "You're a bit too fat, aren't you, Nanimma?" '

'Oh, dear,' Sheila says, wiping her eyes. 'Out of the mouths of babes and sucklings.'

Sunita groans, patting her hips. 'I suppose I ought to lose a stone or two.' She eyes the plate in front of her and her dimples appear. 'All the same, this stollen cake is very good – maybe just one more little slice?'

Fourteen

As the party breaks up, everyone thanking Sheila and sharing Christmas wishes, Pat says to me, 'I think I'm going in your direction. I followed your example and didn't bring the car today.'

Muffled in our coats, we say our thanks to Sheila and everyone parts with Christmas good wishes and Kim hugs us all. The others peel off in various directions or go to their cars. Pat and I can walk part of the way together.

Pat is wearing black ski-pants, a padded, pale blue jacket over her jumper and a knitted hat in cherry-and-cream stripes. She's a pleasant person, I realize, but suddenly, with a pang, I miss Ange's vibrant presence by my side. Pat seems nice, but somehow bland in comparison. Still, nice is a good start. We chat about everyday things: cooking Christmas dinner, relatives. I tell her about Dorrie and she says I'm lucky. She laughs about her own mother-in-law, saying she gets on really well with her now she's no longer alive and this sharp honesty takes me by surprise. Maybe she's not as bland as I thought. Soon we reach the corner where she will turn off.

'Well,' I say, about to add, 'Merry Christmas,' or some such, when Pat turns to me, putting a hand on my arm.

'I do understand a little bit of what you're going

through.' Her voice is quiet but urgent and I wait, bewildered at this sudden change in the tone of the conversation.

Pat glances in each direction as if she's afraid someone might be listening in.

'I lost ... I mean, our first baby ... our little girl. She ...' She speaks all in a rush, then looks down for a moment, her face creasing, before managing to compose herself. 'She just stopped moving – late on sometime. I mean, I noticed, but ... Anyway, I had her but she ... well, she never lived. Fred doesn't like to talk about it, so we never do. Course, we had the boys. But ...'

She looks up at me, a desperate appeal in her eyes. 'I never talk about her. My little Becky. They – I mean, at the time – they never told me where she was buried. They just took her away. And I could never settle. I never could forget about it. I know I've never been the same since that morning when she was born. I mean, I found out later where she was, much later ... so that made things a bit better, but ...' She makes a gesture with her hand as if to cut to the present. 'It never goes away. Not completely. I know that. You just have to learn to live with it – and you will, Jo, I promise.'

Walking home after that, alone, I feel the afternoon's chill wrapping itself about me after all the warmth – not just from the fire – of Sheila's house. But for the moment, the flag game and all the chat is pushed out of my mind by what has just happened with Pat. I tried to say the right things, how awful and that I'm sorry ... And I'm stunned to find out that I feel just as hopeless and as doomed as anyone else would, not to open my palm and hand her just the right small offering of solace.

112

A memory comes to me of the afternoon after Paul died, sitting on the sofa in our old house, Ange beside me, struggling to find words as if there were any: Ange with her two sons alive and well. And how impossible it all was because what no one can say is, *You are going to be trapped in this for years to come and no one else can feel it, no one else can reach your endless grief and you can't escape it and if you did escape you would feel as if you had let him down. You will wake some mornings for a few seconds believing you are the person you were before, young and free, single and running hopefully into your future and then you will open your eyes to the day and it will crash over you again, pressing you down into this deep, cold, lonely furrow that no one else can reach . . .*

In those seconds, I had seen that Pat knew. She knew, the way I know. The way Dorrie knew too, and at the time just let me come to her and sit and grieve.

On the face of it I could see Pat was trying to be help-ful. Of course she was. She was a kindly woman, trying to say what everyone says: that time is the great healer, that I have gone on and you will go on . . . And yet, in those moments, I found myself looking at a woman carrying inside her a lagoon of unspent emotion, as if she herself needed my help almost as much as I might need hers.

Fred doesn't like to talk about it . . .

Anger swells in me again. I seem to be angry all the time as well. Is it something about men? Ian never wants to talk about what happened to Paul, whereas I need to say it – to myself, to *someone* – over and over again.

I felt calm, almost happy for those moments when I left Sheila's. But now, opening the door into our house, I feel stirred up and raw.

113

I can sense that someone else is in the house as soon as I go in, but still I jump violently as Ian comes out of the kitchen, holding a mug.

'Oh, my God!' My whole body feels jarred. 'What're you doing here? You scared the life out of me.'

Ian has already changed out of his work clothes, into navy track pants and his thick grey fleece. He looks put out.

'I came home early – thought you'd be pleased. Where've you been? I went round to Mom's thinking you were there and she said she hadn't seen you.'

'Well, she has seen me.' I can forgive Dorrie for forgetting things that I say to her, but I definitely told him I was going to his mom's. I might as well not waste my breath. 'I was with your mom this morning, she must've forgotten. And I've been round to see the yoga group – I told you. We have a cuppa every Thursday.'

'Oh. Right.' But he sounds very put out.

'Hang on.' I realize I need to make things better. 'You go and sit down. I'll just get myself another cup of tea.'

I find Ian sitting on the sofa, not in a relaxed way. He's perched on the edge, arms resting on his thighs, still holding the mug half full of tea. Cautiously I sit beside him. Inside me, my own bell of need is ringing: *Speak to me, look at me* . . . But I can see that something is wrong and I must try, for him. From the back, his head – with a crown at the top right, the coil of salt-and-pepper hair around it – and his neck and shoulders, all look both aged and boyish at once. I pull myself forward so that I can look into his face.

'How's it going? You managed to knock off early.'

Slowly he shakes his head. 'Not great.' He puts his mug down on the floor. 'Gideon – he's moving on.'

I'm taken aback by this. Gideon? Who's Gideon? I have to rake through my mind to remember. Gideon – like the Bible.

'Moving on? How d'you mean? I thought he was your apprentice?'

'Well, that was the idea, I thought.' Ian sighs. 'We hadn't sorted anything formal but I was going to. Had my hands full . . . He's a good lad, though . . .' He stops, seems really emotional. 'He's been offered another job. Said he thought he'd get on there a bit better. All very polite, he was, but . . .' His voice thickens again.

And then he lowers his head and his body starts to shake. He's sobbing, as I have never seen him before, brokenly, from the depths of him, hands over his face.

I'm so startled and bewildered that I just sit there for a moment, almost unable to believe what's happening. In the past two years I've only known Ian to cry twice – once at the funeral, not sobs like this but tears, certainly. You couldn't not. And once, in the same brief way, after Dorrie had her little stroke. Yet now, all these deeply buried tears, all this feeling, finally releasing itself over a boy I have never even met and have barely been aware of the existence of. How hopeless we both are, I think, how impossible we have found it to grieve straight, all of it coming out instead at odd angles and at odd times.

'Ian?' I put my arm round his shoulders. He shakes and sobs and I wait, feeling glad that these tears have come, and yet also strangely distant from his emotion. I have had too much locked-in emotion of my own, have felt too alone and we have moved too far from each other.

'I just thought . . . he'd stay.' The words are muffled by his hands.

I keep caressing his back, gradually leaning closer, making comforting noises; trying, really trying.

He straightens up at last and gives a few heaving groans, as if relieved but that he can't believe himself, his emotion. He pats his pockets for a hanky.

'Hang on.' I go out to the back for kitchen roll.

Ian mops his face. He seems dazed, exhausted. He screws up the ball of tissue in his hand, still sniffing. Eventually he turns to me, looking almost ashamed.

'What the hell?' he says.

I can't think of anything to say. Quietly I sink down beside him again.

'I've cooked – there's a shepherd's pie. Shall we have a nice quiet one – cuddle up and watch something together?'

It feels like trying to comfort Paul: sofa and cuddly blanket, TV, close, side by side. And I want to give comfort. But there's an angry part of me thinking, needing. What about the bit where he puts his arms around me, says, *I know you're hurting too*? Have I scared him off somehow, become so forbidding that he doesn't know what to do?

Ian nods. His lips twitch into a smile for a second, sort of bashful as if he feels he's being humoured but wanting it all the same. 'Yeah. All right.'

Fifteen

BOY AT THE DENTIST

2015

I sit in the corner of the dentist's waiting room, my nerves shredded by the endless grizzling of a round-faced toddler with cropped, blond hair. The constant problem of *other people's children*. How dare they still *have* children?

The kid is happy neither in his buggy nor out of it, despite his harried mother's attempts to quieten him. '*Shh*,' she keeps saying. 'C'm'ere, Jackson, come and have your juice.' Jackson shakes his head, then his whole body, turning up the volume, his face pinking up. The buggy wheels squeak on the grey floor tiles. An immaculately dressed couple, probably in their eighties, sitting across from me look on in what seems to be mute disapproval.

I couldn't get an appointment before Christmas – this was the first in the New Year. The waiting room fills up with people coming and going. Receptionists keep answering the phones. A couple of people tut at the racket.

When the boy, in red dungarees, veers close to the elderly lady, she forces a smile, showing a neat set of dentures, and says, 'Hello, dear. Here – d'you want to play with these?'

She dangles a little set of keys in from of him. Roaring, he hits out and knocks them from her hand before running off. The lady looks shocked and rather hurt.

'Jackson!' His mother is overweight, looks weary and defeated. 'Sorry,' she says to the lady, who makes kindly signs of never-mind-dear. 'I dunno know what's got into him today. Jackson – c'm'ere.' She picks him up and wrestles him into the buggy, where the screaming picks up several notches, his arms and legs thrashing. I can see how worn down with it she is, with the day-to-day endlessness of it. And I remember all this; the weariness and tedium mixed, the joy that can be forgotten in the exhaustion. I want to grab her by the shoulders and yell at her, *He's your child, your boy, your miracle: you have him, here, alive and in the flesh. Love him, take every moment, you've no idea what you have . . .* But of course, I'd look like a madwoman. I feel like one sometimes.

A moment later, to everyone's relief, the receptionist calls the toddler's mother in. Maybe she's been bumped up the list. A blessed quiet comes over the room and I close my eyes for a moment, recovering, wondering what the elderly lady would have done if her own child had behaved like that. So much has changed. Children are not eating the same foods they once did, are seeing different images, too many of them, maybe, flashing into their brains. I catch myself thinking the sort of things that older people say, that Dorrie might have said.

We spent Christmas Day at Dorrie's, Ian and me and Cynthia and her husband, who made a rare visit with one of their twin boys, Michael. I cooked: beef, Dorrie's favourite, all the trimmings and a Christmas pudding and trifle. It was a relief to do it for Dorrie, not to be in our own house, to be busy. Ian and I pulled together and tried to get along with Cynthia, who can be a bit superior to put it mildly. But I could see Dorrie was overjoyed to have everyone together for once.

Then there was the afternoon at Mom and Dad's with Mark and Lisa and all the family, watching Amy's antics, catching up with my nieces, Emma and Clare. Mom had done salmon and cucumber, all laid out perfectly; Dad was full of excitement about a new extension, spread his plans on the table after dinner and bent over them for ages with Ian and Mark while the women chatted. I sat, smiling until my face hurt, trying to stop my mind constantly jabbing at me. *This time three years ago, when he was still here . . . Four years, five.*

Lisa, my sister-in-law, is a hairdresser but she was on about her new idea of doing Botox treatments on the side.

'You can earn as much in a day by just doing two treatments,' she said. 'Work from home – what's not to like?'

She looked sleek, beautiful, her long brown hair falling forward over one shoulder, subtly iced with blonde highlights; sheer tights, high heels. Her girls are lovely to look at too, and more down to earth – I'm really fond of both of them. I told Emma I had booked a dental appointment for the New Year and she said, 'Oh, as soon as I'm fully qualified you'll have to come to me, Auntie!'

'I will.' I put my arm round Emma and squeezed gently. It was lovely to see her – her youth and sweetness and her face which had strong echoes of her dad, my brother. And Clare, more like her mother, has already grown into a little mother herself, on the go non-stop after Amy, a tiny blonde whirlwind. It was an aching pleasure to have their vibrant young life around me: all that went from our household in one stroke.

And as soon as Christmas was over – it passed busily,

cracks being papered over as usual – Dorrie fell ill with a bad cold. So I've been looking after her ever since, going along to the house early morning, late at night and on and off all day. Ian even slept over one night. But she's looking a bit brighter today.

In all that time Dorrie has not once said to me, 'Have you read the writing I gave you?' Because the truth is, I still haven't finished reading all of it. When Dorrie gave it to me I thought, by the way she said it, that there was something she wanted to tell me. Something secret and important. But what I've read so far, although it was interesting, seemed to be just a collection of rambling memories. But I feel bad that I haven't finished it. I realize for the umpteenth time what a selfless person Dorrie is, always one to step back and let everything be about everyone else as if she's of no importance.

More people come into the waiting room – another family, three kids. Oh, no. Why didn't I make the appointment for after the school term had started again? Another woman sits opposite me and seems to be trying to catch my eye. The last thing I want is a conversation. In desperation I reach over to the pile of dog-eared magazines.

There are *Auto* mags, others on home decoration, months-old *Cosmopolitan.* There's a weekend colour supplement – that'll do. The date on it is December – not too far back then.

Thumbing through . . . an article on somewhere in Eastern Europe, the boom in holiday homes; a sparky comment piece by some young journalist about dyeing hair – 'To dye for?' Her mugshot shows a young, pretty face surrounded by tumbling ginger waves. What the hell would she be doing bothering about dyeing her hair?

Turning a page, my eyes lock on to the words while at the same time the photograph seizes my attention, disorientating me. For a moment it seems so odd seeing them both together that I have to look again and check, almost like hearing my own thoughts called out loud by someone else.

The boy is Paul . . . No, he isn't, yet he is – in essence. The photo is a close-up of a face, or three-quarters of a face, the left side cut off and fading into shadow. The boy is looking down, the light just catching his right eye, which gleams in the shadow. The eyebrow is thick, black. As I focus I realize the boy is Indian, hard to tell his age. But he is Paul – similar in age, the dark brow and sombre, closed-in expression. There is that essence of a deep sadness which we could feel coming from Paul as he grew older, emphasized by the fact that the face is framed by darkness.

'That Night,' it says underneath.

That Night.

It takes me a few seconds to absorb the whole headline.

'*That Night:* 30 Years of Agony for the Children of Bhopal.'

My eyes skim over the words. Bhopal. The name is familiar, an echo in my memory.

'The night of 2 December 1984, thirty years ago this week, Nasreen Iqbal, then a young mother of four children, settled down for a night's sleep. Theirs was a humble dwelling, no more than a shack alongside the railway, a neighbourhood on the north side of the city of Bhopal in central India. Nasreen and her husband Ghusun shared this cramped home with his mother and uncle. Nasreen had no idea that by the end of that night she and her six-month-old baby would be the only members of her family left alive.'

'Mrs Stefani?'

I jump, gasping.

'Sorry – didn't mean to startle you! Would you like to come through now?'

Gathering my things, I scoop up the magazine and take it with me.

Afterwards, I pop in to see Dorrie, heat some soup and carry it up to her in bed. The sunken look she has had for the last few days has lifted and she smiles as I walk in. I'm so relieved, I go and kiss her. I don't know what I'd do if I lost Dorrie now as well.

Like the rest of the house the bedroom is immaculate: pale green walls, pretty curtains dotted with green and mauve flowers, bed with a pale green counterpane, dressing table, chair, a picture of the old Pears Soap ad on the wall, showing the little lad blowing bubbles. A small framed photo on the bedside table shows Ian and Cynthia when they were kids. Little else.

'You look a lot brighter,' I tell her.

Dorrie tuts a bit, adjusting herself to get comfy. We bought her a little table to go over the bed, like in a hospital.

'Proper old nuisance, aren't I?' She waves away my protest. 'I don't feel quite so anyhow today. Thanks, bab – I'll see if I can get some of this down me.' Her shaky hand lifts the spoon with infinite care. 'You not having any?'

122

'I'm all right. I'll have something at home.'

I wait with her until she has had what she can manage – half a tin of tomato soup, a soft white roll with margarine spread, a small banana. Not bad. I watch her, fondly, thinking, I've been so wrapped up in myself. I've never really asked her anything much about herself, her life.

'I'll leave you to have a nap and I'll be back later.' I take the tray and help her settle for a rest. She looks dark against the pillow, wizened and sweet, like a little animal. 'I've not had the chance what with Christmas,' I say. 'But now I'm going to settle down and read the rest of your writing – you know, what you gave me.'

'Oh, ar . . . Well, don't strain yourself.' Dorrie seems a bit embarrassed, almost as if she doesn't want it mentioned. Closing her eyes she says, 'You're a good wench, you are.'

Sixteen

Dorrie's velvet-soft envelope rests on the sofa beside me.

But first, I pull the magazine out of my bag and read about India. About a chemical plant making pesticide, owned by an American company called Union Carbide. About the way the cows started dying from drinking water in waste ponds around the factory soon after it started production. And about the early hours of 3 December 1984, the clouds of choking, poisonous gas which escaped from the plant, drifting across the slum neighbourhood where Nasreen Iqbal and her family, along with thousands of others, were settling to sleep.

I read about the horror and panic as crowds of people tried to flee the toxic cloud enveloping their neighbourhood, many of them falling to the ground, vomiting, frothing at the mouth, their eyes and lungs burning.

Nasreen set out in panic with her family. She was carrying her little baby, covering his face with her shawl as she ran. In the mayhem she was separated from the rest of the family. She never saw any of them alive again.

I read about the bodies piled in the streets the next day, the rows of people sitting with cloths over their eyes, trying to relieve the burning pain. I read about the mass graves, the panic in hospitals whose staff had no real idea how to treat the effects of the gas. The way the company, in calculating denial, would not reveal what the gas was.

The compensation this rich, Western company finally paid out, for the gasping, agonized survivors who could no longer work or live a life that anyone would want, amounted to roughly 7p a day – an average depending, of course, on how long they survived.

But 'that night' was far from the end of the story.

A photograph on the second page shows the old plant, a gaunt collection of corroded pipes under a rusting roof standing like a bleak skeleton over a neighbourhood in which it caused such havoc, such pain and suffering. It stands there to this day, its abandoned chemicals still poisoning the water because no one will take responsibility for clearing it up. The poison is spreading year on year.

The facts of this filter into me. Thirty years since the gas leak. I remember it now, just. In 1984 I was busy in my first proper teaching job. December 1984? I struggle to think. Some of the images are familiar. An item on the news which I was mostly too busy to watch or read. News which I have assumed to be ancient history, one of those other awful events, but resolved long ago. Now, it's all brought up close – what those people, the ones who lived, have been suffering every hour of every day since. But it seems that it's not just them – the poison continues into the second and third generation, babies affected by its presence in their parents' bodies, before they have even begun.

For long minutes, I stare at the face of the boy. He's *so like* my boy. I stroke my finger down his cheek, almost expecting him to raise his eyes to look back at me. I lift the page to kiss his paper face, this boy of some other mother.

'What's your name?' I whisper.

I lay the magazine down beside me, his sombre face my companion, and stare at it for a long time. Finally, I pick up Dorrie's envelope and find the end of the page I had got to before.

'What are my memories of my mother, in our little house in Deritend . . . ?'

Turning to the next page, though, the colour of the paper changes slightly and the ink is a darker blue. I finger through the pages to see if they have got out of order, but seeing nothing that seems obviously to follow on from the last one, I read from where I left off. Dorrie must have written for a long stretch to begin with. After that, it's all more fragmented, as if she was snatching time between other things.

People nowadays have no idea just how filthy everything was back then.

When I was a girl in the 1930s it was all coal fires and the air was thick with it, gritty on your face – and that was on top of all the muck pumped out by the factories. You could hardly see across the streets and some days you'd be almost afraid to breathe. Keeping a house clean was the devil. They started sorting it out more after the war and the smog that killed all those people in London – but we had our share of pea-soupers in Brum I can tell you. The air left soot and metal on your tongue. I've seen washing turn colour on the line – there were always smuts but sometimes the whites would turn a sickly yellow. And everyone was coughing, all the time. You could hear them at night, people out on the street, hawking and spitting. My poor little sister Irene hardly had a day free of pain all her life which ended soon enough. God took her when she was only six years old.

Horses were everywhere, of course. I miss them. There was one used to come round with a cart with all the blocks of salt – lovely big brown and white horse he was and he'd sort of sniff at your hand if you held it out and I loved stroking his nose. Their muck was all over the roads, they brought on the flies in the summer like a green cloud and oil and mess everywhere.

On the next piece of paper:

I often think of my aunt Beattie. What a frightened young woman she must have been, left all alone with six young brothers and sisters to look after. Of course, by the time I knew her, her life had got to a point of calmer waters. I loved Beattie like no one else, not even our mother. I'm not ashamed to say it.

Mom was a harsh, unhappy woman. You might say she looked like a prizefighter. She must have weighed sixteen stone, she was dark as a gypsy and fierce with it. Drink gave her a tongue like a lash and she wore a little cat o'nine tails at her belt which didn't go unused. Poverty and unhappiness and the drink make poor but frequent bedfellows.

I can see our mother now, in that rotten little kitchen full of steam from her boiling pot and the condensation running down the walls. It wasn't the only thing running down the walls in those

128

verminous houses either. No one has any idea these days.

She'd be wearing that big pinafore apron, the poker or a ladle or whatever the latest weapon was in her hand, waving it about and we kids cringing close to the walls or flying out the door. We lived out on the street all we could – most kids did, the cramped state of those houses. The thing was . . .

Another sheet of paper begins:

Our poor old Pa wasn't much of a specimen, but he wasn't cruel. Our mother was another story. By God she had a pair of lungs on her. You could hear her bawling from here to next Friday – no wonder our father almost lived in the Spotted Dog and came home too kalied to take any notice. Looking back now I've got to an age she never lived to see, I think to myself, Ethel Parsons, our mother – who was she really?

Dad did the one thing in his life that showed any initiative which was to leave her. It was the only time I ever saw her cry other than when he died – but I think it was more from worry and fury at being a deserted woman than from lost love. And she was no age when she died – forty-nine and it was cruel, everything about it. I wish she'd had a better life and maybe she'd have been a happier person, but I don't have many good memories of her. She had a big laugh and on the rare times we heard it, it felt as if everything would be all right.

RIP, Mom.

On the next page:

The day that stands out in all my childhood was when Aunt Beattie took us to the zoo. I'll never forget that, me and my brothers – tram rides and then to this new place they had opened not long before. It was shortly before the war, the summer of 1939. When we rode on the tram we saw the barrage balloons on ropes over Birmingham. So I would have been nine when we went and that would make Eric six and Bert nearly four. We'd lost our Irene by then.

All day the sun shone, not a cloud in the sky, and there was the Earl of Dudley's castle with a moat and caves and then all the animals. So many I can't say now but there were zebras, bears and elephants . . . so many different things. It was quite something for us kids who'd hardly seen anything but pet cats and dogs and the odd parrot in our old streets. Our life was lived going back and forth to Fazeley Street School, which was a happy enough place for me, and to the coal wharf when we had to make ends meet, picking up nubs of coal off the barges. And suddenly here we were in this paradise.

There was a little pony called Dot and you could stroke her. Her nose was like a velvet cushion, I love a horse's nose, and she smelt lovely and she breathed on my neck. Beatt said, 'Oh, she's taken a liking to you Dorrie, she's giving you a horse kiss!'

We had a picnic – and ice cream. Eric and Bert fell asleep on the way back, but I sat next to Aunt Beatt and she talked to me almost as if I was a grown-up. There aren't many days in your life when you're all

buzzing with happiness, as if all of you is alive and
skipping about in every part. I've had one or two
days like that but that's a story for another day.

'What're you doing?'

I just about hear Ian come in, later on after work, but I'm glued to the screen of my laptop, immersed in the website I'm reading.

'Oh – just looking something up.' I turn to look at him.

This is all I feel I can say. I find that I don't want to show him the photo, can't tell him, not yet, that something in me is grinding into movement, tiny grains shifting on the rocks which have been blocking all the light, in a way that I don't even understand myself.

Ian nods politely, seeming distracted, and does not ask any more. In his work clothes, his hair untidy, he looks crumpled and forlorn. Even under the swarthiness he has inherited from Dorrie, he looks pale.

'Tea's nearly ready,' I say, shutting down the laptop. Sauce for spag bol has been bubbling on the cooker for the past hour.

'Smells good. I'll just get changed.'

Soon I hear him moving about on the floor above. In the kitchen I curse, finding the sauce sticking to the bottom of the pan. I've been too absorbed in reading, in looking at the photographs of Bhopal. There was one picture I knew I had seen somewhere before: the face of a dead infant. The picture was taken just as the child was being buried, its face and unseeing eyes the only part of it not cradled in dark earth. A man's hand is gently stroking the dust from it, as if the father could not help but caress his child one more time before parting from it for ever. Unlike Nasreen Iqbal's little baby, this one had not survived the gas.

While waiting for the pasta pan to boil, I stand under the bright kitchen lights, staring ahead of me. Eventually I tease spaghetti down into the boiling water, then grate cheese into a little blue bowl. Every day I go on doing what has to be done, cooking meals, bits of cleaning, wondering why I'm bothering.

There is a clinic in Bhopal now, I have read, especially for the children. These are children conceived long after the gas disaster. I saw a picture of a boy born with the bones in the lower parts of his legs curved like crossbows. He is looking up at the camera, a yellow flower held between his fingers as if it is something sacred. The clinic is called Chingari and it means flame, or 'spark' – the kindling of the fire of life within a person.

'How's Mom?' Ian says, once we are sitting at the table with bowls of spaghetti. He sounds exhausted.

'She's getting there,' I say. 'She's had some soup and she's eating quite well now. I went in at tea time and made her some scrambled egg. You could go and check she's all right for the night?'

He nods, chewing.

'Any luck finding new people for the job?'

'Yeah. It's not hard, actually.' His voice is flat. 'Quite a few lads in need of work and there's an older bloke looks good. I'll give him a try.'

I watch him as he twirls more pasta round his fork. *Where are you? Where have you gone?*

Seventeen

Over the next few weeks I can't seem to stop looking at websites. I read every word I can find about Bhopal, about what happened on that chill December night in 1984 and what has happened since.

It fills my mind and it's a relief to have something else to think about other than my own misery.

I read about people's suffering – the dead who fell to the ground convulsing, frothing at the mouth and unable to breathe; the women miscarrying as they tried to escape, the burning eyes and lungs.

And I read about what happened afterwards: Union Carbide in the USA, who built and kept a controlling share in the company in India, would not release the name of the poison gas for days – it was, in fact, methyl-isocyanate, one of the most dangerous and volatile chemicals in the industry. One of its components is phosgene – one of the gases used in the trenches of the First World War. In the face of that, medical staff trying to help had only basic eyedrops and antibiotics.

I read about the man who, ten years later in 1994, came to Europe looking for help when many people thought everything was long over and sorted out in Bhopal. Then, Union Carbide and its dance troupe of lawyers insisted that it had done all it had to do. It had paid out its miserly sum for sick survivors to live on, decreeing that that was 'enough for an Indian'. And still, there was no proper medical help. An appeal was set up, the Bhopal Medical Appeal, a clinic built called Sambhavna, which means 'possibility' and 'esteem' and 'togetherness' in Hindi.

I can't seem to stop thinking about those women. Those children.

That night.

Senseless. It's a word I seem to be forever reading to describe a death. A 'senseless death'. A death which lacks timeliness, is impossible to fit into any scheme of meaning that says it is about something more than raw loss. There is no story about it that can be made comforting. *It was his time. She was suffering. It was a release . . .* No, no, *no*.

After Paul's GCSE results, Ian and I sat down with him and we all talked about what next.

'I dunno.' Paul looked out sideways from under his fringe. It hung in a thick layer almost covering his eyes so that in order to see he often had to give his head a sideways jerk to flick it out of the way. He was quite tall by then, at sixteen. I was often startled by how big his hands were.

'You don't have to stay on at school,' Ian said. He was impatient with schools, with anything academic, had not been able to get out fast enough himself. 'Come and work for me if you want?'

I could hear the hesitation in his voice and Paul must have heard it too. Paul was not handy, not the sort to get on well as a mechanic. It was just so hard to see, at this point, what would be the best thing for him.

He shook his head, though not angrily, more defeated. 'No. Thanks, Dad. Don't think so.'

We explored with him. Did he want to go to a tech? Leave and try to find a job? Any thoughts of him being steadily academic had disappeared a long while back. Did he want to work in a shop for a bit and wait and see? He didn't seem to know.

In the end he stayed on at school for want of any other ideas. I supported him. I'm a teacher. The more qualifications you can get under your belt the better, supposedly . . .

He lasted most of a year. I started to notice marks on him, as if someone had been beating him. I kept advising him to keep out of their way, went to the school to talk to the staff. It took me a while to grasp that Paul was putting himself *in* their way, bringing it on, somehow. And in the early summer, something else began.

I noticed the wound because the weather was too hot to be muffled up. A raw, red scar across the inside of his right arm. Paul was left-handed. There were other, older marks.

If things had felt difficult before, this was the beginning of our four years of hell. Soon after that he dropped out of school and we set off, without realizing we were doing it, into the new, for us, land of mental ill-health. It was like reaching an unknown country full of unforgiving, frozen mountains, pits stumbled into in darkness, unseen swamps and no map available. And on that journey, I did not, for very long, feel that I was walking hand in hand with Ian. He and I were blundering about in the dark, occasionally crashing into each other. Mom and

Dad were hopeless. The only person who helped – with no real idea but with an instinctive sympathy – was Dorrie.

Paul would catch the number 50 bus out to Maypole to visit her sometimes and she was always pleased to see him, asked no questions, got him to do odd jobs for her and fed him cake and cups of tea which she got him to make for her. There was some kind of, not understanding exactly, but a comfort between them. Paul knew he could just be with Dorrie, be somehow free with her, and that was that.

But there were the drugs, prescribed, then changed, the periods of self-harm, the counsellors and psychologists, all of which in the end I sorted out for him on my own. Ian worked and worked. He did seem to listen when I told him things, sometimes, anyway. But over all, I felt alone – abandoned. Perhaps he felt the same. I was so wrung out trying to help Paul that I had no energy left to find out.

One day, I came home from work and found the house quiet in a way that felt wrong. Upstairs Paul was on his bed, seemingly asleep: except for the bottle of gin, the empty packets of paracetamol. We got him to Selly Oak hospital just in time. He had a stay in a psychiatric ward and came out seeming a bit calmer. For a while, he made various attempts at getting a job – in WH Smith, for a bit, and then in a bakery. Then one day he gave up, saying he couldn't do it, and he mostly stayed around the house, where he seemed to feel safest.

'I wonder,' Dorrie said, during this period, 'whether he'd like a dog? I'd get him one, if you like.'

I almost laughed at this. It seemed such a simple, children's story remedy. But any remedy might help at this point.

'What d'you think, Paul?' I asked him. 'Dorrie says would you like to have a dog?'

He turned his head and with more animation than I had seen for a while, said, from under his hair, 'Yeah. A dog. Yeah.' Nodding. For the first time in months my heart sang a little song.

We got Scraps from the dogs' home. Paul said he wanted a dog that someone had given away, just as he had been.

'Given away to someone who wanted you more than anyone in the world,' I told him for the umpteenth time. But there was no getting around the fact.

Scraps was a rambunctious Jack Russell, one ear black, one brown, and with odd patches of both colours dotted over a white body and a black-tipped tail – you could see where he got his name from. He chewed everything in sight, he wee'd on Dorrie's carpet, he barked and yapped whenever there was any noise outside and generally caused havoc. But, for the first time in ages, he made Paul smile and Ian took to him as well. I adored Scraps for both those reasons.

Towards the end of those four years, Paul really began to surface. Over time, Scraps got him into regular habits. He slept in Paul's room and dragged him out of bed to feed him. He had to be walked regularly and Paul got a key to the little private park and walked round the lake every morning. In the afternoon they went to Highbury Park in Kings Heath. He was not instantly better, but something in him lifted, very slowly, week after week. Soon, I started thinking, he'll want to get in touch with his friends again, maybe start looking for a job.

And then Scraps disappeared. He went off into a

corner of Highbury Park one day and just never came back. We waited, thinking he had wandered and would, knowing survivor Scraps, just amble home one day. But he never did. It was a mystery and I was horrified by what this would mean for Paul.

He did not, as I expected, tilt back downwards. He was strangely philosophical.

'At least I didn't see something horrible happen to him,' he said. There had been no screeching of brakes outside the house, no rushing to the vet.

I was still afraid his days would slide back into the shapeless twilight of his depression, but instead he suddenly announced he was going to take up jogging.

'I'm used to being out early with Scraps. I like it. I'll just have to go on my own instead.'

'That's great,' I said cautiously. 'Although it might be a bit sad. You'll miss him.'

'I'll miss him but I won't miss picking up his poo,' Paul said. And he gave what was almost a grin.

I stood for some time after he had left the room, in wonder at what had just happened.

This was the summer of 2012. Paul took up jogging. He teased me, saying I ought to come too.

'Oh, no,' I said. 'Wild horses wouldn't get me out running about like that. Anyway, I'd hold you up.' I didn't say, *After the past few years trying to look after you, to make you want to live and to be happy, I feel weary to my bones, to my very cells.*

But that was when Ian and I started saving for a trip. Things eased, even between us. We started to find each other again, more relaxed, able to joke.

'You always said you'd never been anywhere,' I said to Ian. 'And we've never taken Paul anywhere much. Where shall we go?'

We never quite decided. The USA? Australia? A safari? We wanted something that would excite Paul, enlarge his world.

Paul got a job. It was in a pub up the hill from where we lived, along the Moseley Road. The landlord was a big, no-nonsense, reassuring sort of bloke and Paul worked a few shifts a week. It wasn't all that far – not even a mile away – and he could do late shifts and easily walk home.

By the time the summer of 2012 was laying itself down into autumn, that lovely interval of slanting light and the smell of leaves trodden on the paths, the terrible heaviness of the past four years began to lift. Not a day went past when I wasn't scared. I felt as if I was almost holding my breath, waiting for everything to fall apart again and ruin this respite of at last having some sort of routine, of having my son back – and my husband.

Paul no longer had that permanent look of being shut in, lost to us behind a shield of sadness. He was almost cheerful some days. He started talking about the future, about doing something at college – maybe something to do with social care and working with the elderly? He would be wonderful, we all told him. Dorrie told him.

Autumn came and the weeks when the days shorten and those decaying leaf and gunpowder smells fill the air, when it seems that the whole city is letting off fireworks for days on end, the night sky crackling and flashing. At school I'd be teaching kids about Guy Fawkes, about

Diwali – the Festival of Lights symbolizing the triumph of light and hope over ignorance and fear.

That Friday night, Paul was working an evening shift, staying until closing time. The clear-up afterwards often took quite a while, Paul chatting with one of the girls and the landlord. I was glad – it was good for him, being with the other staff, getting along. He was a likeable lad and it felt as if he was beginning to like himself a bit more. He had smiled as he left for work that evening, something I hold in my heart, that I never want to let go of.

I always listened for him coming in afterwards, his feet on the stairs by midnight, his bedroom door opening and closing, and then I would be able to sleep. But that night, I realized later that I had already fallen asleep, exhausted after a day at school. And did I, half-dreaming, hear the ambulance tearing along the Moseley Road? When the phone rang by our bed, I jolted awake hardly knowing where I was for a moment.

'Yes?' I sat up, groping for the light switch, Ian stirring now, muttering, *Who the hell at this time of night . . .*

'I'm calling from Accident and Emergency at the Queen Elizabeth hospital.' The woman's voice sounded gentle, careful. 'We have a Paul Stefani here in A & E . . .'

'Oh!' I cried. 'Oh, my God – what's happened? I'm coming, hold on, we're coming . . . Is he OK?'

'Well, he's been brought in after an accident.' She sounded young, but well trained. 'I think the best thing would be if you come. We're doing everything we can.'

We were fumbling out of the house into the car in minutes, barely knowing what we were doing.

'How did they get our number?' Ian kept saying, driving like a madman, and I didn't stop him.

'Well, he'd have told them – or maybe . . . well, the number's on his mobile – or in his wallet . . . ?' We made fractured guesses until we were halfway there and then we were silent, tearing along the night-time Bristol Road, just desperate to be there, come on, come on . . .

All I can really remember is walking into the hospital from the car, which we left slewed to a stop. It was very bright and we were trying to find the right place and there were people all around, and other faces which ironed out their smiles into something more careful and solemn when we came near and they heard our name.

And Paul on a trolley. They told us he had died soon after the ambulance brought him in. I wanted them to be mistaken, for it not to be him. But it was him, his lovely dark waves of hair in the sterile cubicle, the length of him, his cheeks, mouth and eyes, closed as if asleep.

'Paul?' I leaned over him, stroking his forehead. His face looked strange, discoloured.

I looked at Ian and never will I forget the look on his face, the helpless, loving horror.

'Mr and Mrs Stefani?' The doctor, a white lad not much older than Paul, with kind, exhausted eyes, came into the cubicle with us. 'We really did do all we could.'

We found out, gradually. As Paul was walking home that night, a driver, at least three times over the limit and in a stolen BMW, had come roaring up the Moseley Road, lost control on the bend and mounted the pavement.

Afterwards, I wondered, did they arrive at the hospital in the same ambulance, Paul and his killer? Was Lee Parry, that feckless, selfish moron who killed Paul, in fact lying in a cubicle nearby when Ian and I went in? And was he still lying there, alive, as we walked out to that car park again, propping each other up as we had to leave our dead son behind, our lives ripped open?

Eighteen

'Hello, love – how're you?'

Rolling out my yoga mat on the hall floor, I look up and make myself smile.

'All right, Sheila? I'm OK, thanks.'

'Good.' Sheila touches my shoulder, holding my gaze for a moment, and I'm touched. She doesn't say anything but it's sincere, the caring way she looks at me. Coming to the class, week after week, I'm beginning to feel at home. Usually it's just the seven of us, counting Fred, and it really feels like a group I can trust. There are not too many demands and I can tell that by just turning up, week after week, there will be kindness and a gradual building of friendship. For a moment I feel a twinge of sadness over Ange. Have I let Ange down – or is it her who let me down? Either way, that's something else that seems to have died with Paul.

Sheila rummages in her bag, pulling out a sky-blue blanket and a bottle of water. Pat and Fred come in, Fred saying, 'Hello!' and, 'All right!' jovially to everyone. Soon his laughter sounds round the hall as a small group forms, chatting, over the other side.

'Sorry to hear about poor Herbert,' I say to Sheila. I have heard, over a cup of tea with Pat, that the old dog

143

has somehow managed to break his front left leg and is all strapped up. 'How's he going along?' It's good to have a dog to talk about. A sweet, devoted old fellow who, when he finally dies, can leave you with a pure, uncomplicated grief. And today is a better day for me than some. Ian and I had a normal, on the surface, sort of chat before he left and I feel able to look out of myself, to ask about other people.

'He's feeling very sorry for himself,' Sheila says. 'There's him going about, dot and carry one – and now Roy's gone and broken his toe. Heaven knows how, messing about in the garden . . .' She gives an exaggerated shrug. 'I'm surrounded by suffering males.'

I'm surprised at the sound of my own laughter. 'Suffering in silence?'

'Oh, I should be so lucky,' Sheila says with one of her eye rolls. 'Anyway – it's the Red Cross tonight, so I can leave them both to it.'

I go over to Kim to pay for the class. Then Hayley arrives and sets herself up in the space next to my mat. She's wearing tight Lycra leggings in pale blue and black which seem to sculpt her legs into an even more beautiful shape than they no doubt are already, a tight electric-blue vest under a black zip-up top, and a swinging ponytail. She also goes over to Kim to pay, fluid on her bare feet. She comes and sits back down, cross-legged, her back effortlessly straight. Beside her, I feel suddenly aged and lumpy.

'Hello.' She gives her lovely smile. 'How're you?'

'I'm OK, thanks,' I say. 'How's it all going?'

'All right – I think.' Hayley puts her head on one side, serious now. 'I'm trying to sort out my college applications. But my nan's been a bit under the weather.'

'Poor thing. How old is she, Hayley?'

'Oh, she's getting on – she's seventy-six.'

I almost laugh. Hayley's nan, who she talks about as if she is as old as Methuselah, is not much older than Sheila.

Hayley stretches, legs straight, reaching for her toes. She is extraordinarily bendy.

'I don't know what I'll do,' she says, 'if she ... when she, you know, passes. She's been everything to me, Nan has.'

I'm surprised and touched by this admission.

'I expect she'll be around for a good while yet, love.'

Hayley smiles and leans back on her hands. She looks like a model, but seems sweetly unaware of quite how beautiful she is.

'I expect you're right. She just seemed a bit, I dunno, older today. It's because she's got a cold.'

'God, Hayley!' I can't help the words leaving my lips as I suddenly notice. 'What on earth have you been doing – your poor feet!'

Hayley looks startled, then worried. 'What d'you mean? Oh, yeah ...'

The tight-fitting leggings taper down from her lovely figure to pale ankles. But her feet look almost as if they belong to someone else. The toes are reddened with calluses and are showing signs of being pushed out of shape, too close together. And she has blisters and sores on the backs of both heels, one covered by a plaster.

'Oh, yeah ...' Hayley blushes, drawing her feet underneath her again. 'They do look bad. I just – I don't always wear the best shoes.'

'You mean for work?' I wonder why Hayley would

145

feel it necessary to wear shoes that kill your feet that badly, just to stand behind the bar of a pub.

'Yes. They like us to sort of glam up a bit, you know,' Hayley says in her lisping voice. She shrugs, seeming really ill at ease. 'Silly, I know.'

'I can't see why you can't just wear trainers for bar work,' I say. 'It doesn't seem worth doing that to yourself.'

'My trainers are covered in mud,' she jokes. 'I don't think I'd get away with that.'

'D'you run then?' I ask her, just as Kim sits down gracefully on her mat to begin the class.

Hayley nods and whispers. 'A couple of times a week.'

Kim settles herself, cross-legged. It's the usual crew here.

'I hope you've all had a good week?' she smiles. 'Right – let's centre down, everyone, and get started. We'll have a few minutes for any news at the end as usual. Now today, we're going to begin lying down.'

After the hour of yoga, finishing with relaxation, we sit on our mats for a few moments.

Sheila gives news of the male afflictions of her household and makes everyone laugh. Sunita says her daughter in Canada is expecting another baby. She seems a bit low in herself though, I sense, discontented, as if something is weighing on her. No one else has much news. Kim says she will be going on her open day to see about being a doula this week.

'I'm really excited,' she says. 'I can't wait to get started.'

There is no obligation to say anything, but I suddenly find it's my turn.

146

'Well.' I look round at the friendly faces and words start to come out of my mouth without me really even knowing I am going to say them. 'I've just . . . well, I've been reading about this charity, on the Web. A lot. I s'pose I've been sort of obsessing about it because . . .' It sounds crazy to say I have seen a picture of Paul – only it wasn't Paul, it was a boy in India . . . 'What happened there was so terrible.' I try, in a few sentences, to explain Bhopal.

Kim is nodding, and Sunita. The others look blank.

'Anyway . . .' Words come spilling out. 'I read on their website that they do this sponsored run – not just them, I mean, it's the London 10K run and people do it for all different charities – and I've never done anything like it but I'm wondering whether I might give it a go.'

Until now I have barely thought about this, not as a real possibility. Saying it to the others – and I have said nothing to Ian – makes the idea seem frighteningly real.

'10K?' Pat says. 'Hang on – how far's that?'

'Six and a bit miles,' Fred says. 'A good stretch.' He shakes his head in an amiable way but as if to suggest that what he's hearing is complete madness. I feel irritation prickle in me – and the challenge of it.

'Do you run, Fred?' I ask. He has tanned, lean legs and you could believe he might go out pounding round the paths.

'Me? Oh, no,' he says dismissively. 'If I'm doing exercise I like it to be something useful – you know, the garden and that. I come along here to keep the wife sweet.' He winks, with a sideways grin towards Pat. 'You won't catch me jogging – especially not six miles.'

'Oh, my –' Sunita pulls a face – 'I don't think I could run one mile. I'm too fat!'

'Well, good for you, Jo,' Kim says, getting to her feet, and the others make encouraging noises.

No one seems to think it too crazed an idea – apart from Fred, apparently.

'If you want any training tips, I could help,' Hayley tells me as we're packing up.

And by the time I have put away my mat and blanket, I begin to feel, in an unreal sort of way, as if I might have somehow committed myself to something. Why did I open my mouth?

As we all head towards the door, Pat moves quickly ahead of her husband and says to me quietly, 'Good for you. See you at Sheila's on Thursday?'

Nineteen

'Oh, no!' I say, walking into Sheila's living room on Thursday. 'Now what's happened?'

Herbert looks up at me from the rug by the hearth, a plastic shield round his head like a lampshade. One of his eyes is half shut, as if he's winking at us.

'Eye infection,' Sheila says. 'He kept rubbing at it.'

'Poor old Herbert.' I get down beside him and make a fuss of him. It does me good seeing Herbert. 'You are in the wars.'

'I don't know why I bother going to the Red Cross,' Sheila says, stalking off towards the kitchen. 'I feel like Florence Nightingale in my own home.'

I stay on my knees, comforting the old dog. Maggie the cat watches from the sofa, with an expression of undisguised scorn.

'Yeah, you can gloat.' I make a face back at her.

I'm glad I've come now, but it was a bit of a struggle. Why on earth did I blurt out all that stuff about the run on Tuesday? This has not been a good day; it's been one of those when I can hardly get up in the morning, let alone start running around. I look down at my scrawny, unpromising-looking thighs, wrapped in my old jeans.

This feels like an enormous deal. It's in London – and *six miles*! What was I thinking?

'D'you know,' I whisper to Herbert. 'I used to be quite a feisty young thing once upon a time. I used to go clubbing and I travelled all over the world.' Now that feels like another life; something that happened to a different, braver and happily oblivious person.

Herbert eyes me sympathetically, or so I choose to believe.

'Yes – I bet you were an adventurous young feller once, weren't you?'

The doorbell rings and I kiss Herbert's shoulder, since his head is trapped in the lampshade thing, and go to answer it.

Soon we are all round the table, what has come to be the usual six of us: Sheila and Kim, Pat, Sunita, Hayley and me, drinking Sheila's tea and eating a coffee and walnut cake Hayley said she baked this morning.

'I made one for Nan as well,' she says. 'It's her favourite.'

'You're a good'un you are,' Sheila tells her fondly. 'I could do with a granddaughter like you. Ours are all lads.'

'You know you were talking about that run?' Hayley says after a while. She's sitting by the window, the other side of the table from me, in a fluffy pink polo-neck jumper. 'I had a look and I think it's a lovely idea. I was wondering if I could do it with you? I mean – that's if you want anyone to?'

For a second all I feel is panic. What on earth have I started?

'Where's it for again?' Sheila says, before I can answer.

'It's in India . . .' I begin.

'Oh . . .' Sheila sounds doubtful and, to my surprise, a bit dismissive. 'Why don't you do something for a local charity? There's plenty going on round here without having to look further afield!'

None of us is quite sure what to say.

'I took a look at the website.' Hayley glances at Sheila, seeming a bit unsure of herself but carrying on anyway. 'It's – it looks like a really extreme situation. I mean, I know we've all got our problems here, but nothing like this . . . And the run's not until the twelfth of July. We've got time to get in shape for it. I'd like to do something – you know, for a good cause.'

I smile gratefully at her.

'Sheila,' I say cautiously. 'I think if you saw the effects it had on the children there . . .'

'Well,' Sheila says rather stiffly, 'I suppose I think charity should begin at home on the whole. But why don't you tell me more – show me where I can read about it. I'm not trying to be difficult.'

'No!' I say. 'Of course you're not.'

We all look at each other. Hayley appears stricken, as if she has started something she didn't mean to.

I'm just a bit lost for words. How to explain about the picture, the boy . . . None of it really makes any sense, not sense that I can explain. I just want to say to Sheila, *Of course charity begins at home, with the people closest to you. But does it have to end there?* But I don't want to argue.

'It's just . . .' Pat speaks up then. We are all awkward, accepting Sheila's hospitality, not wanting to get into an argument. 'Sometimes –' she glances at me as if for

151

confirmation – 'some things just get to you. Get under your skin. You can't always explain it.'

'It was terrible – what happened in Bhopal,' Sunita says. 'I remember when it happened.'

Kim hands round the plate of cake slices as if to ease things.

'Do you go back to India often?' Hayley asks Sunita.

'India – oh, *no*,' Sunita laughs. 'I've hardly ever been to India – I was born in Uganda! We came here in seventy-two, after that madman Idi Amin kicked us out. We lost nearly everything. I was fifteen. My family is Indian, of course, but I've only been to India on a visit a few times. To Gujarat – that's where the family are. I have been to Delhi – but nowhere else much in India. You see . . .'

She holds out her plump little right hand, palm out and facing downwards.

'See, if this is India –' she points to the thumb joint – 'Gujarat is round about there. And here – down a bit and in a bit, in the middle – that is where Bhopal is. It is supposed to be a very nice place. It has big lakes. What happened there . . .' She shakes her head. 'Wicked. Very terrible. The way people died – it was horrible. Poison gas. And still now, so much sickness.'

There is a sudden silence. Sheila pours more tea and I'm wondering whether I ought to change the subject altogether. I'm uncomfortably taken aback by the narrowness of Sheila's attitude. On the other hand, I like her very much, respect her and I'm grateful to her. Things suddenly feel strained.

'The thing is –' Pat's quiet voice breaks in before I can come up with anything to say – 'I think it's a really good

152

idea. I'd . . .' She hesitates. 'I'd have a go with you. Only –' she looks worried, embarrassed almost – 'I'm not sure what Fred'd say.'

'Fred?' Sheila says to my amazement. She's peering into the teapot, the lid in her hand. 'What's Fred got to do with it? You're not asking him to do it, are you?'

'I thought you didn't approve?' Pat laughs.

'Well, it's not my cup of tea, certainly,' Sheila says. 'But honest to God, we're not living in the Victorian age, are we? I'll get Roy to have a word.' She pushes the tea cosy back on to the pot. 'At least he's taken Roy out to the club with him today, even if he can't play. He's driving me round the bend, limping around here like Long John Silver – and the complaining! Suffering in silence isn't on my dear husband's radar, I don't think. The dog's more stoic than he is.'

We all laugh and things feel better. I can see Sheila beginning to come round to the idea.

'Well,' Pat says doubtfully, 'Fred can be a bit funny about some things. But I'd like to.' She looks at Hayley. 'Yeah?'

I find tears in my eyes suddenly. 'Really?' I'm looking at Hayley and Pat. 'Both of you?' I pull out a tissue and wipe my eyes and Kim gives me one of her hugs. 'God, I've come over all weepy. That's so nice! But you're both really fit – I don't think I could run to the end of the road.'

'Oh, it doesn't matter,' Hayley says. 'You just have to start somewhere.'

'Good for you,' Kim says. 'I wish I could – but what with the kids and work I just can't fit it in. We can cheer you on, though!'

Sheila gets up and goes into the kitchen and it feels as if she's distancing herself from the conversation. The rest of us exchange looks.

'Well,' Sunita says, 'I'm too old for all that sort of thing. But I wish you luck.' She sounds wistful.

'You're not *old*,' Hayley says, with great earnestness. 'You're really not. There's a man in his nineties who runs the London Marathon every year!'

'*Ninety?*' Sunita makes one of her round-eyed faces. 'Well, that may be so. But he's a man. And he's probably a bit mad. I don't think my knees would stand it – I'm such a fatty.'

'Oh, Sunita,' Pat says. 'You're too hard on yourself.'

'That's what my grandchildren call me now,' Sunita says slightly huffily. 'My son-in-law's mother is "Thin Dadi" and I am "Fat Nanimma". What can I do?'

'Take up jogging?' I tease her.

'Huh.' Sunita folds her arms. She is still looking put out. 'Since when do grandmothers go jogging?'

Only when I get home does the reality of what I seem to be letting myself in for really dawn on me. Thinking about it, we've got four and a half months to get ready for this event. In the past year I have barely walked anywhere, let alone run.

If I'm going to take part in this thing, that means I basically, obviously, need to start running. Not just thinking about it, but actually doing it. Now, this week.

I wander into the kitchen to start cooking for me and Ian, half-hearted since I am still well fed on cake. I'm just pulling chicken thighs out of the fridge when I realize it's probably been two hours since I last thought about Paul.

Really thought about him, not just about the boy in the photograph. Pain slices through me. An actual physical pain of guilt and regret.

'I'm sorry,' I say out loud. 'I'm so sorry, my love – I haven't forgotten you, I haven't. I never will . . .' The pain of it drains me and I feel suddenly exhausted.

Chopping onions in the quiet kitchen, I feel utterly despondent. It's hard to get to the cemetery to visit these days. Finding that I have not thought about Paul almost every minute, and instead have been thinking about doing this run in aid of people suffering in a faraway place Ian will probably never have heard of, for something he will find hard to understand – I wonder if this is all a big mistake. Or might he be glad to see me just getting involved in something – anything?

Soon I hear him come in and I go into the hall.

'Hello!' I force myself to sound cheerful. And in that moment I actually feel suddenly in better spirits. There's no accounting for my moods these days.

Ian looks wary. 'All right? How's Mom?'

'She's OK. I've been in, as usual. So – how's your new guy getting on? Carl, is it?' Ian has employed an older man, in his late forties, who was eager for the work.

'Yeah . . .' He fishes in his bag for his sandwich box. 'Yeah, he's OK, actually. Good bloke. Knows what he's doing, all right.' He doesn't seem to know how to deal with my good cheer. 'I'll just get changed.'

I watch him go upstairs, hoping that once he's fed and relaxed a bit, it might be possible to hold a conversation.

155

Twenty
WE SEEM TO BE TRAINING

The park is swathed in mist and the cold air stings my nostrils. Wythall Park is the best part of a mile from home and from the moment I set off to walk there – as soon as Ian has left for work – my chest has been tightening and my stomach clenching with nerves.

In the murk the brightest thing I can see is my trainers. These are the one thing I have had to buy. I hid them in the cupboard upstairs because I'm still not really sure I'm doing this. Otherwise I'm wearing old black leggings which I hope won't keep falling down, a T-shirt and navy sweatshirt. The blue-and-white trainers seem to glow at each end of my feet. They make me look as if I'm some sort of sporty person who knows what she's about and so I feel a fraud wearing them.

'There's a track round the park – about a mile,' Hayley told me. 'We could do that to begin with?'

Before I have even got across the car park to get right into the park, I see a figure appear through the mist in tight black sports leggings with a bright blue contour stripe down the sides and a similarly blue top, jogging with a beautiful fluent stride. Hayley's ponytail swings back and forth and she runs out of the park to meet me like some gorgeous Serengeti gazelle. In comparison I immediately feel like a clapped-out old goat.

'Hi!' Hayley waves, her face glowing with health. She has evidently already done at least one lap of the park. 'Well done – you got here.'

'Well, if I couldn't even manage that I wouldn't have much hope, would I?' I say, feeling faintly patronized. 'Have you seen Pat?'

'Here she is!'

A small silver car pulls into the misty car park, Pat waving from the driver's seat.

'Oh!' Hayley says. 'Look who's with her!'

Getting out of the other side of the car, we see Sunita.

'Look who I found,' Pat says, grinning. As ever she is neatly dressed in navy and white.

'The Creak and Groan running team,' Sunita pronounces with her usual self-mocking face. 'Well – not you, Hayley, of course. I thought, Well, come on, Sunita – why don't you give it a go?'

She is wearing a cherry-red top and loose navy tracksuit trousers and her hair is fastened back, covering her ears.

'Oh, am I glad to see you,' I say. 'I thought I was going to have to run with these two fit ones on my own.' I eye Pat's athletic-looking figure.

'I told my husband,' Sunita says, in her emphatic way, 'and he said, "You should give it a try, it's good for you. It will make your heart stronger."' She tilts her head melodramatically. 'That's if I don't have a heart attack.'

'What did Fred say?' I ask Pat.

Pat looks sheepish. 'I didn't really tell him.'

'I haven't told Ian either.' We both laugh. 'Mad, isn't it?'

'Shall we begin with a few stretches?' Hayley suggests. I can see she's starting to feel cold.

'I don't think I can do it.' I'm suddenly full of panic. 'I don't know why I said I'd do this. I've hardly done any of this sort of thing since I was at school.'

'Yes, you can,' Pat says with sudden firmness. 'Come on – you come with me, Jo. Hayley, you go with Sunita.' I find my arm being taken by Pat. 'All it is, is putting one foot in front of the other. You can do it. We'll start by walking fast, OK?'

'That will probably finish me off,' Sunita says, so gloomily that we all laugh.

The path hugs the edge of the park, a wide, flat, grassy space with a few scattered trees. No big hills, anyway, I think, as Pat and I start off in front, walking faster and faster, in fact needing to just to keep warm. I feel the pull on my thighs, the strangeness of being aware of my body. Pat matches my pace. I feel comfortable with her. Since the day she confided in me about her baby, we have not talked about anything like that. We've met for a coffee a few times, kept it light. But we know these deep things about each other and there's a quiet understanding. Behind us, Hayley is making encouraging noises to Sunita.

'Now, we'll take this up to a jog – just for a while,' Pat says. She must have been a good mother, I think. She is gentle, positive.

And we are running. Not fast, in fact very slowly, like lumbering little bears – but we've begun.

'You're running, Sunita!' Hayley cries, like a cheerleader.

'I know,' Sunita grumbles. 'And I can feel my bottom – it is wobbling like a jellyfish.'

Pat and I look at each other and laugh and we can hear Hayley giggling. 'You mean a jelly?'

'Jellyfish, jelly – it's all the same,' Sunita mumbles. 'Very wobbly.'

My grin is almost as unfamiliar as the air stinging in my nostrils, the sudden awareness of how much the ground pulls you down, the effort needed to drive myself forward. It feels all right for a few minutes and then my lungs start to pull, my chest seizing up. But I'm doing it . . . I'm running. The guilt comes again, the bitter waves which wash through me: here I am, alive – if running isn't a testimony to feeling alive what is? – feeling really alive, for the first time since . . . While he lies in the dark, cold earth . . . My chest tightens unbearably as the rush of emotion takes over again and I need to stop. I'm about to gasp that I can't carry on, when I am saved by Sunita.

'Oh! I am stopping now,' she groans wheezily. 'Let me walk – my heart is pounding!'

I stop immediately, panting, bending to rest my hands on my thighs. With a huge effort I manage to get a grip on my emotions and just breathe. Not now – I don't want to do this again. Not here . . .

'You OK?' Hayley asks as Sunita and Pat walk on ahead.

'Yep.' I straighten up and ram my face into a smile. 'Just needed to get my breath back.'

A few minutes later Sunita, suddenly full of enthusiasm, turns and calls to us, 'Right, let's run again!' And I find that once I have got my breath back, I'm bouncy in these new trainers and keen to go too. I feel suddenly as if I'm overcoming something, reclaiming myself.

'We're *training*,' I hear Sunita say with definite proudness and I find myself smiling.

I'm doing it. I'm talking to Paul in my head as I jog along with Hayley. *I'm doing it, love – for you and for that boy.* I feel now that I can hardly distinguish the two. It feels as if the boy is Paul.

We walk a bit, jog a bit and so on and it doesn't feel all that long until we are back where we started.

'Well –' Pat beams at us both – 'that didn't go too badly for a first try, did it?'

'But six miles,' I groan.

'We shall pretend we are in a film,' Sunita announces. 'You know, like . . . Oh, I can't think . . .'

'*The Loneliness of the Long Distance Runner*?' Pat says, grimacing.

'*Chariots of Fire*?' I suggest.

'No, *no*,' Sunita says. 'Something with a bit of glamour . . .'

'The ladies of Hollywood run round their park,' Hayley says.

'Hollywood? *Bollywood*?' I say. 'Maybe we should have our own song? The Creak and Groan song.'

'Hollywood-Bollywood.' And Sunita rises up on her toes, humming and singing something none of us can understand but which is obviously from Indian cinema. And the next thing is she's whirling round, doing arm movements and making exaggerated faces, one minute thunderous and sulky, the next smiling as if at the love of her life. Sunita, tubby and dressed in the baggiest of clothes, is not a bad mover. Her hands, as I watch, are beautiful and expressive.

'Sunita – you're *great* at dancing!' Hayley cries. All of us are laughing in amazement and Hayley goes and dances beside her, trying to imitate the moves.

'You like dancing?' Sunita stops. Hayley looks suddenly embarrassed. 'Yes – well, sort of. I used to dance at school.'

'We need our *own* songs,' Sunita says. She seems really enthusiastic, amused by the idea. 'Our own Hollywood-Bollywood. I will think of a song – or we can make them up.'

'Oh, I'm no good at that sort of thing,' Pat says.

'Don't be silly,' Sunita insists. 'You say that about everything. What about thinking positive, eh? I'm no good at running but I'm doing it, aren't I? And,' she adds, 'I'm going on a diet. No more Granny with her bottom stuck in the chair. Next year I will be sixty and if I don't do something I will just go on eating cake and getting bigger and bigger and . . . one day I will not be able to get into the shower!'

As she says it her eyes protrude with horror at the thought and she looks so funny that we all end up laughing.

I realize, surprised, that Sunita is only a couple of years older than I am and younger than Pat. She seems to think of herself as an old woman – or that's how it has looked up until today. I find myself feeling inspired. Pat looks pretty lit up as well.

'Good for you,' I say, as we walk back across the car park. And with a lightening feeling, I think, we're going to do this.

*

'So we went for our first run round the park this morning,' I say.

Dorrie looks at me over her teacup. As ever, she's in her chair by the fire and somehow she seems even smaller. I see her every day, often more than once, but for some reason I notice this today.

'You went running round the park?'

'Yes – four of us. I've met some nice women here.'

Dorrie replaces her cup on the saucer. 'I don't know why everyone has to rush about so much these days. If you want to give money to charity, what good's running round the park? Why don't you just give them the money? You'll wear yourself out.'

'I think it's just . . .' Again, I can't really explain properly. It's wanting to do something, be involved somehow, but Dorrie, though active, has never been one for expending unnecessary energy. She comes from an age when people literally worked themselves to an early death, never mind going for runs around the block.

'Why that, anyway?' she says. 'I mean, there're all these charities these days – so many . . .'

'I s'pose . . .' It's hard to explain. I don't feel like telling her about the boy, the picture. It all sounds a bit mad. I think about what Pat said, about things getting under your skin. 'It's a bit like . . . You know what Bogey says in that film, *Casablanca*? "Of all the gin joints in all the towns in all the world, she walks into mine." It's just how it goes – some things just get to you.'

Dorrie nods, slowly, as if this makes some sort of odd sense.

'So,' I say, 'they're coming about the stairlift on Wednesday?'

Dorrie nods, stiffly. 'If you say so.'

My heart buckles. I know Dorrie doesn't want to admit how difficult she's finding things, that even getting up to bed at night is a tortured ordeal.

'It'll make everything easier,' I say gently. 'You'll soon get used to it and you'll be glad you've got it, Dorrie – I'm sure you will. It'll mean . . .' I try to find a tactful way of saying it. 'You can stay here, in your own bed for as long as . . .'

Dorrie nods but she's staring ahead of her, a blank look on her face as if she doesn't want to talk about it.

'I was thinking,' she says. 'Of how no one remembers now – about how things were.'

'That's because most of us aren't old enough to,' I point out.

'Things were . . . Everything was so dirty. And food – there's so much food now. People went without for days sometimes . . .'

I feel a prickle of unease. Dorrie does not seem herself this morning. She seems frail and wandery.

'You lived through amazing times,' I say. 'And Dorrie –' I lean towards her – 'I've so enjoyed reading about your memories. I'm sure Ian would love to see them – and Cynthia. I read the bit you wrote about how you met Tom, Ian's dad. It's lovely – what you said and everything.'

'Tom.' Dorrie seems to come back to herself. 'My Tom. Yes, Tom Stefani was my husband. Husband for four years – that was all. He was a good man, Tom was, 'til they did that to him . . .' Again she trails off, sinking into her own world.

There are all sorts of things I want to ask her, but I feel

164

shy. Dorrie has never been one for dwelling on things or talking about herself. I have read nearly all of her pages of writing now. What started off quite fluently, written when she was younger, has become more and more scrappy – odd things she must have jotted down, the handwriting different, shakier. There are also big gaps in what Dorrie chose to write about. Among the descriptions of her childhood, she often says she is about to write about something – her mother, for example – and then she doesn't, or at least if she ever has, it is not there among the pages that she gave me.

The trip to the zoo with Aunt Beattie is there, though next to nothing about school. Nor about what she did when she left school, except that eventually, at some point in her twenties she met Tom Stefani in a pub, where she must have been working. It's not quite true that I have read absolutely all of it. Lately I've found myself resisting going on with it, somehow worried that I might find something I don't want to read. I'm still wondering what it is that Dorrie is trying to tell me by giving me the pages.

'Til they did that to him. What does that mean? Yet in a way I am not sure I want to know.

'Are you a bit tired today, Dorrie?'

She fixes on me again, seeming to shake herself. 'Ar, bab, sorry. I didn't sleep very well last night. Feel a bit anyhow today.'

'Well, let's get you a bit of dinner and then you can have a nap, eh?' I say.

At home I take out Dorrie's sheaf of papers again and turn to the pages near the end.

Twenty-One

I met my Tom when I was 26. Over the hill of course according to my dear mother. She was full of charming remarks about how I was an old spinster.

The thing was I never really said anything much to her about Frank, who I wasted three years of my life on. I lived in hope, being a yes woman and walking out with a man who could never keep a promise. Many a bitter tear I shed over Frank, the handsome so-and-so. I don't know now why I put up with all his nonsense for so long but you do when you're young.

It was in the Adam and Eve that I met Tom, one fine summer day. In he walks, on his dinner break. He was working at one of the factories in Bradford Street then and he had a pal with him. Life was mostly work back then, there wasn't much free time.

'Hello,' he says, and even his voice sounded just right, funny how something just feels right, his eyes, face . . . I liked him straight away. I was dark in looks myself of course, dark-eyed and black hair and I think he thought I must be an Eytie as well which I'm not of course. But it felt like looking in the mirror and seeing someone I recognized. I probably did recognize him

because he grew up not far from us in Bartholomew Street where a lot of the Italians were, but it was more than that. He felt it too. As if we'd known each other before somewhere almost in another life and met again. We were chatting away within minutes and he asked me out. And that was that.

Tom was the greatest bloom of my life – with my children of course, though in my mind they all go together. It surprises me looking back how much I loved Tom, coming as I did from such a loveless household. The heart must know what to do of itself.

I started to catch the rose-scent of Tom right from the word go. We went out that night and never stopped talking. It felt as if we never stopped talking until he died. He was that sort of man – open and friendly and gave of himself. And we clicked and that was that.

'Dorrie,' he said, when I told him my name. He was Brummy born and bred, as were his mom and dad, but his accent was still tinged with his Italian grandparents who lived with them as he was growing up, all crammed into their little house near the viaduct. Old Man Stefani had come over a like a lot of the Italians, in the 1870s, sent over by one of the padrones, men from the district who'd been abroad somewhere, here or America, to make their fortune and gone back.

The Old Man – Giuseppe – was no child when he came. He brought his wife Theresa and worked as a hawker before they set up that fish and chip shop – 'Stefani's' near Scratchem's Corner – it was very popular, was there for years. All of them were

*clever with food – sweets, ice-cream – it was a good
part of town to be in.*

*But there wasn't much love lost between the men
in the Stefani family. Tom was already living in a
lodging house a few streets away to get out from
under his own father Luigi Stefani – my father-in-
law as he became. He was always all right to me but
then I didn't have to live with him. There were too
many kids to share the business, Tom was one of
nine, and he went out and got other work. When we
married he took a job over at Smethwick for the
wages. They weren't the wages of sin, but death
came along with them all the same.*

*He was lovely to me, Tom was. That's the only
way to say it. I found a man who was good and kind
and there was love between us all right. I couldn't
wait for him to get home of an evening – almost as
if every night was a date, even if all we were doing
was staying in, in our little house with our few
sticks of furniture. But it was a palace to me. I
remember saving up for a scrubbing brush – two
and nine it cost and I saved my pennies until I could
go and get it. I had a lot of pleasure out of that –
simpler times they were then. People waited more for
things.*

*It's no good wishing to turn the clock back, but
time and thorns stole my love from me. It left me a
widow at the age of thirty, with my small boy and
another baby on the way.*

The very last page is a sheet of plain paper, but slipped in
front of it is another, smaller scrap, from a cheap, lined

writing pad that I hadn't noticed before. At a glance it seems nothing to do with the rest – it's yellowed at the edges and the writing on it looks almost like someone else's. But the first line tells me that it could only be Dorrie who wrote it.

He's gone, taken from me my Tom my husband . . .

The writing is much steadier, younger. The writing of the heartbroken Dorrie of 1959:

He's gone, taken from me my Tom my husband. I loved him I loved him I loved him. I don't know what to do. What am I going to do? It didn't have to be like this. None of it should ever've happened. Someone should hang for what they did to him my poor husband. But what can I do? No one will pay any heed to me. I've got nothing – who am I? But he's gone and I'm all alone and my baby will never know its father. What can I do?

Under it, several lines are scored across, cutting into the page. It's the last thing in the folder of papers.

'What did actually happen to your father – how did he die?'

We're at the table that evening: stir-fry, bottle of soy sauce, Ian's bottle of Budvar. Red peppers shiny with oil glow in the gloom, seeming weirdly colourful and out of season in an English February.

'Why?' Ian sits back, putting his fork down. His eyes

meet mine, then flicker away. I can't tell what he feels about me asking but he does not seem hostile. Head back, he takes a mouthful from the bottle.

'Just something Dorrie said.'

Lowering the bottle, he looks at me. 'She OK?'

'*Yes*. I'd tell you if she wasn't, wouldn't I? It's not that. It's just, somehow we've just never really talked about it.'

And why am I picking that out among all the other things we're not talking about, Ian and I who used to talk about everything?

'New trainers?' Ian said when he came in and saw them in the hall.

'Yes,' I said. 'I just wanted something more comfortable. It's fine you taking the car most days but I do a lot of walking here – to the shops sometimes, to yoga.' I have not told him about the running yet. Why? I hardly know, other than that any change feels as if it is loaded, threateningly, on top of too many others.

'Well, I think he had a heart attack.' Ian sits back, holding the bottle to his chest. He looks puzzled. 'I can only just remember him. He was in hospital – or at least . . .' He pauses. 'I never got taken to the hospital to see him, but that's where he was, I think.' He glances at me, vulnerable. 'I dunno. That's what she told me. It all feels a bit of a muddle in my head. I can only remember him before, just a bit, sat by the fire, smoking – laughing.' He smiles. 'No bad memories, just, well, that's about all there is. He was all right, though, my dad.'

'He sounds more than all right.'

'Has she been talking about him?'

171

'A bit.' Why do I not tell him about Dorrie's writing? I feel awkward that she has shown it to me first. 'You know – good memories. He sounds like a really nice man. I wish I'd known him.'

Ian shrugs sadly. 'Yeah – me too.'

Twenty-Two

The next morning, at nine-thirty, I tap on Dorrie's door. It's actually locked for once and I let myself in with the key, calling 'Hello!' as I close it behind me.

There's no answer. No one in the front room. I stand for a few seconds in the doorway, staring stupidly at Dorrie's empty chair, her blanket folded neatly on it, the unlit gas fire. And then I go cold.

'Dorrie?' I tear up the stairs, my heart pumping horribly hard. Don't let anything have happened, no, please, no . . .

As I rush into her bedroom I hear a little sound – Dorrie stirring in bed.

'Is that you, Jo?'

'Yes. It's only me.' Thank God, thank God . . . 'You all right? It's not like you to have a lie-in, Dorrie.'

'Why? What time . . . ?' Dorrie pushes herself up on one elbow to look at the clock and gives a chuckle. 'Oh, my word – it's getting on for ten o'clock! Well, fancy – what a lazy old thing I am these days.' She lies back, her olive skin and white curls exotic against the pillow. But she seems quite chirpy.

'I didn't sleep well early on – and I got up to spend a penny some time – I don't know, about four, I think. And

173

then I fell asleep – and d'you know, I've had the best sleep. I feel like champagne.'

'Well, I could nip down to Sainsbury's for a bottle if you like.' I grin at her, bubbly with relief myself.

'You know what I mean. But I must get up, idle old sod.'

'No, you stay there. This is your big chance for breakfast in bed – not that you couldn't have it every day if you wanted.'

Despite Dorrie's protests, she sits tight, seeming to enjoy the treat. I bring up her usual Weetabix and a slice of toast and fill the brown crock teapot. I still feel light, celebratory with relief. Last night I lay for a while, thinking about Dorrie, wrenching my mind away from its usual loop: Paul, the night of the accident, Lee Parry's pale, blank face. I found myself wondering about Ian's mom and dad, about what had happened. But it feels impossibly difficult just to ask her. I think of those ink lines scored deeply into that cheap little sheet of paper.

The heating is on and her room's cosy, with a faint smell of the hand lotion Dorrie uses – something fruity. There's a kind of sensual pleasure in looking after someone else and I arrange Dorrie's pillows as she sits up, then put her mauve cardi round her shoulders and swing over her little table round with the tray on it.

'Well,' Dorrie says, seeming amused by all this. 'You going to sit with me?'

'Yes. Someone's got to help you get through this enormous pot of tea.' I move Dorrie's clothes carefully from the wicker chair and sit down.

Dorrie nods. 'Nice to have you here, bab.'

She eats her Weetabix surprisingly briskly and starts

on the toast. We chat idly, and soon she indicates that she has finished with the tray.

'Thanks, bab. I'll have another cup of tea if there is one.'

'Oh, there is!'

Settling back in the chair after tea duties, I look up to find Dorrie watching me beadily.

'Dorrie?' I hold my mug close to me, two-handed. 'I read everything in your envelope. It's taken me a while, I know, but . . .'

Dorrie nods. 'No rush.'

There is a silence.

'I don't quite understand –' I feel my blood speed up, not sure if I am about to say all the wrong things – 'why you showed it to me and not Ian.'

Dorrie draws her legs up and hugs them with her arms. It's a youthful kind of movement, making her seem almost like a girl. She sighs.

'I don't know either really. It's the shame, you see. Well, it was then.' She shakes her head. 'Though what in God's name any of us had to be ashamed of. But a boy – his father . . .' She seems to stall for a moment, then sits up, bracing herself. 'I do want you to know.' She starts to talk, still clutching her legs, staring ahead of her.

'After we were married, as I told you, Tom and I moved over to Dudley – near there anyway. He wanted to get away from Old Man Stefani – his dad, Luigi I mean, more than old Giuseppe. He and his dad never saw eye to eye – on at each other all the time. I don't know what it is with men, fathers, sons – they can be like flaming stags, banging their what-d'you-call-'ems together. Anyway, the pay was better there – he hadn't much

175

experience but they took him on and he soon learned. It was a rolling mills. It's heavy work – you need to be strong and tough. And Tom was that. There was lots of Indian lads working there then – hard workers all of 'em.

'He'd been there, oh, best part of three years. What they did there, see, they take these big billets of steel and they heat them, red hot, and they go on to rollers, on sort of tracks, like, to be made into other shapes – longer or thinner or rolled flat, whatever's wanted. It's hot, filthy work – Tom used to have a thirst on him when he came home. "Get me a bucket of water – I want to drink the well dry!" he used to say.' Her lips smile, but the smile doesn't get as far as her eyes.

'He didn't mind it there but he used to say he was a right fool to leave the Italian quarter. "I could be selling *gelato* or chips, like Ma and Pa, not breaking my back in there," he'd say. But he knew he wasn't going back. "This'll do us for a while, Dor – we'll save up a bit and get ourselves a nice little place, a little business of our own." He worked with some nice fellers though, good blokes. He made friends easily, my Tom. And weekends we'd go out somewhere, take Ian to the countryside, breathe some better air. It's bad in the Black Country – always has been.'

She pauses. I stop breathing for a few moments, flex my spine, remind myself to take another lungful of air.

'Anyway, this one Monday he went in. Course, I didn't know anything had happened until after. His mate had to come round and tell me. Bill Riley, his name was. He was more of a pub pal, sort of thing.' She stops for a second, as if bracing herself. 'When I saw him on the doorstep ... I only had to look at his face and it was,

"What's happened? It's Tom, isn't it? Is he dead?" He looked that bad. "No, Dorrie," he says, "no, he's not, but there's been an accident. A bad one. They've taken him over to the infirmary on Dudley Road."

'They'd been working over the weekend, some of them, and I heard later they'd had trouble – it was the nine-inch mill, they said, and the metal was twisting as it came off – wrong like. It shouldn't have done that. On the Monday they started up and Tom was standing close to it, adjusting summat. The billet that was passing through veered off, came off the track – red hot, of course. It just came up at him and kept coming. It caught my Tom right in the belly, took him up in the air –' She motions upwards, then winces at the pain in her shoulder. 'It drove him right across the factory before he dropped to the floor. Bill said a whole group of the Indian lads ran over and picked him up and someone called an ambulance.' She stares ahead of her. 'They was all ordered back to work, but they refused – the lot of them. Production stopped. They were all too upset at what had happened – that no one had seen to it that the machine was fixed properly.'

I sit completely still, listening.

'Thing was, Tom was badly injured – very badly. You should've seen him.' She stops. She's all hunched up now, arms folded close to her, behind her bent knees, as if the memories have chilled her blood. 'But he did sort of recover over the next few weeks. They sent him home. But he was never my Tom again, not really. Course he'd hit his head when he fell, but when he tried to talk about it . . . I kept hoping it'd all just sort itself out, but thinking back, it's clear it did summat to his mind. He'd banged his head hard, of course. But there was summat else. It was the force of it. He tried to say to me what it was – like being taken over by summat too big to reckon with, like an electric shock. If you ever get a little electric shock . . .' She looks at me for a second. 'You think, how would a really big shock be? And this was like that – that's what I think. This great big inhuman *thing*, coming at you and the force of it, it plays on your mind. It did summat to him, like a sort of torment he was in but he could never really explain it.

'It was summer when it happened, just before the factories went on holiday. I was expecting Cynthia and Ian was little. Tom came home from hospital at the end of September. I thought he'd get better like, you know – it was early days. He was home for about five weeks . . .'

She stops talking for so long that I think she must have said all she wants to say. She shakes her head gently a couple of times.

'I was worried he'd have to be buried in unconsecrated ground,' she says. For a moment her voice seems to have lost all strength, is barely a whisper. 'That was how it was back then. But Tom was Catholic and the priest said they wouldn't deny him a funeral . . . We went back over to the parish near his family in Birmingham . . . So his grave is in Lodge Hill Cemetery. But in them days it was . . . I never wanted to tell Ian, you see. There was what other people would think. And it felt as if it was all wrong, as if *I* was wrong, as if I hadn't looked after him right . . .'

I'm only just beginning to take in what she's telling me. What does this mean? Was it a heart attack that finally killed Tom Stefani – or what?

Dorrie stares down at her knees, speaking so softly that I have to lean close to hear her.

'He wasn't right – not right at all. Terrible nightmares he had and he did go back to work after a couple of weeks. But he was like a shell, sort of thing. I kept telling myself it would be all right but he was a stranger to me really, the things he said to me. And then he . . . I . . .'

I wait, hardly breathing. Almost, I don't want Dorrie to say it.

'I found him. I'd been out, taking Ian to play with another little lad. When I came into the house there was a feeling. I don't know – just how quiet it was . . . He was upstairs. There was blood everywhere. He'd never have done it – not done that to me – if his mind hadn't been affected. Not my Tom.' She keeps shaking her head. 'That wasn't him. Not the husband I knew. My Tom had gone and someone else had taken his place. It was his shaving razor – he'd stropped it sharp and cut his throat, you see. And I couldn't . . .' She gulps in a breath. 'Over the years, I mean – how could I tell Ian and Cynthia that?'

I find myself shaking. As I pull myself to my feet, my already stiff legs will hardly hold me. But I go to Dorrie, sit on the bed and wrap my arms round her. Dorrie is shaking as well. We sit for a long time, me holding on to her, and neither of us speaks.

179

Twenty-Three

'Jo?'

'Oh, hi, Hayley!' I've got the phone tucked into my neck. 'I'm just getting my trainers on. Are you all right?'

'No – well, yes, I'm OK.' Hayley's lispy voice sounds even more childlike over the phone. It warms me that she's called me, that Hayley will run and spend time with people old enough to be her mother – or older. 'I've gone and sprained my ankle. Had to go to hospital after work in the end. It's not broken, but it's quite a bad sprain. I'm so-o-o fed up with myself.'

'Oh, you poor thing – how did you do it?'

'I just sort of – I fell down a step in the pub. Went right over on it. I thought it was all right to begin with but then it really hurt – and then it was agony. I'm not in plaster, but it's all strapped up so I'll be out of action for a while. I'm so frustrated!'

'Well, you've got a head start on the rest of us, that's for sure – but we'll be sorry not to see you.'

'I'll get to Sheila's on Thursday,' Hayley says. 'Have a good run, won't you? No slacking,' she teases.

'No, all right – no slacking!'

*

The air holds a touch of spring now March has arrived. Daffodils jiggle in the breeze in front gardens and the park is full of birdsong and sunlight.

'I have news,' Sunita says, as soon as the three of us get there. She's looking mighty pleased with herself. With a little twirl, hands on her tummy, she says, 'I have lost four kilos in weight.'

'That's fantastic!' I say. 'That's loads, Sunita!'

Sunita is looking trimmer, more alert somehow.

'What's that in real money?' Pat says.

'About eight or nine pounds,' I suggest.

'Wow.' Pat runs her gaze admiringly over Sunita's slightly less portly figure. 'I just can't stop eating. I get to ten at night and I want a cheese sandwich! Where's Hayley got to?'

I explain.

'Oh, dear,' Pat says as we wander across to our starting point, she between me and Sunita. 'Well, she'll soon catch up, bless her. Shall we go?'

As we settle into a gentle jog, I say, 'Where does she work, anyway?'

'Not sure,' Pat says. 'Some pub in town, I think.'

'She's a nice girl, a good girl,' Sunita says. 'Very caring. Looking after her grandmother.'

'Yes, she's unusual,' Pat agrees.

We string out into single file for a moment to let a dog walker pass. The dog, an elderly boxer, stares as if mesmerized at our legs.

'Fred wants a dog,' Pat says, when we are all in a row again. 'I keep wondering whether to give in.'

'Have you told him you're running yet?' I ask.

'No.' Pat's quiet for a moment.

'What is his problem?' Sunita says bluntly.

'Fred? Oh –' Pat sounds weary – 'I don't know really. He finds any sort of change difficult – anything he doesn't understand. I sometimes think I'd have done a lot more things with my life if . . .' She stops herself. 'Don't get me wrong, he's a good man, Fred is. Heart of gold and I love him to bits. But things have to be within what Fred can sort of cope with.'

'Is that why you work as a childminder?' I ask her.

'Partly. It fitted in with my own kids, of course. But, I don't know . . .' She sounds wistful. 'I never really questioned it. We've had a nice life and Fred always brought in enough money. But I wish I'd branched out a bit more.'

We are silent for a few yards, all feeling the increasing pull on our lungs. I enjoy the tingle of the winter sun on my face and the fresh, cool air. My body is getting used to this, gradually, but getting warmed up for each run is always hard work. Slowly I'm feeling stronger, hungrier – and even despite having to get over the guilt of eating, of living and nourishing myself, I'm beginning to feel much better for it.

'I told Ian,' I say eventually. Ian didn't take much notice. It's just something I do when he's out of the house so he doesn't see it as affecting him. 'I just said I was going for little runs with some friends. I didn't tell him what for.' Just another thing I don't seem to be telling him. How can I pass on to him what Dorrie has told me? How would it help him to know?

The image of the boy in the magazine passes through my mind again, that sad, closed expression. I see Paul's face and then, of course, Lee Parry in the dock – the usual loop of thought that I can never seem to get away from for long.

'What about your husband, Sunita?' Pat says.

'Oh, he's all right,' she says. 'He thinks it's good for my health – he was teasing me about getting fat. He's quite easygoing really. And he's sponsored me!' She takes a few more breaths and then starts humming for a moment. 'What about these songs then? Our Hollywood-Bollywood songs?'

Once again, she sings a few scraps of a tune, as her breathing will allow, and falls into one or two little dance moves. The tune is so catchy that we can't help joining in to the rhythm, though we can't make head nor tail of the words.

'What's that, Sunita?' I ask her.

'It's from a film,' she pants.

'There's this one tune I can't get out of my head when I'm running,' Pat says. 'It's quite annoying . . .' She la-la's a few bars of the tune.

'Oh, "Candy Girl",' I laugh. 'That's a blast from the past!'

We are running on the path between the trees at the far side of the park and there's a pause in the conversation while a whole clutch of fluffy dogs, of varying sizes, goes charging past.

'Come on, ladies,' Sunita says afterwards. 'If we can run, we can sing. Very good words, that song. It is all about having troubles and if you walk with someone else, your troubles are halved, before they are double-double.'

'Oh, I heard you say double-double – I just thought I got it wrong!' Pat laughs.

'Double-double,' I say. 'Well, at least we can manage that bit.'

Sunita starts humming again. For a moment she whirls on the path, dancing on her short, plump legs.

It's strange how Lee Parry has become a part of my life even though I've only set eyes on him once. Like today, during our run, I find myself thinking of him.

Before we went to court, I had built him up in my mind. All I knew to begin with was that he was still in his teens and at the time of the accident had been driving a stolen BMW. My mind was full of images of the flash, swaggering, shameless monster who had killed our son.

Lee Parry in the flesh came as a shock. He was eighteen, it was true, but looked younger. He had obviously dressed up to come to court, in a black suit and a shiny pale-blue tie. He kept pushing a finger into his shirt collar, tugging as if it was too tight, whereas the suit looked too big on him. His mousey hair was cropped convict short even before any sentence was passed and he had fishy-white, terribly pimply skin. He sagged in the dock as if he had never developed muscles in his limbs.

On the night of 26 October, when he had stolen the car, drunk God knows what and was driving at almost eighty miles an hour up the Moseley Road, the police were already on his tail. He didn't even seem to be very good at stealing. If he had been anyone else I might have been wrung with sorrow for him, the pitiful little runt. He cried, standing there in the dock, snivelled like a lost child. You can cry now, can you? I thought, then. That's it, cry – try and get time off your sentence, you little bastard. All I could think then was: this pathetic specimen is here, alive, and Paul is not.

We learned a little bit about him from his defence lawyer. Lee was the middle child of three brothers and the youngest was disabled in some way. His mother's health was not good either. There was not much mention of his father. Lee had spent most of his school days either truanting or excluded and was unemployed. There was nothing in his attitude that spoke of defiance. He looked beaten down and hopeless.

The judge gave him five years: he would likely serve half of that.

Ian and I left the court, numb, speechless. When we got home, Ian finally said, 'I suppose whatever time he got would never have been enough, would it?' Soon he'll be out again, getting on with his life.

Twenty-Four
SUGAR-SUGAR, DOUBLE-DOUBLE

Over the weeks of early summer we settle into our training habit and it does wonders for me. There's the running for one thing. Twice a week, meeting in the park after my warm-up walk. We run one lap, two, then three.

'There's no need to run six miles very often,' Hayley says. She is soon recovered and back with us. 'Not unless you want to. You'll do it on the day when you have to.'

We all say we'd at least like to have a go, just so we know we can make it. We jog along gently, have stops if we need them to walk a few paces. But gradually we cover the distance, dodging dogs and Canada geese, running in pairs which change, slow enough to chat. And sometimes to sing, in a broken-up, gasping way.

Sunita is a changed woman. It's as if this is something she has been waiting for all her life. Now and again she breaks into a little dance on the path, singing Bollywood show tunes. Our favourite is the 'double-double' song which is says is called '*Kashmir Main, Tu Kanyakumari*', about two people who are opposites but need to be together. The jigging tune suits us all fine and we join in whenever she gets to the double-double bit, which is in English, and try to pick up other lines but we're pretty hopeless. We sometimes have to stop because we're laughing too much.

'Doesn't running make you hungry, though, Sunita?' Pat asks, when Sunita announces she has lost six kilos.

'Hungry?' Sunita frowns. 'No, not really. A lot of times I am only eating because I am bored at home. You know, nibbling at this and that. Running makes me not so hungry and anyway I have something to do, you know? I am reading a book about running. It is called *No Need for Speed*.'

'Good title – sounds ideal,' Pat says as we laugh.

It is Pat who constantly surprises me. I feel ashamed of my first impression that she might be rather boring, a bit housewifey (after all, who am I to judge?) and too much under her husband's thumb. They might be things that life has somehow forced her to be, but I can see there is a Pat who is longing to break out.

'Right,' she says one morning, when we have been running together for a month or so. We're gathered in the car park, valiantly ignoring a light drizzle. She tugs a folded sheet of paper out of her trouser pocket. 'I've been thinking about some more songs.'

'Wow!' Hayley says, giggling. 'You guys will be *so fit* – all this running and singing.'

'Well, Sunita's already doing her Hollywood-Bollywood routines,' Pat grins. 'So I thought ... OK, how about this, to the tune of that "Sugar, Sugar" song you were talking about, Jo ...' She stands now, bashful but determined and sings, tapping one foot, to the tune of the chorus:

'We're the ladies
Of Hollywood – and
We're running for Bhopal!
For the mums and children there ...'

She looks round, laughter in her eyes. 'That's as far as I've got.'

'That's fantastic, that's brilliant!' from all of us.

'Do it again,' Hayley says. 'And we can learn it.'

And we all set off into the damp, trying to remember the words . . . 'We're the ladies, of Hollywood . . .'

A few dog walkers look startled, then smile, more often than not. And we laugh and pant and sing.

I decide it's time to tell Ian about it all. When he gets home one night, over our meal, I explain about it, and what's it's for. He eats with his head down while I'm talking.

'Oh. Right,' he says, finally looking up when I go quiet. I feel deflated. I want to tell him everything – about the boy in the magazine, how this happened and made me look out of myself. But I can see he's not really interested.

'Don't you think it's a good idea?' I say. Suddenly I feel almost close to tears.

'I dunno. I'd've thought you're getting on a bit to be running about that far. You want to be careful.'

I sit, thinking, I'm being careful, very careful – not to tip my plate of dinner in your lap.

I find I am spending more time with Pat. Now and then we have a coffee after the run, at one or other of our houses. She lives about half a mile from me in a similiar sort of street. Pat and Fred's house is immaculate, even though she is a childminder. I have once glimpsed into the garage when Fred left the door up and I have never seen such a well-ordered place, every kind of tool you could want, all in regimented lines.

Sometimes we meet at dinner time, or I pop round for

a cuppa once she has picked up the two children she cares for after school. They are a brother and sister of five and eight and seem so tired – their mother leaves the house at seven – that they are content to have snacks and watch telly, or play out in the garden, where Pat and Fred have a little slide and a sandpit.

Fred is mostly out somewhere doing something busy when I call and Pat and I chat, sitting at the table or responding to the kids in between. I find I don't mind being with the children, which surprises me.

One sunny afternoon we are sitting out on the little patio with a cup of tea, watching Jack and Ruby play. The garden is a rectangle of green stretching away from the paving slabs, with flowers round the edge, all very organized. There are biscuits and cups of squash on the table for the kids and they come up every now and then and take a few gulps, their big blue eyes taking us in us, before seizing a custard cream and running off again.

'Don't run about while you're eating,' Pat warns them.

'At first, I couldn't stand being around any children at all,' I say to Pat. 'It's funny. I feel OK now. Ish, anyway.'

She smiles gently at me.

'I was the same with babies for a long time. How dare anyone else be happy sort of thing.'

We both smile at the sadness of this.

Cautiously, I say, 'And Fred?'

She looks away for a moment and I hear her sigh. I know I must have touched a nerve and I begin to regret saying anything.

'The thing is,' she says, looking back at me. 'My Fred had an absolutely terrible childhood. He's a good man and I love him, always have . . .'

I go to say something about how I didn't mean to be rude, to intrude, but she waves a hand.

'He can be very irritating and he always needs to be in control. But in a way I know he's amazed that he's got this far in life, that he's even made it to this age, the way his father was. But where it really affects him is, he needs life to be very settled and predictable. It makes him feel safe. Even things in the house – well, you can see.' She laughs. 'When we lost the baby – it was just too much for him, I think. It wasn't that he didn't feel anything, he just had no idea what to do, how to . . . You know . . .'

She's finding it difficult to speak. I nod, understanding.

'Ian's been much the same. It's lonely.'

She looks seriously at me. 'It is. But then we had our boys and things went on . . . It's just, it's been hard. No – that's not quite right . . . What I mean is, I suppose I've trimmed myself back to fit him all these years, hardly even noticing I was doing it. You do when you've got a family anyway, don't you? Cut back on yourself – you have to, to make room for other people. It's just that now they've grown up it's hard to get Fred to see that we don't have to stay the same . . .'

I'm just about to ask whether he knows about the London 10K yet when we hear the front door bang shut and Fred's voice, 'Pat? You there?'

'Every time –' she makes a face, half-resigned, half-exasperated. 'He can't come into the house without yelling for me.'

'Here!' she calls back. 'Jo's round for a cuppa.'

Fred soon comes out through the sliding door at the back. He looks very healthy, as ever, in long olive-green shorts and a white T-shirt which hugs his muscular chest. His mobile features move into a grin.

'All right, ladies?' He says it with a coyness that grates on me. But I feel annoyed with myself because I can see he's a good man. 'All right, are you, Jo? Nice to see you.'

'There's tea,' Pat says. 'I made a pot.'

'Oh, no, you're all right. I had some with Maureen – my sister,' he tells me. 'Just popped in to see her. So.' He sits on the third white plastic chair. 'How's all the running going?'

So he does know. Here we are, I think, 2015 and we are still worrying about what our husbands think of us for doing something different.

'All right, thanks,' I say, smiling at him. It seems as if he's OK with it.

'Nice for you all to train together – get a bit of exercise,' he says, crossing one leg over the other. 'Not my thing, but they say it's good for you. That young dolly-bird's coming along as well, I hear?'

'Hayley?'

'Yeah. Pretty little thing, isn't she?'

'Oh, stop it,' Pat says, reaching out to play-slap his arm.

'She got some sort of rough boyfriend, has she?'

Hayley appeared last week for our runs and for yoga with an injury on her left cheek, the bruising spreading round her eye.

'No,' I say. 'I don't think so. She's never mentioned any boyfriend. She seems too busy one way or another. She had a fall at work – or so she said.' All this does seem odd to me, but I don't really feel I can challenge Hayley on it because I would be accusing her of lying to us and she doesn't seem the type to do that.

'I'm not surprised, the shoes she insists on wearing,' Pat says. 'Have you seen the state of her feet? Cut to ribbons.'

'Funny girl she is,' I say. 'Lovely though. You can't help wanting to look after her, can you?'

'You lot want to get yourselves ready for a marathon or something,' Fred says. I can feel that he's trying to wind us up. 'Have a goal for all your training.'

My eyes meet Pat's. So he knows we do a bit of jogging, but he doesn't know about London yet. Goodness, I think to myself. Life does seem unnecessarily hard work at times.

Ian, on the other hand, does know. While not expressing any view on the subject at all, he is clearly not happy. In general. I'm finding it hard to read what's going on. He's so closed in and forbidding, I'm afraid to ask. He's over at the business working away every hour possible, it seems, despite the new guy Carl being apparently very good, very capable.

Communication between us is not great. There are a few good moments but mostly it all feels distant as if we live in different worlds. It's still weighing on me, all that Dorrie has told me, but I don't feel I can sit Ian down and tell him anything – not the way things are at the moment.

Twenty-Five

I go to Lodge Hill Cemetery every few days now, instead of daily. It's so far and I hardly ever have the car. In the beginning it was the only place I wanted to be. That's what I did, some weeks, once I'd stopped pretending I was coping at work and left the school. I used to spend half of the day on buses. Having to leave his body at the hospital that night, after it happened, was like being torn apart. All I could do to survive was to be close to him, to his body, which I was so attached to and could not yet take in that he was not. If I didn't go for some reason, I was weighed down with guilt.

I took him flowers, read him things from the paper, told him everyday bits of news. I remember wandering round and round those paths lined with the dead, in the winter cold, sometimes under an umbrella. Time was a blur, especially when I had taken sleeping tablets. Once or twice I remember screaming. It would have been better if I had been able to cry.

When I can go now, I still offer him flowers like a present. Sometimes I think of taking chocolates and then realize how ridiculous this is. I tidy up as if I am arranging his bed for him to come home to. I talk to him. I tell him over and over again how much I love him and miss him, how I will always love him.

But less and less, these days, does it feel as if he is there. It is a grave, with grass sprouting round the stone, leaves spiralling down and settling, spiders weaving tiny veils of grey, and lichen spots appearing. It is a marker where we can commune with him – as his bedroom was before we left the house. But now we are not living there, and he is not here to answer me. His remains are here, lying, as he does, in a garden full of markers of the long dead. But not him. My boy with his quiet way and sensitive eyes. And now I am feeling that, suddenly, like a chill wakening to reality.

And so I have reached a point where there are chinks in the black wall of my own pain, through which I can see out around Paul, even though hardly a beat of my heart passes without my thinking of him.

Dorrie seems to need to talk now, urgently.

All along, since I have known her, Dorrie has said so little, despite her long life and the loss she has experienced. She has kept it tight inside her. I must ask her about her happy years, the life with Tom before he died. Must hear anything she wants to say, because who has ever been there to listen to her? Not her own mother, by the sounds of it.

'She must want someone to know,' Pat says when I talk it over with her. We grow closer by the week. 'Or why would she have written it all down – or at least why show it to you? She wants you to ask, maybe to tell your husband because she can't, somehow – don't you think?'

So I try to give her a chance to begin. One warm day,

I say to her, 'Would you like to sit out at the back, Dorrie? I can get the garden chairs out?'

'Oh, no – I can't be bothered.' She waves this idea away and we sit, as usual, in the front room with tea, Dorrie huddled up in a rug. I think it's probably warmer outside than in today.

I have to steel myself to start because I'm used to the way older people often just don't talk. Some of them have never been given the words for their own feelings, or been allowed to take them seriously. Breaking through the surface of that feels invasive, rude almost. So all I say is:

'You've never really told me much about your Tom, Dorrie.'

She sits forward as if she has been waiting all along for me to ask.

'He was a wonderful man,' she says. She's not starry-eyed, not that type, but instead, matter-of-fact, which makes it more moving. 'I don't think it's just that I didn't have him long. He was one in a million and other people said so as well.'

She takes a sip of her tea, remembering. 'We were happy, me and Tom. Happier than any other married couple I knew. And because I didn't have a very good start – my mother and father like wasps in a bottle and Mom was still kicking up – well, I knew I was lucky. I knew what I had – that's the thing that keeps me going, thinking of it. I never took it for granted.'

Smiling, she says, 'It was a good time to be young and in love. I met Tom in 1955. Course, Birmingham was ever so scruffy after the war years – all knocked about and like a building site. But at least they'd called off rationing, finally – fourteen years we'd had of it altogether. I hardly knew what sweets were! But everyone wanted to get on with their life and have some fun. And we did. We worked hard – long hours. But in the time before we was married and had Ian, Tom and I were off somewhere every night. Mom didn't half mither about it. She was used to having me under her thumb and suddenly I had someone else.

'Tom wasn't keen on dancing – there was a lot of dance halls but he said he had two left feet. I never minded. I didn't know how to dance and I was shy of that sort of thing. We went to the pub, walked out round the park in Sparkhill – this was before we moved to Smethwick. Or just walking the streets was enough. It was free and we were that happy to be together, arm in arm, sort of thing. We were saving to get married although we didn't wait long!

'If there was one thing Tom really loved, it was a fun-fair. He'd go miles for it, Tom would – Aston, Kings Norton – wherever you could go on the rides and be out there with all the flashing lights and the smell of onions frying and candyfloss – oh, I can smell it now.'

She laughs, her wrinkled face lighting up, then stops, looking down as if she has lost her thread.

'He was a good'un – always good to me – and his family, most of 'em anyroad. But then . . .'

Her expression changes and I suddenly have that cold feeling you get when you walk from a sunlit street into cold blue shade.

'Yes . . .' She drifts. 'We had our times, Tom and I. And then Ian . . . You see, when Bill Riley came round he told me there was summat wrong with the tracks in the factory . . . There were two sort of levels, you see, on the machine – a double thing.' She makes gestures, trying to explain the rolling machines. 'The metal went in on the lower track and through the rollers, then it bent round and passed through another set of rollers to get the right thickness. And there were steps up and like a platform along the side for them to keep an eye, make adjustments and that. So Tom was standing on that when the metal – and it was red hot – bent off the lower track and just came at him.

'Bill said he guessed what was wrong – the tracks weren't adjusted right or the floor was uneven – but Tom wasn't the first. No one else had died but there'd been near misses. One feller was off weeks after one of the bits they were rolling came off and wrapped itself round him, terrible burns he had. It was all in the accident book, but so far as I know no one did anything. It was like that in them days, you see. People'd say, "Oh, that's just part of the job," but of course if anyone actually died . . . Well, that starts to look different. And they just wanted everyone to go straight back to work after, with Tom. They didn't want to stop production.'

'Incredible,' I say.

Dorrie looks at me. 'Oh, there was no care. Not like now. People moan about safety regulations but most of 'em have no idea how things used to be.'

'What about – I mean, did you get any help? Compensation?'

She gives me a look as if to say, *You are joking?*

'Make no mistake . . .' She's leaning towards me, grim-faced. 'When it comes to making money, no one cares. It's profits they're bothered about, nothing else. They have to be *made* to care – you have to have laws.'

199

She subsides, sits quiet for a moment, huddled with her arms wrapped round her.

'So. That was that. I had Cynthia and I just had to get on with it.'

This statement buckles my heart. 'Oh, Dorrie,' I say.

'They were hard years.' She sits up, flexing her spine. 'It was when our mother really started to . . .' For the first time, to my surprise, I see real distress pass across her face and she looks down.

'Your mother?' I say, not sure whether to ask.

'Oh –' Again, the dismissive wave of her hand as she looks up. 'Enough. You don't need to hear all this old nonsense. Ancient history now.'

'I do, Dorrie,' I tell her. I look searchingly into her eyes. Something passes between us. I see her understand that I am really listening.

'How about putting the kettle on again, bab?' She prises herself to her feet and I go to help. Dorrie is quite bent over now. 'I'll spend a penny while it boils.'

Once we are settled again, she has had time to think and she begins in a considered way.

'Both our mother and father were drinkers. The unhappy man's consolation – and woman. And drink does terrible things to you. So I look back and think of all our mother said over the years – terrible things sometimes, cursing us all high and low. Was that really her or was it just the drink talking? And I don't know – I never really knew her. Ethel Parsons. Who was Ethel Parsons?' She shrugs. 'She was never a happy woman, that I do know.'

'What about your father?'

'Well, he wasn't too bad really. Not in himself. Could

be quite good with us kids at times, given the chance. But of course, the way they were together . . . And he was out at work or down the pub. We didn't see a lot of him really. It was her always there, carrying on. My father died in 1953 – just before the Coronation. His heart it was, I think. And that's the only time I've ever seen our mother cry. She bawled and bawled, made a right carry-on. Heaven knows why really – I think it was just her way of getting attention . . . It's not as if they were even married any more. It was Aunt Beatt who found out and had to tell her about it. Course, Eric and I – Bert took off years before, we never knew where he'd gone – we could hardly believe it, her going on like that after all that time as if he was the love of her life.'

Dorrie takes a shaky sip of her tea and holds the mug in her lap. It seems to take a long time.

'So there she was. She'd been living on her own for a while since I moved out. I wasn't even married by then, but I just couldn't live with her, even though I felt I had to keep going in to see if she were all right. I was restless myself, moving from job to job – I'll say that, there was plenty of work in them days. But I couldn't stick living under the same roof as that harridan, heaven forgive me. Beattie popped in to see her – and I went to see Beatt more than I ever did our mother. But Mom just went from bad to worse. She'd always been a drinker but after a certain point she really hit the bottle – it became a full-time thing with her. Terrible.'

She looks down again, seeming to be ashamed.

'She got herself into a bad state. Very bad. I kept trying to say to her, "Mother, you've got to stop this, you're making yourself bad." I'd go in sometimes, find her passed out on the couch – she'd've wet herself and every-thing. She didn't seem to care at all. Oh, she was a dirty old thing. She was always a bit that way – you know, careless of herself. But she was going downhill fast … And the thing was, her mind went. You never knew whether what she was telling you was real. And on top of that, of course, she was always after money …'

'This went on for quite a time. Aunt Beattie – she was more my father's sort of age, a good few years older than Mom … Beattie was kind but she'd had enough of Mom's nonsense over the years. She used to say, "I know you do what you can for her, Dorrie, but don't let her ruin your life. She's not been much of a mother to you and she's on the downward path of her own choosing." I was grateful to Beattie – lovely, she was. She had no other family of her own, after all, so she was stuck with Mom and the rest of us. And her life had been the hardest of the lot, but she never went the way Mom did.

'See, by this time – this'd be 1955 – Tom and me was thinking of getting married. So with our mom playing up in the background it wasn't easy. I never wanted Tom to meet her – I was ashamed of her, to tell you the truth. But he insisted, said it didn't reflect on me. He wanted to see who my mother was and what I was having to deal with. He said he wanted to support me and it was no word of a lie – he always did.

'So I warned her one day that I was bringing my intended round to meet her. Not that I was asking her permission – I was twenty-five, after all, and quite old enough to make up my own mind by then. Well –' She gives a strange chuckle. 'I could hardly believe it. We went over to Deritend as arranged, me with my heart in my mouth as to what state the old girl might be in or what she might say. I say old – course, she was only in her forties but she was a wreck. When we got there, she come to the door all dressed up like a fourpenny rabbit in her best finery – the finery being her own wedding dress that she'd kept somewhere. I mean, I'd never seen it before. It was all cream lace and such but it had gone a horrible shade of yellow and she could hardly squeeze into it – it wasn't done up at the back and she was all bulges. And her skin was almost as yellow as the dress.'

Dorrie puts her hand over her mouth, remembering. 'Oh, my Lord.' She shakes her head. 'You've never seen anything like it. She'd put lipstick on and piled her hair up – and even that was a funny colour. Course, she'd gone grey but her hair had a yellowish tinge as well. I looked at Tom and he could see in my eyes, I think, that . . . Well, that this was unexpected.

'"Come in," she says, all grand. I just don't know what had got into her. She knew who Tom was, that the Stefanis were from a few streets away. They were prosperous enough for the time but it wasn't as if I was marrying the Prince of Wales.'

Suddenly she sits back, rocking with laughter until tears run down her face and I can only join in.

'Oh, Jo, it was terrible – you've never seen anything like my mother that day. Tom and I couldn't look at each other. She made tea as if she was the Queen and put a cloth on the table – an embroidered thing I'd never seen before either. All the cups were cracked – mine never even had a handle. And she'd bought a packet of biscuits and laid them out on a plate. I just don't know now what we talked about.' She's still shaking with laughter, crying a little. 'Dear, oh, dear. Her mind was going then but . . . Anyway, after we got out of there – we only stayed an hour, if that – I said to Tom, "Well, she's going to be your mother-in-law – so now you know." I'd told him a fair bit about how she really was. And as we walked along the street, he in his Sunday best to meet her, he just drew my arm through his and he said, "Never mind, Dor. She needn't bother us. We've got each other and that's all that matters." And I tell you – if it was possible, I fell even deeper in love with him that day.

'She carried on like she was, and Tom and I married – I never told her when it was happening – and got on with our lives. I went in now and then, screwed myself up to do it – but we were living a long way off. I'd take Ian over, very occasionally, for her to see him. He wouldn't remember her though, he was too small.

'But then I lost Tom . . .' She stops abruptly

I sit, waiting. I feel tense, sick, waiting to hear even more pain.

'That was 1959, so you can imagine by then she was getting pretty bad. I went round to see her one time and I don't know how long it'd been going on but I realized she couldn't walk. She tried to get up and fetch summat and she must've forgotten she couldn't and she just fell flat on her face. The place smelt terrible. I helped her up, of course, and I went to see Beattie. She had some idea, but we both knew it was all getting worse – much worse than we realized. A lot of what she said didn't make much sense any more, either. By then she was forty-six. No age, is it? Even then it wasn't. And she was a wreck. A complete and utter wreck of a person.

'Beattie was living in a little house in Sparkbrook and

204

I knew where my duty lay. I couldn't stand the thought, but I said to Beattie, "Well, she can't go on like this. She'll have to come and live with us and be looked after." I don't know why I said it, really. There was me, a widow with a small child and another on the way, but it felt as if it was laid on me. I was so sorry, so ashamed of her and even being near her – it was like an aversion. Terrible to think she was really my mother. I could hardly stand to be in the same room. But still, I felt I had a duty to her. Eric was no good – he's never made much of a life and he was still just lodging in one room. And our Bert was nowhere to be seen.

'"Oh, no, you don't," says Beattie. "I'm not seeing you ruining your life by taking her on. What she's done, she's done to herself and there's no blame on you. You've got quite enough on your plate." Well, Aunt Beattie was a rather splendid-looking woman by then. She had a rounded sort of figure, very straight-backed, waist nipped in with her corset, and she still wore her hair up as she'd always done and brown lace-up boots. And she stood there, hands on hips – this was out in the little yard at the back of Mom's house. "I'm not going to stand by and watch her drag you down," she said. "She may be my sister, but that doesn't mean I have much respect for the way she's gone on."'

'But what can we do, Auntie?' I said to her. I really had no idea.

' "Well," Beattie said. "I'm sorry to say, but Ethel is no longer in her right mind and she'll have to go and be looked after where other people go who are in that state."

'I just stood there gaping at her. Surely she didn't mean what I thought she was saying?

'"What?" I remember whispering it. It was so frightening, so shameful. "You mean the asylum?"'

Even now, Dorrie's face registers shock. She can't seem to look at me as she says it.

'And Beattie looked me right in the eye and nodded. "I think it's come to that," she said. "I can't manage her and neither can you. She'll have to be looked after in there."

'It was terrible really, the relief of it. I've never told Ian or Cynthia. They think their grandmother died at home when they were very small. I never took them to see her. I was too ashamed. The thing was, of course, once she got there – they took her to All Saints asylum – they wouldn't let her drink in there. They dried her out and she improved in some ways. But she'd already done too much damage to herself – she hardly ever knew who I was when I did screw myself up to go and see her. But she lived on and on, for twelve years. If she'd stayed on the way she was at home it would have been another story . . . It was her chest finished her off finally, in 1967 – pneumonia.'

She looks down at her veined hands.

'Beattie died in 1978, bless her. She and I were the only ones at Mom's funeral. And I never told anyone – not a soul – that I still had a mother or where she was. Seems terrible, doesn't it?'

She looks up at me cautiously, and I can see all the shame she has been unable to shake off over the years.

'You couldn't have done anything else,' I say gently. 'You did the only thing you could. Beattie was right – wasn't she?'

Dorrie nods. 'She was. I know she was – only it seemed a shameful thing. She wasn't a nice person, our mother.

She was very bitter and she could be cruel and violent with it. But she was unhappy. I thought I should be able to save her somehow – but there was never a way.'

'No,' I say. 'There wasn't. It's very sad.'

She takes in what I say as if she needs to hear it. After a moment she looks away and reaches out to put down the empty mug.

'Well, there you are,' she says. 'That's how it was.'

I wait a moment and we sit in silence.

'D'you want me to tell Ian?' I ask. 'Any of this?'

Dorrie shrugs. 'Sometime, maybe. When things are a bit easier, eh?'

It's my eyes that fill with tears then. Without my even saying anything she seems to know that we are not doing very well.

'All right.' I get up and touch her shoulder, give a gentle squeeze. 'The right time will come, I'm sure.'

Dorrie smiles as I let go. 'Are you off to see your friends this afternoon?'

'Yes,' I say, getting my things together. 'I'm going to be drinking a lot of tea today!'

'Nice, that they do that. Sheila, you say – the person whose house you go to?'

'Yes. She's very kind.' I go to the door. 'I'm surprised you haven't come across her.'

'Hm. Can't place her,' Dorrie says. 'But then I've never been one for church.' She twinkles at me. 'I expect I'm bound for the Other Place.'

Twenty-Six

There are only the four of us at Sheila's that afternoon – Pat, Sunita, Sheila and me. We sit inside, but with the window open over her immaculate garden. Pots and hanging baskets spill fuchsia, geraniums and Busy Lizzie. Sweet peas are weaving themselves up a lattice on the side wall of the house.

Herbert, the old Labrador, who has had his neck protector off for some time, comes and rests his jowls on my leg.

'Hello,' I say, stroking him.

'Oh – you're the Chosen One,' Sheila says. As usual she's moving stiffly back and forth to the kitchen, refusing offers of help.

'I know.' And I do feel ridiculously honoured. Herbert's warm presence is like a comfort blanket. I keep my hand on his head. Maggie the superior-looking cat is nowhere to be seen.

'No Hayley?' I ask.

'I haven't heard,' Sheila says. Hayley usually turns up pretty regularly.

'There's something about her that worries me,' Pat says. She's voiced this to me before. 'D'you think she's got a boyfriend? She never mentions anyone. But the way her face was the other day. I didn't say anything but that didn't look like something you'd get from falling.'

'You mean someone is hitting her?' Sunita says.

Pat shrugs. 'I don't know. She just seems . . . sort of secretive. Evasive – about some things. I don't like to push it with her.'

'Oh, hang on – I know what she said.' Sheila comes back, bringing a plate of home-made shortbread. She's missed the rest of the conversation and so we end up changing the subject. 'Something about college. An open day, I think?'

'Good for her,' Sunita says. 'Everyone should go to college, that's what I think. Ooh, shortbread – delicious.' She bites into it with enthusiasm, our new, streamlined Sunita, who looks the picture of health. 'Running is good – I am eating everything I want and still losing weight!'

'You look great,' I say.

'So do you.' Pat nudges me. 'It's put roses in your cheeks.'

'How's it going?' Sheila asks. I can hear the slight reluctance in her voice and realize she feels left out.

'It's going fine,' I say.

'You're all absolutely mad.'

'You'll come and watch us, won't you?' Pat says to her. 'On the day, I mean? We'll need someone to cheer us on.'

'What – in London?' Sheila seems taken aback.

'Why not?' Sunita says. 'It only takes two hours to drive – less. Early on a Sunday morning the roads will be quiet. You don't need to be there right at the beginning.'

Sheila looks pleased suddenly. 'Well, I suppose I could ask Roy. We could make a day of it.'

'There's a picnic afterwards,' I tell her. 'Or you could go off and see the sights.'

'Are all your husbands going?' Sheila asks.

'Mine is coming,' Sunita says. 'My brother lives in Wembley – we can stay with them.'

Pat and I look at each other.

'We're not sure yet,' Pat says.

I'm trying really hard at home. I know a lot of things are my fault, the way I have been so shut in with my own feelings, the way I resented Ian for not grieving the way I understood we should grieve, for not sharing it with me, for seeming to have energy only for work.

All the same, sometimes I feel like just screaming at him, 'You're not the only one who's lost your son, you know! What about me? Why can't you *talk* to me?' But so far I've managed not to – not because I'm especially self-controlled but because in the end I know it wouldn't be fair, and even more to the point, that it wouldn't actually make any difference to anything. Ian can't help the way he is – really can't, any more than I can – and that's how it is.

I'm there a lot of the time, making the house nice, cooking, looking after his mom – not that that's a hardship – trying to be open to him. And I'm trying to find a way of getting back on my own feet, of having a life and not staying in the tomb as someone once said to me. We moved house partly to try and drag ourselves out of that tomb.

But this new life is what seems to worry Ian. I'm making friends, going running. He doesn't want to know – not about the friends. And as for the running:

211

'You're not still doing that, are you?' he says, a few days later when I mention that we have been out for our morning jog. I don't say too much about it but he asked – although not as if he really wanted to know – what I've been doing all day. I try not to take that as a criticism of my not working at the moment. He wants me to be there for Dorrie, after all. And I know he's grateful that I can be there for her.

'Well, we're training,' I tell him, as I dish up food at the table – chicken stew, potatoes. He's already showered and changed. It's not as if I'm throwing information at him the second he's stepped through the door. And he asked, didn't he?

'We've got to be able to run ten kilometres. It's a quarter of a marathon – just over six miles.'

He picks up his knife and fork, shaking his head as if I'm saying something absolutely ridiculous. I feel myself getting more and more annoyed, but I swallow it down and manage to say:

'D'you have a problem with me doing it for some reason?'

He shrugs off the question. 'No.'

'So what about a bit of encouragement? It's in a good cause.'

'India?' He says that too, as if it's something absurd, distasteful almost.

'Well, your mother's sponsored me, anyway.' Generously too, I think. Five pounds a mile. And she's listened to me telling her what it's all about, tutted when I say what's still happening with the children in that area of Bhopal.

'Wicked,' she said. 'Absolutely wicked. It's always been the same with rich bosses.'

As she wrote her name shakily on the sponsorship form, she said, 'There's suffering everywhere, bab. None of us can do much really – but if this helps do summat about a single thing, then good for you.'

'I just think . . .' Ian puts his knife and fork down. But he can't seem to think what it is he just thinks and picks them up again.

'Why don't you come down and watch?' I say, still trying to hold on to being positive when I feel hurt and undermined. 'Some of the others've got their families coming. They're making a day of it.'

'When is it?'

'I've told you – the twelfth of July. It's a Sunday.'

Without looking up, he says, 'I dunno – I'll have to think.'

'Right,' I say. 'You do that.'

Later, when I come out of the bathroom to get into bed, he seems to be asleep. The light's still burning on my side of the bed and as I climb in, he rolls over and looks at me. His face appears more textured than I remember it ever being: bags under his eyes, the cleft between his nose and top lip deeper, lines round his mouth. We are all more textured – by the years, by Paul. He looks anxious, almost afraid.

'Sorry,' he says. 'About earlier.'

'How d'you mean?' I hold back, still hurt. I'm not just going to say, *It's all right*, and let it go straight away.

'I'm just not . . . I don't get why you're doing it. I mean, you don't know any of those people . . .'

213

'OK,' I say, still curbing my impatience. I've told him several times what it's about. 'Imagine it was you, there – like now, just getting into bed, asleep maybe. And you find you're waking up and the house is full of poisonous gas and you get up and try and get away and find that maybe all your family die on the way. Or some of you survive and you can never work again because you can hardly breathe and you're in constant pain. And on top of that you find that the water you're drinking is poisoning you and your family day after day because no one will take the trouble to clear the place up . . .'

I'm crying, great heaving sobs. Ian shifts closer and takes me in his arms. Tightly, rocking me, making comforting noises. When I'm a bit calmer, he says:

'You're hardly cried. Before, I mean.'

'Nor you.'

We lie close for a moment and I can feel his heart beating against my shoulder.

'I just don't know why you're getting so upset about people over there – so far away. It's their government should be sorting it out, not us.'

'The Indian government have been rubbish as well,' I say. My nose is blocked and I sit up for a moment and reach for a tissue. 'Pretty much everyone has been. But in the end, the Americans designed it and had the biggest share in it. They wanted all the court cases to be held in India – and then every time there's any kind of hearing they just don't turn up because they won't recognize the jurisdiction of the Indian courts. What really gets to me is companies using poorer countries to make profits and do just what they like without giving a toss about the people.'

214

'That's business, I suppose.'

'But it doesn't have to be, does it?' I'm almost shouting. 'Who says it has to be that cruel, ridiculous way and why do we all go along with it?'

Suddenly I remember all that Dorrie has told me. Ian's dad – his own father's life devastated by an industry taking short cuts, gambling with people's lives. Should I tell him – now?

'But why them?' he's saying. 'Of all the things to get upset about?' He has pushed up on his elbow.

I almost tell him about the boy, the boy from Bhopal who looks like Paul. But then I realize I have hardly thought of him in these past weeks – that it's not about him any more – it's about them, the people there who I have read about, what they're going through … More tears find their way out, surprising even me.

'I suppose I just feel for them,' I end up saying.

Ian hugs me again and even if he doesn't really understand, he strokes my hair.

'Will you come?' I say eventually.

After a hesitation, he says, 'Yeah – OK then.'

And at the time I think he means it.

Twenty-Seven

July 2015

The last few weeks of training have been bittersweet. I feel better for it; much better. I run, talking to Paul – he is beside me for so much of the day. But something has shifted – I can smile, I am making friends. Stronger threads of light are warming the dark, lonely place into which I had crawled. I like Pat a lot. I have begun to feel a kind of love for these women I am running with. That's what it does, I suppose, struggling for something together like that. We've even managed, last week, to run 10K for the first time – with little bits of walking along the way.

But when it comes to the men, things have not been so easy.

Pat had to get on and tell Fred about the run because Fred plays golf with Roy, Sheila's husband, so he would have found out in any case.

'What did he say?' I asked her, when she popped round to see me afterwards. I couldn't believe he could say much, really. What was there to make a fuss about?

Pat pulled a face. 'He wasn't too happy. D'you know – I've only just realized this myself, but Fred and I have never had a night apart.'

'What – *never*?' I was gobsmacked. 'In how many years?'

Pat blushed. 'Forty-four.'

'You're kidding me?' I just sat there gaping at her.

'Oh, no, come to think of it, there was one night, when his mom was dying – he spent it in the hospital.' Smiling, she shook her head. 'Met him when I was sixteen, married at seventeen. That was that. Where else would either of us go?'

'You do realize we're going to have to go down the night before – we wouldn't make it from Birmingham in time, not by train.'

'I know,' she said calmly. 'I've told him. He'll come round. Basically, he's going to have to.'

We looked at each other as if to say, *How hard can this be?*

And for me, while I may have been out running, at home we've been limping from week to week. There have been a few moments of closeness, glimpses of something better, more like old times, brief and hopeful. But Ian also seems resentful of me running, of what I am getting into, as if in opening a door for myself I am closing another one on him.

There is also something going on at his work and I can't make sense of it. First Gideon left, and now he has Carl. Carl is older, experienced. This, you would think, was a good thing. On the face of it, Ian agrees that it is, but something is bothering him. I can't get him to say anything about it. Maybe he doesn't even know himself. I try – I don't know what else to do. He moves further away from me again, so that I feel I can't reach him.

When I told him that we will have to go to London the night before the race, he looked really put out.

'Come on,' I tried to joke. We were just finishing

breakfast. 'I'm talking about *one night*. Since when have you been a Victorian patriarch?'

'Where will you stay?' He sounded really suspicious. Men, honestly. Who exactly does he think I might hook up with for the evening in a city where I know precisely no one? Since when has he been such a control freak? He never used to be like this.

'Sunita's brother lives there – they've got a house in Wembley and she says they'll put us up. We can go in on the Tube then. We have to be there by about nine-thirty at the latest.'

'Right,' he said, putting his plate in the sink. He still hasn't met Sunita or any of them, except Pat.

'They've sent us a race pack with a race number and safety pins to put it on with and everything!' I told him, wanting him to share the excitement.

'Right – nice,' he said, sounding anything but interested. He looked as if he was about to leave the room, so I went up to him, put my arms round him. He stood stiffly, not responding. 'So if you come down early in the morning, from Euston, you should be able to make it in time for the end of the race at least . . .' I give him a gentle squeeze. 'It'll mean such a lot having you there, love. This is for Bhopal – but it's for Paul as well.'

'Oh,' he said, with flat sarcasm. 'Seems like it's for you and your mates more than anything.'

This stung me into such anger that I recoiled from him, turned away and folded my arms tightly to stop myself lashing out.

'Sorry,' he said, after a few seconds. 'I didn't mean it – not to come out like that.'

'I should bloody well think you are sorry.' I turn back

to face him, my jaw clenched as I speak. 'Yes, it's for me too. Yes, I'm getting something out of it – like some point to my stupid little life, like friends. Is there something wrong in that?'

He was looking warily at me, as if he sort of didn't know who I was any more.

'No,' he admitted. 'I s'pose not.'

And so we go on.

The Thursday before the race, we all meet at Sheila's and sit out in the garden. Sheila, having been a little bit sniffy about what we are doing at the beginning, has confessed to going online, reading about the children of Bhopal. She is upset and appalled. And, besides that, she's excited about coming down for the race.

'I couldn't believe it. Roy's booked us into a hotel, says why don't we make a weekend of it? We're going to see a show if we can, on the Saturday night!'

'Good for you,' Pat says. She makes a wry face at me. 'Fred suddenly announced this morning that he'd decided he'd drive me down on Sunday morning – no need for me to stay with Sunita's family. If we start off at six the roads'll be quiet and we'll get there in plenty of time, etc. etc.'

We all look at her.

'So?' Sunita says.

'I just realized, when he said it . . .' Pat plays up her excitement, almost like a little girl. 'I'm really, really look-ing forward to it. It'll be like a girls' night out. I've hardly been anywhere except the cottage in Wales for years. So I said, "Fred, love – I'm sorry but I'm going and that's that. You come and join me the next day."'

'Yay, good for you!' I say and the others clap her – all of us laughing at ourselves at the same time.

'Are your brother's family still OK with it?' I ask Sunita.

'Yes, yes, all fine,' she says. 'They are very happy.'

A moment later, Hayley arrives and we can all see immediately that something's wrong. We watch her sink into a chair as if her body hurts and she has dark rings under her eyes.

'What is it, love?' Sheila asks eventually.

Hayley looks up, obviously upset. 'I'm not sure I'm going to be able to come on Sunday.'

'What?' we all cry. 'You've got to – you're our leader. Our trainer. You can't not come!'

'The trouble is –' she looks down – 'my manager's being difficult. Saturday night's our busiest time at work, you see, and he doesn't want me taking the night off then . . .'

'Oh, for goodness' sake,' Sheila says. 'You're entitled to time off, surely?'

Hayley looks up and her face is tense. 'You don't know what he's like.'

We all stare at her, bewildered.

'It's just a pub job – why don't you go and work some-where else?' Pat says, her tone gentle, motherly.

'It's . . . it's complicated.' Hayley's looking really uncomfortable now. 'I just . . . I just really need this job.'

I look at her, wanting to ask what exactly is wrong, but she seems so uncomfortable I don't like to. Hayley's become like a kind of daughter to me as well and if we were on our own I might ask, but it doesn't seem right now.

We carry on chatting about the race, about plans for travelling down together, having a meal somewhere – curry, pizza?

'I don't think curry the night before a race,' Pat says, with a comical raise to her eyebrows.

Sheila makes a face. 'Rather you than me. Come on, ladies –' She lifts the plate in front of her which holds a big chocolate cake Pat has made. 'You need to build up your energy.'

After a while, as we all tuck into the cake, Hayley bursts out with, 'Oh, I can't not come! I just can't!'

'What's the worst that can happen?' I say. 'You won't be there much longer anyway, will you, if you're going to college?'

She looks at me as if seeking reassurance. 'No. I s'pose not.' She gathers herself. 'It's just . . . I'm not even sure if . . .' She pushes her doubts away. 'No – you're right. I'll tell him. If he fires me I'll just have to . . . Well, I'll find something. I've got to come and do it – and I've got people who've sponsored me, like my nan, for a start.'

Twenty-Eight
MILK STREET

Walking home afterwards, part of the way with Pat, I feel happy and excited for the first time in as long as I can remember. It's a warm afternoon, the sun is on our backs and my body feels stronger and at one with itself.

At this thought the guilt crashes in for a moment. *I haven't forgotten you, Paul. I love you – I'll always love you and I'm thinking of you, always . . .*

But I am here with a friend, someone who wants to be with me, and who I know, to some extent, understands. We have talked about her little girl: at least, I let her talk and talk about the birth and how she held her and called her by her name. She needed to tell me, in every detail she could recall, how lovely her little Becky was, pale and perfect as if she was asleep, though not a breath ever passed through her.

'I was lucky, I suppose – they let me hold her. And the nurse was so kind. She washed her and wrapped her in a little white blanket. She was upset herself.' Her eyes fill as she looks back. 'I know with some mothers, they snatched their babies away and they never got to see them.'

There is a quiet, kind understanding between Pat and me. When we reach the corner where we part she says:

'Well, this is it. See you on Saturday!'

'I can't believe we're really doing it,' I say. 'And I'm so impressed with the way you've all just joined in and seen it through.'

'It's in a good cause,' Pat says seriously. With a wave she takes off towards home.

I pop in and visit Dorrie, who seems to be all right. Each time I've been lately I hedge around, seeing if there's any more she wants to talk to me about, but last time I visited, she said:

'I've got things off my chest, Jo. What happened to my Tom should never've happened – people should be better taken care of. And our mother . . . Well, it's all over now. I don't need to keep harping on it. You're a good girl, listening to me maundering on.'

'Dorrie,' I say seriously. 'You've really been there for me – through all this. It's the least I can do.'

And exactly what she has done is be there. Not saying much or doing much – simply being, especially in those early days after the accident when all I could do was sit there and she let me. Like an old, loving tree, as Paul said. And it's meant the world to me.

After I've sorted out a bit of tea for her I go home and cook for us. Fish and chips, cutting up potatoes, watching them turn a lovely golden brown, lifting them to drain. I'll save the last fry until Ian gets home.

In the meantime I go into the living room, kick off my flip-flops and take out the magazine I found at the dentist's. I sit for a long time looking at the boy, at his sad, shadowy face. It seems a face full of pain and I want to make it better, make everything better. Suddenly I'm crying, as if pain is invading me from everywhere, and not just my own. I sit sobbing for a time – I don't really know how long, immersed in both my own grief and theirs, those faraway mothers. And then, having felt it, I find I can stop. I go upstairs and rinse my face, looking in the mirror at my blotchy cheeks. But I feel better for crying, as if each time I do it empties something more out of me, just a little.

Ian is usually home by seven. At ten to I start cooking the chips again, put the fish under the grill. The house fills with nice smells. Air breezes in from the open window.

By half past, I text him. *Are you nearly home?*

There is no reply.

After another fifteen minutes: *Can you let me know how long you're going to be, love? Xx*

Nothing.

Eight o'clock: *Ian, where are you? Can you text me back please?*

I try ringing his phone and keep getting his voicemail. I call the landline at the garage although it's now after eight and they surely must have shut up and gone home? I'm trying hard not to get annoyed or worried, but this is just not like Ian, this not getting in touch. I tell myself that maybe he and Carl have gone for a drink. After all, that's a perfectly reasonable thing to do. It would be good if Ian would socialize with someone – I've been encouraging him to – although it would have been nice if he'd bothered to let me know.

Although I've cooked I don't feel like eating so I leave the food for us to heat up later and go back to the front room. I pad around barefoot, switch on the TV, flit through channels but can't concentrate on anything and then switch it off again.

Has he gone in to see Dorrie maybe? But he wouldn't stay this long. I don't want to go down there though, because it would worry her.

Eventually I pick at a bit of the food I've cooked, watch some TV, keep checking my phone, still telling myself not to be ridiculous, even though all the time my nerves are on alert for any sound. Ian's never deliberately nasty or tricky, I tell myself. Some emergency has come up or his battery's died – or he's gone to the pub and forgotten to take his phone.

Which works quite well until pub closing time, then more than enough time for him to get home, and all the panic I've been trying to keep under control starts to take over. Where the hell is he? There's still no message. He's got the car, otherwise I'd go out and drive round everywhere – the garage, the pub. And then it's nearly midnight and there is still no sign of him.

I don't know what to do. I feel sick, the blood pounding round my body, and I'm back in that night when Paul didn't come home and there were fireworks and sirens and all at once the skin of our life, which had been slowly healing over, was ripped into unrecognizable shreds.

'Where are you?' I'm whimpering. I'm way beyond anger – just really scared. I go to the front door and stand looking out as if this will bring him driving up the road, or walking – anything so long as I see a living person come back to me. My ears are pricked for the horrible sound of ambulances. 'Come home. Where are you?'

I can't call the police, not this soon, can I?

There's no way I can just stay in sitting here, so I pull

a fleece on and head outside, striding the mile to Ian's garage along the dark, almost silent roads. The air smells of summer night – cooling concrete, grass, the exhaust of passing cars. The garage is all locked up, of course. I go along the alley at the side, hearing something crunch under my trainers. There are no windows, no sign of light.

I stand there for a while, obsessively calling his phone, sending texts. *Where are you?* I rack my brains trying to think who else I could call. I have no number for Carl and there really isn't anyone else I could ask – not at this time of night especially. And if there was any trouble, if he was in hospital, they would ring me, surely?

Next I try a couple of pubs. I'm hardly even sure where they are but I just keep walking until I find them. They're all locked up as well and by the time I get home after nearly two hours pounding the pavements, my blood sugar has sunk and I feel shaky and weepy.

He'll be home by now! I think, half-jogging the last stretch of our road to the house, despite feeling so wobbly. Hands shaking, I push the key into the lock.

'Ian?' In the hall.

But there is only silence.

Eventually I go upstairs and lie on the bed with the light on. There is no sleep to be had – just a half-waking state in which I keep jerking up, grabbing my phone to see the time, to check for messages, my body jangled with fear.

By eight the next morning, I am round at the garage again, still in last night's clothes and my trainers, waiting by the kerb. My body is in a state of emergency, beyond hunger or tiredness.

Soon, a rescue truck drives up with a small silver car strapped on to it. I see a man, who must be Carl, at the wheel, dressed in bottle-green overalls. He's in his fifties, a lean guy with curly grey hair and a tanned, humorous-looking face. His expression, however, is not particularly jolly at this moment. He eyes me as if I'm a challenging job he's got to deal with, brakes, switches off the ignition, gets a sheaf of papers off the passenger seat and finally climbs slowly out.

'Morning.' He has a deep voice with a smoker's gravel in it. He doesn't seem all that surprised, as if there is something predictable about my standing about on the pavement at eight in the morning.

'Where's Ian? I'm Jo, his wife – where's he gone? He never came home last night,' I gabble at him. I'm near tears, but there is something about this man's dignified demeanour that makes me want to keep my cool.

He looks at me as if judging what to say. 'Has he not been in touch?'

'No. I kept phoning and messaging him – I've no idea where he is.' My voice starts to crack. *Don't,* I scream inwardly at myself. *Just hold it together.*

Carl puts his head on one side and the pitying impression this gives suddenly makes me want to go up and punch him, scratch his face, anything. *You know where he is – tell me, you bastard.*

'Thing is,' he says finally, weighing his words. 'I thought he was going to be in touch with you. He should have done that.'

'What d'you mean? Just tell me where he is and stop

228

messing about!' I'm shouting, waving my arms. Carl holds up a hand.

'He's all right. Don't fret – he's fine. He just said he wanted a bit of . . . well, space. Time away. Nothing to worry about. He's been a bit down, like, and he just wanted to sort his head out, I think.'

'D'you know where he is?'

Carl's eye wanders. 'Only in general terms.'

I go up close to him. His overalls have been ironed, creases down the front of the legs. He must have a very efficient wife.

'Carl, please – what's going on?' I'm caught between worry and fury with Ian. Here I am, worried sick, exhausted – just before our run, so that I wonder whether he's done it on purpose even while I'm concerned about him.

Carl shrugs and I see that he really doesn't get it either, not really.

'Tell him to get in touch with me – will you? Tell him to text me back. *Please.*'

'I will, bab,' he says.

And he sounds kind now and this undoes me. I turn to walk home, cold and deflated, tears running down my face all the way.

Twenty-Nine

At home I make black coffee and sit in the kitchen sipping it, asking myself if this is all my fault. Then I get angry and decide it's all Ian's fault. And then I rock realistically into the middle of these accusations and decide it's all part of *shit happens*, that I do need to worry about him but that the stupid sod still should have texted me . . . Has he any idea what he did to me last night?

Tomorrow I am supposed to be going to London and the day after that is the race. At this moment, overwrought and exhausted as I feel, with a missing husband and sense of catastrophe, this now seems impossible.

I'm about to phone Pat and say . . . what? That I won't be coming? That one of the Bhopal Runners of Hollywood is going to pull out . . . ? Or just, *Help me* . . . But then I hear my phone beep and grab it immediately.

Ian. *Sorry. Am fine, no worries. Just need to get away for a bit. Will be in touch.*

You bastard, I think, flushed with relief. I message him: *Are you coming back today?* I should put, *Are you OK?* Something kind and concerned. But I'm too angry. *I* have to stay here. *I* have to feel all this. What the hell is he playing at?

231

Seconds later the phone beeps. *I don't know. Probably not.*

This drives me to my feet. Right. Fine. If that's how it is I'm not going to just sit here in case he deigns to turn up.

As I cross the room, the phone rings and I run back like a maniac. My mother – oh, no, please . . .

'Jo? Oh, good – I'm glad I've caught you,' she says, as if I'm some busy tycoon who never has time to answer the phone. 'How are you, love?'

'Oh, I'm fine,' I say manically.

'Well, good for you.' She sounds reassured. 'Nice to hear you sounding so cheerful. It's about time.'

I grit my teeth.

'Now, I know we haven't been over for a while so your dad and I were thinking maybe we'd pop over tomorrow afternoon and see you both? Come late afternoon so we can see Ian after work as well – maybe have a barbie or something? If you haven't got one we could bring ours over?'

'Mom,' I say. 'I won't be here tomorrow.' As I say it I know with sudden certainty that I won't be here. Whatever Ian is up to he's not here and I have something that I very much need to do.

'Oh? Where're you off to then?' Her tone is coy, as if she thinks perhaps Ian and I are off for some kind of dirty weekend. As you do when you've been together for over thirty years and your only son has died.

'I'm going to London with friends. We're doing the run on Sunday morning – it's the London 10K, for charity – for the Bhopal Medical Appeal.'

'Oh!' She sounds astonished. 'What? Since when has this been on the cards? What's the . . . the *what* appeal?'

'Don't worry about it, Mom,' I say coldly. 'Anyway, as I say, we're going down tomorrow and I'm staying with my friend Sunita's brother.'

'I see.' She very clearly doesn't. 'Well, all right. So we'll make it another time, love. Is Ian all right? Business doing OK and everything?'

'He's fine.'

'Oh, *good*. Well, we'll see you soon, pet. Let me know if there's anything you need.'

How do you spend the day when your husband has gone missing, you have no job and no child, and you have already sorted out every inch of your new house? For a start you call on your mother-in-law and pretend everything is fine. Then you do what any self-respecting person would do which is to get on a bus – with a kind of exhausted defiance, needing to be ceaselessly moving, needing *something* but not really knowing what – and head into the Bull Ring.

The day is hot and in town, all around me, are colourful sleeveless dresses, saris and head wraps and guys strutting in jeans and T-shirts – an atmosphere almost of carnival because the sun is shining for once.

I wander amid the fruit and veg and shouting vendors, buy bananas and peaches from a stall where all the fruits are portioned out in plastic bowls, then walk up the ramp and mooch aimlessly round the shops for a couple of hours. I don't buy anything, don't really *see* anything because I'm thinking about Ian – where is he, what's he doing? And Paul. Trying not to go down that path that says, *Now you've lost everything . . .*

I drink a cup of coffee looking out at St Martin's church while the shoppers go milling past outside. I have deliberately left my phone at home, daring myself to detach, not to be waiting minute after minute for Ian to call or text. Maybe I need some space as well . . .

But now, feeling very low, I sit wondering, in an unbelieving sort of way, whether Ian has actually left me. Whether I have, in fact, lost everything.

Knots of dread twist in my stomach. I begin to sink. I take deep breaths and tell myself not to do this. Not to assume the worst. *But has he?* The worst can happen – it has already happened. Is this Ian's cowardly way of just going, not even telling me or dealing with anything? Images start to fill my mind, tender memories of all our past – meeting Ian at Sam Wellers, the first days when we moved into our house, full of 'happy families' excitement, our lovemaking and teasing, all that lovely day-to-day life, so easily taken for granted. And the days when we first had Paul . . . It's only seconds before I can't stand it and I get to my feet, almost overturning the table in my rush to get out, so that people turn to look.

I start striding towards the stop for the bus home, but I'm forced to slow down by the crowds in the city centre. I find myself thinking about Dorrie and all she has told me. I stop and turn round. Why go home? All I'll end up doing is sitting there by myself, waiting and fretting. Why not try and think about something else?

After making my way down past the spire of St Martin's church again, I cross over Digbeth, the main road leading out, eventually, towards Stratford. Deritend, the neighbourhood where Dorrie grew up, is somewhere I have only been once or twice. It's one of the few bits of Birmingham that still looks almost unchanged, at least from the outside.

The blue brick arches of the viaduct straddle a number of the streets, casting cool shade in summer and a dank gloom in winter. And the streets are a mixture of factories and a few tightly packed rows of terraces. No one lives in back-to-back houses on yards any more. The last ones, about a mile away, have been turned into a museum. But there are still small firms here, where you can hear radios playing and the turning of machines, glimpse sparks from soldering, hear men's raised voices. A lot of the businesses seem to be something to do with car repair now, rather than making things, but there's still an atmosphere. It's mainly men about the streets, with oil-black hands and overalls. The only women tend to be in offices or running the cafés on the corners of streets.

Desperate to push away thoughts of Ian and me, I turn along Floodgate Street, under the cool of the viaduct. Soon I reach Milk Street, where Dorrie spent her early years. I don't know much about the history of how it all used to be, and there's nothing much here to show me now. I walk along the street, which is flanked on each side by a mess of little factories, some brick, some more modern, ugly, as well as parked cars, rolls of razor wire atop walls and fences, graffiti. There is nothing much left in the way of housing. Even here, where everything is not yet all glass and concrete the way the city centre is going, it is hard to find the ghost of little Dorrie, or the horses and carts and gas lamps, the neighbourhoods of back-to-back houses packed full of factory workers.

No one remembers old Brum now, Dorrie said. I've come here to try and think about someone else but, walking in this neighbourhood which has been bombed and knocked about and rebuilt into an undistinguished confusion of functional buildings, begins to drag me down as well. *Change and decay in all around I see . . .* All the lives that were once here – and soon, all the Dorries who can lift a corner of our version of the present and show us another city, a city crammed with industry in an age of barrel organs and flat caps, milk carts and children playing all along the street – will be gone for ever.

As I sit on the bus home, the heartbreak of change and loss settles on me. I have to make a huge effort to shake it off. You can spend your whole life thinking about what has been lost.

By the time I get down from the bus, it's three o'clock and I am now frantic to check my phone. I end up tearing along the street with my bag of fruit. Inside, I stare, heart thudding, at the phone's blank screen: no message, nothing. Of course, he must be at work. I could just walk back to the garage. But how would that be? Desperate and pathetic – especially in front of that Carl bloke, who knows Ian wants to get away from me.

So I go and see Dorrie again for tea. Thank the universe for dear Dorrie.

Back home, later, I am trying to decide how to get through the evening when Ian texts.

You OK?

I carry the phone to the living room, sit on the sofa and stare at the message for a long time. Those two words make me feel so much better. Some sign that he actually cares about me, that he's not just locked up in his own head, has not just gone off for ever. I'm not sure what to answer. Eventually, I text back:

OKish. I'm going to London tomorrow – leaving home about 4.30. You'll need to go in and see your mom later on.

There's a long silence. I sit waiting. Then I text again: *R u ok?*

I can't stand it any longer when there is no answer and add, *Are you ever coming home?*

The silence goes on. He must have switched his phone off after the first message, as if he can't cope with any more from me. Or maybe his battery's died? Reasons, there must be a good reason.

An hour later, when I'm certain he is not going to reply, I send a last text: *Please, Ian – come to the race on Sunday. Ends Whitehall – near Charing Cross Tube. It's only for a few hours. It'd mean so much to have you there. Xx*

Thirty
FAMOUS FOUR

'Jo!' Pat comes trotting along the platform, weaving through the other waiting passengers. She's wearing cornflower-blue cropped trousers and a crisp yellow shirt, and has a small rucksack looped over one shoulder. 'The others are up here – we decided to get out of the crowds.'

We had arranged to meet on the platform because New Street station is in the throes of being rebuilt and it's mayhem. Following her in the shadowy light of the platform, I catch sight of Hayley's blonde hair scooped up into a knot at the back. She's in a strappy sundress, white with big sunflowers on it, and Sunita in cerise trousers and a bright orange top. They see us coming and both of them wave.

'Oh, I'm so glad to see you lot,' I say. Even though my emotions are very up and down, I've decided to be as cheerful as I can. A better night's sleep has helped and it's great to have this to take my mind off things. I shan't say anything about Ian. He'll come to the race – I'm sure he will. No one needs to know what has happened. 'I've spent the morning getting more and more nervous.'

'I know,' Pat says. 'And Fred's been fluffing about non-stop. "Have you got this, have you got that . . ." I felt like telling him the train was two hours earlier than it really is!' We all laugh.

'You've got a lot of luggage there, Sunita,' Pat says. While she and I each have a little rucksack and Hayley's got a sports bag on one strap over her shoulder, Sunita has an entire wheelie suitcase and a bulging carrier bag.

'Oh, well . . .' she says vaguely. 'You never know . . . Anyway, I bought presents for the kids, and –' she lifts the bag, which seems to contain various plastic boxes – 'a few snacks for the journey.'

We're almost like kids ourselves as we settle into seats next to a table. It feels like a school trip. The others don't go anywhere much and it's been a long time for me too. In fact, as I was putting everything in my rucksack – overnight things, my running clothes and the race number and pins – I felt suddenly excited, in contact with my younger self – the Jo who used to pack a bag and take off across the world.

'You managed to get here, obviously,' I say to Hayley. 'I hope you're not getting the sack because of it?'

'No.' She grimaces. Once again, talking about work, she seems uncomfortable. 'They weren't very pleased. But they're short-staffed anyway so they don't want to lose me.'

'I should think not,' Pat said.

'Right.' Sunita hoiks her bag up on the table and starts pulling out boxes and a big bottle of 7 Up. 'Time we all had something to eat.'

She pulls the lids off to reveal a delicious-looking array of snacks – pakoras and samosas, sandwiches, biscuits and grapes – and is met by appreciative cheers.

'That's the beautiful thing about this running,' Sunita says, happily biting into a samosa bulging with potato. 'I can eat just whatever I want!'

Eventually we find ourselves walking through the low sunshine of a Wembley evening, past fruit and veg stalls and rows of booths selling mobile phones and phone cards, as well as curry shops and lots and lots of people. Pat and I follow Sunita, who parts the waters of the crowds with her loud, rumbling suitcase, until we turn into a side road of large terraced houses. We stop at a white door with a small window in it, the glass patterned with flowers.

The door is opened by a woman so small and doll-like that for a second I wonder if she is a child of the family. She is dressed in jeans and a peach-coloured T-shirt and her hair is cut neatly at shoulder length.

'Hello!' She beams in welcome. 'Come in, come in!' She greets Sunita first with a hug and then we go through the introductions. This is Janu, Sunita's sister-in-law. Two boys, who look about eight and ten, peer out of the back room and then abruptly disappear again and a sound starts up that sounds like an electronic racetrack.

'My nephews,' Sunita says. 'Hey, you two – come and say hello to your auntie!'

As the boys come out shyly for hugs and introductions, Janu urges us to put our bags down and come and sit down in the front room. Seeing that she is barefoot and that there is a shoe rack, we all take off our sandals and pumps and walk into a large room, the thick pile of the crimson carpet like a luxurious lawn beneath our feet. The air smells faintly of curry and of something scented.

The room has long windows, swathed with black-and-gold curtains held back each side and big, cream-coloured sofas arranged along three sides of the space. There is a big flatscreen TV on the wall to the left.

'Now,' Janu says to us as the boys hover, curious. 'Prem, my husband, will be home in a moment. He has gone to buy some nice sweets – we have a good shop along the street. You are very welcome – and I wanted to tell you about where you might sleep. We have one spare room –' she counts off the options with her fingers – 'and there is an office with a fold-out bed. Thirdly, it is very possible to be comfortable down here – all these cushions and we have duvets and covers …' She smiles. 'You might like to be together, I don't know.'

'Let's do that,' Pat says. 'It would be fun – we can all camp out here together.'

'Like the Famous Five,' I say.

'Without the dog,' Pat adds.

The front door opens then and we are greeted by a man of medium height, with a round but slightly saggy face which has hints of Sunita's. Prem, Sunita's brother, who comes and shakes our hands. Little blue plastic bags dangle from one of his wrists.

'So,' he says. 'Bhopal, is it, you are all running for?'

'It was Jo got us into it,' Hayley says, looking at me.

Prem comes and shakes my hand, holds on to it for a moment. He has tired-looking eyes and a friendly expression.

'Terrible – a terrible thing that was,' he says. 'My friend, some of his family, aunt, uncle, kids, lived in that part of the city. North side, isn't it? Many people dying. My friend was about eight or so when it happened. Most of the family survived but he is almost blind – the gas affected his eyes very badly. He has had big problems finding work. The whole family have faced many problems since that time.'

There is not much you can say. I sense – and I can feel it from the others – that it is being brought home to us again why we are doing this.

'Come.' He turns away, suddenly more cheerful, and says something quickly to Janu, who scuttles out to the kitchen. 'We have food for you – some tea and snacks. You need a good amount of energy for tomorrow!'

Later, as we lay out cushions and duvets and pillows all over the wide floor, I realize how much I am loving all this. Of course, I'm nervous, but not like this morning when all I could do was fret about Ian and worry about packing and wait for it to be time to go. Ian finally texted me, *Will do my best . . . Will go to Mom's beforehand*, and my heart sang. He'll come. I went to see Dorrie just before I left – she needn't know anything and things will be all right. It's going to be all right . . .

And right now, it's just fun. We had a lovely time sitting and eating with Prem and Janu. They are very hospitable and their boys, Ijay and Tapu, ran in and out and were cute and talkative. Sunita has a light-hearted, teasing relationship with them. They talk about cousins, other relatives. I find myself envying her large, scattered family.

Laying out all our stuff feels like camping, getting changed, taking it in turns to go into the downstairs loo and clean our teeth. It's like travel and adventure and, now I begin to think about it, it's something I have missed.

The night is warm. Sunita slides the window open: 'I

hope there won't be burglars – they will get a shock if they come in here!' And eventually we all lie back on our makeshift mattresses under light covers. Pat and I are side by side, foot to foot with Sunita and Hayley. Pat is the last to clean her teeth and get to bed.

'Right, ladies –' She stands with a hand on the light switch by the door. 'Everyone ready?'

'Yes!' we all chorus, like kids. Darkness comes over us. The thick curtains block light from the street, except a crack down the middle, a yellow glow from a street lamp outside. I like the feeling of them all here with me – of having other human beings breathing around me.

Sunita is sitting up and I hear her give a little burp before she settles again. 'Tomorrow is the day,' she says. Her voice sounds older, now she is lying down. We are all quite old, come to think of it – except Hayley, of course. I have not thought about my age for weeks. We've all just had this goal in mind and have been heading for it.

'Did you ever think you'd be doing this, Sunita?' Pat says.

'No,' Sunita says. 'My daughter is still always saying, "Mummy is running – I just can't believe it." And Leela, now she is saying, "I am going to go jogging like Nanimma – she is a fit athletic lady." '

We can hear the pride in her voice. I grin in the darkness, remembering Sunita's description of getting her bum stuck in the chair. How long ago it seems now, but it was only February. It's life – new life.

And as I'm musing, I suddenly realize Hayley has started talking. I think Pat asked her something but I had gone off into my own thoughts. I turn on to my back to hear her better.

Pat must have asked something about Hayley's grandmother. Hayley's saying how good her nan has always been to her, how kind, how the old lady doesn't understand why her own daughter, Hayley's mother, has been so irresponsible, how uncaring of her own child.

'I think she feels bad – about my mom,' Hayley says in her soft voice. 'And I never want Nan to be upset about anything. The thing is . . .' She hesitates, sounding upset, on the brink of confiding something. There's a silence. We've all wondered about Hayley, about exactly how she got those bruises, what exactly is going on. In the end I say:

'What's up, love? I'm sure you can tell us. I mean, if you want to.'

'I'd like to. I don't like not being truthful with people, and . . .'

'It's all right, Hayley.' I sense, rather than see, Sunita sitting up again to speak. 'You are with friends here. If you want to say something, say it, darling.'

'Thanks,' Hayley says. 'You guys are so nice. You're like another family.'

I smile. This feels true. But I wonder what we are going to hear. Does Hayley have some awful boyfriend – is that why she had injuries to her face?

'Well, OK,' she says. 'Now or never, I suppose! Just don't judge me – OK?' I hear her take a breath. 'It's just – you know I want to go to college? I mean, I'm not even sure what I want to do now. I thought beauty therapy or something but now I'm wondering . . . Anyway, doing this race, *why* we're doing this, has made me think about it. I know I want to go to college, but I want to do something to help people. Anyway, that's another thing and I'm not really sure what yet.' She pauses for a second.

'Basically, though, I don't want to be any burden on my nan. I know no one in the family can afford for me to go to uni now the fees have all gone up and everything. I don't want her to think I have a load of debt. I know there are some loans and things, but I want to save up so that I've got enough to get through – or most of it, anyway.'

This we already know – and admire her for it.

'My nan doesn't have much idea about money now – except for the basics, you know. Every time she buys a pint of milk she tells me how much it cost in – I don't know, the nineteen thirties or something! She's got no idea how much uni will cost. And she doesn't know how much I earn . . .'

'Pub work's not very well paid, is it?' Pat says.

I hear Hayley take another breath, almost a gasp. 'That's the thing. Nan thinks I'm working in a bar but . . . Well I am, but . . . The thing is, I'm not telling her the truth but I want to be truthful with all of you because you've all been really good to me and I hate lying to people.'

God, I think to myself. What on earth is she doing?

'I'm actually earning good money – much more than Nan realizes – because I work at Flighty Aphrodite's, in town.'

Ah.

'Flighty what?' Sunita says.

'It's a dance club.' Hayley sounds really awkward. 'I mean, it is a bar, but there are girls and we dance, you know, there's a pole for dancing . . .'

'What – topless? One of those all-bosoms-hanging-out places?' Sunita sounds scandalized.

'I know a lot of students are stripping to get by these days,' I say, trying to make her feel better. I can see how good she would be at it as well. She's gorgeous, a good dancer and very physically flexible – she's certainly got assets she can make use of, though heaven help her for having to.

'I'm not the only one there who's into going to uni,' she admits. 'There's a girl already at Aston. I really don't like it – I don't like the way the men are. It's . . . ugh . . . But the stupid thing is, I'm really good at it. I can already dance and I've learned a lot of moves on the pole. I can earn big money some nights, in the VIP rooms – you know, they pay for private dances. There're one or two men who . . . Anyway, that's why my boss didn't want me to be off tonight. It's Saturday . . .'

'But it must feel very disgusting with all those men staring at your bosoms?' Sunita asks, rather relentlessly I can't help feeling.

'Hey, Sunita!' Pat says, in a gentle attempt to shut her up.

'You just have to switch off and give them what they want. It's a seedy world and that's the truth.' I can tell Hayley is reaching the limits of how much she wants to tell us, especially as Sunita sounds so judgemental.

'It's nice of you to tell us,' Pat says kindly. 'I can see why a lovely-looking girl like you gets on well. You're a good'un, Hayley – and don't let anyone tell you other-wise. Sometimes you have to do things you don't want to, just to get to where you do want.'

'Yeah,' I say. I don't want to judge her, but I'm really not sure what to think.

'Aah.' Hayley sounds almost tearful. 'Thanks, guys.'

'I don't think I could take my clothes off like that,' Sunita says. 'Not in front of strange men and all.'

'Don't worry,' I tease her. 'You most likely won't have to – not in this lifetime, anyway!'

'The other week, when I had that cut on my face,' Hayley says, as if wanting to complete her confession while she can. 'It was one of the punters – he punched me.'

'Oh, my God!' I say, as the others exclaim as well. 'Why?'

'Dunno,' Hayley said. 'You just don't know with some people what they're going to do. He just lashed out at me and it really hurt. I tell you, I'll be out of there the moment I get enough money.'

'I wouldn't let my daughter do it,' Sunita says. I feel cross with her for keeping on like this, but in a way, I have to admit I feel the same.

'Your daughter's been better supported,' Pat says. 'Thanks for telling us, Hayley. You're doing what you need to do at the moment – and we all think you're great.'

I say something similar and, I'm glad to hear, so does Sunita. We chat on for a bit longer until Pat yawns and says:

'Anyway, wonderful women – how about us getting some beauty sleep?'

And after lots of 'night-night's and 'sweet dreams's we all settle, cosy together. But of course, I'm full of food and not sleepy. I lie there, thinking about Ian, hearing an occasional car outside, footsteps, and Sunita's little rhythmic snores. I keep going over things in my head, all that's led up to where we are. I imagine us all running over the finishing line tomorrow and Ian coming out of the crowd and hugging me and being pleased. And then I'm full of doubt about tomorrow and whether he'll come, about everything. It's a long time before I get to sleep.

Thirty-One

Race Day, 12 July

All of us wake early, jittery and giggly with excitement.

'You will need a very good breakfast,' Janu says, already waiting for us in the spacious kitchen. 'Very special, energy-giving.'

'Good, but not necessarily big,' Pat cautions her. I can see she's thinking of the huge spread of snacks and fruit Janu and Prem laid on last night.

'Well,' Janu laughs, her eyes lighting. 'Bananas I have – they are very good. And I can make porridge, toast, eggs?'

Pat and Hayley opt for porridge. Sunita and I have toast – mine thickly spread with peanut butter. And soon we are setting off, Sunita leaving her luggage, planning to come back later.

'Good luck, see you there!' Janu hugs us all, Prem comes out in a red plaid dressing gown and the boys, bushy-haired from bed, climb on the front wall all excited, shouting, 'Good luck – run very fast!' The four of them wave us along the road.

As soon as we get on the Tube there are quite a few of the other passengers wearing running gear. It's a bit early on a Sunday to be up for anything else. We all give each other knowing looks and smile. Some sit adjusting their i-Pods, then we all pin race numbers on each other and fasten the little timer tabs on our trainers.

'I suddenly feel like a pro.' Pat looks up, grinning, admiring the tab fastened to her laces. She looks happy, lit up, and I feel a rush of affection for her.

'I expect there'll be some real pros running at the front,' I say. 'They'll soon put us in our place.'

'Well, it's not about winning, is it?' Hayley says.

'No. More like being on the motorway,' I say. 'All just moving along from A to B.'

'I can't believe we're really going to do it.' Sunita smiles, full of delight. 'Fatty Nanimma is running around London!' Suddenly she breaks into a song: "We're the ladies, of Hollywood . . ."

We all join in, ridiculously extrovert. Other runners look startled, then grin. What does it matter? We are away from home and after all, it's a day of goodwill.

And then, after the bag drop, we are at the top end of Piccadilly in this warm, hazy morning, each with our bottles of water. Standing in the excited, limbering crowd, we can see, from the back, the memorial for Bomber Command, a group of bronze men in their flying gear, many who would have been going off to their deaths, gazing endlessly out over London, silent and dignified.

The road is divided in half by barriers and all the runners are corralled into the left-hand side which slopes gently upwards. There are thousands and thousands here, at least twenty-five thousand people for this charity race, almost all about to run on behalf of someone else. We four, in our red Bhopal Medical Appeal vests – somewhere there will be others in the same vests – are surrounded by a sea of shirts in different colours with a huge variety of slogans. There are banners, a few brave souls running in costumes, and an atmosphere of excited goodwill.

We limber up gently, sing softly, fret quietly. When will we start? But it's fun – a band plays, someone passes us in a giant sunflower costume, a parade of horses goes by on the other side and suddenly, after half an hour or so, the crowd eases. We see people start to appear through the pink inflatable starter arch at the top of the slope, two young, compact men, Kenyan athletes, going like mad, other runners intent on making good times, and then the crowd thickens into the charity runners and we all surge forward.

Round the top, towards the arch . . .

'Oooh,' Hayley skips up and down, suddenly looking like a little girl.

'Save your energy, kid,' Pat smiles at her.

And we are through the arch and gradually breaking into a trot and we are running – slowly – but we are. It has begun: between the grand buildings of Piccadilly, which feel like being on a film set, music blaring, and all the crowds clapping and cheering us on and we drift, the first kilometre mainly downhill and it feels easy, almost like flying as we warm up. All of us beam at each other.

On we go, getting gradually out of breath. We double up along Pall Mall, go along Regent Street. I imagine our friends and families all setting out. Kim has said they have to go to a wedding and can't come, but there'll be Fred in his car, Sheila and Roy, Prem and Janu on their way with their excited boys. And my Ian. My stomach lurches. It's my turn to feel like a child, excited that someone will be watching, cheering us through to the end. Things will be all right. He has needed time to think. I knew something was wrong, and I feel myself sending him love and strength. It's been so terrible, the worst, but we'll go on together – we will. And I know Ian – he has never deliberately let me down. He'll come, I know it.

The worst is the middle. It always is. Far enough in to be feeling tired, not quite close enough to the end to feel it is in sight. Miles four to five – kilometres six to eight. The sun has come out and we are red-cheeked and flagging. The ground is strewn with discarded water bottles and their caps from the water stations and we have to keep skipping round them. Ahead of us, someone is running gamely in a bear costume – how do they do it in this heat?

'Oh, my God,' Sunita groans. Her face is running with perspiration. 'Let's stop for a few minutes.'

I'm relieved. My chest hurts, I'm drenched in sweat and I feel low on energy. It feels endless, pounding along the pavements, as if we are now going to be doing it for ever.

We are in Charing Cross Road. They keep making us do loops along roads and back again, which is demoralizing because as you run, all the time people are coming back the other way on the other side and you realize that's what you are going to have to do, as if you are getting nowhere . . . Next, the Strand. People by the side of the road wave and cheer: 'Come on, you can do it – not far now!'

'Huh – not far for you,' Sunita mumbles. 'Still more than two miles.'

We take a few moments. Breath returns surprisingly quickly and after a few sips of water we are ready to go again.

'Come on,' Pat says, 'let's get singing.'

Suddenly Sunita breaks into life and starts on her

'*Kashmir Main Tu Kanyakumari*' song. As she does so she takes some jigging steps, though no twirls – too risky in this crowd – and we all join in. The people around us start cheering.

'We have some great dancing here!' the loudspeaker announces. 'Someone running for the Bhopal Medical Appeal who's got the breath to dance *and* run as well!'

Sunita grins and shakes a fist triumphantly.

People around us laugh at this raggle-taggle bunch of singing women – all good-naturedly.

'Come on,' Hayley says. 'We're the ladies – of Hollywood …'

Gasping and panting we manage to sing, until I see the tag by the road. 'Hey, only two more K to go!'

We are in the process of cheering this – almost the end: still, 2K is 2K! – when Hayley goes crashing to the ground beside me.

'Oh, no – Hayley!'

All of us stop. One of the race marshals comes over, in a fluorescent yellow tabard.

'I'm all right,' she keeps saying. 'It's my ankle again …' I can see she's grazed her knee and elbow badly. People surge on past us – a sea of feet passing and passing, water bottles skittering across the road.

'You should rest that by rights,' the marshal says. He's a young, friendly white guy. But he can see she wants to finish.

'I can do it,' Hayley says and I see the lad blush as this gorgeous girl hauls herself to her feet using his shoulder. She rotates her ankle, grimacing, and takes a few steps but it obviously hurts. 'I don't think it's broken.'

'We'll help you,' I say. 'Won't we? Come on – we'll carry you to the end if necessary!'

253

Sunita takes Hayley's water bottle off her and Pat and I, who are closer to her height, get on either side, pulling her arms over our shoulders.

'Right,' I say. 'Come on, girl – we're going to do this.'

'You've just got to get round Parliament Square and you're there,' the guy says. 'Good luck. It's not far now!!'

This is understating the case a bit but we are determined to be cheerful.

'Oh!' Hayley groans, frustrated, as we hobble along together. 'I'm holding you all up.'

'So what?' Pat says. 'We're all going to get there in the end.'

'Motorway, remember?' I say. 'Who wins on the motorway?'

'It's the same ankle,' she says. 'The one I ricked before.' She starts giggling suddenly, realizing she can tell us. 'I was wearing six-inch heels to dance in, all sparkly – and I fell right off the stage and ended with my bum sticking up in the air. It was so undignified I can't tell you!'

We are so intent on keeping Hayley going, limping and talking, singing and fooling about, that we hardly notice the Houses of Parliament passing us by and the long haul up and along Whitehall.

What we do notice, suddenly, is that ahead of us we can see another pink rubber archway swaying in the gentle breeze.

'Look!' Sunita is skipping around again. 'The end – nearly there, Hayley, come on!'

Seeing our plight, people in the crowd are cheering us on, and suddenly a little figure who has somehow broken through the barrier comes running up to us.

'Come on, come on, Auntie!' It's Ijay, the older of Janu's two boys. 'You can do it!'

He probably shouldn't be there but who's going to stop him at this point?

'Run with me!' Sunita takes his hand and he runs along with us, cajoling and shouting, and we are surrounded by cheering as we labour our way up to the archway and – finally! – jog through it, high-fiving and cheering. We can stop – at last we can stop!

Almost as soon as we are beyond the finish line, Janu and Prem arrive with Tapu and there are hugs all round, Janu fondly scolding Ijay for escaping. 'You are lucky the police did not take you away, naughty boy!'

The whole area is full of people hugging and laughing and celebrating. The rest of us look round for family and as we do, we suddenly see Sheila and Roy hurrying up to us, beaming and waving. They look so happy that I realize what a great opportunity this has been for them to get out and have a change.

'Well done, all of you – you were fantastic!' Sheila cries, hugging us as well. 'Oh, Hayley, what have you done?'

'I'm all right – I just ricked it a bit,' Hayley says and I watch her, seeing that she is probably never going to tell Sheila exactly how she injured that ankle in the first place.

Then Fred comes bouncing up, grabs Pat and hugs her as if she has been away for at least six months.

'What a bunch of champs!' he cries, beaming round at us all as Pat laughs, hugging him back. Over her shoulder he says sweetly, 'Never thought you could do it – but you did! Congratulations, all of you!'

I'm so pleased to see them all but inside, my own

feelings are sinking. Even while talking I'm looking round for Ian. Since there are thousands of people milling about and he is not familiar with London, it's really not that surprising he is not here this second, but all the same I had hoped. I wanted him to see us running across the finish line, the moment of triumph and happiness – to see that we had really achieved something.

Hayley, I realize, also has no one of her own here to greet her. It only truly comes home to me now, how isolated she is in her life when it comes to family. No brothers or sisters and her nan's too old to come down for this. I stick with her and give her my arm as we all drift away along the street, to be presented with our medals – heavy bronze rectangles with Big Ben and the Houses of Parliament on them, with bright red and white ribbons. Sheila and Prem take photos of us and I'm smiling away, happy, but aching inside.

Where are you, Ian? Please be here somewhere – please.

And I know Pat knows that I'm looking for him and we all hang around for as long as possible as the other runners move off for picnics and celebrations.

'I s'pose we'd better go back and pick up our stuff,' I say, trying to sound matter-of-fact. At least then I can check my phone. Maybe there was a problem with the trains.

As we head off, I take one more look round, hoping still that he might come running up through the crowds, full of *Sorry I'm so late . . .*

But there is no sign.

Thirty-Two
THE NIGHT BETWEEN

A cheap medal is nice – it hangs, heavy and substantial, round my neck. But it is an empty thing compared with seeing the face of someone you love greeting you at the end of all this effort, these weeks of preparation. But we waited until most people had moved on and still there was no sign of Ian.

I trudge along with Hayley. It feels a long way back to the bag drop. I don't want to show her, but I feel hurt, angry and close to tears. Could he not have managed this – just this, for me?

Hayley seems to sense my mood.

'Your husband not got here in time?' she asks sweetly.

'Apparently not,' I say, afraid of crying. But then, because she has been honest, I say, 'To tell you the truth, Hayley, I don't really know what's going on with him. He hasn't been home for three days. It's all been pretty weird since Paul died. But he said he'd come. I never thought he'd do this . . .'

And tears are running down my cheeks.

'Oh, my God, Jo – I'm so sorry,' she says, an arm round my shoulder. 'What, seriously – he hasn't been home?'

Put that way, it does sound really bad.

'Yeah, well.' I wipe my eyes. 'Sorry. I think my blood sugar must have dipped.'

We wait for our bags. By now I'm jittery with impatience and I pull my phone out straight away. There'd better be a message, Ian Stefani, I think savagely. Or I'll . . . Or I'll what?

The screen leaps into life. A few seconds later it beeps.

Jo – Mom's been taken bad. Looks like another stroke. We're in the QE. Sorry not to make it today. I wanted to. Please get here soon as you can. I need you here. Love Ian x

Oh, no . . .' I turn to Hayley, feeling as if I've been kicked in the belly. Dorrie, my lovely mother-in-law. I should have been there. I'm the one who's being selfish, not being there to look after her. 'I'm sorry, Hayley – it's Ian's mom. I've got to get straight back to Birmingham – now.'

The train is quiet and I am glad now to be alone. Hayley offered to come back with me, but I sent her off to join the others at the picnic.

'It's sweet of you, love – but there's nothing you can do when we get there. I'll just be at the hospital. Go and celebrate – give them all my love.'

I wasn't there, I think, guiltily, watching London fade behind me as we head north. I should have been there. But at the same time, I can hear Dorrie's matter-of-fact voice: *It's just one of those things, bab – you weren't to know.*

Dear, dear Dorrie. When I went to see her yesterday before I left, I fussed over her, making her lunch and saying Ian would be in later (I was sure he would).

'I'm all right, Jo,' she said. 'I'm not a complete vegetable yet, you know . . .'

I was about to apologize, but she twinkled at me.

'I'll be all right. You go and do your thing down there – and good luck to you. I admire you for it. I've got the money for you, when you get back.'

'Oh, Dorrie – you're so kind,' I said. 'I'll be back as fast as I can.'

'I know you will. Now stop fussing. You go and do your run – eleven o'clock, is it? I'll be thinking of you.'

When I left, she said, 'Bye-bye, bab. Keep together and do your best.'

She seemed fine, bless her – quite lively. There was no sign of anything amiss . . . But I still feel terrible for going off and not being there.

My mind keeps hammering, Don't die, please don't go and leave us. The train seems to be crawling. All I want is to be there, but there's nothing I can do so once again I force myself to think about other things.

The race quickly seems like a dream. *But we did it, Pauly*, I say to him, reaching for the space in my head where I talk to him, on and off all day. The Paul I talk to is the one who came back to us just before he died – Paul and me walking round the little lake, his laughing at *Blackadder* DVDs and *Family Guy*, getting up in the morning, talking about the future. Basically being my boy again.

Then, fondly, I imagine all my new friends having their picnic and feel lucky to have met them. But for the first time in ages, I find myself thinking sadly about Ange. It would be good to see her. I can see her face now, catching sight of me here on the train, still in my running clothes, looking at me, head on one side – *God, look at the state of you!* It makes me smile.

I change at New Street for the train out to University station.

Getting close – which ward? I text Ian.

Only when I get off the train do I remember that the Queen Elizabeth hospital is still a bit of a shlep from here. So I ask directions, swing my bag on to my back and, cranking my tired legs back into action, start running.

Ian looks up as I approach the bed. His dark eyes are directed blankly at me for a moment, as if I am a stranger. I am chilled by that look, until I realize that his mind is trying to triangulate the face he knows so well with the pink, sweaty, messy-haired apparition in front of him, clad in running shorts and vest. It takes a few seconds. He stands up, looking almost shy, confused.

'Got here as soon as I could,' I pant.

In that moment I realize that if Dorrie was able to speak, she would have said wryly, *Run all the way from London then, have you?* But her eyes are closed and the figure on the bed looks tiny and shrunken and very ill. Oh, Dorrie. I can feel the dismay overtake my face as I look up at Ian again.

He beckons me away and we go and stand outside the ward. Memories come rushing back. My body goes cold. Here we are again – this hospital, the shiny-floored corridors and hushed atmosphere. And there is still a distance between us, a real awkwardness.

'I went in this morning – that's how I found her.'

Ian's control begins to crack and I can see he is close to tears. I put my arms round him and we hold each other for a moment. It feels nice, but still we are far from each other, too many things unsaid and unresolved.

'I'm a bit sweaty, sorry.' I try to smile, pulling back.

He doesn't quite manage a smile either.

'D'you think – I mean, had she been like it long?'

'I don't know, that's the trouble.' He looks away, along the corridor for a moment. 'Could've happened any time in the night. She was out of it when I got there. I just called an ambulance and . . .' He gestures towards the ward. 'They say it's on her left side, which apparently means it's the right side of her body that's affected. She did come round for a bit – she looked at me, in the ambulance.'

I feel my heart lift with hope. Indestructible Dorrie. She'll come through this, won't she? But I also know that with a stroke, you need to get help soon and there's no knowing how long ago it happened.

'Have you let Cynth know?' I ask him.

'Yeah, she's coming – soon as she can. Tomorrow, I think.'

'Right. That's good.' I nod slowly. 'Look, shall I get us a coffee or something?'

'Have you had anything?' Suddenly he is considerate Ian again and my heart lights with hope.

'No – well, a bottle of pop after the race.'

'I'll go and find us something – you sit with her.'

Grateful, I go back to Dorrie's bed. A couple of the other visitors on the ward eye me with puzzled expressions. Perching on the edge of the chair I lean forward and reach for her hand. She is on her back, huddled-looking, as if she is cold. Her left hand lies out on the pale blue blanket and I reach for it, a bit scared of how it

261

might feel. Her hand is cool, but when I take it, I feel a faint reaction, a squeeze, as if she is glad someone is there.

And then she opens her eyes. My heart starts to thud.

'Dorrie! Dorrie, it's Jo. We're both here, Ian and me. You're in the Queen Elizabeth. Everything's all right – we're all looking after you.'

I'm not sure if she can focus because her eyes look vacant. But again, I feel that minuscule squeeze of her fingers before her eyes slide shut again and I sit stroking her hand, her arm, and I tell her about the race, about how we did it and how I'm sorry I wasn't at home when she was taken ill. I just keep talking softly, not sure if she can hear but hoping the sound of my voice is some sort of comfort to her.

Ian comes back with coffee, biscuits and a cheese roll for me. As there's only one chair he stands and it all feels a bit strained. After I've finished eating, and have drunk my coffee, he says:

'Look – you go home and have a shower, get changed and everything.' He fishes in his pocket and gives me the car key, tells me where to find the car outside. 'Come back a bit later, yeah?'

'OK.' Grateful, I stand. 'I'll come and take a turn when I've got cleaned up.' Our eyes meet. We are both being careful with each other, shy. But I can't bear it any longer.

'Are you coming home?' I can only whisper and my eyes fill with tears. I don't want to be angry. I want him home and I want harmony.

Ian looks upset. For a moment he turns away, then back to me, looking almost afraid. 'Yeah.' He nods. 'Yeah – I'll come home tonight.'

Thirty-Three

We take it in turns to sit with Dorrie. She just seems exhausted and she sleep and sleeps. I take over from Ian late in the afternoon and stay on until eight o'clock when the other visitors start leaving. I have slipped into a kind of emergency mode, imagining that I will be camped by her bed all night. But as the ward empties, one of the nurses comes over to me. She is young with a pink, kindly face and gentle voice.

'Go and get some rest,' she says. 'Visiting's over and really, there's nothing to be gained from you getting exhausted. Mrs Stefani is stable and if there's any change we'll let you know at once.' She smiles. 'We'll look after her.'

I have already been dozing on the chair, exhausted by the long day, so I'm quite thankful to be told to go home.

Nurse told me to come home, I text Ian. I wander outside, worn out and disorientated. It seems strange that it is still light as today seems to have gone on for ever. It takes me a good while, after wandering bewildered round the car park, to remember that Ian took the car.

When I get my phone out there's already a message: *On my way.*

*

We talk about Dorrie, how they think she must have had the stroke some time in the middle of the night.

'She's still just asleep,' I tell him. 'It must take it out of you. I expect she'll pick up.' I don't know if I believe this. At the same time, I still find it hard to take in that Dorrie might not be indestructible. It's too unbearable to think about.

'Yeah,' Ian says, as we head south along the Bristol Road. He nods. 'Maybe she'll be better tomorrow.'

When we get in, he says, 'You must want something to eat?' I can smell food, something microwaved. He has dashed to get me, leaving a half-eaten plastic container of pasta and tomatoes. 'I bought a couple of things . . . Spag bol? Cheesy pasta?'

'Oh . . .' I don't feel like eating but I suppose I should. 'Go on then. I'll have the cheesy one.'

Things feel almost normal. We take the food through and eat on the sofa. It's only when I've got some nourishment into me and I start perking up again, that I can cope with the idea that things are not normal at all. But I also have a terrible realization that having Ian back in the house makes me feel worse. When he was away, I was upset, full of grief and bewildered. But it felt different. I grieve for Paul every day – it never ends. But the grief was just mine when Ian was away. Now he is here, I can feel it expanding again, so that for a moment I can't breathe. It's my grief, Ian's grief, *our* grief – as if they are three distinct and gigantic things swallowing me up.

Putting my plate down on the floor, I straighten up and pull in a deep breath. I can feel Ian looking at me. We have to deal with this, somehow. Only now I see that this is how it has been for a long time.

'I'll make us a hot drink,' I say, getting up. I need coffee. Waiting for the kettle to boil gives me time to think.

'So,' I say, handing him a mug and sitting back down. I keep my voice calm. 'Where have you been?'

Ian crumples suddenly. He physically sags.

'I just . . . Well, the first night Carl and his missus put me up.'

'Right. He didn't think to tell me that.'

'No. I know. Sorry. But then, anyway, I thought, I can't stay on here. It was awkward, him having his son living there and everything. And I just wanted . . . I dunno.' He looks down miserably. 'Time, I s'pose. I wanted to be on my own and try and think things out. So I just went into town – Travelodge, Travel Inn, or something.' He shakes his head. 'Sorry,' he mutters. 'If you were worried. I never meant that.'

I bite back the sarcastic words that have come to mind: *Did he not think I might be worried etc.* I try to think what to say.

'Carl – he seems nice,' is what comes out, to my surprise.

'He is, yeah. He's a bit . . . I mean, he's only, like, five or six years older than me, but he's a dad – he's like a dad . . .' And suddenly he's crying. Really crying, sobbing and shaking, bent over. I watch for a moment, then I put my hand on his back, gently stroking it as he falls to pieces in front of me.

'I don't know what's happening to me,' he says, from behind his hands, once he can speak. 'I can't seem to . . . Nothing's right. Not since Paul. But Carl's been . . . I mean, I wish . . . I just wish I'd had a dad for long enough to remember him properly at least.' He sits up, his face wet and creased. 'I was sat next to Mom yesterday in the hospital and I thought, all these years I've never got around to asking her about my father. Cowardice really. I know he was supposed to have died of a heart attack but I never felt that was all of it – that there was something else she never said. But somehow, I could never ask. And now – well, I don't know if she'll ever speak again, do I?'

Tears trickle down his face and I move closer and put my arm round him. I can't tell him now – not this minute. It feels too much. Not only that one of the things that killed his father was someone else's gross negligence, but that he took his own life and left Ian and Dorrie behind. Both things feel too brutal for the way he is at this moment – a man who has lost both his father and his only son.

'I'm sorry,' he whispers. He sags against me, putting his hand on my thigh, and we lean on one another. 'I'm no good to you. I feel all over the place – as if I've got nothing left in me.'

I want to say, *Don't worry, it's all right, I understand,* and in a way, I do. I see that he has had loss upon loss and has never really sorted anything out in his head. I want to be kind and helpful, but I have nothing much left to give him either. And so we sit, warming each other, as if we are stranded on a rock somewhere, surrounded by dark waters, instead of in our own living room.

'I s'pose we'll get through it somehow,' I say eventually. I look round at him. 'Maybe you could get some help?'

'What d'you mean?'

'A counsellor or something.'

He looks uncertain, pushes his hair back and shakes his head, hard.

'Oh, God. I don't know. Maybe.'

Upstairs we don't say much. We make love, quickly, as if it's the only thing to do, and it's a release for him, if not much for me, but it feels nice lying holding each other in the dark.

'I'm scared I'll lose you as well,' he says eventually. And then he's crying again. 'It feels as if you've gone so far away . . . All this stuff about India.'

'I'm not,' I try to tell him, thinking, am I? Is that what's happening? 'I don't mean to be. But you're not here most of the time and I have to . . . You know I have to do things for myself . . . And I feel strongly about it – it's terrible there, what's happened.'

'I know,' he says, sniffing. 'I know. I'm sorry.'

'Ian.' I roll over to face him fully. 'You're not losing me. Not unless you push me away. I love you – and I love your mom. You know she's been family to me, more than my own. I'm not going anywhere, not with my heart. Just don't shut me out.'

'Mom loves you. And you've done such a lot for her.' His eyes search my face, earnestly, then he wraps his arms round me, with force, pulling me to him and we lie together, raw, frightened, warming each other.

Thirty-Four
WHAT DO WE DO NOW?

Dorrie, other than a few moments of wakefulness, sleeps on. In those rare moments, she opens her eyes and looks calmly round, though it is not clear how much she can see. She does not seem to focus on our faces. But her good hand will meet ours with a faint movement. The nurses tell us that the right side of her body is so weak that she is all but paralysed. I spend as much time as I can there. Ian takes a day off. Cynthia arrives from down south. She's rather like Ian to look at, both with dark, attractive Stefani eyes. She is short, curvaceous, her hair dyed an auburn colour. Even today she's smartly dressed – sort of office smart – but she's upset and is nicer than I remember. We take turns at Dorrie's bedside so I don't see a lot of her. She says she'll sleep at Dorrie's house. After the first day, Ian goes in every evening.

On the third day, the young nurse with the pink cheeks and kind eyes sees me come on to the ward.

'Mrs Stefani's looking a bit brighter today,' she says. 'I'm sure she'll be pleased to see you.'

A huge surge of joy rushes through me. Dorrie's getting better! And hurrying to her bed I somehow expect her to be her old self, sitting up, smiling, chatting to me. What I find is her lying there, as before, on her back, with her eyes closed. Something in me folds up at that moment and puts away hope that she will ever get back to anything like she was. They say she may recover language and some mobility. Each person who has a stroke has a quite individual outcome. But looking down at her that morning, her face the palest and most withdrawn I have ever seen it, I know I don't really believe it will happen.

'Dorrie? Hello, love. It's Jo.'

Taking her hand, I sit down and lean towards her. A tiny flex of her fingers answers mine.

'How are you today?' I say. 'Cynthia's gone home for a little rest and Ian's at work, but he'll be in later to see you.' I struggle to think of things to tell her. I have already talked about the visit to London and staying with Janu and Prem and how the race was. Now, I tell her, as I do every time, that everything is all right and Cynth is looking after Sweep and that he is missing her.

Her eyes open suddenly, almost as if she has been startled by something, making my heart beat faster. She looks angry for a moment, then it passes. I can't see much wrong with her face, no obvious distortion or anything, but then she has not tried to talk.

'Hello?' I say, leaning in to her field of vision. 'Can you hear me, Dorrie?'

Another tiny squeeze of the hand.

'Cynthia says Sweep is eating up all his dinner and she's watering your plants . . .'

Dorrie lies there, eyes open, I assume listening to me. There's an atmosphere of quiet about her, of acceptance, the way Dorrie has always somehow had to accept things.

'I love you, Dorrie,' I say, close to tears. 'You do know

that, don't you? You've been a mom to me – more than. You've been a friend as well – all through everything . . .'

Do I imagine her mouth twitching slightly? The old Dorrie would have been waving away all this sentimental talk – *Go on with you* – and changing the subject. This Dorrie slowly, driftily, closes her eyes again.

There's no yoga for the six weeks of summer, but the next afternoon, as Cynthia is sitting with Dorrie, I go over to Sheila's. It's the first time we've met again since the race, though I have seen Pat briefly. Kim is away on holiday with her family so it's the rest of the usual suspects. Everyone exchanges news about their weekend: Pat and Fred went to the Tower of London and had a good look at Buckingham Palace but did not pay to go in; Sheila and Roy had a great time seeing *The Lion King* at the Lyceum, stayed overnight and went on the London Eye and walked all along the Embankment. Sunita stayed on with the family in Wembley. Only Hayley came home after the picnic in the park.

'The people from the charity brought us all these curries and beers!' Pat tells me. 'It's a shame you missed it. We sat out under the trees and the food was very nice.'

But they all ask after Dorrie and as I tell them, I realize it doesn't sound very good.

'Some people make very good recoveries from strokes,' Sheila says. 'My brother-in-law had a bad one three years ago and to be honest, although he's had to make a few adjustments to his life, he's really done well.'

I'm grateful for her optimism, and you never can tell with Dorrie, but it does feel as if, every day, she is slipping further from us.

And despite the news and all the excitement of the weekend, everyone is feeling flat.

'Well,' Sunita says, after a while, looking round at us. 'That was all very nice. But what do we do now?'

Three days later, on Sunday morning, Ian's mobile rings. Immediately, he is bolt upright.

'Yes,' he says. And then, 'Oh.' Immediately, I know what's happened. That dear old lady, all her love, all her memories, the person who held us all together, has left us.

Even as he is still speaking, grief begins. I think of her when I said goodbye to her on Saturday, before the race. *Bye-bye, bab. Keep together and do your best.* And there was I thinking she would be there to hear all about it when I came back, that she would always, somehow, be there. The thought of her not being there is so awful that tears are beginning even as Ian clicks off his phone and our eyes meet.

We each reach out and hold each other, we, the ones left standing.

And now, I realize fully, I am entrusted, when the time is right, with telling Ian what really happened to his dad.

Dorrie was never religious and the funeral, ten days later, is a simple crem do, followed by a pub wake. It turns out to be a strange day, and in the way of these things, somehow seems not to have much to do with the person whose life we are celebrating. It feels peculiar having to dress in a smart black linen dress, bought specially for the occasion. I'm not sure why it's always necessary to wear black, but I think Dorrie would have thought that was the thing to do so I do it.

Cynthia and her family all come and she and Ian move carefully round each other. It goes off all right. Cynthia and Ian each give a short tribute to their mother, as does Michael, one of Cynthia's twins. I sit thinking, would Paul have had the confidence to stand up and do that for his nanna? Probably not. I ache with missing him, knowing how sad he would have been today.

To my surprise, my own mother and father turn up for the funeral as well. Mom is dressed to the nines in a black suit, black patent shoes with four-inch heels and a black hat with a dashing stripe of white along the brim. Dad has got out his best suit, with a hanky-triangle pointing up from the breast pocket.

Afterwards, in the pub, Mom makes for me and sits beside me with her plate of filo-wrapped prawns and baby pakoras and cherry tomatoes. I'm not sure what Dorrie would have made of this food. She would have preferred a good sausage roll, I think. But then she's not here, which is the whole, sad point. We are all perched at little round tables which you can barely fit everything on.

'You all right, love?' Mom says to me, head on one side. It seems to occur to her that she could see me better if she took the hat off and she lays it on the padded seat beside her, patting her hair, which is, as ever, immaculate and tinted with blonde.

'Yeah. It's been a bit of a couple of weeks,' I say.

'You'll have a lot to do – the house and everything.' Mom keeps looking at me, intently. I see her working up to something and then she says, 'She was a lovely lady, Mrs Stefani – and I know she was very good to you.'

I'm surprised by this, touched even, and I find tears in my eyes. I realize my own mother is somehow nervous of me, especially since Paul's death, hopeless at talking about it, forever worried about saying the wrong thing and often saying it anyway.

I'm nodding, not really trusting myself to speak.

'And,' Mom goes on, 'Cynthia was talking to me about that run you did. I wish you'd told us earlier!'

'Why?' I say. 'I mean, sorry.' I mentioned it to her at some point, I'm sure, but I didn't think they'd really be interested. 'I just . . . I didn't get round to it, I suppose.'

'Well, Cynthia said she sponsored you – quite generously, I believe?' This, to my amazement, also true. I didn't get many sponsors but Cynthia was really nice about it. She's been nice about a lot of things, even saying she'd take Sweep and re-home him – her boys would like to have him. 'We'd have sponsored you, you know. It takes a lot of effort doing something like that. But I suppose it's too late now.'

'Never mind,' I say, astonished. 'It's a nice thought. And maybe we'll do it again.' We're going to keep running, the others were saying on Thursday. More money is always needed – why not?

'Really?' Mom sounds doubtful.

'You could run as well,' I tease her. After all, she does step classes.

She laughs then, properly. And laughing together feels nice. 'Oh, I'm not sure about that.'

Thirty-Five

September 2015

'OK,' Kim says, walking over to her mat on the hall floor. 'Let's get settled now, shall we? I've missed you all over the summer – it's good to be back.'

And it is. The free, shapeless days of August have passed and we are back into purposeful September, when terms starts, new projects begin and there's a feeling of freshness and knuckling down to things.

I look round at the group. Pat's next to me, cross-legged and neat as a pixie. We meet up every few days for a coffee and a chat. She feels like a good, comfortable friend now. Sheila, who has difficulty sitting cross-legged, sits with her legs half-stretched out, massaging her stiff knees and looking round smiling at us all, as if she is our mom, which in a way she is. Sunita is rummaging in her bag looking for something. She has some new, shocking-pink leggings and a yellow top and looks curvy and muscular. Kim seems much as ever – and happy, I think to myself. And Hayley looks ... well, Hayley always looks marvellous, hair in a high knot like a ballerina, her skin clear, eyes eager. And I feel a great surge of love for them all. My group, I think. My tribe, as they say.

Kim begins the class and soon we are flexing our spines in cat-cow poses. Saluting the sun, moving into cobras and lions and generally flowing along yoga's quiet, benign current. As I move, images fill my mind. I let them pass through: Paul jogging along round the little lake in Moseley, with Scraps tearing about him; Paul walking down the Moseley Road in air smelling of fireworks, moments before death would rush to meet him . . . I think of that pathetic boy Lee Parry, in Winson Green prison. Lee who never seems to have had much of a life anyway, and this is all part of the horror. And my mind fills with memories of Dorrie: the day she bought the ice creams, Dorrie and Paul, her teaching him to crochet; Dorrie sitting in her chair with her mug, talking to me.

I miss Dorrie, at times almost unbearably. We have cleared her house, Ian, Cynthia and I. It did not take long. She owned few things – a modest number of clothes, her furniture and proud bits of cutlery and china, kept in the back room 'for best', a very few books, photographs and magazines. Sweep is adjusting to a Berkshire village and the house is about to go on the market. Already it has long been empty of the essence of the woman I knew and loved.

And in my drawer, upstairs, I still have *Roses with Thorns* by Dorrie Stefani. In one way I wish she had not left me with this. It feels a heavy responsibility. But I understand why she did. I just don't think now is a good time to tell Ian.

We both miss Dorrie but it's he who has been in bits. He was already going to pieces, even before she died. He's fragile, exhausted, easily emotional. Now that we've done all the things that immediately needed doing, sometimes he just sits and stares, for ages.

'I don't know who I am any more,' he said to me one day.

On another: 'I just feel stuck. I don't know what to do.'

He was just sitting there in the kitchen, late for work. He looked up at me and his eyes were scared. He looked like a little boy. I went over and put my arms round him, rocked him gently. The weird thing is, I feel stronger. As if I'm coming through something, even though some days I still feel as if my body is weighted down with stones. But I have got something – just a little – to give to him.

And while I miss our Dorrie, all her love, her modest, self-effacing, humorous kindness, I have put everything I can into trying to help and support Ian over these weeks. Because I can see he's near the bottom – close to really losing it. And I've found love and strength from my Creaking and Groaning tribe. They know what's going on – I talk to them now. They give me advice and support.

I sit with Ian for hours, hold him, listen to him, suggest he might want to talk to a professional counsellor because much as I love him I can't be everything for him. I think he's coming round to the idea.

'I never thought I'd be one of those people,' he says, embarrassed, when finally admitting he might need help. This evening, he came home from work and just cried for over an hour.

'No,' I say. 'But there're a whole load of things we never thought, aren't there?'

After relaxation we all sit up, in that calm, dazed state that the end of a yoga class brings on.

'Any news?' Kim says. She sits, limber and cross-legged.

'You go first?' Pat suggests.

Kim smiles. 'Well, we've had a good summer. Mike and I and the kids went to Devon and . . . Yeah,' she nods, 'it's been good. But the other thing is – last night I was with one of my moms. She asked me to be her doula a couple of months ago and she was already quite far on. But she's the first one I've got to know and seen through – it was her first. Last night she had a little boy and I was there with her and the midwife all the way through . . .' Her eyes fill with tears although she's smiling. She wipes them away. 'Sorry – it's really emotional. I mean, I can't hack being a midwife any more, but it was really special. A perfect little boy called Charlie.'

Everyone makes happy noises and Sheila pats Kim on the back. 'Good for you, love – I knew you'd work something out. Sounds just right for you.'

'It really is,' Kim says. 'Anyway – that's me. What about the rest of you? Other than a certain run, obviously! I'm *so* sorry I missed it! The photos looked fab – you all look really fit and amazing! Are you all still running?'

There's a silence.

'It's been too hot,' Sunita says. But she seems a bit subdued.

'What have you been up to then?'

'Oh,' Sunita says. 'Summer holiday is all children, children. I haven't had time for anything else.'

Pat has no real news – she and Fred went to Wales for ten days.

'And Hayley?' Kim says. 'I thought you were going to college? What are you doing still here?'

'But I am!' Hayley beams round at us. 'Uni doesn't

start yet. I applied quite late, but I've saved up quite a bit of money now - and I suddenly had a brainstorm about the kind of thing I'm interested in. I've got a place at Birmingham Uni to study Environmental Science. I had to write and beg them – but I think someone had dropped out and they actually found me a place!'

We all take this in.

'Well, that's a bit different from beauty therapy,' Sheila says carefully.

'Have you got A levels?' I ask her. 'I mean – sorry, of course you must have!'

'Oh, yes, I've got what they ask for. In fact, they ask for ABB and I've got AAB – A's in biology and history and B in chemistry.'

'*Have* you?' Everyone seems amazed. None of us had ever considered that she might be so well qualified.

'That's *fantastic*!' I find I'm laughing. 'Good for you, Hayley. And you'll live at home, will you?'

'Oh, yes, I don't want to pay rent. I can live with my nan – keep an eye on her – and go in from here. I'm going to get a little car. It's not far. And depending on my classes, you never know, I night even still be able to come to yoga!'

'Environmental Science,' Sunita says. 'Is that pollution and all?'

'Well, it's all sorts of things,' Hayley says. 'Sort of a mixture of geography, chemistry, biology – anything to do with the way the earth works. So yes, chemical pollutants are one thing. To be honest, after all this, learning about Bhopal and everything, I'd be really interested in studying more about that.' She grins – especially at me. 'So thanks, guys!'

We cheer her on. She's like our little mascot. Then they're all looking at me.

'Well,' I say, 'it's been a bit of a summer. As you know, my lovely mother-in-law left us a few weeks back so we've been pretty busy. And Ian, my husband – he's needed a bit of looking after. I suppose soon I'm going to have to look for a job, now school's beginning again. Although I'm not sure that's even what I want any more.'

'So what about the running?' Kim says. 'How much did you all raise between you?'

'Eleven hundred pounds.' Sunita announces this proudly. 'Between us.' She raised the most – no one in her enormous family got away without sponsoring her.

'That's amazing!' Kim says. 'Are you going to do it again next year?'

We all look at each other.

'We don't know,' I say.

What we do know is that everything feels flat. We have done what we set out to do, the money has gone to the charity and, effectively, we are back to square one. And none of us was especially happy with square one in the first place.

I'm concerned about Ian. I am doing everything I can to help him, care for him. But something in me is rising up, protesting. I have no Paul, no Dorrie. Do I just go and get a job like before? When nothing else is as it was? Something is birthing itself in my mind, slowly and quietly. A thought – a seemingly impossible idea that I keep trying to ignore but which keeps prodding and nagging at me.

When we meet at Sheila's later that week, everyone seems restless and a bit fed up.

'I don't know what to do,' Sunita says. 'My husband says I am being very grumpy because my body is addicted to running about and I am not doing it any more.'

'Well, why don't you all just go for a run?' Sheila says, plying us with chocolate muffins that I made to bring along this time. 'There's nothing stopping you, is there?'

Sunita takes a cake and stares at it in her hand with an air of fate. 'I am going to get fat again.'

'No, you're not,' Pat says. 'Look, come on – we can all go out, even if it's only once a week. I know Hayley won't be here to keep on at us . . .'

'Well, I might be,' Hayley says. 'Depending. But no, realistically I probably won't. Why don't you get everyone going, Sunita? All you have to do is your song-and-dance routine and everyone will be running behind you!'

'Double-double.' I grin at her. 'Yes, come on, why don't we? We could do the run again next year. We need something to aim for.'

'It's just that asking everyone for sponsorship money again,' Pat says, 'feels a bit . . . well, cheeky.'

'They can say no,' Sheila says, to my surprise. 'Every little helps. Most people can afford a pound or two at least and it mounts up.'

'So – shall we?' Sunita says. I can see her perking up already.

'OK,' I say. And then it just comes out. Just like that. 'The thing is – the thing I *really* want is to go to Bhopal.'

I wait for a chorus of ridicule or at least of incomprehension.

Pat, sitting beside me, turns and without missing a beat says, 'Right. I'll come with you.'

Thirty-Six

'I know it's mad.'

It seems to be the first thing I say to everyone. As soon as I say it to the group, I can't stop saying it. And in the end, I have to say it to Ian. Bhopal. The bafflement of anyone else is nothing compared to the arguments I put up in my own head. What's the point? You'll just be in the way. What use are you, another white Westerner coming and just looking at the situation? (After all, it was a Western company that caused all this in the first place.) Who d'you think you are? Are you just looking for that boy because of Paul – so that in the end it's all about you? Etc., etc.

I can't really answer those questions. It's not about the boy any more, that I do know. All I know is, I have to go. I am involved whether I like it or not and I want to understand better. And that's about it really.

'I'm only talking about a week – two at most,' I say to my baffled husband. 'Seriously, that's all. I'll be back and things will be . . . I'll be here.'

And when one evening as we sit with a drink at the table on the little patio at the back of the house, I explain why – as much as I can – and how I feel, Ian is sweet about it. He's seeing a counsellor one evening a week now, a man called Evan who lives in Kings Heath and it seems to be helping.

'We've got the money,' he says. 'We'd have gone somewhere with Paul.' He looks shyly at me. 'I'd never've got through the last few weeks without you being so – well, so great. I don't know as I've been much good to you through it all. I look back and I think . . .' He shakes his head.

'I suppose we lost each other for a bit when we lost him,' I say. 'But . . . I guess we're still the only people now who really understand, who loved him. Shall we . . .' I hesitate. 'Shall we have a look through the albums later?'

Our albums of Paul, the blue one and the brown one which I made such efforts to compile – the building of our memories, our family. We have never looked at them together since he died.

'Not sure I can yet,' Ian says. But then he tries. 'Yeah, maybe. And Jo – what we were talking about. I thought you were going to get a job?'

'I don't know.' I smile at him. 'I mean, I will – do something. There's no reason you have to earn all the money all the time.'

'Well, it's one thing I'm good for.'

I touch his arm. 'Don't. You know it's not like that.'

He gives me his lopsided smile. 'If you say so.'

'The trouble is, I don't know what to do. I don't know anything any more either – other than that I can't just go back to doing the same job as before. All I know at the moment is that I need to do this one thing.'

'Will you be all right? I mean, you know you've travelled before and everything.'

'Pat wants to go.'

'Pat?' He laughs and it's good to hear it. 'What the hell's Fred going to say?'

'God knows.' I laugh as well.

Pat constantly surprises me. When I next see her – she calls round for a coffee – I tell her I've emailed the British charity and they are fine for us to visit. They've sent advice about nearby accommodation, said there might be an interpreter who could lend us a hand if he's free. She tells me, calmly, she has announced to Fred that she is coming with me and that is how it is.

'Blimey, Pat,' I say. 'That's a bit harsh. The poor man's been used to you never moving more than a hundred yards from the house and now you're talking about taking off several thousand miles!'

Pat giggles. She looks very tanned and healthy and her smile really brings her face to life.

'I know. But the thing with Fred is, I don't think the distance really makes much difference. If I said I was going to Scotland it would be much the same. Anyway, he went a bit quiet and then he said, "The thing is, I was thinking I might go with Len and the other lads on that golfing week they were on about in Majorca. But I didn't like to ask you . . ."'

'What – at the same time?'

'No, it's quite soon. Len told him there'd been a lad pull out. And he wasn't going to ask me because he thought I minded him going.'

I stare at her and then we both start laughing hysterically.

'Talk about Stockholm syndrome,' I manage to say eventually.

'Oh, I don't think it's quite that bad,' Pat says. 'More a case of a great big rut. And neither of us has been used to being able to go far – we could never have afforded it and then it just wasn't something we'd ever done. But now the boys have grown up and . . . well, it's not out of the question. And to give Fred his due, he's been very good about it. Said he'd drive us to the airport if we want – even if it's London.'

Part of me wants to resist this because it just feels like Fred trying to be in control of everything again, until the last minute. But I have to agree it's a kind offer.

'What about the kids you look after?'

'I can get someone to cover me. I think she'll be glad of the money.'

'So you're really coming?'

'If we're really going?'

We look at each other in some amazement and then I say, 'Yes, I think we are.'

We make arrangements – tickets, visas, jabs, accommodation. How things have changed – booking on the Internet is not how I did it all those years ago. We have ten days altogether – almost a week in Bhopal and a couple of days sightseeing in Delhi afterwards. Whenever Pat and I meet, our talk is of flights and arrangements and packing. I am amazed at her. She seems up for anything – not at all the way I would have expected her to be when I first met her.

And in a way Fred seems excited about it. When I see him, in the middle of all this, he says, 'So, got everything sorted out, have you?' He seems to regard me as an expert in the travel department.

'Nearly,' I say.

Out of the blue, whether to impress me or what I don't know, he suddenly announces, 'I've been thinking I might learn French.'

Pat looks astounded by this declaration.

'Great,' I say. 'Brilliant idea.'

As the preparations move forward, I can't help feeling guilty about doing all this without Ian. 'I'll stock the freezer with stuff,' I tell him. 'It'll keep you going while we're away.'

'Don't worry, I can cook some of the time,' he says. 'Time I learned to fend for myself a bit more. Actually, I was thinking, while you're away, maybe I'll go down of a weekend – Saturday night – and see Cynth and the boys.'

'Great,' I say again, to another man who seems suddenly full of ideas. He's never, ever suggested that before! But with Dorrie gone, he and Cynth both know they don't have anyone else much. I'm glad for him. 'You can see Sweep as well.'

Our date for departure is very near the end of October. After Paul's anniversary. I don't want to go before then. Pat confides in me that her baby daughter was born in October too – on the seventeenth. Our visit takes on a feeling of memorial – of honouring them as well as honouring the mothers and children we are going to see. Throughout this time, as the nights darken, the air smells of woodsmoke and the first fireworks start going off, I am glad to have the distraction of getting ready for the

287

journey. So that every second of my day is not spent picturing a drunk Lee Parry, already well out of control, folding his puny body into that car that did not belong to him, revving up and starting his brainless, selfish, death-dealing course towards our son.

Thirty-Seven
FLAMES NOT FLOWERS

A rainbow sunrise fills the sky as the plane lowers itself into Bhopal.

Pat and I lean towards the window and begin to see a yellowish land dotted with bushes, out of which appears a motley collection of buildings at the edge of a city, and then runways, more dry scrubland in the dawn light – it could be just about anywhere. I find myself almost surprised, as if expecting to see a place wrecked and devastated, even now. But, of course, it's not like that.

We're here. I want to tell Ian, to share it with him. But he'll be asleep now – we're five hours ahead and it's about seven-fifteen in the morning here.

He was a bit wobbly saying goodbye to me.

'It's not that I don't want you to go – for you, I mean,' he said, when we lay in bed the night before I left. He was trying his best to be kind, not to guilt-trip me, though goodness knows it doesn't take much. 'I suppose I just . . . I'll miss you.'

I could hear tears in his voice, another reminder of how fragile he is these days, how close to the edge.

'It's not long,' I said, stroking his chest, then reaching up to touch his cheek. In a frail way, things feel so much better. 'I'll be back before you even notice.'

There was a silence.

'What if something happens?'

We know now that things can happen – to us, not just somebody else.

'We'll be OK. I've got Pat with me. I'll text you – every night.'

My mind is so involved with home in these moments that it startles me when I feel the plane touch down and it brings me back. India. My God, I'm in India.

Pat glances at me as the plane careers along, braking hard. She looks as she always does, girlish, curly-haired and calm. But I see her draw in a deep, nervous breath. 'Well, here goes.'

So far all we have seen of India is the inside of Delhi airport while we waited for the early flight to Bhopal. The old airport used to make you feel you had arrived in India. In the newly built one, glassy and modern, with a mesmerizingly hectic brown-patterned carpet through-out and everyone glued to their mobile, you could be anywhere.

But now we are somewhere. Before eight in the morn-ing we are in a taxi. The tawny light across the pale earth around the airport has a grainy quality, almost giving the feeling of being inside a painting. The roads are so far surprisingly empty. We sit quietly on the back seat of a white Maruti, which in itself feels strange. Last time I was here, over twenty years ago, almost every car was a bulb-ous Ambassador with a fifties retro look.

As we move towards the centre of Bhopal, for a moment I remember Sunita holding out her hand as a map: *Bhopal is almost in the middle.*

Trucks, a few cars, black-and-yellow auto rickshaws . . .

At the edges, thin, sleepy-looking men on bicycles, some laden with milk churns or a pile of buckets or textiles strapped on the back, press down on pedals with feet protected only by plastic push-on shoes. We glimpse the lake, through trees, looking wide as a sea; swallows and house martins wheel through the air, while people, cows, goats and dogs mingle with the traffic. Gradually the volume of it increases: the noise of hundreds and hundreds of motorbikes, the endless beeping of horns and roar of trucks. I peel the scarf from round my neck – it's getting warmer.

In the brightening light we turn into a side street, dusty and scruffy, and for a moment I wonder why we are stopping outside a small, grey Hindu temple. But on the other side, somehow unexpectedly in this little street, is our hotel. Most likely built in the eighties, I think, looking up at its tall oblong, with a glass-fronted foyer. It's functional and in the right part of town – just what we need. Inside there are shiny stone floors, glass and metal, grey and black – nothing soft or colourful.

We are shown to the fourth floor, to a narrow room with a double bed and tiny bath cubicle attached. Pat goes to the window and flings it open, letting in the sound of traffic and blaring horns from the main road a short distance away.

'Oh, my goodness,' she says, as I throw my rucksack on the bed. She starts laughing.

'What?'

At the window, I am confronted with so many things to take in that I hardly know where to look. The back of the hotel faces over the rear of the blocks along on the main road – a chaotic array of buildings, stained brown and yellowish-white, a telephone tower in the middle: some with rectangular windows, others with curved tops. The space between those and our hotel is taken up by a mess of half-built structures, some with metal struts sticking out of the roof which announce the intention of building higher. On one, work is already in progress, a man squatting over a pile of bricks. Thin trees have forced their way up from any corner where they have managed to find a toehold. On the ground, in the shade of the buildings, lie heaps of pallets, tumbled like jackstraws, and curving sheets of rusted corrugated iron, weeds forcing up around them. A stray white cat weaves between the scrubby plants; and for some reason, squeezed into the narrow alley amongst everything else, is a big shiny blue-and-silver coach.

I take in the sight, grinning. 'We've arrived. I like this place. Shall we go and find a cup of tea somewhere?'

This first day we spend getting used to things. We go out to see the city or at least the part of it where we are staying, just off the Hamidia Road in the old Muslim heart of Bhopal. The name is familiar, because there is a Hamidia hospital. On the night of the gas leak in 1984, its corridors were overwhelmed with people trying to get help, lying dead or dying in numbers far greater than the staff could cope with. Over the following months, many of the babies born in Hamidia hospital were handicapped and malformed in ways not seen before, the state of some so horrific that people could hardly bear to speak of it.

But we are not here to visit the hospital. Today we are tourists. We set off along crazy-busy Hamidia Road. The stone-slabbed pavements are hemmed in by a phalanx of hundreds and hundreds of parked motor scooters, the scruffy buildings along the road house shops and work-shops, all with signs in blaring colours advertising retail wonders. 'Alpana Talkies,' a cinema announces. Every-where is so busy – shops, fruit stalls, cinemas, traffic and more traffic, mostly auto rickshaws and motorcycles – that you hardly know where to begin looking.

We are in the heart of an area of mosques, of markets, of commerce. Side streets give us glimpses of minarets and domes. Small shops spill their displays out across the pavement: one moment heaps of coiled ropes, the next, office chairs and desks, plastic buckets, galvanized buckets, iron bedsteads, tables, shoes, a mountain of safety matches in bright yellow boxes, a slight man sitting cross-legged on top. The white light of welding sparks arc across the dark interiors of workshops; oil seeps across a pavement, its stink adding to the fumes from the traffic, the smell of rotting papaya skins as we pass a stall . . . And all around us, the racket of hammering, banging, shout-ing, beeping horns. Seeing the men squatting in their oily workshops, I wish for a moment that Ian was here to see. He'd be fascinated.

We wander about for some time, mesmerized, growing exhausted. It takes energy just to get along, dodging people, having to move into the road when the pavement is blocked by a stall, a motorbike, a crowd, having to watch your feet while trying to look about you. It's growing hotter and our senses are quickly saturated. I look at Pat, wondering how she feels about it all. She looks fine – gazing about her, drinking it all in.

'Cup of tea?' I say.

'Where will we find one?' Now I can see she is

bewildered. 'I've never been anywhere like this ... Well, maybe Sparkhill. Not really, though. It's like Sparkhill on steroids!'

At this point we discover the Manohar Dairy – a shop that looks nothing much from outside, but which inside is a wonderland of steel surfaces, tables and what seems an almost endless menu. To one side is a whole section with glass cabinets displaying vast quantities of sweets and cakes. On the other, a canteen-style restaurant with a list of possibilities so extensive that I feel too tired to choose. The waiters wear bright yellow polo shirts and a lot of the tables are occupied by people slurping tea and speedily eating morning snacks.

'Shall we start with toast and tea?' I say to Pat. 'We can come back for something else later.'

'Yes, good idea.' She gazes around her in wonder. 'Look at all those cakes! It's amazing.'

'It does take a while to acclimatize,' I say.

'Yes.' She looks solemn for a moment. 'I certainly feel like a foreigner. I've never been so aware of being *white*. Good lesson, I suppose. But I'm glad you've been here before. I wouldn't know where to start.' Just as the waiter comes up to take our order, she suddenly beams at me. 'You know, I'm tired out and I have no idea what's going on – but this is great!'

And the waiter is met by her lovely smile. Soon afterwards, braced by toast and our first cup of *chai*, thick, hot and sugary, we are fortified for more of our jet-lagged day.

Even though we're tired, we can't stop exploring. It's a pleasantly warm day, not too hot, and we are dressed in jeans, long shirts over T-shirts, trainers. With some food inside us we are comfortable to walk for hours, tying the shirts round our waists as the heat builds. We pass through a market, stalls laden with papayas, guavas and pomegranates, with stacks of snow-white eggs, tomatoes, aubergines and the long-tailed green trails of spring onions. We ride in an auto rickshaw to the lake, an experience which reduces Pat to hysterical laughter.

'It's like being in a video game!' she squeals, clinging to the metal door frame. The roaring little vehicle, like a motorbike with two back seats and a roof, swerves deftly through the traffic, between cars and cows, motorbikes and pedestrians who seem to have taken it into their heads to wait in the most perilous-looking spots possible in the middle of the road. Buses, bicycles and scooters come flying skilfully at us from a variety of directions, seldom the one you would expect. 'D'you remember that game, Asteroids? Where all those things are just coming at you all the time?' Pat laughs and laughs. I grin, enjoying seeing her so lit up. 'I've never seen anything like this!'

We spend the whole journey with our heads hunched down trying to see out, to take everything in as we weave through the narrow streets of busy shops, cross a flyover and peel off down a bumpy, tree-lined road beside the lake where it is suddenly much quieter. Boat Club, we are told.

And we stroll back, amid the milling holidaymakers and food vendors and offers of pony-rides and rickshaws. The lake, lit by the sun, is dotted with boats. Flocks of geese and ducks bob about with the pleasure boats: a fountain shoots up rainbow spray before it falls back into the steel grey water. Huge letters alongside the water spell, 'WELCOME TO THE CITY OF LAKES'. And its life echoes distantly across the water.

Later, in the glow of late afternoon, we find ourselves in the compound of the city's biggest mosque, the Taj-ul-Masajid. Approaching it, we see its terracotta walls mirrored in a pool along one of the outer walls, a beautiful image, perfect as glass despite the filthiness of the water.

Inside, in the spacious compound at the heart of the mosque buildings, people mill about, many seeming to use the place as a passage through to somewhere else. Along a path leading to the mosque itself, we stop to watch a heated game of cricket played by a group of boys, mostly aged about twelve or thirteen, all in white, lacey caps. Seeing us stopping to watch, some of the fielders standing round the edges crowd round us.

'Selfie? Selfie, ma'am?'

'OK,' I give in. 'Selfie' apparently just means, *Please take our photo, selfie or not*. Grinning, they strike up a variety of poses, arms draped round each other's shoulders, fingers arranged in 'cool' V signs. Then they are keen to see the pictures and cluster round me, giggling. For a moment I feel like a teacher again.

'OK, bye-bye,' I say, and they go back to their game, apparently satisfied.

By the time we have managed to get back to the area where we are staying we are both completely exhausted. We collapse into the Manohar Dairy and eat plates of rice spiced with ginger and chillies, drink sweet lime sodas and tea.

'We might just as well eat here every time,' Pat says, looking round with apparent fondness already. The place is only just round the corner from where we are staying. She yawns. 'What time did you say he was coming tomorrow – the interpreter guy?'

'Ten, I think.'

'Right. That's good. I'd better text Fred and then I'm off to sleep. I shan't need any rocking tonight, I can tell you.'

'No, nor me.'

When it comes to it, though, I don't sleep well. We are sharing the rather firm double bed and Pat seems to drop off quickly. But I lie awake in the dark, hearing the distant mayhem of the Hamidia Road, and have a kind of dark night of the soul. I remember now, not having travelled for a long time, that it sometimes has this effect on me – at first, anyway. Lying in a bed in a strange place where no one knows you, or has any idea where you are; the life of a strange city going on all around you, the expanding realization that you are a little random dot on the face of the earth.

So I lie on my back, wondering what in fact the hell I am doing here. I'm glad I didn't come on my own now. It's nice to have Pat's gently breathing form beside me. But I'm full of doubts. Tomorrow we are going to start seeing and meeting people who have been involved in the chemical leak, the poisoning of their lives by the water. Many will have lost a lot of members of their families, or are enduring terrible physical afflictions. And there are people who have worked there for years, living each day and every injustice that has been visited upon them. And then there is me, walking into this with some vague idea of being able to help somewhere along the line, even if

297

only by raising money. I feel stupid. One photo in a magazine and here I am rocking up. For what?

On my last visit to the cemetery before I left, I tidied Paul's grave as usual, laid some roses on it, told him in a whisper that I love him – will always love him. Leaving even for just ten days made me feel horribly guilty and I got Ian to promise he would go, regularly, to see our boy. But – and this makes a big difference – not too far away, in a grave where there is already a gravestone for 'Tom Stefani, b.1926, d.1959, beloved son of Lorenzo and Ida Stefani', there is a little temporary sign beside it, as we wait for them to add Dorrie's name to the stone, where we buried her ashes. 'Doreen Stefani, 1929–2015'. And I went and knelt by it.

'Hello, Dorrie.' I stopped as tears ran down my cheeks. They come more easily now, at any time, as if some rusted-up mechanism in me has been freed and I can finally begin to move it. 'Well, we're off to India tomorrow – Pat and me. You never met Pat but you'd like her. She's sort of quiet and you have to get to know her. But she's got a lot to her. And I admire her. She's one of those volcano women – you know, waiting to burst out.'

I squatted down and tidied round Tom Stefani's grave. Now that Dorrie's here, and it feels as if she can see everything that's going on anyway, I can tell her anything and everything.

'I miss you, Dorrie. Miss you like mad. I don't suppose you realize quite how much you meant to me. Or maybe you did. You'd never have said really, would you? I miss you just being there – us chatting.' I look across the wide space of the cemetery, the tranquil rows of gravestones. 'Anyway, what you told me, about Ian's dad and everything ... He hasn't been too good lately, in himself. But he's getting a bit of help now as well. We went through a really bad patch after Paul – I can see now just how bad. When he left, I didn't really know if he was coming back, even if I didn't admit it to myself. I never said anything to you then because I didn't want you to worry. But he's back now – he really is. Properly back. And I think I am too. I know things'll never be the same but ... Anyway, we're trying ... So what I was going to say is, I will tell him. In a bit. When I get back and when I think he's going to be able to deal with it. I promise.'

I smoothed my hand over the earth covering her ashes, with that sudden, awful empty feeling you have of knowing the person really is not there. There is earth and flowers, a stone and loving words, but not them – ever again. I lowered my head, tears falling on the bare crumbs of soil. Then I wiped my eyes and got to my feet.

'Look out for Pauly, won't you, Dorrie? I'll be back soon, love – to both of you.'

Ta-ra, bab. I could almost hear her, as if she was speaking straight to me. *Just mind how you go. Don't worry about me.*

And she's with me now as I lie in this strange bed, with her simple, kindly good sense. As I set off on some mission that I passionately know I have to fulfil. For what? A boy's face? For the company of other women who know the horror of the words, 'That night'?

I don't know. And I'm scared. I have no real idea what any of this means for me – for Ian and me. But I just know I have to be here. In this particular gin joint, as Bogie would have said.

Eventually, I sleep.

Thirty-Eight

Ten o'clock finds us waiting in the hotel foyer. A worried-looking man in black trousers, a white shirt and shiny black shoes washes and polishes the long panes of glass looking over the street. From here you can see the little temple with its strings of bright marigolds dangling just inside. Another man is mopping the already shiny stone floor.

'Oh, dear,' Pat says, watching him. 'We're going to have to walk on that in a minute.'

I can see she is nervous. I certainly am. And I still feel foolish. There is something about India that I had forgotten. It makes me feel idiotic: too big, among these small-boned people, too pink, too *English*, as if we embody the colonial folk memory that none of us can ever quite shake off. And I feel rather like a child thrown into the company of adults who have to humour me because they really have far more pressing things to do.

Dead on time, I see a motorbike draw up in the narrow street, wheel round and stop. A slender young man hops off, dressed in black trousers and a pale blue polo shirt with a maroon puffa jacket hanging open over it. He pulls off his helmet, props the bike up and comes into the hotel. He is of medium height, his hair neatly cut. He has a thin face and lively, enquiring eyes which settle on us immediately. As we stand up, he hangs the helmet on his left wrist and comes to shake our hands.

'Good morning, Mrs ... Jo? I am Aasif, from the Bhopal Medical Appeal. I work on publicity and information and I will be your interpreter.'

'I'm really grateful for this,' I say, after the introductions, as we go outside into the warmth. I wonder, nervously, if he expects us both to squeeze on the back of the bike. 'Only – if you've got other things to do, we don't need to take up much time.'

'It's OK,' Aasif says cheerfully, fetching his bike. 'Some times are very busy, but this week is good. We are happy to show you round. You guys have been raising some money, right?'

'Just a bit,' Pat says quickly. It feels so little.

'It's good,' he says. 'People come, they see and learn. That is my job. Anyway –' he points along the street – 'come. We will go and find an auto for you.'

'We're not going on your bike then?' I say, just a bit disappointed.

Aasif grins, looking suddenly impish. 'Maybe another day. The auto rickshaws stop on the corner there by the Dairy. Today we will go to Chingari – this is the clinic for children.'

The life of the street explodes in on us. It's rush hour, the main road full to bursting with traffic. Sunshine slants down, leaving our side of the main road in shadow. There is so much racket of engines and beeping scooters that it has become normality rather than noise.

Pat looks pleased. In this very short time she has become

addicted to riding the streets in an auto rickshaw and as soon as we are on the way, her face lights up again. She gives little squeaks of excitement as we wheel off into the swirling, fume-filled, blaring street. Aasif hops on his bike and rides beside us like an escort. Soon we are turning right somehow, in the face of the oncoming barrier of traffic, and down another road. This one is lined with piles of gravel, carts laden with fruit and trinkets, goats and vendors of piles of second-hand white containers, of the sort you might buy full of plaster or Polyfilla, to use as buckets.

The light is already strong, picking out sharp shadows. We pass over a flyover and Aasif is leaning in shouting something at us.

'Over there – the company building. Union Carbide.'

Twisting round, we catch sight of the hunched, rusting skeleton of a building, standing higher than the tangle of low buildings around it.

'Very bad,' the auto driver shouts back to us. 'Gas, gas – 1984.' We have yet to discover that every driver who brings us this way will tell us, *Kampani, Union Carbide, Dow, very bad.* The open wound of Bhopal.

'Yes, yes,' we shout, as the deathly structure fades into the distance.

A few moments later we follow Aasif's bike into a side street and pull up beside a shabby, orange-painted building. I hand rupees to our driver and he turns the little vehicle nimbly and disappears back into the street's turmoil. On the wall in front of us, making patterns all across the peachy orange paint, are the handprints of children in varying bright colours. Painted in blue along the white border at the top, in English and Hindi, is the exhortation:

In seconds we are aware of busyness all around us. A little white van with CHINGARI TRUST painted across the front is unloading nearby. Children and a few mothers, some carrying their infants, emerge from it and hurry in through the gate and along the front of the building. A moment later the white van drives swiftly off again.

'Come,' Aasif says.

He leads us along the front of the building, saying good morning to people as he passes. We are in a long, stone-paved area about five metres wide covered over by a green corrugated-plastic roof that sheds a botanical light on everyone beneath. To the right, opposite the building, is a low wall with potted plants arranged along it, into which are embedded the iron struts which support the roof. And beyond it, a strip of garden, and then the main wall which divides the garden from the street.

We wait under the shady overhang, amid an atmosphere of purpose and bustling activity. Children who can walk come in from the street or from the little people carriers, greeting each other, laughing and chatting. All of them are wearing grey V-necked jumpers with a crest of some sort on the breast.

'Is that a special uniform?' Pat asks.

'Yes,' Aasif says. 'When they are registered to come they are all allocated this – the Chingari uniform. Actually, it also makes them easier to find when we go to pick them up from the street. Now – oh, hold on . . .' Someone is calling Aasif's name, a middle-aged woman, beckoning him along the corridor. 'Just wait here one moment.'

A number of women with woolly cardigans over their sarees walk back and forth, looking efficient and taking people into the building. Just outside the main door is a pile of shoes and flip-flops. One of the women comes round with little paper cups of *chai* and we are offered one as well.

'Take tea,' Aasif suggests, rejoining us. 'And we will wait here a few minutes. People are arriving. Then we will go inside.'

As we stand watching, we begin to see the world of Chingari and what it is for – what has been done to this place. A tiny, thin woman carries a boy into the building. She has him clutched closely to her and the boy's age is hard to guess – perhaps eight or nine. His body has a wooden stiffness. I catch a glimpse of a face, the eyes more widely spaced than would be considered 'normal'. The woman's exhaustion transmits itself to me. Looking after able-bodied, healthy children is tiring enough – but seems as nothing compared with this: all this lifting, struggling to feed, striving to manage, day after day after day in the summer heat, in the cramped, deprived living space of the *bustees* – miles of slums.

Because most of these parents are the poor. It was the people living in slums so close to the factory who took the brunt of the poison. I hear Pat make a sound, an out-breath of horror and sympathy as she catches sight of some of the children being carried in.

'OK – come.' Aasif takes our empty cups. We unlace our trainers and leave them by the door, following him inside.

'We just have the ground floor here,' he says. 'The rest is offices. Actually, this used to be the main Sambhavna clinic until they moved to a bigger place. It is quite cramped, as you can see. There are a number of different therapy rooms and clinics and people are coming and going in the morning time, for different treatments.' He looks gravely at us both. 'This is the only place in Bhopal where gas- and water-affected children can have a specialized treatment for no charge. There are government hospitals but you have to pay. But those who come here have a certificate saying they are gas-affected or water-affected – and they can get treatment.'

Inside is another long corridor. The atmosphere is colourful and jolly, with a red-and-white chequered floor and lime-green walls with children's paintings pinned up and colourful doors. On the floor on each side of the corridor are huddles of mothers and children, all waiting to be seen.

A row of lads, all wriggling and grinning, stands together signing at each other. The mothers sit chatting, some with children on their laps: the Muslim women mostly in black, the Hindu mothers in sarees and cardigans. The place is full of life and noise.

As we stand just inside the entrance amid all the activity, I become aware of an unusual movement just to my right, near the floor. Turning, I see a little girl, maybe ten years old, dressed in the Chingari jumper, her head covered by a black scarf, moving along on her belly; pulling herself, fishlike, on her arms, her legs trailing uselessly behind. She has a bright, lively expression and is clearly intent on getting somewhere. We are in a place of profound disability. And of course, ability. The lively, gesticulating boys all wear hearing aids; some of the children, locked in wooden expressions, are not speaking; others simply lie close to their mothers, limbs so wasted they are not able to get up and play.

'Now, here –' Aasif shows us into a small room which is remarkably quiet once the door is closed – 'this is where we work with the deaf kids – we can do tests.' He tells us some more before we move on into a much bigger room where several mothers are sitting cross-legged on the floor. To one side, bent over a little massage bench, one of the physiotherapists, a young woman wearing loose trousers, a blouse and headscarf, is working on a child. She glances round and smiles at us.

'This is the sensory room,' Aasif says. 'You see – things for climbing, touching . . .' There is a small wooden slide, ropes for swinging on, a big inflated ball, cushions and rugs. Against one wall is a vertical wooden frame to which a boy is strapped, standing to try and strengthen his legs. His mother sits looking up, encouraging him.

'Bless him,' Pat says softly. She smiles at the boy. His features are unevenly arranged, but he nods and grins, seeming to be interested in our appearance.

Pat and I move round, smiling at the mothers, exchanging a few words through Aasif.

'There are many disabilities here,' he says. 'Children are still being born with deformities, with no lips, or noses – wasting in the legs, as you have seen. Many problems. Some are the children of gas-affected parents but much of it is chemicals in the water. The factory has never been cleared up and is still poisoning the water supply. For example, they have found lead in the breast milk of mothers – this is from the water. Only many years later, we have water brought into this area from elsewhere – most of the time, anyway.'

I see Pat's face, the emotions registering in it, and I can only imagine mine looks the same. Imagine breastfeeding your child – that primal, instinctive giving of love through your body – and finding you have poisoned your baby in doing so.

Going over to the physio, we see that she is working on a little girl. The child is bone thin, and looks very frail. One side of her body is wasted, as if only half of her has truly been given life. The physio works on her weak side, bending her leg, trying to develop the muscles. The child winces, lets out a small whimper and the physio makes comforting noises.

'You are from England?' she asks us. When we nod, she says, 'We are grateful to you guys. This is what keeps this place going – the money you raise.'

It feels so insignificant – a tiny breath in a vast world of air.

'This little girl,' I say, smiling down at her. She has a pink ribbon in her hair and her eyes are fixed on me, wondering, I suppose, who these pale strangers are. 'She is . . . ?'

'Her mother was gas-affected. She is . . . as you see. Severe wastage of the limbs and she is also deaf and dumb. We are trying to get her to walk – one day, per-haps.'

We learn that there is a pool for hydrotherapy, rooms for speech therapy, help with autism and mental-health problems, a little classroom where children can learn basic skills. Outside, at the far end of the garden, is a small playground, the play equipment surrounded by soft, pale sand. On the back wall is a beautiful mosaic of a pregnant woman, in mirror glass which catches the light. We meet some of the other parents there. Some are enter-taining siblings while their child has treatment inside. I'm interested to see that there are quite a few fathers there, minding children as well.

'My son, Sanjay, he is autistic.' A lady comes up to me, tells me, as if she needs me to know. She is small, with a round, friendly face, and she speaks a little English. The boy, about thirteen years old, stands close to her like a wooden statue, and she ushers him about. 'His brother is OK. But this one – very bad. No speaking – nothing.'

'Were you here in 1984?' I ask her.

'Me? No. I was further out.' She waves a hand vaguely. 'But my husband . . .' She shrugs, as if the rest of the story is obvious, and I don't like to keep on at her to tell me more.

We play with children, pushing them on a little round-about, cheering as they slip giggling down the slide. It comes easily to us – we have both brought up kids. And while it brings back memories of Paul, here my own grief feels contained by this larger grief around me and I can let it be without collapsing into it. The parents are friendly. Even talking to those with no English, we some-how manage to make something understood. Sanjay's mother sits on the wall, her son beside her, both of them silent, watching. More people arrive, others leave. The little white people carriers come and go.

Chingari – flames. I think of all the *bustees* that we have seen extending away from here, the many, many other children who could be treated but for lack of space and resources. The women struggling day after day. The enormity of it all.

Pat comes over to me, her bare feet in the sand, after a conversation with another of the mothers.

'Jesus,' she says, her face tight with emotion. 'Has

anyone from that company ever even been here, to see what they've done?'

By the evening we are exhausted, jet-lagged and swamped with new impressions. We eat a bowl of fried rice and go straight back to our room.

'Quite something for your first ever day in India,' I say to Pat as she emerges from the bathroom.

She sinks down on the bed. She has a pale pink summer nightie on, a towel wrapped round her hair.

'It's very upsetting.' She sits staring ahead. I can see how much it's got to her, the anger she's feeling. 'I mean, *all these years*. What is it? Thirty now, more? And kids being born like that. It's wicked – I never knew ... I mean, if this was America they'd do something, wouldn't they?'

'Well, maybe.' I lie back on the bed. 'If the people concerned were the right colour. Dow's poisoned things in America too – just not quite on this scale. This is the biggest industrial accident there's ever been, I think. Dow didn't actually own this place then. They didn't cause it. They took over in 2001.'

Pat looks at me.

'They bought Union Carbide's assets,' I explain.

'So it's up to them then. They wanted all the profits they could get, presumably? They ought to take the rough with the smooth.' She adds a few choice and out-of-character expletives. 'I've never seen anything like it.'

We're silent for a moment.

'Are you going to text Fred?' I hold my phone up. I've just emailed Ian, telling him as much as I can about today, asking how he is. I'm longing to talk to him. On and off

310

all day, I've been thinking, Imagine if Ian could see this. But no message could really begin to cover what we've seen. *I do wish you were here to see,* I finished it. *Lots and lots of love – I miss you xxxx*

Pat stares at me for a second as if she has forgotten for the moment who Fred might be. 'Oh!' she says, reaching for her phone. 'Yes. Of course.'

By the next morning there's a text from Ian.

Sounds amazing. You'll have to tell me. Really want to hear about it. Everything OK here – cooked spag bol all by myself last night! ☺ *Love you, Ian xxxx*

I sit up in bed, grinning. It feels so good, getting a normal, loving message, and it makes my day. I text back: *Brill to get your mssg. Will phone tonight – be in! Love, love xxx*

Sod the expense. I really want to talk to him.

Thirty-Nine

Aasif has told us for that for the next two days he can be at our disposal. After that he has to look after visitors from Japan.

He turns up regular as clockwork the next morning, soon after we have finished our breakfast of eggs and toast. It feels chillier today and he is wearing a rather fetching yellow woolly hat instead of the cycle helmet.

'So,' he says. 'Today we are going to see the main clinic, Sambhavna. There we will meet Nalika – she is a community health worker. We can take you to some places. And we will see the evaporation ponds.'

He sees our puzzled look.

'The factory was putting chemical waste into ponds a distance away from the plant. But they had a very thin lining which was torn in many places – plus they flooded during the wet season. This has been a big factor in poisoning the water supply. Actually, a lot of the contents have been dug out and buried somewhere else, but you can still see what remains.'

'We're in your hands,' I say and Aasif smiles.

As we pass our time with him we get to know him a little. He has a wife and two young sons in the newer part of Bhopal but comes north to work. We walk with him

313

to find an auto rickshaw. Conversation, if any, is made at the tops of our voices, over the sounds of traffic and a building site on one corner, a cement mixer turning, drilling sounds, women smashing up piles of stones. And it is also hard to hold a conversation together since we are constantly on the lookout so as not to be mown down by something in the street.

'Very sensible,' I yell to Aasif. 'Using a motorbike.'

'Actually, I have a car,' he shouts back as we reach the main road where it gets even noisier. 'But I don't use it much in the city. It is much quicker to come here on the motorcycle!'

And we are off again into the tumult, the throaty sound of the auto rickshaw in our ears, gritty air blowing in our faces, a whirl of sound, movement, smells.

I think of Ian at home, asleep, getting up later, going about his day. It's strange how, being here, sometimes home feels very close in my mind, sometimes so far away that it is like another world and I can hardly believe it exists.

Just now I am close to it, as the little engine labours along the road, the skinny shoulders of the driver in front of us in a cheap, dark green jumper, a checked scarf at his neck billowing behind.

Further on, we pass the stall heaped with its mountain of yellow matchboxes. And I wonder if there are women all round town sitting on the floors of their houses gumming those endless numbers of little boxes together, just as the women in Dorrie's family sat in their rooms in Birmingham, glueing by candlelight, late into the night.

We have turned into a filthy street, lined with warehouses and vehicle workshops. Lean men, bare to the waist, hammer sheets of metal and haul on the handles of carts. There is an atmosphere of oily dirt, of metal and rust and back-breaking labour. A pothole opens up in the road, so huge that the auto rickshaw has to do a swerving detour round it. Yet a moment later we are turning in at a gate, seeing before us a brick building surrounded by trees. Everything suddenly feels serene and peaceful. The Sambhavna clinic.

'It's lovely,' Pat says, seeming to be relieved after the sight of the quarter we have just ridden through. I see her clear eyes taking everything in.

An older man and woman are sitting waiting on the low wall outside, the woman wrapped in a shawl as if she is cold. Both nod to us. There are trees, and plants in pots near the steps.

For the next couple of hours we are shown round this airy building, which feels like a cross between a clinic, a school and a retreat centre. It offers free care, both Western allopathic and ayurvedic and herbal remedies. There are clinics, a dispensary, examination rooms, quarters for volunteers who work here, a herb garden, a playground. People who are able to get to the clinic wait on benches in patient lines.

'Of course, they also do home visits,' Aasif tells us. 'Many people are too sick to come here. This is the only clinic in the city where treatment is free. In other hospitals it is money that talks – but many of these people are very poor. Some have been unable to work since the night of the gas. They are too sick, too weak.'

The garden, full of medicinal plants, is at the back, green and serene. There is a whole department for making herbal medicines – pans boiling up various roots, pill-pressing machines. So many people who need treatment have already suffered such a toxic overload in their bodies that Western drugs just add to their problems. Several people are working hard in the gardens. We walk round full of admiration.

'The water for drinking here now has to come from another place – it is piped in,' Aasif tells us. 'If you walk the streets you will see that the water pumps are tied closed – the water supply contains dangerous levels of chemicals. But of course, sometimes the water in the pipes does not come and people are forced back to using the poisoned water for the necessities of their daily living.'

'So people are still getting sick from it?' Pat asks.

Aasif gives a complicated nod. 'There are many difficulties. Later we are going to some of the living quarters here – if you visit almost any house close to the factory there is a problem. People still sick from the gas, children with deformities, many cancers. And other physical sickness, breathing problems, mental-health problems also and mental retardation.'

We stand silent, listening.

'You see, water has been badly contaminated – and it is spreading further each year.' He is insistent that we take this in. It's not just about one night, one gas leak – it's about thirty years of poisoning, generation after generation.

He stops in the garden, close to a section of tall, sword-like leaves. Turmeric – very medicinal, he tells us.

'The organization Greenpeace have given us the title "Toxic Hotspot". They did testing on the water, some years back. Many chemicals, and many, many times more than safe levels. For example, dichlorobenzene – this causes anaemia and leukaemia, damage to liver and kidneys, skin problems, vomiting, even damaging chromosomes of the body. That is just one chemical in the water. There is very much carbon tetrachloride, causing dizziness, vomiting, sickness – even coma. And others ... chloroform, tetrachloroethane ...'

He seems to have the report off by heart. All we can do is listen, appalled, to the cocktail of toxic horror visited upon these neighbourhoods.

'No one is wanting to take responsibility – the chemical companies, Indian government and state government. Chemical plant is still there. No one is now prepared to say they own the site, which is still putting chemicals in the water, even a very rich country like the USA – they wash their hands of it. They handed the site to our state government as a gift.'

'A *gift*?' Pat says. She is silent with astonishment for a moment, then she asks, 'Why do people stay here? Why don't they just leave?'

Aasif looks at her almost pityingly. 'Where should they go? A few have left, but for many people they have nothing and nowhere to go. This is their home. They have family members who are sick. At least there is some treatment here.' With sudden change of tack, he says, 'You will take tea?'

'Oh, no, it's OK, thanks,' we chorus.

'OK then. We will go to meet Nalika. Now is your turn to ride a motorcycle.' His solemn face breaks into a grin again. Pat and I look at each other.

Nalika is a quiet, serious young woman in a tidy

orange saree and grey cardigan, who pats the back of her motorbike. I scramble on obediently behind her. Pat, making a comical *Well, here goes* face at me, hops on behind Aasif and off we go. After a few minutes, we are beaming at each other. No helmets, mad – though not very fast-moving traffic. A risky, heady freedom, the sun shining, wind through our hair. I wonder what Fred would say if he could see us, I think, almost giggling.

But I feel quite safe with Nalika, who steers her little cycle expertly through the traffic, until we can see the looming old factory again and turn into a narrow street lined with tiny, brick dwellings piled one above another, some of them painted in bright colours, some with satellite dishes all pointing in the same direction.

People, stalls, cows and dogs all compete for space and we wind our way through to the point where the roughly paved street gives way to a muddy track lined with still more houses. Most are brick but there are some shacks made of old pallets and bits of plastic. They would all have been more like that once – in 1984. Back in those days, many people had just arrived in Bhopal from elsewhere and had found a few square feet to set up home. These places almost back on to the wall of the chemical factory.

'We will meet two families who are happy to greet you,' Aasif says, once we have come to a halt and scrambled off the bikes again.

Nalika stops at a door and calls out. A tall man in white invites us graciously inside and leads us to what must be the room for visitors – bare except for brightly coloured walls, yellow and green; a shelf with some artificial flowers. We meet his wife, his son. All of them smile and shake our hands. And then his daughter. Immediately we can see there are problems. She is twenty years old, we are told. She is tiny, looks perhaps fourteen, and her face is not regular; boss-eyed and vacant-looking. She has a sweetness about her and smiles at us.

'She knows nothing of what is going on,' Aasif says. 'She cannot speak – she has no education.'

'Selfie,' the boy says. He looks about sixteen. 'Photo?'

So we do family shots and shake hands and thank them and are on our way again.

'Are people not sick of strangers turning up, taking pictures?' I ask Aasif. I feel we are invading people's privacy.

He looks at me. 'They know they have to keep telling their story. They already feel forgotten – that nothing is being done. Tell everyone you can. That is one thing we can do.'

In a second home we meet a young woman who greets us from a squatting position. It only takes seconds to realize how unnatural the posture is. Her legs are splayed impossibly far apart so that each one is at right angles to her body. She cannot stand or walk but is condemned to shuffling about on her haunches. She is eighteen years old and Aasif tells us she was born like this. But, she tells us, smiling happily as he translates, she is married and expecting a child. She very much hopes the baby will be born normal. Her proud mother stands nearby, nodding and smiling.

I think of what Aasif said: in every house you find a problem.

And soon we are on the bikes again, turning to stop on a patch of rough ground under a flyover.

'Actually,' Aasif says, having almost to shout again, 'the flyover is new – it cuts through the middle of where the evaporation ponds were.'

Just nearby, in an open expanse of ground where grey cows graze and kids play games of cricket, is a wide, sunken area. The evaporation ponds. The idea of dumping toxic waste and letting the sun evaporate the liquid did not work too well in a country where the monsoon can flood any body of water over its edges on a regular basis. And as for the lining . . .

'Here.' Aasif calls us over to a lip at the edge of what was an original pond and squats down. 'See?' Along the edge we see the frayed, remaining edge of some black plastic. The lining which was put in to protect the local people from toxic waste. For one of many times that day, we find ourselves staring in appalled disbelief.

'God,' Pat says. 'That's like the lining Fred put in our pond.' She looks at Aasif. 'Is that even legal?'

He laughs up at her. 'Legal. Ha ha.' Standing, he says, 'Soon after the Union Carbide company came here in the early eighties, the locals started noticing their cows were dying. People were getting sick – water tasting very bad. This was before the gas leakage. Many years ago now.' He pulls his shoulders back. 'For these people living here, the disaster never ends. Poison gas, drinking poisonous water – this goes on and on, into next generation and the next. We do not know how it can be finished.'

We all stand in the warm sun, Aasif and Nalika, Pat and I, looking across the open space dotted with pools of water and, at its far edge, the jumbled, crowded neighbourhood beyond. The traffic roars on the flyover behind us. I find myself wondering what exactly is in the soil

320

under our feet, in this place where people have been apparently far more disposable than the toxic material itself. About the mental state of the people running those corporations. Perhaps greed should be defined as a mental illness: the crazed, loveless desire to protect shareholder profit and absolutely nothing else?

'So,' Aasif says as we go back to the bikes, 'I have the pass now, for tomorrow. We can go to visit the abandoned site.'

'Jo? Hi!'

It's so good to hear Ian's voice. I'm sitting down in the foyer of the hotel, leaving Pat in peace upstairs. There are not many people about, but I lean forward, hugging one arm around myself, trying to hold on to our privacy.

'You sound cheerful,' I say. He does sound really pleased to hear me.

'Yeah,' he says, considering this. 'Not bad.'

'This is the day you see the counsellor, right?'

'Yep. Yeah. It's . . . good. I think it's helping.'

'That's great,' I say. 'I'm really glad.' I don't want to ask him questions now – I'm just happy to hear him sounding OK.

'So – how's it going?'

'It's amazing.' I tell him about the city, all the mechanics and workshops, about the lake and the auto rickshaw rides.

'Pat gets so excited, she's practically jumping up and down in the seat!'

I tell him a bit about the clinics and the plant. 'But there's too much to explain. I wish you were here as well – there are so many things I'd like to show you.'

'Yeah.' He hesitates. 'I kind of wish I was too.'

'Do you?' This is unexpected. Ian has never been one for going anywhere much.

'Well, yeah – sounds good. Important.'

He seems different somehow. More open to things. He tells me he has been to visit Paul and Dorrie, just once, and that generally everything's fine.

There's a pause, and then he says, 'I love you, Jo. And I'm sorry.'

'I'm sorry too.'

I think we both know what we mean.

I lie in bed afterwards feeling warm and loved and hopeful.

Forty

The road we walk on into the factory site has dry, scrubby vegetation on each side. The two government officials lead us along it, at first seeming bored and indifferent. After all, these remains have been here so many years now, festering away. But as we move on and they see our interest, they become more animated and start pointing things out to us.

There are low office buildings mouldering away among the trees and scrub. And then we see the main plant, once a slick new edifice of shiny pipework, of tubes and valves and tanks roofed over but open at the sides. Now the corrugated-iron roof and everything else are brown with rust, some tanks so corroded that their bases have dropped off, spilling heaven knows what into the ground.

It's a haunting place, the structure wound round with creepers and leaves, small trees forcing their branches between what was once the bodywork of one of India's finest industrial hopes: a giant pesticide factory. Pesticides to keep crops alive, to increase yield and wealth. The creators assured everyone it would be 'inoffensive as a chocolate factory'.

But this place was no Cadbury's.

Three giant storage tanks, long and rounded with thick

spouts at one end and looking like large abandoned railway locomotives, lie in the shrubbery. The tanks once contained one of the most dangerously toxic and reactive chemicals in the industry, methyl isocyanate. One of its components is phosgene – used in the trenches in the First World War. And one of the factors which keeps it safe – not reacting, in other words – is that it needs to be cool, kept below a temperature of no higher than zero degrees Celsius. In Bhopal, even in winter the temperature never drops below fifteen degrees. And in summer . . .

By 1984, the plant was no longer operating. The Americans had realized it was not as profitable as they had hoped and wrote it off. The skilled engineers who had taken pride in it left one by one. Costs were cut at every turn – with no thought of the ultimate cost to the people living round the plant. Disregarding the huge quantity of lethal chemical still sitting in those tanks – something that would not be allowed in Western countries – in October, the refrigeration was turned off, thereby saving a few dollars a day.

We walk in silence, looking, imagining. I try to visualize it in its heyday, a modern vision of progress, pride and hope (and, of course, profit). Then began the downward slide, the cost-cutting, the fact that the safety systems were not maintained in working order. Eventually, on 2 December 1984, came the events of 'that night'.

Afterwards, Union Carbide put forward theories blaming Sikh terrorists for what happened. Following that, they attempted to blame the actions of a 'disgruntled employee'. Neither of these theories have ever been supported by evidence. The version of events from the technicians present on the site at the time was that they began a routine cleaning operation in the neglected plant with its clogged pipes. This resulted in water backing up into the tank of methyl isocyanate. Its reaction with the water resulted in a massive build-up of heat and pressure. Gas came hissing out of the pressure relief valve to form a deathly, heavy cloud which soon seeped its way into the houses nearby. One of the gases it broke down to under heat was hydrogen cyanide.

The area of the site is not all that big – maybe a kilometre square. Along the back wall, only metres from the plant, are still the slum dwellings. Close. So close.

As we go out, a different way from where we came in, Aasif shows us a figure standing at what was once the main entrance to the factory.

'This was built in 1986, by a Dutch lady,' he says. 'Her mother and father died in the gas chambers at Auschwitz.' A stone figure on a plinth, of an anguished woman with a baby in her arms, another child at her skirts, running from the gas. It is called *Mother and Child.*

It's a long time before either of us feels like saying anything.

As we go back to find Aasif's bike, he says, 'Is there anywhere else you would like to go?'

'Yes,' I say. We have agreed on this before. 'Just once more, we would like to go to Chingari.'

This afternoon there is a different set of children at Chingari. A group of deaf boys has come for treatment and they greet each other with great enthusiasm, laughing and jostling. A few parents are with children in the little sandy playground and Pat and I go to see them, playing with some of the kids again.

Twins of about six appear – two boys. They both hurry over to the little iron seats of the roundabout and jump on. They seem almost manically active and there is something about their faces. Some of the children are obviously profoundly handicapped. With others, you can't quite put your finger on it but you can see that something is not well with them.

'No speaking.' Their mother, a lively-looking woman of about thirty, dressed from head to foot in black, points to one. 'This one –' she indicates the other – 'go to school, but lot of problem.'

They are full of beans, somehow a little too much so, and keen to have attention. Their mother gives way to us as we play with them – takes a rest and goes to talk to another of the women.

And then I see a familiar face appear. The mother of the profoundly autistic boy, Sanjay. What is especially sad is that he does not seem able even to play. Once again, she leads him to the wall and they sit together, watching the other, more active children. Or at least, she is watching. It is hard to know what goes on in Sanjay's mind. Pat stays, turning the roundabout for the twins, but I go over to see Sanjay and his mother.

She smiles gently, recognizing me as I join her on the wall. We both sit with our bare feet in the sand of the playground. She has bright red leggings on today, a dark green shalwar dress and black cardigan.

'Hello, Sanjay,' I say to him. He eyes me, but there is no real reaction.

'No speech,' she tells me again, patiently. 'Autistic boy.'
'Yes,' I say. 'Very difficult.'

She gives a tilt of her head as if to say, *You don't know the half of it.* Which of course I don't.

'What is your name?' I ask her.

She touches her chest. 'Priyanka. You?'

'Jo.'

'Jo. OK.' She digests this as she pulls her cardigan closer round her. I'm comfortably warm in a T-shirt, but so far as everyone here seems to be concerned it's now winter and cold.

'You speak good English,' I say.

Again an incline of the head. 'I learn in school. I was going to the university, to be pharmacist. Then I got married. But now –' she nods at her son – 'he is my life. That is all.'

There is a quiet, long-accustomed anguish about her. Our eyes meet. There is nothing really to be done.

'D'you mind telling me what happened?' I ask. 'That night? I mean, maybe you don't want to talk about it . . .'

'It's OK.' She clasps her hands neatly in her lap. When she talks it is as if she is repeating a story she has told numerous times before. 'My husband's father was an engineer here in Bhopal.'

'At the Union Carbide plant?' I ask, startled.

'No. He was civil engineer,' she explains, talking with her hands as much as her voice. 'He was out of the city for a few days. That night he was coming back – by train. So his wife went to greet him at the railway station over here in Bhopal. She take with her their little ten-years-old son – my husband – and her two other children, boy, girl. When train came in, very late, already the gas was there. They tried to stop the train coming into the city but message did not get through. My husband's father died on the railway

327

platform, from the gas. Many people there, many crowds, so many people dying of the gas. His wife try to save her children. They run away. Balram, my husband, he say his mother took her woolly –' she fingers the edge of her cardigan to demonstrate – 'she take it off, tell him, "Cover your face." His brother died, and his mother, a few days later. Baby sister is living. The two children were left alone.'

I watch as she speaks, looking ahead of her. Her voice is flat.

'Where did they go?' It's so unbearable I can hardly take it in.

'Father's brother and wife took them.'

'And your husband – how is his health?'

'He has some lung problem – and his seeing. Sometimes very bad. I do not know if he will live long.'

She turns to me, rolls her eyes. She is friendly, tired, resigned. Then she looks at Sanjay and her face clouds.

'We are here now to help him – but one day we will both die. Then what?'

I can't answer this. There is no answer. We sit in silence for a moment.

'You – children?' she asks.

That question – one I would dread from anyone else, feels different coming from her.

That night, I think to myself. That night, something terrible must have happened inside the body of your husband, resulting in this wooden boy sitting beside you. And my 'That night' . . .

'One son,' I tell her. 'But he died. Two years ago. Someone killed him – with a car.'

She nods slowly. As we sit side by side, looking ahead, she takes my hand for a moment. Hers is small, the skin dry.

'Only one child? No more?'

I nod. I don't want to have to explain that Paul was adopted. What does it matter? He was my son – the son I brought up, loved, feel I failed in many ways. But still my son.

She strokes my hand for a moment before letting go.

That evening Pat and I go to a restaurant on the high ground overlooking the lake, when it is already sunset. We sit looking out at the boats bobbing on the darkening water, the pale blue arc of the sky fading to orange and rust.

We order beers and spiced vegetables and rice and the air cools so that we need jumpers on. From below we can hear the chatter of pleasure-seekers alongside the lake, the roar of motorbikes and every now and then the clop of hooves, the rowdy screech of a goose.

Pat's phone beeps and she reads a text.

'All well?' I say.

'Yes – he's fine. Been playing a lot of golf. He says he's missing me, though!' She twinkles at me.

Ian has sent me a few more texts and he seems all right. At the weekend he is going to see Cynthia down south.

'Are you glad you came?' I say.

Pat nods. She puts her fork down and sits back. 'D'you know, I've never even been to France.'

We both laugh.

'No, I know,' I say. 'Still, we'll do more sightseeing in Delhi when we get there.'

'But yes, I am glad I came.' She takes a mouthful of beer and holds the glass to her chest. I see the lights at the edge of the restaurant terrace, little bright dots reflected in her eyes. 'More than glad. I feel . . . as if everything has got bigger. In my life, I mean. But also . . . You know, when you hear about something bad – seeing it is another thing. It's wicked what's happened here. Completely wicked.'

I think of Priyanka, her gentle despair.

'It's as if these companies can just do what they like, get away with anything. As if they're not people any more – they're just these *things*. Sort of monsters with no faces.'

We sit quietly. The waiter comes and removes our plates. We order tea.

'D'you think Fred would ever come?' I say. Because a tiny, poppy-seed-sized idea is beginning to plant itself in my mind.

'I doubt it,' Pat laughs. 'You know how particular he is about everything, and about safety as well. Can you imagine him here – on Aasif's motorbike? I mean, seriously?'

'Oh, I don't know. He's interested in things, isn't he? He might love it.'

We start laughing and can't stop. It's a rinsing out of the tension, from the awfulness of what we have seen in the last few days. We laugh until we're hysterical. The waiter, bringing our tea, gives us a concerned look as if we might have become deranged in the few minutes between ordering tea and the prospect of drinking it.

'Thank you,' I say, trying to sound sober and sensible.

'What can we do?' Pat says, wiping her eyes with one of the little white paper napkins. 'What can anyone do about all this? I can't think of anything at the moment – except running.'

'Well, I suppose that's the least we can do,' I say. 'It doesn't seem like much though, does it?'

330

Forty-One
LION'S BREATH

We arrive into Heathrow's Terminal 5 that Sunday, to find Fred beaming at us in the arrivals hall. He sweeps Pat into his arms, looking relieved, bashful, somehow embarrassed to be the one waiting at home, the passive one, standing there as his wife strides up energetically, loaded with a rucksack almost like a teenage backpacker.

He and I give each other a brief hug as well.

'I told Ian I'd bring you both back safe,' he says. 'He asked should he come, but I said to him, "You get yourself a lie-in, son, you work hard all week."'

I smile, knowing that he and Ian would be hard-pushed to manage a conversation all the way from Birmingham to here and that it was better that Fred came on his own.

We make our way to the car park and England's chill, grey winter wraps itself round me. It feels as if we've been away for months.

'I brought a flask of coffee in case you needed it,' Fred says, clicking open the doors and lifting our rucksacks from the trolley and into the boot.

'You sit in the front,' I say to Pat and she gives me a grateful look. 'I can have a doze in the back.'

And in the warm comfort of their Hyundai saloon,

that's what I do, as we head smoothly west and north, head home, to the silky muttering of Fred's satnav.

Ian sees the car pull up and is at the door. He too looks shy and unsure. But as soon as we have said our goodbyes to Pat – *See you at yoga?* – Ian pushes the door closed behind us, props my rucksack up in the front room and turns to me.

'Well, home again,' I say, feeling shy myself.

He comes up to me looking emotional and we step into each other's arms.

'Ooh –' I hold him tightly – 'it's so good to be here.' And it is, although my head has not quite arrived yet. I am still full of jangled energy from a flight and not enough sleep and being somewhere else for ten days. And I have so many things to tell him – but not now, not yet.

'Let's have a cuppa,' I say. 'Tell me what you've been up to.'

We sit at the table in the kitchen and chat for a bit. He says things are going well in the business. He went to see Cynth and she seems keen to get along these days.

'Yes, I thought at the funeral she was getting over herself a bit,' I say. 'And now your mom's not here she's got to get in touch herself instead of leaving it to her to tell all the news.'

'Yeah.' Ian thinks about it. He smiles suddenly. There is something about him – as if something, slightly, has loosened inside him. 'It was all right. Surprised me a bit. I s'pose I'd set myself up for her being all – you know. And the lads are all right too – played a bit of football with them and – yeah. It was good, really.'

I reach over and put my hand on top of his, give it a squeeze.

'Did you go . . . you know, again?'

Ian looks down a moment. 'Yeah. Course. Took some flowers – for both of them. They haven't finished Mom's stone yet, but I made sure it was all tidy and everything.'

Our eyes meet for a moment, hovering above our shared well of grief, and then we look away.

And I tell him things, about the flight, the hotel, the sightseeing we did in Delhi – the Red Fort and Government House, all the Lutyens stuff along Rajpath, the old city, classic Delhi sights.

Somehow, I can't begin on Bhopal, not in any detail. It feels too much, too emotional. I tell him a few basics about what we did, about Aasif and riding on the motorbikes, which makes him laugh.

'I'll tell you about it later properly,' I say, finishing my tea. 'And you can see my photos. You'd love it there, you really would. I'd better go and have a shower now, though.'

Ian gets up and takes my hand, pulling me to my feet. He looks down into my eyes and I see my Ian, the Ian who looks at me, full on. He pulls me close.

'I think I'll come up with you,' he says, leaning to kiss me.

I didn't mean to say any of this – not yet. I planned to tell him all about things, let him get used to the idea, before saying anything.

But by the time we have tumbled on to our bed and made love – slowly, taking care, both there with each other, really there – and are lying together in the cosy bedroom with the side light on, I feel as if we are more together, more *us* than we have been for a long time. Something in the way of love and trust is knitting itself back together like a cobweb protecting a wound. And lying holding Ian, his arms round me, it all just comes spilling out.

I tell him about the city, the mosques and the huge lakes, the mayhem, the workshops with people welding right by the pavement. And about the clinics, Chingari especially. I feel him listening attentively, as if he really wants to see into where I've been.

'Did you see that boy?' he asks. 'The boy in the picture?'

'No!' I laugh. 'I mean, there are so many people. But I did meet a boy called Sanjay . . .' I tell him about Sanjay and Priyanka, about what happened to her husband's family.

'Bloody hell,' Ian says. The vision of hell that was that night in Bhopal is truly hard to take in if you were not there.

I'm on a roll now. I tell him about the Sambhavna clinic and all they do. And about something that happened while we were there that I have not even told Pat about.

While we were having our tour of the clinic, Pat asked Aasif if she could go to the bathroom. While he showed her where to go, I waited in a corridor, outside some offices, where people were moving back and forth to treatment rooms. While I was standing there, a tall man came out of one of the offices, in jeans and a shirt. He wore black-rimmed glasses and a red-and-white turban wrapped casually round his head. He looked about my own age.

'Hi.' He seemed surprised to see me there. He had a kindly expression. 'Can I help you?'

'Oh, no, it's OK, thank you.' I explained that I was waiting for Aasif.

He asked me the usual basic questions, where was I from, and I told him England, that my friend and I had heard about the clinics because we had run for the Bhopal Medical Appeal.

'Ah,' he said. 'I see – our loyal supporters.'

And because I could tell he was something to do with the place, that he worked here in other words and did not seem to be a patient, out of my mouth came the words, 'Am I right in thinking that you have volunteers who come to work here?'

'Yes,' he said. 'There are quarters for the volunteers upstairs. You can get information about it from our website. Why – are you interested?'

I realized I must be, because why else would I have asked?

'I'm not really sure I have anything much to offer,' I said, feeling pretty silly.

He put his head on one side. 'Everyone has skills. If you are interested, there is always something you can do.'

Just then I saw Pat and Aasif coming back along the corridor. Pat looked questioningly at me, but Aasif clearly knew the man I was talking to and just wandered up. Pat said hello and off we went, the man saying, 'Don't forget to look at the website!' to me as he turned back to his office.

'So,' Aasif said as we walked on, 'you met Sathyu.'

I looked at him.

'He runs the clinic. He was very influential in getting it set up.' He draws us close to the wall and stops. 'Let me tell you about Sathyu Sarangi.'

By the time he has finished I have heard the story of a young man who, in 1984, was studying engineering in another part of India. When he heard the news of the catastrophic gas leak in Bhopal, he travelled to the city thinking to stay a few days and help. Amid the chaos and great suffering, he and others carried people to hospital and helped bury the dead.

'In fact,' Aasif says, 'he has been here ever since – given his life to this place. He has fought many battles.'

'He just seemed very kind,' I say to Ian, 'and brave. I read about him afterwards. He's been to the US, trying to get justice for the gas-affected people, and he's been beaten up by the American police, the Indian police – the lot.'

'Why would the Indian police beat him up?' Ian says, bewildered.

'Good question. You'd think they might be on the side of their own people, but I suppose he was challenging the government or the state or something. There's not been much sympathy officially in India either. When they built the first little clinic to try and help the gas-affected people, the police had it torn down.'

'That's mad.'

'I know. It really is. But, Ian . . .' I push myself up on my elbow. 'I just . . . Look, I'm just going to say this. Why don't we volunteer? The two of us – we could go over together.'

'What?' He looks at me as if I'm insane. 'What're you on about? We can't do that.'

'We could – we'd be able to sort something out. He said there are all sorts of ways we could help – you can do all sorts of practical things. We could work on the garden if nothing else, they always need that!'

But Ian's pushing back the bedclothes, getting up.

'For God's sake, Jo – live in the real world. It's all very well you taking off there for a week or two, but that's not something you can just do. I've got a business to run. Not go mucking about like that.'

Ian gets up huffily and I lie back, cursing myself. Why did I just blurt it all out like that?

He disappears into the bathroom and locks the door. Conversation over. Apparently.

Forty-Two

All around me in the cemetery is the sound of rain steadily falling. Everything is green, dripping, the grey stones gleaming in the wet. I'm layered up in jeans, boots, my coat with the collar up, a scarf and gloves. The cold is a shock.

Carrying my two bunches of roses, I go to Paul's grave first and stand, hearing the tippling of drops on my red-and-white striped umbrella, which creates a tent-like glow around me. There's no way I can sit on the ground beside him now, as if I'm reading him a bedtime story – it's far too wet. The summer is gone and the weeds have died back. There are half-withered pink carnations in a jar which Ian must have brought. I bend, balancing the umbrella handle across my shoulder, and manage to replace the dead flowers with the fresh crimson roses. I straighten up again, feeling helpless to do anything else, as I have felt so many times before.

The place rushes in on me again. The last ten days are the longest time I have ever been away from it. A terrible guilt washes through me. Did he miss me? Did he feel abandoned? And I know this is mad because he's dead, he's not here. Yet I feel it, overwhelmingly, all the same.

I close my eyes for a moment and the image comes to

me of Priyanka, sitting quietly on the playground wall with her dead-in-life son. For a second I imagine Sanjay as he might have been: a sweet, handsome little boy running, playing … Another picture flashes in – that messed-up lad Lee Parry, in his prison cell; a lad whose upbringing left him like a booby-trap waiting to be sprung. My heart hurts and I press my hand to it, trying to ease the ache and the thought of them, the thought of all of it.

'Hello, love,' I say softly. 'I'm back. I brought you some flowers.'

Tears run down my cheeks. As if Paul would ever really have wanted flowers. But what else can you bring to someone who is not here except something that blooms and dies alongside them?

'I've been away – in India. I met a lot of children there. What's happened to them is a terrible, terrible thing. It would've upset you.' Would *have*. Past tense. Before, I would always have said *would upset you*. Present, not gone. This makes me cry more – the beginnings of my acceptance, which also feel like another betrayal of him.

I tell him a few things about our trip, then lean over and pat the gravestone.

'I'll see you soon, love. I love you. Bye-bye for now, sweetheart.'

I carry the other roses, white ones, over to the Stefanis' grave. Still the stone has not been taken away to add Dorrie's name but the little wooden plaque is there. 'Doreen Stefani, 1929–2015'.

'Hello, Dorrie.' For a moment I feel foolishly awkward, as if, because it is their joint grave, Tom Stefani must be listening in on my conversation as well. I don't even believe in the afterlife, not really – but when someone dies it brings the dead close as if they are all there watching. I tell myself not to be so ridiculous. At least she's with Tom now – maybe that's where she really wants to be.

'We're back from Bhopal. I wish I could tell you all about it. Well, I can here, obviously, but I'd've loved you to hear even though it's upsetting. I'm not really sure Ian's OK with things.' Instead of describing our visit I find myself telling her what happened last night.

'It was really stupid of me. I should never've said anything. But then, it was a pretty daft idea anyway, even thinking about it. I knew he wouldn't want to and why should he? And it was selfish of me, I s'pose. He's gone through all his life with no dad and now Paul's gone. And there's me just sitting around at home now – I really need to help him out, get some sort of job. I might go and ask at Sainsbury's, just for something on the tills or whatever to tide me over.'

The sky seems to be lightening and I realize the rain has almost stopped. I look across the cemetery, loving the way it's like a piece of timeless space amid the distant noise of the city.

'I still haven't told Ian yet – about his dad. About you, Tom, and what happened to you.' I feel bashful suddenly, talking to this strange man. 'It was a really bad thing that happened, Mr . . . Tom. And I do think Ian should know the truth. I'll get to it, I promise. At the right moment.'

The sun comes out, brightness breaking over everything, lightening all the colours. And I say goodbye and walk back out from the sparkling wet cemetery, into the everydayness of things.

There are hugs all round when I get to yoga the next day. Pat and I are greeted as if we've been away for months. But it's not until we're at Sheila's on Thursday that we all have more time to talk.

The six of us are there as usual: Sheila, Kim, Sunita, Hayley, Pat and me. Herbert lies snoring by the fire as usual. Maggie the cat sits nearby, watching us all with a green, unnerving gaze. Sheila fills the teapot repeatedly and we are there longer than usual, catching up. Hayley is loving her course at the uni and says she can probably make most Thursdays as long as she's not having a work crisis. She seems to be very organized. I don't ask if she's quit her night work yet – that's her business, bless her.

We tell them everything we can think of. They all shake their heads a lot in the face of some of the facts.

'Government is no good,' Sunita says.

'What – the Indian government?' Pat asks.

'Government, state government – all!' She makes a sweeping gesture, her face puckering in disgust. 'All corruption and taking bribes. And these big American companies – no one is anything to them except big profits. All they can see is dollar sign.'

'Aren't they all supposed to be terribly religious?' Hayley says.

'Huh!' Sunita shifts in her seat, looking disgruntled. 'Religion of money.'

'You know,' Kim says, 'my kids were really impressed with you doing the run. They said we should all do it next time.'

342

'All three of you?' I say.

Kim nods. 'They'll be fine – they're pretty fit already.'

'Good. Let's do it,' Sunita says. 'I miss it. I need to get going.'

Pat and I look at each other gladly. 'OK.' We both grin. 'Let's do it. D'you want to start meeting regularly again?'

'You're all mad,' Sheila decrees once more. But I realize that she's still feeling a bit left out.

'You know,' I say to her, 'you really don't have to do this thing fast. You could basically walk round if you got going near the beginning. Some people look really unfit – and there's others in all sorts of costumes. I don't know how they don't pass out.'

'Oh, don't be daft.' Sheila waves a hand at us, but I sense she is being drawn in.

'Yes,' Pat says. 'Go on, Sheila. Everyone at their own pace. It's *why* we're doing it that matters.'

'You could come out to the park and practise with us,' Kim says. 'Us lot'll have to do it later in the day if the kids are at school. Come on – be brave. Lion's Breath!'

Sheila picks up the plate of flapjacks and passes it round.

'I might just think about it,' she says. 'Though I must be off my head.'

Forty-Three

Ian and I have been moving carefully round each other all week. Both of us avoid any difficult subjects. He's been quiet, as if he's dwelling on certain things, but not in an angry way. And I'm not angry with him either. I threw something into the ring at the wrong time, when he's already not quite right in himself. Neither of us is – and it was probably a mad idea anyway.

So we pretty much get back to what normal seems to be these days. He works a lot, I keep house, go to yoga, see Pat and the others.

'I went into Sainsbury's today to ask about jobs,' I say to Ian on Thursday night, as we're having tea.

'Sainsbury's?' He gives me a puzzled look. 'You do know you don't *have* to work, don't you? Not if you don't want. I'm earning enough.'

He's still really old-fashioned like that, Ian is. Some men really resent having to earn all the money but I think Ian quite likes it. It makes him feel he's doing what a bloke is supposed to do.

'No, I know. But I feel I want to get out and do something. Going back to teaching would be too much – I know I just couldn't hack it at the moment. But it'd be something, wouldn't it. Maybe towards a holiday or something?'

We both know I'm talking nonsense really. We'd saved up quite a bit in our 'holiday of a lifetime' fund to take Paul, and my trip to India certainly didn't use all of it.

'We could go away in the spring. Somewhere like Italy – look for your roots!'

Ian laughs. 'Yeah. Maybe.'

Things feel easier. He's pleased I'm home and I'm pleased too. Why rock the boat?

'Carl all right?' I ask, giving him the last portion of chicken.

'Yeah.' He polishes off what's on his plate. 'Got to hand it to him. He's an opinionated so-and-so but he does a good job.'

I look at him, full on, and ask carefully, 'You OK, Ian? You know – with the counsellor and everything?'

'Yeah. I think so.' He seems embarrassed, but somehow a bit looser in himself. 'Takes a while, I s'pose.'

'Is he good, d'you think?'

'Well, I've nothing to compare him with but he seems it, yeah. Can't complain.'

I lean over and take his hand. 'D'you want to talk about any of it? I mean . . . I've been thinking a lot about you – you know, about losing your dad, and Paul. It's a lot to cope with.'

His face takes on a sad, vulnerable look and he squeezes my hand. Looking down at the table, he says, 'Yeah, I'm starting to realize that. I'm just not . . .' He shrugs and looks up at me, seeming embarrassed. I know this is well out of Ian's comfort zone. 'I'm just pretty rubbish at talking about things.'

'Well, if you want to?' I keep my eyes fixed on his, not wanting to close things down if he needs to talk. I feel very tender towards him because I know how difficult he finds things like this.

'Yeah.' He releases my hand then. 'I will. I mean, when I can. It's good to go into things. I'm beginning to realize that now.'

I stack the plates, thinking that while he's seeing a counsellor, while there's some backup for him, I'd better tell him.

I wait until the weekend, plan a nice Saturday night in. It's a dark, overcast sort of day and I stay in while Ian is still working and put a pot of meat sauce on to simmer for hours, the smells of wine and oregano filtering through the house. Later I make a cheese sauce and assemble lasagne, his favourite. I toss a salad, open a bottle of Chianti and lay the table nicely, with a rose in a glass. And having done my best to be mamma at home, I prepare myself to talk to him and tell him, as gently and lovingly as I can, about the father he hardly knew.

He comes in at five and sniffs the air.

'Something smells tasty!'

There's a kind of energy about him as he comes through the door today. Usually after work he is tired and not conversational until he has eaten, and not always then. But today he seems lively, sort of nervous. I feel nervous myself, but I can't see why he would.

'Did you have a Mars bar on the way home or something?' I tease, going to kiss him.

'Ah – found out!' He grins. He really seems . . . What? Happy? Excited about something. It's hard to tell. 'Yeah, I did. But I can still eat.'

'It's not ready yet anyway,' I say, heading back to the

kitchen. 'It's in the oven – half an hour at least. D'you want a cup of tea to take up?'

'Hey – this is fantastic!' he says, coming down later after getting showered and changed.

I've put a cloth on the table and lit a candle. The red peppers and tomatoes gleam on a bed of lettuce and rocket.

'What's brought this on?'

'Can't I cook a nice meal for my beloved, hard-working husband?' I say, teasing. Opening the oven, I see the lasagne has just reached golden, bubbling, cheese-topped perfection. Ian groans with pleasure when I bring it to the table.

'Well, I'm not complaining.'

'Pour us some wine, will you?' I say, fetching the dressing for the salad.

And so we sit and eat. It's not often I hand it to myself with cooking, but this lasagne is flipping delicious.

'Oh, my,' Ian says, taking a mouthful and closing his eyes. 'I see God.'

I watch him tenderly. I have no intention of dumping the tragic facts he needs to know into the middle of the meal. I want to be able to sit next to him, while he is feeling loved, and tell him gently.

But after a few mouthfuls he puts his fork down.

'This is fantastic. Thanks, love.' He looks down, and again I can see he is nervous. 'And I'm sorry.'

'What for?' I'm really not sure what this is about.

'I just – I want to say something to you. I've been thinking about it all week . . .'

God, I think, what now?

'I'm sorry – for what I said the other night. For being so negative. I was . . . Well, I behaved like a bit of a dick and I didn't mean to.'

'You mean about us volunteering? Oh, it's OK.' I pick up my glass and take a warm, red sip. 'Not one of my more realistic ideas, I know. Don't worry about it.'

'No, but I know it matters to you. All you've been doing, training and that. Going down to London – and I never even managed to get there . . .'

'That was your mom, though.'

'Yeah, it was. I really was going to come . . . I mean, when you first said it, I just thought – well, it seemed something just right off the screen for me. Do people even do that sort of thing? And me – I'm doing my thing, the business and all that. And it's going well, but sometimes I think, that's all I've ever done and when you're running your own place it's like you can't do anything else. It feels like it'll just go on that way for ever, 'cause you're in charge of it. And sometimes, if I'm truthful, that makes me feel bloody depressed.'

He pauses to take a sip of wine. 'Umm – lovely.'

'So what're you saying?' This is all a bit confusing.

Ian sits for a minute, thinking, looking down at his plate as if he doesn't want to say anything he'll regret.

'I think I'm saying . . .' He hesitates as if he's scared to commit to what he's going to say. Then he looks up at me. 'What you said made me think. The way I've been feeling lately – I can't just go on like this. It's not as if we need a lot of money, is it? Not now it's just . . .' Just the two of us. He doesn't need to go on. He looks up at me. 'We don't even have a mortgage any more.'

He drains his glass and reaches for the bottle.

'It's not that I hate work. I like it, in a way. But lately – I dunno. It's like, I look at my life, look at the years ahead and think, Is this it? Is this all I'm ever going to do from now until the grave? And if I'm honest it doesn't seem like much. I feel as if I need to get out and I don't know where to begin, really.'

'But what would you like to do?' I ask cautiously. I'm really trying not to impose anything on him. He's been a good worker, a good dad, never asked for much. He needs room to blossom like anyone else.

'I dunno. I s'pose I've never given it much thought. I've never been adventurous like you. It's just – what you were talking about . . .' He looks bashful now, not sure how to say it. 'Well, it's something important, isn't it?'

I frown. 'What about the business though?'

Ian hesitates. 'Well, the one over Moseley's doing all right. And I reckon Carl could do everything that needs doing down here – for a bit. It's not as if it's for ever, is it?'

And suddenly we are talking, animated, excited. It's as if a door has sprung open, offering possibilities that I wouldn't ever have expected from Ian. So much so that I can hardly believe it.

And I start to try and tell him more of what it has meant to me. I tell him how I feel about what happened in Bhopal, the anger and horror. The way big companies can lie and damage and get away with it again and again.

Ian listens closely. 'But do they really need us to come?' he says after a while.

'Us?' I find myself laughing. 'No, of course not. Not us specifically, anyway. But they do like people to come, to see them and understand what happened. After all the crap they've had poured over them for thirty-plus years

350

it must be nice to think that anyone cares. But I know it helped me. We can help a bit – we won't make any real difference to anything, but maybe we can all help each other.'

'Yeah.' He gives a tired nod. After a moment he looks up and says, 'Maybe. That'd be nice.'

Later, we move through to the living room with a cup of coffee. It feels as if things are warm and close after talking for so long across the table. So why not now? I put both our mugs down on the table and sit beside him on the sofa.

'Look, love.' I turn myself sideways so I can face him. 'There's never going to be a good time to do this, but there's something I need to tell you. That your mom wanted me to tell you – when I could.'

When he looks back at me with those dark eyes, he does not seem all that surprised. As if there has been something he was waiting for.

And gently, simply, I tell him what happened, about the horrific accident, the red-hot length of steel that changed his father into a damaged, traumatized man.

'I know it's a terrible thing – that your dad should take his own life and leave you behind like that,' I finish. 'But your mom said he would never, ever have done that if his brain had not been injured. He wasn't the man she knew. What happened took her Tom away from her – and from you – even before he decided to end it.'

Ian sits for a while, digesting this, resting his elbows on his thighs, hands clasped. After a time, he heaves a big, emotional sigh and sits up, rubbing his head with both hands as if this will help the information sink in.

'I always knew there was something,' he says finally. 'I mean, I wouldn't have guessed that, but there was something about the way she talked about him – or didn't talk – about his death for all that time. It was like a kind of blank and I don't even know how I picked up that he was supposed to have had a heart attack. I don't think she ever actually said that. It was just somehow the way it was.'

He slumps, puts his hand over his face and breaks down for a moment. And then the wave passes and he straightens up again.

'Poor Mom. God.'

'She was pregnant with Cynthia.'

'And she never said – all this time.' More tears run down his face.

'She was ashamed, I think. Different times.'

'Did anyone do anything?' He looks at me. 'Did they put it right? Was there – I mean, did she get any help or anything?'

'No. I don't think it occurred to her to ask. It was just like, that's how it was in those days, I think. Maybe if she'd been more confident, or had some help . . . I don't know. That place he was working for got away with murder – that was what killed him really.'

Ian rubs his eyes with the heels of his hands. 'It'll be a while before I can take all this in.'

'Sorry.' I put my arms round him. 'Another thing.'

'Yeah. But all the same – I'm glad I know.'

He rests his head on my shoulder and we sit, rocking gently back and forth.

Forty-Four
IF I CAN DO IT, ANYONE CAN!

January 2016

A month of arrangements: emails to make sure that our coming to volunteer at Sambhavna is welcome. They seem keen to have Ian's technical know-how. For me there will be work with the children, and perhaps in the garden. I am happy to help in any way I can. And there are tickets to sort out, visas, jabs for Ian.

The others have started running again minus Hayley, who is immersed in her classes at the uni. Sunita is now fully in charge. And for the time being, I am running with them. It seems a good idea to be as fit as possible to go to India.

'Does this mean you'll miss the London 10K?' Sunita says, slightly huffily, one morning as we jog along.

'I don't know. It depends how long we stay,' I tell her.

'July? That's months away. You'll be back before then. You won't be able to stand it there – it will be hot as hell.'

This may be true, but I just don't know. We don't have a return date at present.

As well as organizing us, Sunita has now set up another women's running club in the Hollywood–Wythall area. Its logo, 'If I Can Do It, Anyone Can!' is embroidered across the brow of her yellow baseball cap. She is organizing ladies into groups of abilities, making rotas. She has had club T-shirts designed – also bright yellow, for visibility, she says. Now and then I come across small clusters of them staggering along the pavements, their expressions varying from valiantly cheerful to desperate.

'All we women need to make the best use of our bodies!' she instructs them. She's obviously having the time of her life.

'If not this year,' I tell her, 'definitely next, OK?'

Amid the excitement, the feeling that Ian and I are really doing something together at last, inside I feel agonizingly torn. We are going away for some months, probably – and leaving Paul. My feelings, my heart, are stuck to that sweet, silent rectangle of ground in the cemetery. Ten days was one thing, with Ian still here – but this time we don't even know when we are coming back.

I know both of us feel it. It's as if something in me is being stretched away but without being released, as if I am being pulled back constantly. I feel guilty and anything but free.

'I know it's silly in a way,' I confide in Pat. She's round at ours, both of us drinking coffee at the table.

'It's not silly,' she says gently. 'It's just how it is. All that time I didn't know where they had buried Becky, it was as if . . . I don't know. As if I just couldn't settle. It was a bit like having a part of yourself lost and floating about somewhere and I'd let her down by not taking care of her.'

Her eyes fill and, undramatically, she wipes them.

'Look, I can go,' she says, looking across at me. 'I'll look after him for you. Becky's in there too – she was buried with someone else who died that week. We have a little stone for her now. I'll go as often as I can, OK?'

'Oh, Pat.' Now I'm the one filling up. 'That would be so good, knowing you're doing that. There's no one else I can ask really. My mom and dad – well, they wouldn't. And they live quite a way away. And would you mind looking in on my mother-in-law now and again?'

'Course I will,' she says. 'I might even persuade Fred to come and see his mom as well.'

'Has he recovered from you being away?' I ask, grinning.

'He's fine,' she says, in her calm way which suggests that however daft Fred can be he's her man and he'll always sort himself out in the end. 'He's hell bent on buying a campervan and taking off to France – maybe even Spain.' She smiles. 'So what's not to like?'

And so we part, for the time being, with our new friends. They've come to mean a lot to me over the months, these women, and I feel a tug of sorrow at going. But we'll be back. And I'm sure I'll be running around the paths of Hollywood again, with our Hollywood-Bollywood songs and Sunita bossing us all about.

The night before we leave, while Ian and I are packing, I go to the cupboard under the stairs and drag out the box of Paul's things. Taking out from it one precious object, I carry it upstairs, this token of our boy, holding it behind my back.

Ian is bent over a new rucksack, stuffing clothes into it. He looks up, hearing me come to the door.

'Look who's coming with us.' I bring Paul's favourite-ever toy out from behind my back: Rex, the cowardly dinosaur. 'Ta-dah!'

Ian stares at the green plastic Tyrannosaurus rex with

its daft expression. *Toy Story*. Our eyes meet and his face breaks into a sad, complicated smile.

The night before we are due to leave, I slip out to the nearest letterbox to post a card. Standing by the box, I read through it again.

Dear Ange,
  Ian and I are off on some travels for a little while. We're in need of some healing. But I miss you. When we get back, let's get together, eh, chicky?

Love,
Jo xx

WRITING *MOTHER AND CHILD*

The Boy

I was not at the dentist's when I saw that picture of the boy. I have a book of pictures by a professional photographer, Alex Masi, who spent time in Bhopal photographing families affected by the toxic legacy left to their city, in particular by the contaminated water. The book is called *Bhopal: the Second Disaster* and the boy, whose sad face sparked the writing of this story, appears on the cover. You can see the photograph on my website: www.anniemurray.co.uk.

Incidents and Accidents

A number of times over the years while I have been writing about Birmingham's history, I have come across a story that goes something like this: 'My father worked at so-and-so. He was a—[insert skilled or semi-skilled manufacturing job]. But then something happened.' An accident causing burns from molten ferrous or non-ferrous metals, an item of clothing or hair being caught in machinery, a fall from a great height while maintaining equipment . . . If things were really bad, the man's working life was over. 'He lived with constant pain. He was no longer the man he'd been before. He could no longer work to feed his family.'

Sometimes this became so unbearable, or the damage was so great, that the father of the family had seen no other way out than to end it all.

Not to mention the countless stories of working with substances either in factories or in the house, having taken 'outwork' to do at home, that affected eyes, made you cough or perhaps had longer-term effects not obvious at the time.

I based the story of Tom Stefani on a reported incident that took place almost thirty years later than it happens to Tom in the story. In 1988, a man called Tara Singh was tending to a machine in a metal-rolling mill in the Black Country when a red-hot steel billet broke loose. Tara Singh died there and then in the factory. This 'accident' was written up in a report published in 1994 by the West Midlands Health and Safety Advice Centre. The report is titled *The Perfect Crime? How companies get away with manslaughter in the workplace.*

Though the last major Health and Safety at Work Act was passed in 1974, this by no means changed everything overnight. Of course, there had been a number of Factory Acts before that as trades unions drove the campaign to safeguard industrial and other workers. And over time, since the 1974 Act, there has been an estimated 85 per cent reduction in workplace deaths (though that figure does not include public services such as the police). Those figures speak for themselves.

But industry is, and has always been, a dangerous business, as Tara Singh's story shows. In that particular case, there had been clear, previous near misses and apparently unheeded warnings that something was wrong in that factory. There was also, by 1988, an expectation enshrined in the law of 1974, that employers must ensure, so far as possible, the safety of everyone in their employ.

There are human errors, unseen flaws, mistakes. And then there is just plain negligence.

What does it mean for something to be an 'accident'? I looked up some definitions.

Accident: An unfortunate incident that happens unexpectedly and unintentionally, typically resulting in damage or injury.   *Oxford Living Dictionary*

An accident waiting to happen: A very dangerous situation in which an accident is very likely.
Cambridge Dictionary

Negligence: Failure to give enough care or attention to something or someone that you are responsible for.   *Cambridge Dictionary*

Manslaughter (UK), Culpable homicide (US): The crime of killing a human being without malice aforethought, or in circumstances not amounting to murder.   *Oxford Living Dictionary*

In Britain, in 2007, the Corporate Manslaughter and Corporate Homicide Act was passed – a landmark Act. For the first time, companies and organizations can now be found guilty of corporate manslaughter as a result of

361

management failures resulting in a gross breach of a duty of care.

So where does Bhopal fit into all this?

It is not too hard to find a definition from this list. What is so difficult to understand about Bhopal is not that 'accidents happen'. They do at times, even with the best of safeguards. What is harder to get your head around is the lack of safeguards right from the beginning and especially in the time immediately preceding the leak of gas, when the skilled engineers who had once taken more pride in the plant had all left and only a reduced and less skilled workforce remained.

This appears to us like complete contempt for other human beings when the only bottom line is shareholder profit and, as a consequence of this, like the behaviour of a company that would apparently do anything at all to protect itself, with dire consequences for some of the poorest on the planet.

I'm sure there are definitions for this as well.

Mother and Child

In writing this story I wanted above all to portray the empathy between women and children everywhere, even if we do not share the same land or language. For all the elements of the story, there seemed no better title to choose than the simple one, *Mother and Child*.

It was only later that I found out about the *Mother and Child* statue, which stands at the gates of the old Union Carbide factory. In 1986, a Dutch sculptor called Ruth Waterman-Kupferschmidt created a statue of a woman with her children trying to escape the gas, as a memorial to the night of 2–3 December 1984 in Bhopal.

Ruth Waterman clearly identified with the women and children of Bhopal who had suffered this horrific experience. Ruth's own parents were gassed at Auschwitz, a system of murder that had nothing accidental about it whatsoever, but which gave her a strong feeling of connection to what happened in Bhopal.

You can see a picture of the statue on my website: www.anniemurray.co.uk.

Visiting Bhopal

In early 2018, I went to Bhopal with my husband, Martin, in order to get a real feel for a place I have been reading about for many years. Some of what we experienced appears in the story. We met some unforgettable people, including Rashida Bi and Champa Devi Shukla, who won the International Goldman Environmental Prize in 2004 and devoted all the prize money to setting up Chingari, the clinic for women and children. A few of their stories and more photographs can be found on my website.

35 YEARS OF BHOPAL

The leak at the Union Carbide pesticide plant in Bhopal happened on the night of 2–3 December 1984. This factory, the consequence of an expanding market during India's 'Green Revolution', was built to produce a pesticide called Sevin, to tackle pests and thereby try to increase harvests.

What happened 'that night' in 1984 caused the deaths of thousands of people and the ongoing suffering of thousands more. For survivors affected in Bhopal, 'that night' has never ended. In addition, the poisoning of the local water supply has continued for more than thirty-five years, adding to the sickness, the suffering and the sense of injustice.

So, as this shameful thirty-fifth anniversary comes round, here are thirty-five steps through the history of this disaster.

....

We decided to remove this section before publication. Even now, matters involving Bhopal are unfortunately live and unresolved. The matter is still so sensitive that we came to the conclusion that the contents – however thoroughly fact-checked – might lay us open to the possibility of legal proceedings, something that would not serve any useful purpose either to us or the people of Bhopal.

....

Never before except in Hitler's gas chambers have so many people died at one time by exposure to industrial chemicals.

'Never before', wrote the Bhopal Group for Information and Action, in 1990, 'have so many victimized people struggled for so many years for justice, accountability and the right to a dignified, disease-free life.'

That was written twenty-nine years ago. They are still waiting.

FLAMES NOT FLOWERS

'We are not expendable. We are not flowers offered at the altar of profit and power. We are dancing flames committed to conquering darkness and to challenging those who threaten the planet and the magic and mystery of life.'

Rashida Bi, gas survivor, on receiving the prestigious 2004 International Goldman Environmental Prize, the money from which was used to set up the Chingari Clinic, for gas- and water-affected children.

When I visited Bhopal, I was privileged to meet Rashida Bi and Champa Devi Shukla. Both lost a number of members of their families on the night of the gas leak. Rashida is from a humble background, but has become an inspiration to many women – including me. She is a few years older than I am and does not speak English, so we spoke, briefly, through the interpreter.

'So – you walked all that way, to Delhi?' I asked her. She had taken the lead in all this. And after all, it's 500 miles to Delhi from Bhopal.

Rashida's kindly face turned to me with a wry expression.

'Yes,' she said. 'But I was thirty years younger then.'

The following is an account of their journey, as published in an article in the *Bhopal Marathon*, a publication of the Bhopal Medical Appeal. The stories were related to Colin Toogood and Syed Tabish Ali.

THE WOMEN WHO WALKED: 1989

'We'll go to see the PM.'

It was Rashida's idea, this much everyone agrees. When she said this, all of us were happy. Yes, of course. The Prime Minister. He'll listen to us. It was our only way to be heard.

'Where's the Prime Minister?'

'He has a so-big house in Delhi.'

'Where is Delhi?'

Nobody knew for sure, but a couple of people reckoned it was quite a way off.

'How will we get there?'

Rashida and Champa Devi said, 'We have no transport, so we will have to walk. It will show we're serious. We'll all go together.'

'When?'

'As soon as possible.'

'Tomorrow then.'

We agreed to meet early next morning and set out. We'd bring a bit of food and, if anyone had any, a little money might come in handy.

After the angels

When the angel of death opened its wings over our city, bodies were piled in heaps in the streets and our old lives were gone.

Most of us worked hard at heavy manual jobs. Now we weren't able to do that work any longer. We were ill, breathless, coughing all the time. Our children were ill. We had no money for medicines or food.

What do you do when there's no food? You bind a cloth tightly round your middle to fool your stomach. If your children cry with hunger you fill their tummies with water. But how long can you live like that?

A promise of work

Then the state government got a large amount of money from Delhi to create jobs for gas-affected people.

It decided to train some women to work in one of its printing presses. About 100 of us took up the offer. We trained for four months on a stipend of Rs 150 a month (about £2), not enough to make ends meet. The bosses told us that when qualified we'd earn a proper salary, but after the training they said there were no jobs. There had never been any. We might as well have trained to be astronauts.

That was when Rashida and Champa Devi spoke up. What was the point of training us, they asked, if there was no work. The bosses said we should be grateful to be trained at all. If we wanted to work we should set up our own printing press.

So we made a petition and took it round to the Chief Minister's office. After some time came a reply that we would be employed in the State Industrial Corporation. We should just show up, work would be given.

We were thrilled. On the appointed day, we went to the gates of the factory and waited. Come back tomorrow, they said. Next day it was the same story. After a month we had had two days' work and earned each Rs 6–12 (8p–12p).

Did no one explain to you, they said, that you are piece workers, here on sufferance? You have no right to demand anything.

We get angry and wise . . .

Well, we'd had enough of excuses and of being pushed around and lied to. We warned the civil servants and bosses, look, day after day we waited outside your gates, you people shut your eyes and ears. You have hearts of stone. So be it. We'll take direct action and don't say we didn't warn you.

The officials relented and began giving us work. For the next two and a half years we earned Rs 10–12 a day – about 12p.

. . . and angrier and wiser

Around this time, someone found out about a thing called the Factories Act and Minimum Wages Act.

It turned out that we had not been paid a proper rate, plus during that period we were underpaid, the press made a profit of 400,000 rupees.

We went to the bosses and asked for our rights: minimum wages and regular employment. We asked to be treated according to the law.

371

The bosses were shocked, they said, disturbed by our ingratitude, but they would be generous, would try to find us a bit more work and offer a small increase in wages.

So we told them what they could do with such generosity.

We learn politics

We did not know how to protest, but we had heard of sit-ins, so we went to the state assembly and sat and slept there for several days.

This had no effect.

People gave us new ideas and we tried rallies, roadblocks and even a procession at night with burning torches, which the children enjoyed very much. But none of this worked.

Then we got wind that the Chief Minister was canvassing for election in a particular region. We issued a statement saying that half of us would go there and canvass against the Chief Minister, while the rest protested at his office.

This had a magical effect.

The Chief Minister immediately instructed that our needs be met – salary, everything. Wages rising to Rs 535 a month.

We are ungrateful

In our ignorance, call it innocence if you prefer, we held out for what the law prescribed, a salary of Rs 2700 a month for a skilled worker, and a proper employment contract.

A lot of the officials were horrified. Again, we had shown ingratitude. It began to dawn on us that they, coming from more affluent backgrounds than us, did not think of us as deserving of the same rights they enjoyed. Maybe that – or they didn't like being pushed around by a lot of women like us.

So, we gathered one sunrise in the summer of 1989 for the grand send-off from our families, who thought us mad but garlanded us with marigolds and roses.

We did not know how far Delhi was, nor the way there, nor how long it would take. We didn't know what we'd eat or where we'd sleep. We did not know how tough it would be. Many of us had our kids with us. There were a few men too. Each of us carried a small bag with a few necessaries: a blanket, bedspread, spare clothes.

Soon, the children and many of us women had blisters on our feet. We'd treat them with herbs found along the way. At night, exhausted, we forced ourselves to cook and eat.

No one said, 'Let's go back.'

At first, we walked 8–10 kilometres per day. As time passed the pace picked up and we could walk 35–40 km per day, kids and all.

We got up early, about 3 a.m., to escape the cruel sun. When our sandals wore out we tied leaves to the soles of our feet. Often people would walk with us from one village to the next as a way of showing support.

The road passed through some wild places. Far from anywhere, we'd sleep in the grass, a wide bedroom under the starry sky, three or four of us keeping watch over the rest.

In the dawn we were shocked to see dead scorpions and snakes killed on the road during the night. Many more must have passed among us as we slept and we never knew . . .

No food or money

Most of us had brought only a small amount of money. When it was spent, the women sold ornaments to get cash for medicines and food for the children.

We had to beg for food from villages where we stopped for the night. Country folk are extraordinarily kind. Some days they would cook for us or give us food to cook ourselves.

Telling our story

Occasionally when we begged we would be scolded, 'You seem healthy and capable, can't you work for food like everyone else?'

Or, more cynically, 'You must have received good compensation from the government after the gas disaster. Why are you still making more demands?'

Then we would try and explain what had really happened in Bhopal. How people were ill and the compensation was a joke. We told of having to pay officials. People were angry then and they helped us.

Sometimes the local police would arrange food for us and put us up in government houses with guards for our protection.

We are all one

We walked in small groups – the quicker ones would leave pounded rice on the road to mark the way.

We were Hindus and Muslims, but in our group all differences melted away – we cooked together, ate together, shared our troubles and slept side by side. We began bonding with one another and the people we met saw no differences among us.

We were one.

During the walk, the group are warned that there are groups of 'killer' bandits, or dacoits, in the locality . . .

We weren't scared. Who would waste time robbing people who had nothing?

The dacoits got to hear about us and sent word that they would not touch a hair of our heads.

The local police inspector said he believed this, but just to be sure, he and his men walked alongside us for almost 40 km.

At the edge of his territory, he parted from us in tears. 'If I had the power, I would have agreed to all your demands long ago and saved you this trouble.'

Pain and loss

During the days of our walk, those who were menstruating were the worst sufferers. We used folded cloths as pads and walking with a cloth created rashes on the tender skin of the upper thighs. Walking became extremely painful, but we kept on.

Yashoda, who was five months pregnant, tragically lost twins she was carrying soon after we got to Agra.

And then there was Abeeda, who would faint every few kilometres. Gendabai's 7-year-old son Rajendar was sick during the journey. His head would reel and his legs would give way under him.

We keep on

In spite of all the hardships, not once did anyone say, 'Enough, let's go back.'

After crossing twelve districts in four states in 33 days, we finally reached Delhi.

We were utterly exhausted, but our problems weren't over. We did not know where India Gate was or how to meet the PM.

We were finally told Rajiv Gandhi was out of town.

Unlike the villagers who had supported us, Delhi was cold. Nobody offered to help us. Instead, they sneered at us. 'What makes you think the Prime Minister of India would want to meet women like you?'

Tricked by our MP

We were camped on the grass by India Gate. The rains were due and no one would meet us.

Then our MP came along. He talked us into going back to Bhopal and assured us that once we got back, matters would be resolved. He promised personally to take care of our case and get our demands met. We trusted him and decided to go home.

All his promises he broke.

We won't be fooled again

We are together still and we now know that we should not have come back empty-handed, but our long march had turned us into gritty, determined fighters.

We even got our audience with Rajiv Gandhi. He was

in Bhopal at a public meeting. We forced our way in. After walking all the way to Delhi to meet him, were we going to let a few fat police wallahs stand in our way?

Rajiv Gandhi apologized to us. He said, 'I didn't know you had come all the way from Bhopal on foot to meet me. If I had known, I would have come to India Gate to meet you myself.'

Oh yes. A likely story.

In 2006 a group from Bhopal, mainly of women and including Rashida Bi, walk to Delhi once again to see Prime Minister Manmohan Singh, demanding the basic right to clean water for their families. They find support from many people including students and trades unionists and Amnesty International. In one demonstration in Delhi, Sajida Bano, fifty-five, whose husband and son were killed by the gas, is beaten and kicked by police before ending up in hospital.

As the PM continues to ignore them, two months after leaving home they stage a die-in on a street in Delhi and some of the women go on hunger strike. The temperature is over 100 degrees Fahrenheit. Finally, the PM promises to meet four of their six demands. But at any mention of anything which would affect trade with Dow Chemical, the PM puts his hands over his ears. After five days the strike is called off. Some of the women protesting outside are locked up and beaten.

None of these promises was kept by the government.

All this, for clean water.

Once again – they are still waiting.

IF YOU WOULD LIKE
TO KNOW MORE

There are some good films about Bhopal which you can watch free online. There are also all sorts of clips if you google 'Bhopal'. A full-length dramatization of the events of 2 December 1984, as well as various documentaries, can be found on YouTube. The film *Bhopali* can also be watched free on Amazon Video.

A number of excellent books have been written about Bhopal. *Five Past Midnight in Bhopal* by journalists Dominique Lapierre and Javier Moro is a really good read. There is also the novel *Animal's People* by Indra Sinha, who has been active for many years in the Bhopal situation. *The Bhopal Marathon* – a history with many first-hand accounts – is available from the Bhopal Medical Appeal, www.bhopal.org.

Another new group involved with campaigning for justice and a clean-up in Bhopal is www.actionforbhopal.org.

You might also enjoy a look and singalong to the running songs used in the story by Jo, Pat, Sunita and Hayley!

'Kashmir Main Tu Kanyakumari' from the film *Chennai Express* and 'Sugar, Sugar' by The Archies can both be watched on YouTube.

ACKNOWLEDGEMENTS

Our work as writers of fiction is one that deals in the business of empathy. So, my thanks first of all to Jeremy Trevathan, the head of fiction at Pan Macmillan, for listening to my idea of writing this story and for agreeing to fit another book into the already crammed publishing schedules. A big thank-you also to my editors Trisha Jackson and Jayne Osborne for their kind support and editorial insights, and to the other Pan Macmillan staff who have contributed their creative energy at every stage of the process.

I owe a particular debt of gratitude to my long-time, wonderful agent Darley Anderson, who not only gave generous moral support to this book, but also contributed all the normal agency fees to the Bhopal Medical Appeal.

Another big thank-you to Colin Toogood, the British Campaigns Manager of the Bhopal Medical Appeal for his help in setting up our visit to Bhopal in January 2018. In Bhopal Martin and I would not have got far without our interpreter Syed Tabish Ali, to whom we owe thanks for his quiet patience and steady management of a motorcycle in the Bhopal traffic. To Satinath Sarangi (Sathyu), who found time for a chat at the Sambhavna Clinic and to the parents and children at the Chingari clinic who it was a privilege to meet.

My thanks also to Tim Edwards, Executive Trustee of the Bhopal Medical Appeal for taking time to fact-check the text of the end material.

Also to Dave Lyddon, retired academic from Keele University, who gave his time by pointing me in the direction of fascinating information regarding accidents, industry and the law in Britain.

Special thanks to Sally Stinton who kindly welcomed me to her home to tell me about her neighbourhood. My apologies for any liberties taken with Birmingham's Hollywood!

And to our lovely yoga class here in Purley-on-Thames who have been an inspiration, but I promise you none of you appear in the book . . .

To the other brilliant writers who helped – friends in Oxford Narrative Group and above all to Sophie Morgan, Katy Murray and Polly Wright, who took the time to read all of it and give their comments and insights.

And above all to my husband Martin, an engineer well-versed in the prevention of industrial accidents, whose first-ever visit to India plunged him into the life of Bhopal and the Bhopal Medical Appeal, hair-raising motorbike rides, a visit to the ghostly remains of the Union Carbide factory and many other things. Our particular thanks to the Manohar Dairy on the Hamidia Road in Bhopal, which was a case of love at first sight. Thank you for coming with me, Martin – it would never have been the same without you xx